THE
MERCIES

ALSO BY KIRAN MILLWOOD HARGRAVE

The Way Past Winter
The Girl of Ink and Stars
The Island at the End of Everything

THE MERCIES

A Novel

KIRAN MILLWOOD HARGRAVE

Little, Brown and Company

New York Boston London

Copyright © 2019 by Kiran Millwood Hargrave

Little, Brown and Company
Hachette Book Group
1290 Avenue of the Americas, New York, NY 10104
littlebrown.com

First Edition: February 2020

Little, Brown and Company is a division of Hachette Book Group, Inc. The Little, Brown name and logo are trademarks of Hachette Book Group, Inc.

The publisher is not responsible for websites (or their content) that are not owned by the publisher.

The Hachette Speakers Bureau provides a wide range of authors for speaking events. To find out more, go to hachettespeakersbureau.com or call (866) 376-6591.

ISBN 978-0-316-52925-9
Library of Congress Control Number: 2019956201

10 9 8 7 6 5 4 3 2 1

LSC-C

Printed in the United States of America

For my mother, Andrea,
and all the women who raise(d) me

THE
MERCIES

BY ORDER OF THE KING

If any sorcerer, or faithful man, had the sacrifice of God
and His Holy Word and Christianity, and devoted himself to
the dævil, he should be cast down on fire and incineration.

FROM

Denmark–Norway Trolddom (Sorcery) Decree 1617,
ENACTED FINNMARK 1620

STORM

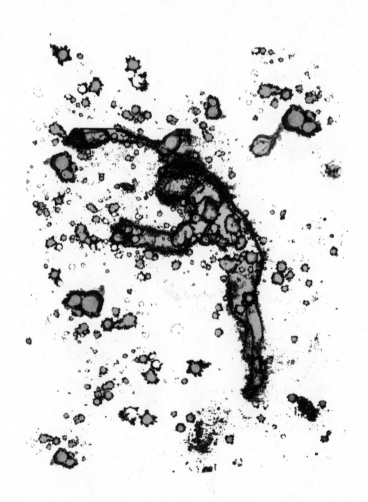

VARDØ, FINNMARK,

NORTH–EASTERN NORWAY

1617

Last night Maren dreamt a whale beached itself on the rocks outside her house.

She climbed down the cliff to its heaving body and rested her eye against its eye, wrapped her arms across the great stinking swell. There was nothing she could do for it but this.

The men came scrambling down the black rock like dark, swift insects, glinting and hard-bodied with blades and scythes. They began to swing and cut before the whale was even dead. It bucking and all of them grim and holding like nets tight about a shoal, her arms growing long and strong around it— so wide and fierce she held it—until she didn't know if she was a comfort or a menace and didn't care, only watched its eye with her eye, not blinking.

Eventually it stilled, its breath melting out as they hacked and sawed. She smelt the blubber burning in the lamps before it stopped moving, long before the bright roll of its eye beneath her eye wore down to dullness.

She sank down into the rocks until she stood at the bottom of the sea. The night above was dark and moonless, stars scarring the surface. She drowned and came up from sleep gasping, smoke in her nostrils and at the dark back of her throat. The taste of burning fat caught under her tongue, and would not be washed away.

ONE

The storm comes in like a finger snap. That's how they'll speak in the months and years after, when it stops being only an ache behind their eyes and a crushing at the base of their throats. When it finally fits into stories. Even then, it doesn't tell how it actually was. There are ways words fall down: they give shape too easily, carelessly. And there was no grace, no ease to what Maren saw.

That afternoon, the best sail is spread like a blanket across her lap, Mamma and Diinna at its other corners. Their smaller, neater fingers are working smaller, neater stitches into the wind-wear tears, while she patches cloth over holes left by the mast fastenings.

Beside the fire there's a stack of white heather drying, cut and brought by her brother Erik from the low mountain on the mainland. Tomorrow, after, Mamma will give her three palmfuls for her pillow. She'll wrench it apart, stuff it earth and all into the casing, the honey scent almost sickening after months of only the stale smell of sleep and unwashed hair. She'll take it between her teeth and scream until her lungs wheeze with the sweet dirt tang of it.

Now, something makes her look up and out towards the

window. A bird, dark against dark, a sound? She stands to stretch, to watch the bay, flat grey and beyond it the open sea, tips of waves like smashed glass glittering. The boats are loosely pegged out against it by their two small lights, bow and aft, barely flickering.

She imagines she can tell Pappa and Erik's apart from the others, with its second-best sail rigged tight to the mast. The jerk and stop-start of their rowing, their backs to the horizon where the sun skulks, out of sight for a month now, and for another month to come. The men will see the steady light from Vardø's curtainless houses, lost in their own sea of dim-lit land. They're already out beyond the Hornøya stac, nearly at the place where the shoal was sighted earlier in the afternoon, worried into bright action by a whale.

"It will have passed on," Pappa said. Mamma has a great terror of whales. "Well eaten its fill by the time Erik manages to haul us there with those herringbone arms."

Erik only bowed his head to accept Mamma's kiss, and his wife Diinna's press of thumb to his forehead that the Sámi say will draw a thread to reel men at sea home again. He rested a hand on her belly for a moment, bringing the swell of it more obviously through her knitted tunic. She pushed his hand away, but gently.

"You'll call it early. Let it be."

After, Maren will wish she rose and kissed them both on each rough cheek. She will wish she had watched them go to the water in their stitched sealskins, her father's strung-out stride and Erik's shambling behind. Wish that she had felt anything at all about them going, other than gratitude for the time alone with Mamma and Diinna, for the easiness of other women.

Because, at twenty and with her first marriage proposal come three weeks before, she at last considered herself one of them. Dag Bjørnsson was making them a home from his father's second boathouse, and before winter was done it would be finished, and they wed.

Inside, he told her, panting hot, scratching breath beneath her ear, would be a fine hearth and separate food store so he wouldn't need to walk through the house with his axe like Pappa did. The wicked glint, even in Pappa's careful hands, brought bile to her tongue. Dag knew this, and cared to know.

He was blond as his mother, delicately featured in a way that Maren knew other men took to mean weakness, but she didn't mind. She didn't mind that he brushed his wide mouth against her throat, as he told her of the sheet she should weave for the bed he would build for them. And though she didn't feel anything at his hesitant caress at her back, too gentle and high to mean much at all through her dark blue winter dress, this house that would be hers—this hearth and bed—sent a pulse low in her belly. At night she'd press her hands to the places she'd felt the warmth, fingers cold bars across her hips and numb enough not to be hers.

Not even Erik and Diinna have their own house: they live in the narrow room Maren's father and brother tacked along the back edge of their outer wall. Their bed fills the width of it, is pressed flush against Maren's own through the divide. She put her arms over her head on their first nights together, breathing in the musty straw of her mattress, but never heard so much as a breath. It was a wonder when Diinna's belly started to show. The baby would be here just after winter left, and then there would be three in that slender bed.

After, she will think: perhaps she should have watched for Dag too.

But instead she fetched the damaged sailcloth and spread it over all their knees, and did not look up until the bird or the sound or the change in the air called her to the window to watch the lights shifting across the dark sea.

Her arms crackle: she brings one needle-coarsened finger to the other and pushes it under her woollen cuff, feels the hair stiff and the skin beneath it tightening. The boats are still rowing, still steady in the uncertain light, lamps glimmering.

And then the sea rises up and the sky swings down and greenish lightning slings itself across everything, flashing the black into an instantaneous, terrible brightness. Mamma is fetched to the window by the light and the noise, the sea and sky clashing like a mountain splitting so they feel it through their soles and spines, sending Maren's teeth into her tongue and hot salt down her gullet.

And then maybe both of them are screaming but there is no sound save the sea and the sky and all the boat lights swallowed and the boats flashing and the boats spinning, the boats flying, turning, gone. Maren goes spilling out into the wind, creased double by her suddenly sodden skirts, Diinna calling her in, wrenching the door behind to keep the fire from going out. The rain is a weight on her shoulders, the wind slamming her back, hands tight in on themselves, grasping nothing. She is screaming so loud her throat will be bruised for days. All about her, other mothers, sisters, daughters are throwing themselves at the weather: dark, rain-slick shapes, clumsy as seals.

The storm drops before she reaches the harbour, two hundred paces from home, its empty mouth gaping at the sea. The clouds roll themselves up and the waves fall, resting at each other's horizons, gentle as a flock settling.

The women of Vardø gather at the scooped-out edge of their island, and though some are still shouting, Maren's ears ring with silence. Before her, the harbour is wiped smooth as a mirror. Her jaw is caught on the hinges of itself, her tongue dripping blood warm down her chin. Her needle is threaded in the web between her thumb and forefinger, the wound a neat circle of pink.

As she watches, a final flash of lightning illuminates the hatefully still sea, and from its blackness rise oars and rudders and a full mast with gently stowed sails, like underwater forests uprooted. Of their men, there is no sign.

It is Christmas Eve.

TWO

Overnight, the world turns white. Snow piles on snow, filling the windows and the mouths of doors. The kirke stands dark that Christmas, that first day after, a hole between the lit houses, swallowing light.

They are snowed in for three days, Diinna portioned off in her narrow room, Maren unable to rouse herself any more than she can Mamma. They eat nothing but old bread, settling like pebbles in their stomachs. Maren feels the food so solid inside her, and her body so unreal about it, she imagines herself pinned down to the earth only by Mamma's stale loaves. If she doesn't eat, she will become smoke and gather in the eaves of their house.

She keeps herself together by filling her belly until it aches, and by placing as much of herself as possible in the warmth from the fire. Everywhere it touches, she tells herself, she is real. She lifts her hair to show the grubby nape of her neck, spreads her fingers to let the warmth lick between them, lifts her skirts so her woollen stockings begin to singe and stink. *There, and there, and there.* Her breasts, back, and between them her heart, are caught in her winter vest, bundled tight together.

The second day, for the first time in years, the fire goes out. Pappa always laid it, and they only tended it, keeping it banked at night and breaking its crust each morning to let the hot heart of it breathe. Within hours there is a layer of frost on their blankets though Maren and her mother sleep together in the same bed. They don't speak, don't undress. Maren wraps herself in Pappa's old sealskin coat. It was not flensed properly and reeks a little of rotted fat.

Mamma wears Erik's from when he was a boy. She is dull-eyed as a smoked fish. Maren tries to make her eat, but her mother only curls into her side on the bed, sighs like a child. Maren is grateful for the blankness at the window that means the sea is hidden from sight.

Those three days are a pit she falls into. She watches Pappa's axe wink in the dark. Her tongue grows thick and mossy, the tender place where she bit it during the storm spongy and swollen, with something hard at its centre. She worries at it, and the blood makes her thirstier.

She dreams of Pappa and Erik, wakes dank and sweating, hands freezing. She dreams of Dag and when he opens his mouth it is full of nails meant for their bed. She wonders if they will die there, whether Diinna is already dead, her baby still paddling inside her, slowing. She wonders if God will come to them, and tell them to live.

They are both of them reeking when Kirsten Sørensdatter digs them out on the third night. Kirsten helps them restack and light the fire at last. When she clears the path to Diinna's door, Diinna looks almost furious, the dull gleam of her pouted lip catching in the torchlight, hands pressed hard either side of her swollen belly.

"Kirke," says Kirsten to them all. "It is the Sabbath."

Even Diinna, who doesn't believe in their God, does not argue.

•

It isn't until they are all gathered in the kirke that Maren understands: nearly all their men are dead.

Toril Knudsdatter lights the candles, every one, until the room blazes so bright it stings Maren's eyes. She counts silently. There once were fifty-three men, and now they have but thirteen left: two babes in arms, three elders, and the rest boys too small for the boats. Even the minister is lost.

The women sit in their usual pews, hollows left between where husbands and sons sat, but Kirsten orders them forwards. All but Diinna obey, dumb as a herd. They take up three of the kirke's seven rows.

"There have been wrecks before," says Kirsten. "We have survived when men are lost."

"But never so many," says Gerda Folnsdatter. "And never my husband among them. Never yours, Kirsten, or Sigfrid's. Never Toril's son. All of them—"

She grips at her throat, falls silent.

"We should pray, or sing," suggests Sigfrid Jonsdatter, and the others look at her poisonously. They have been trapped apart for three days, and all they wish to talk of, all they can speak of, is the storm.

The women of Vardø are looking, all of them, for signs. The storm was one. The bodies, still to come, will be seen as another. But now Gerda speaks of the single tern she saw wheeling above the whale.

"In figures of eight," she says, her ruddy hands arcing through the air. "One, two, three, six times I counted."

"Eight by six means not much at all," says Kirsten dismissively. She is standing beside Pastor Gursson's pulpit with its engraved stand. Her large hand rests upon it, the broad thumb working over the carved shapes her only sign of nerves, or grief.

Her husband is among the drowned, and all her children were buried before they breathed. Maren likes her, has often gone about her tasks with her, but now she sees Kirsten as the others always have: as a woman apart. She is not standing behind the pulpit, but she may as well be: she watches them with a minister's consideration.

"The whale though," says Edne Gunnsdatter, face swollen so tight by tears it looks bruised. "It swam upside down. I saw its white belly shining under the waves."

"It was feeding," says Kirsten.

"It was luring the men," says Edne. "It set the shoal about Hornøya six times, to be sure we'd see."

"I saw that," nods Gerda, crossing herself. "I saw that too."

"You did not," says Kirsten.

"I saw the blood Mattis coughed upon the table a week ago," says Gerda. "It has never scrubbed off."

"I can sand that out for you," says Kirsten smoothly.

"The whale was wrong," says Toril. Her daughter is burrowed against her side so tight she might have been sewed to her hip by Toril's famously neat stitches. "If what Edne says is true, it was sent."

"Sent?" says Sigfrid, and Maren sees Kirsten turn a thankful eye upon her, thinking she has found an ally. "Such a thing is possible?"

A sigh comes from the back of the kirke, and the whole room turns towards Diinna, but she tilts her head back, eyes closed, the brown skin of her throat gleaming gold in the candlelight.

"The Devil works darkly," says Toril, and her daughter presses her face beneath her shoulder, cries out in fear. Maren wonders what terrors Toril has woven into her two surviving children these past three days. "He has power set above all but God's. He could send such a thing. Or it could be called."

17

"Enough." Kirsten breaks the silence before it can deepen. "This will help nothing."

Maren wants to join her in her certainty, but all she can think of is the shape, the sound that brought her to the window. She had thought it was a bird but now it looms bigger and more unwieldy, five-finned and upside down. Unnatural. It is impossible to stop it leaking into the corner of her vision, even in the blessed light of the kirke.

Mamma stirs, as if from sleep, though the candles have been reflecting off her unblinking eyes since they sat down. When she speaks, Maren can hear the toll silence has taken on her voice.

"The night Erik was born," says Mamma. "There was a red point of light in the sky."

"I remember," says Kirsten, softly.

"And me," says Toril. *And me*, thinks Maren, though she was only two.

"I followed it through the sky until it dropped in the sea," says Mamma, lips barely moving. "It lit the whole water with blood. He was marked—it was meant from that day." She moans and covers her face. "I should never have let him to sea."

This brings a fresh wave of wailing from the women. Even Kirsten can do nothing to quell it. The candles stutter as there is a rush of cold air into the room, and Maren turns in time to see Diinna striding from the kirke. What words Maren could offer, as she puts her arm about Mamma, would be bitter comfort: *There was nothing for him but the sea.*

Vardø is an island, the harbour like a bite taken out of one side, the other shores too high or rocky for boats to be launched. Maren learnt nets before she learnt hurt, weather before she learnt love. In summer her mother's hands are speckled with the tiny stars of fish scales, flesh hung out to salt and dry like white drapes of baby's swaddling, or else wrapped in reindeer skins and buried to rot.

Pappa used to say that the sea was the shape of their lives. They have always lived by its grace, and long have they died on it. But the storm has made it an enemy, and there is brief talk of leaving.

"I have family in Alta," says Gerda. "There is land and work enough, there."

"The storm did not reach so far?" asks Sigfrid.

"We will hear soon," says Kirsten. "I imagine they'll send word from Kiberg—the storm must surely have struck there."

"My sister will get a message to me," nods Edne. "She has three horses, and it is only a day's ride."

"And a rough crossing," says Kirsten. "The sea is still fierce. We must allow them time to reach us."

Maren listens as others talk of Varanger, or more outlandishly, Tromsø, as if any of them could imagine life in a city, so far away. There is a small disagreement about who would take the reindeer for transport, for they belonged to Mads Petersson, who drowned alongside Toril's husband and sons. Toril seems to think this gives her some standing over them, but when Kirsten announces she will care for the herd no one argues. Maren can't imagine starting a fire, let alone keeping a herd of high-strung beasts through the winter. Toril likely thinks the same, for she drops her claim as quickly as she took it up.

Eventually the talk falters, finishes. Nothing is decided except that they will wait for word from Kiberg, and send for it if it does not arrive before the week is out.

"Until then, it is best to meet daily at kirke," says Kirsten, and Toril nods fervently, in agreement for once. "We must watch for each other. The snows seem on their way out, but there's no telling."

"Watch for whales," says Toril, and the light hits her face so Maren can see the bones work beneath her skin. She looks ominous, and Maren wants to laugh. She bites down on the tender spot on her tongue.

There is no more talk of leaving. Walking down the hill homewards, Mamma clinging so tightly it makes her arm ache, Maren wonders if the other women feel as she does: bound to the place now more than ever. Whale or no whale, sign or not, Maren was witness to the death of forty men. Now something in her is tied to this land, as tied as she is trapped.

THREE

Nine days after the storm, the year newly turned over, the men are brought to them. Almost whole, almost all of them. Laid like offerings on the small black cove, or else risen by the tide to the rocks below Maren's house. They must climb to fetch them, using the ropes knotted strong for Erik to fetch eggs from the birds' nests woven into the cliffside.

Erik and Dag are amongst the first to come back, Pappa amongst the last. Pappa has one arm, and Dag is burnt, a black line drawn from left shoulder to right foot, which Mamma says means the lightning struck him.

"It would have been quick," she says, not hiding her bitterness. "It would have been easy."

Maren presses nose to shoulder, breathes herself in.

Her brother looks as though he is sleeping, but his skin is filled with that horrible green light she knows from other bodies brought in by the tide. *Drowned*. Not so easy.

When it is Maren's turn to descend the cliff, she retrieves Toril's son, snagged like driftwood on the sharp-toothed rocks. He is Erik's age, and his body slips about in its bones like jointed meat in a sack. Maren smooths his dark hair away from his face, picks a whisper of seaweed from his collarbone. She and Edne must tie him by the waist and ribs and knees, to keep him together as he is drawn up to his mother. Maren is glad she can't see Toril's face when she is brought her boy. Though she is not fond of the woman, Toril's keens prick at Maren's chest like tiny needles.

The ground is too hard for burial, and so it is agreed that they will keep the dead in Dag's father's first boathouse, the cold keeping them frozen as earth. It will be months before they can break the surface to bury their men.

"We can use the sail as a shroud," says Mamma, after Erik is taken to the boat shed. She eyes the mended sail where it lies in the centre of the floor, as if Erik is already beneath it. It is exactly where they had dropped it nearly two weeks before. Maren and Mamma have been dancing around it, neither wanting to touch it, but now Diinna snatches it up and shakes her head.

"A waste," she says, and Maren is glad: she can't stand the thought of sending her father and brother into the ground with anything more of the sea upon them. Diinna folds the sail with deft movements, resting it upon her belly, and in her decisiveness Maren sees some of the girl who married her brother, laughing, a summer ago.

But Diinna disappears the day after Dag and Erik are brought back. Mamma is frantic that she has left to bring up the child with her Sámi family. She says some awful things, things that Maren knows she doesn't mean. She calls Diinna a Lapp, a whore, a savage, things Toril or Sigfrid might say.

"I always knew it," Mamma weeps. "I should never have let him marry a Lapp. They are not loyal, not made like us."

Maren can only bite her tongue, and rub her back. It is true Diinna's childhood was spent travelling, living beneath changing stars even in winter. Her father is a noaidi, a shaman of good standing. Before the kirke was more fully established, their neighbour Baar Ragnvalsson and many other men went to him for charms against rough weather. That had stopped lately, with new laws brought in to ban such things, but still Maren sees the small bone figures that the Sámi say will protect against bad luck on most doorsteps. Pastor Gursson always turned a blind eye, though Toril and her ilk urged him to come down harder on such practices.

Maren knows it was only Diinna's love for Erik that made her agree to live in Vardø, but she doesn't think Diinna would leave like this, not when they have already lost so many. Not with Erik's baby inside her. She would not be so cruel as to take the last part of him away from them.

•

Within the week, they receive word from Kiberg. Edne's brother-in-law comes with news that besides numerous boats moored in the harbour, they lost only three men. When the women gather in the kirke to hear the message, it stokes their unease.

"Why did they not fish?" says Sigfrid. "Did Kiberg not see the shoal?"

Edne shakes her head. "The whale neither."

"So it was sent for us," whispers Toril, and her fear spreads across the pews in muttering waves.

The talk is too loose for a sacred place, full of omens and embellishments, but no one can resist the chance to gossip. Their words are like links they can hang fact upon, tightening with each telling. Many of them seem past caring what is true or not, only desperate for some reason, some order to the rearrangement of their lives, even if it is brought about by a lie. That the whale swam upside down is now beyond question, and though Maren tries to shore herself against the creeping terror their talk brings, she can't hold steady like Kirsten.

The woman has moved into Mads Petersson's house, the better to care for the reindeer. Maren regards her, standing firm by the pulpit. They have barely spoken since Kirsten dug them from the snow, except to exchange words of sorrow when their men were pulled rotting from the sea. Maren thinks to speak with her as the kirke meet comes to an end, but Kirsten is already out of the door, striding to her new homestead, bent against the wind.

•

Diinna is back the day they find Pappa. The first Maren hears of her return there is shouting at the boathouse and she runs, imagining all sorts of things: another storm though she can see for herself the sunless sky is calm, or a man found yet living.

There is a cluster of women about the door, Sigfrid and Toril at the fore, their faces twisted in anger. Before them stands Diinna with another Sámi: a short, square man who watches the women coolly. It is not Diinna's father, but he has a shaman drum at his hip. Between them they hold a furled length of silvery cloth. As Maren comes closer, dizzy with the effort of running, she sees it is birch bark.

"What's the matter?" she asks Diinna, and Toril answers.

"She wants to bury them in that." The woman's voice is close to hysteria. Spit flecks her chin. "Like *they* do."

"Makes no sense to use cloth, not for so many," says Diinna. "This is—"

"And I will not have that, not near my boys." Toril is panting worse than Maren, looking at the drum as though it were a weapon. Sigfrid Jonsdatter nods her approval as Toril plunges on. "Nor my husband. He's a God-fearing man, and I'll not have you near him."

"I don't remember you minding my help when you wanted another baby got upon you," says Diinna.

24

Toril puts her hand across her belly, though her babies are long born. "I did no such thing."

"I know as well as any that you did, Toril," says Maren, unable to keep silent at the lie. "And you, Sigfrid. Many of you came to her, or her father."

Toril narrows her eyes. "I would never go to a Lapp sorcerer."

There is a collective hiss. Maren steps forward, but Diinna puts her arm out.

"I should put a hole in your tongue, Toril. Perhaps it would let some of the poison out." It is Toril's turn to shrink. "And it's not sorcery, and it's not for them."

Diinna turns to Maren. She is beautiful in the bluish light, the planes of her face strong, her eyes thickly lashed. "It's for Erik."

"And my father." Maren's voice breaks. She cannot bear to separate them, and Pappa loved Diinna, was proud of the match made for his son.

"He has come back?" Maren nods, and Diinna clasps her shoulder. "And for Herr Magnusson, of course. We will watch them. And any others that want it."

"And will your mother be happy with this?" Toril rounds on Maren, and she is too weary to do anything but nod, her head heavy on her neck.

Eventually it is agreed that anyone who wants the Sámi rites for their men will be taken to the second boathouse, that was to have been Maren's home. Only two men are moved in next to Erik and Pappa: poor Mads Petersson, who has no family to speak for him, and Baar Ragnvalsson, who was often gone to the low mountain and wore Sámi clothing.

The second boathouse would have made a fine home. The start of the shed alone is as large as Diinna and Erik's room, and the main space rivals the one at Dag's father's house, the largest in the village. Their bed is laid out in planks ready for Dag's careful hands to knock together.

They take the wood for their fire, and lay her father and Erik on the bare ground. Maren has to leave Dag behind in the first boathouse: his mother, Fru Olufsdatter, has not spoken a word to her, will not meet her eye.

Maren snaps a lock of frozen hair from Erik's dark head, places it carefully into her pocket. As she leaves Diinna and the noaidi behind in the silent room, Maren loops around to the first boathouse. She sees one of the women has nailed a cross over the door, and it feels less like a blessing on those within than a warding-off of those without.

When she reaches home, Mamma is asleep, her arm flung across her eyes as though she is cowering from a nightmare.

"Mamma?" Maren wants to tell her about the noaidi, and the second boathouse. "Diinna is back."

There is no response. Mamma seems barely to breathe, and Maren resists the urge to place her cheek over her mouth to check for life. Instead, she retrieves the lock from her pocket, holds it before the fire. It frills into Erik's fine curls. She makes a slice in her pillow, places it inside with the heather.

•

Every day after kirke, Maren returns to the second boathouse, though she can't bring herself to sleep there like Diinna and the man with the drum. He does not speak Norwegian, and will not give an easy version of his name so Maren calls him Varr, vigilant, because it sounds a little like the beginning of what he says he is called before she loses the rest on her unskilled tongue.

Each time she visits her father and Erik she waits outside, listening to Varr and Diinna speak together in their language. They always fall silent the moment she puts her hand on the door, and Maren feels as though she's walked in on something indecent, or else intensely private. That she's broken something, clumsy just by being there.

Maren speaks Norwegian to Diinna and Diinna translates to Varr, her sentences always shorter, as though they have the better and more exacting words for what Maren is trying to say. What must it be like to have two languages in your head, in your mouth? Having to keep one tucked like a dark secret at the back of your throat? Diinna has always lived between Vardø and elsewhere, around now and again since Maren was a girl, trailing alongside her silent father who came to fix nets or weave charms.

"We lived here," Diinna told Maren once, when Maren was still a little afraid of her: a girl in trousers and a coat edged with bear fur that she'd skinned and stitched herself.

"This is your land?"

"No." The girl's tone was firm as her gaze. "We only lived here."

Sometimes Maren can hear the drum beaten, steady as a heartbeat, and she sleeps easier those nights though there is much muttering from the strictest kirke-goers about it. Diinna tells her the drum will clear the way for the spirits to break cleanly from the bodies, and not be afraid. But Varr never plays it when Maren is about. It is broad as a trough, skin stretched taut over a shallow bowl of pale wood. Small markings punctuate the surface: a reindeer with a sun and moon caught in its antlers, men and women linked like paper chains at the hands in the centre, and a twist of hideous almost-men, almost-beasts writhe across the bottom.

"Is that hell?" she asks Diinna. "And that heaven, and us in the middle?"

Diinna doesn't translate to Varr. "It is all here."

FOUR

As winter loosens its grip on Vardø, and their food stores stand near empty, the sun heaves itself closer to the horizon. By the time Diinna and Erik's baby is born, they will have days flooded with light.

Maren feels an uneasy rhythm take hold of Vardø, her time finding shape. Kirke, boathouse, housework, sleep. Though the lines are beginning to be drawn more starkly between Kirsten and Toril, Diinna and the others, they pull together as men rowing a boat. It is a closeness born of necessity: they need each other more than ever, especially as food begins to scarcen.

They receive some grain from Alta, scant tørrfisk from Kiberg. Sometimes sailors stop in the harbour, row ashore with sealskins and whale oil. Kirsten has no shame in talking to them, and manages a good deal, but they are running low on items to trade, and it is clear that when the time arrives to sow their fields, no help will come.

Maren uses the between hours of her days to walk the headland that she and Erik would play upon as children, the scrubby patches of heather healing after a sun-starved winter. They will be knee high before long, and the air will be so sweet with their scent as to make her teeth ache.

At night, the grief is harder to manage. The first time she picks up a needle, the hair on her arms rises and she drops it as though scalded. All her dreams are dark and full of water. She sees Erik caught in stoppered bottles and the gaping, sea-washed hole of her father's arm: its white, white bone. The whale comes most of all, the dark hull of its body crashing through her mind and leaving nothing good, nothing living in its wake. Sometimes it swallows her whole, and sometimes it is beached and she lies with it, eye to eye, with her nostrils full of its stench.

Maren knows Mamma has nightmares too. But she doubts her mother wakes with salt on her tongue, the sea mottling her breath. Sometimes Maren wonders whether she brought this life upon them all with her wishing for time alone with Diinna and Mamma. For though Kiberg is close, and Alta not so far, no man has come to settle with them. Maren wanted time with women, and now all her days are so.

She starts to imagine that Vardø could go on for ever this way: a place without men, and still surviving. The cold is loosening its hold, and the bodies are in turn becoming soft. Once the thaw is root deep, they will bury their dead, and perhaps some of the rifts might be buried with them.

Maren aches for the feeling of soil beneath her fingernails, the weight of a spade in her hands, Erik and Pappa finally at rest, neat in their silver-birch shrouds. She checks the vegetable patch outside their home daily, scraping her nails across the ground.

•

Four months after the storm, the day her hand sinks into the dirt, she runs into kirke to declare they can dig at last. But the words catch in her throat: there is a man planted at the pulpit.

"This is Pastor Nils Kurtsson," says Toril, voice reverent. "He is sent from Varanger. Praise God, we are not forgotten after all."

The minister turns pale eyes upon Maren. He is built slight as a boy.

Ousted from her usual spot, Kirsten slides in beside Mamma and Maren, leans close to whisper in Maren's ear.

"I hope his sermons are not so weak as his chin."

But they are, and Maren thinks he must have done something awful to be posted at Vardø. Pastor Kurtsson is reedy, obviously unused to life by the sea. He offers no words of comfort for their particular trials, and seems a little afraid of the roomful of women who arrive each Sabbath's Day to fill his kirke. He scurries to his house next door after each final *Amen*.

The kirke newly sanctified, the women take to meeting on Wednesdays in Dag's father's house, Fru Olufsdatter reduced to a whisper in the rooms of her too-large home. The gossip is the same, but the women are more careful. As Toril had said, they are not forgotten, and Maren is sure she is not alone in her unease about what this might mean.

The week of his arrival, the minister writes for ten men from Kiberg, Edne's brother-in-law among them, and Maren feels an unexpected envy when they come to bury the dead. It takes them two days to dig the graves, and with the nights' darkness shortening they work late into them. They are loud, and laugh too much for their task. They sleep in the kirke, and lean on their spades to watch the women go by. Maren keeps her head down, but still she walks past the site to watch their progress hourly.

The graves are at the north-west side of the island, dark pit after dark pit, so many it makes Maren's head spin. The soil is heaped beside, and as Maren watches from a safe distance, she imagines the ache in her arms, the dirt tasting like a coin in her mouth, the sweat coming hard from her. It doesn't feel right, after all the women have seen, after gathering their men from the rocks and keeping vigil through the winter, to watch someone else dig the graves. She thinks Kirsten would agree with her, but doesn't want a fuss. She wants her pappa and brother in the ground, the winter over, and the men from Kiberg gone.

On the morning of the third day, their dead men are brought out from the first boathouse, already smelling a little, stomachs swollen in their cloth shrouds stitched by Toril. They are laid beside the open graves, stark white against the freshly turned earth.

"No coffins?" asks one man, plucking at the shroud.

"Forty dead," says another. "A lot of labour for a village of women."

"A shroud is harder work than a coffin," says Kirsten coolly, and Toril's cheeks pinken in surprise. "And I'll thank you not to touch my husband."

Kirsten sits on the edge of the grave, and before Maren understands what she is doing, she has dropped down so only her head and shoulders emerge, arms outstretched.

The men stare wordlessly at one another, and so Kirsten takes her husband herself, and disappears from view as she lowers him down. The next they see of her, she is pulling herself up, her stockinged leg flashing as she climbs out of the grave.

Toril tuts and turns away, and one of the men laughs, but Kirsten only takes a handful of earth from the mound and drops it onto her husband. Then she walks straight past Maren, close enough so Maren can see the tears on her cheeks. Maren should reach out to her, say something, but her tongue feels useless as a pebble.

"So she did love him," murmurs Mamma, and Maren has

to bite back a retort. Any fool could tell Kirsten had loved her husband. She'd seen them often, walking together and laughing like friends. He took her to the fields and sometimes out on the sea. If she had gone with him the day of the storm, the women of Vardø would be even more lost than they are now.

Pastor Kurtsson moves forward to bless the grave. His jaw is tight, and Maren supposes he is embarrassed that Kirsten showed her boldness before these men. "May the mercies of God be upon you," he intones in his wavering voice, saying nothing much over the man he never knew.

"Kirsten should not have done that." Diinna appears beside Maren, watching the minister. Her hand rests on her belly. The baby will come any day, and sorrow grips at Maren's throat: her brother pressed beneath the dirt before his child even breathes. She has a sudden urge to reach out and touch Diinna, to feel the warmth of her stomach and the baby inside, but not even the Diinna of before would have tolerated it. This new Diinna is hard as stone, and Maren doesn't dare ask.

No other woman has a hand in the burial of their kin. The men work methodically: two passing a body down to two in the grave. The families step forward to sprinkle dirt, Pastor Kurtsson blesses the grave, it is filled. No one wails, or falls to their knees. The women are tired, numb, done. Toril prays incessantly, the words rising and falling on the wind.

The cycle repeats until it is time for the second boathouse to be emptied, and Pastor Kurtsson raises a pale eyebrow at the silver-birch shrouds. Mamma plucks at Pappa's, looks from the minister to Maren.

"Perhaps we should ask Toril—"

"I have no cloth left," says Toril.

"I have a sail—"

"No thread neither," says Toril, and she turns her back on

them, walking home, pulling her son and daughter after. Sigfrid follows, and Gerda. Maren is sure that she, Diinna and Mamma will be left alone to bury their dead, but the other women stay to watch as Mads, then Pappa, then Erik, and at last Baar are lowered, covered over.

That night, when the men from Kiberg have left, Maren walks to the graves with Erik's lock of hair in her pocket, thinking to bury it with him. She has decided it is a macabre keepsake, that perhaps it is this poisoning her dreams, letting the sea seep in. The nights are no longer winter dark, and in the gloom the graves appear to her like a pod of whales on the horizon, humpbacked and menacing. She finds she cannot approach them.

She knows what they are: hallowed ground, blessed by a man of God, holding naught but the remains of their men. But here, with the wind whistling through the open channels of their island, and the lit houses at her back, walking towards them seems as ill-fated as stepping from a cliff. She imagines them crashing up, thrashing down, and the world seems to rock beneath her feet. In her confusion, she loosens her grip on the lock of Erik's hair. The wind plucks it from her slack fingers, and spins it away.

●

Later that night, the noise of the door wakes Maren. Mamma is curled on the blankets like a snail in its shell, breathing rank air into her face. She has insisted they still share the bed, though Maren sleeps the worse for it.

Maren sits up, body singing with nerves as the door closes. She can't see anyone, only sense them there. There is a grunting sound, a fast series of almost animal breaths. It sounds like a mouthful of dirt being choked on.

"Erik?"

She wonders if she has called him to her, conjured him with her dreaming and prayers, and it frightens her to the point where she is up and climbing over her mother, towards Pappa's axe. Then she hears Diinna's soft cry, a lurch of pain that sends the woman to her knees and Maren can make out her edges. A spirit wouldn't open a door, Maren chides herself, and an axe would be no help against it.

"I'll fetch Fru Olufsdatter."

"Not her," says Diinna on an outrush of breath. "You."

She guides Diinna to their hearthrug. Mamma is awake and cracks open the fire so its light spills over the floor, brings blankets and heats water, gets a strap of leather for Diinna to bite on, makes soothing sounds.

They don't need the strap—Diinna doesn't make much noise beyond panting. She sounds like a kicked dog: she whimpers and bites her lip. Maren stays by her head and Mamma removes her underthings. They are wet, and the whole room smells of Diinna's sweat. She is pouring with it, and Maren wipes a cloth across her forehead, tries not to stare at the dark mound between Diinna's legs, her mother's hands slick and working. She has never seen a child born before, only animals and often they did not live. She tries to banish the thoughts of slack tongues poking from between soft jaws.

"It is already nearly come," says Mamma. "Why did you not fetch us sooner?"

Diinna is almost dumb with agony, but whispers: "I knocked at the wall."

Maren dabs and murmurs at Diinna's ear, enjoying the closeness Diinna's pain is allowing them, like old times. Soon the light coming through the thin weave of the curtains at the window meets that of the fire, and they are all caught in a foggy white glow. Maren feels shrouded in sea mist as Diinna clings to Maren as if she were an anchor, holding her steady against the tides of pain. Maren presses a kiss to her forehead, tasting salt.

When it is finally time to push, Diinna flaps like a landed fish, bucking her body against the floor. "Hold her," says Mamma, and Maren tries though she has never been stronger than Diinna and cannot hope to be now. She sits behind so Diinna can lean against her, and whispers into her neck. Maren's own tears come to meet Diinna's as she gives another twist and, at last, a scream as an answering wail comes from between her legs.

"A boy." Mamma's voice is bright with joy, and the sharp edge of pain. "A boy. Just as I prayed for."

Diinna falls back and Maren guides her to the floor. Maren holds her, kisses her cheeks, listening to the baby cry, the clatter of metal as her mother takes up a blade to cut the cord, then wipes blood from him with a rag. Diinna clings to her, crying harder, their bodies shaking, damp, exhausted, until Mamma nudges Maren off with her elbow and puts the baby to Diinna's chest.

He is tiny, crumpled, creamy with afterbirth. His lashes are dark against his white cheek. Maren is minded of a baby bird she found struck from its nest in the moss roof, so thinly skinned she could see the workings of its eye under the closed lid, the heartbeat quaking its entire frame. As soon as she touched it, thinking to put it back in the nest, it stopped moving.

His cries heave his tiny shoulders, his small mouth works. Diinna pulls down her nightgown, places her dark nipple into his mouth. There is scar tissue laced across one collarbone, a burn that Maren remembers came from a pan full of boiled water, though she can't recall who threw it. She wants to kiss there too, to smooth it.

Mamma finishes cleaning Diinna. She is crying, pulls herself up to lie on the other side of her, places a hand over Diinna's where it rests on his back. Maren hesitates only a moment longer before placing hers there too. He is shockingly warm, and smells of fresh bread, clean cloth. Her chest tightens, aches with want.

3rd of June 1618

To the Esteemed Mr. Cornet,

I write on two counts.

Firstly, to thank you for your generous letter of the 12th January of this year. Your words of congratulations are most appreciated. My appointment as Lensmann over Finnmark is a great honour and, as you markedly say, a chance to serve our Lord God in that troubled place. The Devil's breath reeks there, and there is much work to be done. King Christian IV is working to solidify the Church's position, but sorcery laws were passed only a year previous, and though they are modelled on Daemonologie they are most lacking next to what our King James has achieved in Scotland and the Outer Isles. They are not even yet enacted in my Lensmannship. Of course, when I take up my post next year I will move to rectify this.

Which brings me to my second point. As you are aware, I am much admiring of your conduct in the 1616 Kirkwall trial of the witch Elspeth Reoch, which reached us even here. As I wrote at the time, while the public praise was all for that popinjay Coltart, I know how much you supported him and that it was your swift action that caught the incident in its earliest stages. It is precisely this pace that is required in Finnmark: men who can follow Daemonologie's teachings to "spot, prove, and execute those who practise maleficium."

I write, then, to offer you a place alongside me, to rout out its particular evils. Many of the issues arise from a segment of the local population, endemic here in Finnmark—a transient

community termed Lapps. *They are somewhat akin to gypsies,
but their magicks deal in wind and other weather. As mentioned,
legislation against their sorcery is established, but weakly
enforced.*

*You being an Orkney man, I do not need to tell you of the
peculiarities of weather or season that come with a place like
this. But I will warn you the situation is grave. Since the storm
of 1617 (you remember it made even the Edinburgh papers: I
myself was at sea and it was felt as far as Spitsbergen and
Tromsø) womenfolk have been left to themselves. The barbarian
Lapp population mixes freely with the whites. Their magicks are
no small part of what we must move against. Their weather
sorcery is even sought out by sailors. But I believe that with
you, and a small number of other capable, God-fearing men,
we can beat back the darkness even in the ever-dark of winter.
Even here, at the edge of civilization, souls must be saved.*

*You would of course be remunerated for your efforts. I have
it in mind to set you up in a sizeable dwelling in Vardø, close to
the castle where I will have the seat of my power. Five years
here, and I would write you a letter of recommendation fit for
whatever endeavour you would wish to undertake.*

*Perhaps keep this offer close to you: I have no doubt Coltart
would sniff it out, but he is not the sort of man I am in need of.*

Think on it, Mr. Cornet. I will await word of your response.

John Cunningham (Hans Køning)
Lensmann over Vardøhus County

FIVE

By the time her nephew is born, Maren's own body is becoming something she carries effortfully, with pity and something like disgust. It is hungry, disobedient. When she stands, it is as if there are bubbles between all her bones, and they pop in her ears.

Grief cannot feed you, though it fills you. They have been ignoring that, but when Kirsten Sørensdatter asks for permission to speak at kirke, a clear six months after the storm, Maren sees it finally in the loose skin about the woman's jaw, and in the tributaries of Mamma's veins standing proud from her arms. Perhaps the others do too, because they straighten from the slump of their sermon-listening, watch her carefully.

"It will not change with more waiting," Kirsten begins, as though picking up a conversation. Her brow is pulled down over her small blue eyes. "Our neighbours have been kind but we all know kindness has its time. We must start carrying ourselves." She straightens: something clicks. "The ice is gone, we have the midnight sun, and there are four boats fit for sea. It is time to fish. We need twenty women, perhaps sixteen. I am one." She looks about her.

Maren expects some of the others, Sigfrid or Toril or

perhaps even the minister, to say something, to raise an objection. But he is thinner too, and he had precious little weight to lose. It is sense, what Kirsten says, however briefly she chooses to say it. Maren's hand goes up with ten others. As she lifts it, she has the same lurching sensation that comes with leaning into the wind, and feeling it lessen just as you find your balance. Mamma eyes her, and says nothing.

"No others? This is crew enough for only two boats," says Kirsten. Eyes drop and the women shift in the pews.

•

They thought it was decided. But though the minister raises no objection in the kirke, Toril arrives at the next Wednesday meet with news that Pastor Kurtsson found his voice, and has written a letter.

"How clever," says Kirsten, not looking up from her work: she is making a pair of sealskin gloves, for helping grip the oars, Maren guesses.

"To the man who is soon to take over Vardøhus," says Toril, and even Kirsten stills and looks up.

"The fortress? Here?" says Sigfrid, her eyes shining at the gossip. "You're sure?"

"You know of another?" snaps Toril, but Maren can understand the question. The fortress has stood empty for her entire lifetime.

Beside Maren, Diinna and Mamma have stopped working too. The three women are salvaging an old net, Diinna resting it upon her lap beneath baby Erik in his cloth sling. She brings her head down so close she looks like a mother bird feeding her young.

It is impossible to forget the last time the three of them worked on mending together, and the needle feels spiteful. Maren places her hand on the fine thread, so as not to lose her place. Dag's mother, Fru Olufsdatter, has set out benches along the edges of her cook room and they sit around them as though they are ranged about the lip of a square boat. The firelight sets the floor unsteady.

"We will have a Lensmann there, Hans Køning. He is under direct orders from King Christian, and will be making great changes, Pastor Kurtsson says, with new strictures on kirke-going." Toril looks directly at Diinna. "And he is looking to settle the Lapps and bring them to God."

Diinna shifts beside Maren, but holds Toril's gaze.

"He will not manage it with men like Nils Kurtsson," says Kirsten. "That man couldn't bring a beast to pasture."

Diinna snorts, and goes back to her sewing.

"Pastor Kurtsson has told me his next sermon will be to stay you," says Toril, narrowing her eyes at the top of Diinna's head. "The Lensmann will not think fishing proper."

"He isn't our Lensmann yet. And propriety doesn't feed us," says Kirsten. "Only fish can do that. I'll not be minding what a Scotsman thinks of it."

"He's a Scotsman?" Sigfrid's eyebrows rise. "Why not a Norwegian, or a Dane?"

"He was in the Danish fleet for many years," says Kirsten, eyes on her needlework. "Cleared the pirates at Spitsbergen. The King himself picked and placed him at Vardøhus."

"How do you know this?" says Toril.

Kirsten doesn't look up. "You aren't the only one with ears, Toril. I speak with the sailors who come to our harbour."

"I see you do," says Toril. "It is most indecent."

Kirsten ignores her. "And whatever Pastor Kurtsson decides to mumble at us this Sabbath's Day, I shall not be able to hear him over the grumble of my stomach."

Maren stifles a laugh. If it had been anyone but Kirsten who had put forward the idea of taking the boats, they should not have entertained it. But she has always been a certain woman, stubborn and strong, and on Sabbath's Day Pastor Kurtsson's mouthful of lukewarm warnings do nothing to stop them. He has had no reply from the Lensmann, and so Kirsten insists they go ahead.

•

Instead of the Wednesday meet, eight of them gather at the harbour's edge. They have lost a few of their volunteers following news of the letter to the Lensmann, and will only take one boat after all.

The women are dressed in their dead men's sealskins and caps, hands unwieldy in thick gloves, oars standing higher than their heads as they regard the jumble of mended nets, unintelligible as the tangle of hair Maren pulls daily from Mamma's fish-spine comb.

"Well then," Kirsten claps her broad hands together. "We need two between us. Maren? Help me."

Though her hands are large, they are more skilled than Maren's, whose fingers chafe and catch on the thin weave of the nets. It is a good day, the sky light but clouded, free of the biting cold they have spent so many months living with pressed against their bones.

They spread two nets out on the harbour side, and the others have to weight them with slick black stones. Then, taking one at a time, Kirsten shows them how to work them into a fold that can be opened easily.

"How do you know this?" says Edne.

"My husband taught me."

"Why?" says Edne, shock apparent in her thin voice.

"Just as well he did," snaps Kirsten. "Now the next."

They are watched on all sides from windows and most keenly from the doorway of the kirke. Pastor Kurtsson's slight frame is backed by the brightness of candles and the wooden cross glowering behind. They are being judged, unfavourably at that.

Finally they load the boat with the nets and themselves. Mamma has made Maren a meal, just as she used to for Erik and Pappa, of flatbrød sprinkled with flax, and a strip of dried cod from Pappa's last catch. She told Maren this detail proudly, as if it is a blessing and not as Maren feels it, an omen. A skin of light beer sloshes over her heart.

Before she steps into the boat Maren does what she has been avoiding for months now, and looks directly at the sea, slapping the side of Mads's boat with careless little touches. *Waves*, Maren corrects. The sea doesn't have fingers, or hands, or a mouth that can open and swallow. It doesn't watch her: doesn't think anything of her at all.

She takes up an oar, and with Edne at her other side, begins to row. None of those watching cheer, or wave them off, and once the women are on their way they turn their backs.

Kirsten matched them according to size. Edne and Maren are of a similar height and age, though Edne is a little thinner. Maren has to temper her stroke to meet her, and from the seesawing of their path she can tell that others have not yet grasped the need to make allowances and adjustments for the rhythm of your partner. The calculation of it is so distracting Maren doesn't much care that land is drawing further and further away, how soon they will be at the harbour mouth and how beyond that is the sea proper, full of whales and seals and storms, and men drowned and never returned.

Her arms ache within minutes. Though none of them live idly, this is a different sort of movement, this folding forward and straining back, all in your shoulders and arms and licking up your neck and down your back, the seat hard beneath your thighs. The birds begin to circle, feinting so low towards the boat that Edne squeals.

Maren's breath has a song to it, a wheeze she can feel tracing down into her lungs and bringing up stale air, tasting like dust. Her hair is dripping sweat and sea spray down the back of her coat, face numb already, lips cracking around her foul breath. It is no wonder that the men kept their beards long: with her bare face she feels as unsuited to the sea as a newborn.

They reach the harbour mouth and suddenly are at open ocean. The wind comes stronger as soon as they leave the inlet, and a couple of the women cry out as the boat rocks against the strengthened waves.

"First net," says Kirsten, voice still steady. Edne and Maren unfold it as the others continue to row. They spread the net as though they are making a bed with fresh sheets and throw it. It settles like a blanket over the waves, and drops down, tethered to the surface by regular plugs of cork. They keep it trailing from the boat with rope and throw the other net over the opposite side.

"Drop anchor," says Kirsten. Magda and Britta heave it overboard and let the heavy metal fall. The men would cast off entirely and go further out to set more, but they are loath to travel beyond the jut of Hornøya island. The ache in Maren's arms has pooled into heaviness, and she is working hard not to look at the stac crouching barely a hundred feet away.

With the boat secured and nets down, something close to joy spreads through them. Magda laughs at the swooping birds and this brings an echo to Maren's own mouth. They fall silent almost as fast, but something has lifted. They slouch back into the curves of the boat and share their meals between them. The clouds sweep aside and though she can't feel its warmth, the sun is starting to redden Maren's nose. She feels tired and happy, and does not think of the whale at all.

After an hour or so, a shadow crosses the sun, clouds turning swift and the sea swelling once again. An awful quiet passes through, but there is nothing to do but wait. Spitsbergen, where Kirsten says the Lensmann fought back pirates, sits beyond a horizon sparkling with ice. It could be that they can see to the end of the world, here.

"Nets," says Kirsten. "Come on."

Maren knows it is good the moment they start pulling. The net is heavy and strains their sore arms, but as the first shift and flip of fish begin to break the green chop of the water they are shrieking joy through ragged throats. Pulling harder and faster, they soon spill a half-net into the bottom of the boat.

Aside from the skrei and other whitefish fit for tørrfisk, there are herring neat and silver as needles, and salmon that thrash until Kirsten picks them up, one by one, and smashes their heads over the sides of the boat. Edne shrinks back but Maren cheers with the others. The other net is nearly as full: a single redfish thrashes bewildered amongst cod. Maren lifts it almost tenderly, and takes firm grasp of its tail. The snap of its head against the boat sends a thrill through her aching belly.

"Well done," says Kirsten, a hand on her shoulder, and for a moment Maren thinks she might blood her cheeks like a man after a hunt.

There is light enough for another cast-off, but they don't want to stretch their luck. They turn for home, and now they are facing the open water, broken only by Hornøya island and its stac of heaped rocks. Edne whispers a prayer beneath her breath, and Maren closes her eyes, breathing the air in deep, feeling the drag of her oar.

The row home feels fast, all of them finding each other's pace more easily, like a well-worn tune. There is no one waiting as they draw in. Kirsten jumps ashore to tether them, and Maren watches the dark water and thinks that maybe the whale was shadowing them all along, and will now rise to break the boat across its back.

But soon she is being helped onto the harbour edge, the ground unsteady beneath her. Land has been made strange from even their half-day at sea: Maren wonders how sailors can stand to come ashore at all. The other women start to gather when they bring the catch to the troughs, Toril at their head. There is a subdued cheer as the nets are emptied, and Maren can barely believe how many fish there are.

"God provides," says Toril, though the ache in Maren's arms tells her it was not God but they who brought this catch home.

Mamma comes to the harbour like an invalid, leaning on Diinna, and Maren can see baby Erik's hat over her shoulder. Diinna's lips are pursed. She doesn't like being left alone with Mamma: recently Mamma has become absent-minded. She gets in the way and does household tasks wrong, darns already mended stockings, leaves the lids off jars so they spoil. Diinna would rather be on the boat than at home with her child and Mamma, Maren is sure.

Maren helps sort the fish, and atop the regular meting-out of their portion, Kirsten gives Maren the redfish she killed. She thinks to tell Mamma what she did but Mamma shrinks away from it, and from Maren. She says, "You have blood on your cheek," then turns and follows Diinna, laden with their share of the catch, back to the house, leaving Maren to seek out the smudge herself.

When Maren reaches home she lets Diinna help prepare all but the redfish. She scrapes it clean of scales herself, draws a line from its mashed head to its narrow tail, and brings out the guts. She settles them beside the board, and doesn't let Diinna throw them away: they are blue and red and translucent.

She throws them instead on the fire, watches them sizzle and dissolve.

Maren uses Pappa's walrus-tusk tweezers to lift out the finest bones of the fish, and when she is done she cooks it straight away, though it would have been best smoked. She wants to eat it now, at its freshest, while she can still remember what it felt like to have it living between her palms.

Mamma watches her from bed with something like disapproval knotting her brow. She will not eat the fish, will not eat at all that night. She doesn't ask Maren what it was like on the boat, or tell her she is proud. She turns her back in bed, and feigns sleep.

Maren dreams, as always, of the whale. There is salt in her mouth, and her arms strain with effort. But the whale is swimming, not beached, and though it is black and has five fins she isn't afraid. She reaches out to it, and it is warm as blood.

SIX

The next months are at once sharp and shapeless. There is no more talk of whether they should go to sea: they do, every week. More women join them, and soon they have three boats going regularly, even as the year switches on its heel and darkness begins to gather at the corners of the sky, like shadows at the rafters of a mighty house.

Pastor Kurtsson watches from the narrow stoop of the kirke, preaches sermons of growing intensity on the merits of obeying the Kirke and its servants. But even as his fervour builds, Maren feels a change, a turning amongst the women. Something darker is growing, and she finds it in herself, too. She is less and less interested in what he has to say, and more consumed by her work: fishing, chopping wood, readying the fields. In kirke, she finds she has drifted, like an untethered boat, and her mind is out at sea with oars in her hands and an ache in her arms.

She is not the only one losing interest in kirke ways. At the Wednesday meets, Fru Olufsdatter questions Diinna about the Sámi way of scenting fresh water, and enlists Kirsten's help in fashioning bone figures to mark her husband and son. When Maren visits Pappa's and Erik's graves, she finds poorly carved rune rocks laid like stepping stones amongst the settled dirt. More than once, she finds a fox skin on the headland, its meat left at the highest point of the hill. Remembrances, charms: she recalls such things from childhood.

She watches the women in kirke, wonders who snared it, bled it out. Who peeled the fur from its flesh and left it hollow, pinned down by rocks, an offering to the wind. She asks Diinna what a skinned fox means, and Diinna raises her eyebrows, shrugs. But whatever the hope wished over it, the women of Vardø are slipping back into the old ways, grasping for anything solid.

Toril must be unaware of it, or else she'd have told the minister. She and her "kirke-women," as Kirsten calls them, spend more and more time in the kirke as the winter draws in and closes over them, atoning for the sins that took their husbands from them.

Still the divide is growing, sure as a crack in the wall tapped upon by ceaseless fingers, smoothed only slightly by fuller bellies. But they are still here, Maren reminds herself. Still living. They have a system—if you need hides you go to Kirsten, swap for dried fish or thread work, which is in turn exchanged with Toril for gut thread or fresh moss from the low mountain, where she refuses to go because it is full of Sámi and once rumoured to be a witches' meet place. All of them have their skills, their uses, interlaced and built up like a haphazard ladder, resting one atop another.

"It's a sort of triumph," says Kirsten one Wednesday. "What would our husbands say?"

"Nothing good," says Sigfrid. She has fallen firmly in with Toril, but can't stand to miss the gossip of the meets. "Pastor Kurtsson says—"

"Has Pastor Kurtsson planned the sermon for Christmas Eve?" says Kirsten.

"I imagine so," says Sigfrid.

"I should like to say something," says Kirsten. "Speak on the storm. I think many of us would. It is time. I am ready."

Maren looks around the room. She sees no likely candidates. She has no true words for it, even a year later. All of them have the same telling of the storm, now, passed through many tongues until its rough, difficult edges are worn smooth as sea glass.

"Maren?" Kirsten is looking at her, waiting for support. But Maren has none to give her, and nor does any arrive from Edne, or Fru Olufsdatter.

The others must feel, as Maren does, a comfort in it, all of them standing at the same point on the flat sweep of bay: as though they are collected and folded an eye behind an eye behind an eye, clustered around the same seeing scope. *The storm came in like that.* Finger snap. She can't remember who first put the action to it: it may have been Toril, or Kirsten. It may even have been her. They agree on this telling, this snap of fingers, as if by accident, though it's a sort of cowardice. She's sure they despise her for it, as she does them. They pull it across their eyes and tongues so they do not have to really remember. How the boats were there, and then gone.

Maren looks to the window. The relentless dark has a tinge of grey to it: a fog rolling in from the north. They come sudden, swallowing, a dampening cold that penetrates skirts, stockings, makes the familiar ground foreign and strange. Out there, beyond the final row of houses, is the harbour. She watches the sea even more carefully now. She is learning not to feel much for it, with their regular fishing expeditions. But with the anniversary soon upon them, she finds she has no desire to dwell on what it took from them, least of all speak about it in kirke.

She can feel Kirsten's disappointment, and seeks her out as Fru Olufsdatter dims the lamps and tells them it is time to go.

"I'm sorry," she says, touching Kirsten's shoulder. "I am sure the pastor would let you speak."

"I don't need his permission," says Kirsten, blue eyes narrowed. "I'll think on it."

•

Kirsten does not speak on Christmas Eve, though Maren wishes she had. Pastor Kurtsson's sermon is full of platitude, a vague repetition of his words over their husbands' and sons' graves. Maren finds no comfort in it, nothing of their lost men, nothing of the altered women left behind. How many times has she wished that Erik and Pappa lived? Pastor Kurtsson could never understand. No man could.

As she watches him bend to the shelf below his pulpit, and bring out a letter bearing a seal and tassel, Maren realizes she hates him a little: his weakness, his power over them. His constant talk of the mercies of God, when it is obvious to her that they do not extend so far north. Is His eye upon her, inside her head as she thinks these things? She holds her breath and gropes inside her mind, as though she could feel God there.

"This arrived yesterday," says their minister, unfolding the letter. The seal is so heavy it bends the parchment almost in half, and Pastor Kurtsson must hold it out before him, so it blocks him from view. "Our Lensmann is soon to take his seat at Vardøhus, from which he will govern all of Finnmark."

Toril shifts in her seat, looks about the room as if to ensure they note it was she who first brought them the news.

"And, in addition, you," continues Pastor Kurtsson, "which is to say, we, are to have a commissioner live amongst us. He will be appointed by the Lensmann, to oversee the town more closely."

"But Pastor Kurtsson," says Kirsten, "is that not what our minister, your good self, is for?"

"It is true that he might assist in spiritual matters," says Pastor Kurtsson, frowning at the interruption. "But I remain your minister."

"Praise be," says Kirsten, too brightly for the minister to do much but look dour.

When the letter is folded, and the kirke-women kneel to heap prayers upon prayers, Kirsten and Maren linger outside. It is so dark they must stand very close to one another, like animals pushing their bodies together for warmth. Kirsten's eyes are hooded.

"A commissioner," she says. "But no mention of his commission."

"Perhaps he will be like a governor, as Alta has," offers Maren.

"In so small a place?" says Kirsten. "Alta has a great many more people. What need have we of an overseer, especially if Lensmann Cunningham will soon be at his fortress?"

They glance instinctively in the direction of Vardøhus, though the fog is pressed so tight against Maren's eyeballs it makes them sting. Kirsten looks back at her, considering. "Would you like to come to my house? I have beer, and cheese."

Maren would like, very much, to see what Kirsten has made of Mads Petersson's house. She has often wondered how Kirsten copes there, without farmhands, and she would like to see the reindeer. But Mamma will be at home and weeping over Pappa, and so she shakes her head.

"Thank you, but I must go."

Kirsten nods. "To be told of the commissioner on this day—is it significant?"

Maren blinks at her, surprised. "I did not take you for superstitious."

"I only wonder what it is the beginning of."

"Perhaps it is an end," says Maren, unsettled by her tone. "A closing of a circle."

"Circles have no end," says Kirsten, and straightens suddenly. "I'll see you tomorrow."

They turn away from each other into the mouthing fog. The houses are quiet as Maren walks from the kirke, past Fru Olufsdatter's house, Toril's home, and to the outskirts where the light from their fire glows weakly through the slatted windows, dispersed into unearthly whiteness by the fog.

Maren wants to keep walking, past Baar Ragnvalsson's empty house, to the headland. It is an effort to place her hand on their door, to push her way into the cloying warmth. Mamma is stoking the fire, worrying at a patch of dry skin at the corner of her mouth, and Diinna is there with Erik pressed to her chest.

"I told her," says Mamma, without looking up. "About the commissioner."

"What do you think?" says Maren.

"Not much." Diinna is rubbing at Erik's gums with clove paste. Drool comes in great strings from his mouth, red in the firelight. Maren wants to shake her. She misses the way they used to talk. She thought Erik's birth would draw Diinna out of her husband's death, but she is more silent than ever.

"At least it will be someone new," she offers. "Another pair of hands."

Mamma's tongue flicks at her cracked lip, and they fall into the silence that marks their evenings, and speak no more of the commissioner.

They imagine he will be like their minister, have as little impact as snow falling in the sea. They imagine that their lives will go on, and that the worst is behind them. They imagine all sorts of silly, inconsequential things, and every bit of it is wrong.

15th of January 1629

To the Esteemed Commissioner of Vardøhus, Mr. Cornet,

New Year greetings to you! I thank you for your letter of the 19th October. I am greatly encouraged that it reached me with such pace. One never knows how the ships will go.

It is with gladness I read of your acceptance, and urge you not to tarry. I will inform King Christian of your agreement—I have his ear and you can be sure your name will be poured into it. The minister at Vardø has already been notified, and will make ready for your arrival. Great things await you here, and I hope we can grow the Lord's estimation of us Scotsmen even further.

I enclose with this letter your passage to Bergen, where you can proceed through Trøndheim, and on to Vardø. I trust you will not find the journey too arduous.

Your idea of a Norwegian wife is a good one, though I should not wait to come so far north. Bergen will have its spread of good young women desirous of a husband of such standing. Use your title and the sum enclosed to bring someone to keep your bed warm. Perhaps someone who can sing? We will be in need of entertainment.

My regards to Coltart, who I had not known reads your letters. There will be none of that here.

Come safely and swiftly.

Hans Køning
Lensmann over Vardøhus County

BERGEN, HORDALAND, SOUTH-WESTERN NORWAY

1619

SEVEN

Siv has lit the fires in the drawing room and hung the best curtains, so Ursa knows there has either been a death, or there is to be a marriage.

"Or maybe a lord come to our house," says Agnete when Ursa has returned with a final warmed jug of water and the information. "Or an actress?" Agnete has recently learnt of actresses, their father having organized passage for a theatre troupe travelling to Edinburgh on one of his remaining ships.

"Then it will be a dead lord, or a lord come to marry one of us," Ursa says, pouring the jug into the tub. "Same goes for the actress, only she will be here for Father."

Agnete laughs, and then winces. Ursa can hear the draw of fluid rattling across her lungs.

"Hush, I should not have excited you." She helps Agnete pull herself up on her pillows. Her leg drags, and Ursa smooths the sheets. "Siv will not forgive me. Here."

She places her hand on Agnete's thin front, leans her forwards over the enamel bowl. Beneath her palms her sister's lungs rattle as she spits. Ursa covers it over without looking as Siv tells her to do: she knows what colour it will be from the thick breathing that came against her ear all night.

When Agnete is done she helps her from her nightdress. It smells of sour sweat and sickness, so common to Agnete that Ursa barely notices it other than when the clean, bright smell of lavender-scented water is in the air. She helps Agnete into the tub, half-lifting her bad leg over the edge, specially scooped for this purpose.

Her sister is still child-thin, child-straight at the waist and hips though Ursa was nearly full-figured by thirteen. The doctors, who come monthly, measure her each time, but none see her naked as Ursa does, the sharp planes of her body hollowed, her bad leg shrivelled off as old fruit.

"Surely there's no one left to die," says Agnete when Ursa has placed the bar across the tub for her to lean on as she soaps. "So it must be marriage."

Ursa had thought the same, and hopes Agnete can't hear the painful thumping of her heart.

"Do you not think so, Ursa? Father has found someone for you to marry!" Her voice is bright and hollow as a bell. Though there are seven years between them, Ursa often thinks Agnete feels what she feels, as they say twins do. Now Agnete is clutching her soaped hand to her bare chest, at exactly the point Ursa's is hurting.

"Perhaps."

It means Agnete will be alone in this house, confined mostly upstairs, with only Siv left to care for her. Father rarely visits them except to say goodnight. Even if Ursa's betrothed is from Bergen, Agnete will have to learn to sleep alone in this room, spend her days with only herself for company. But Agnete doesn't say any of this, only nods for Ursa to pour a jug of water over her head.

When Agnete is out and dried, and in a clean nightdress, she stops Ursa from combing her hair and says, "Come, let me plait yours. Siv makes it so severe."

Her hands are gentle as she wraps and twists Ursa's hair into one long loop that gathers across the back of her head, scooping down to her nape and fastening behind each ear, and looks at her with such evident pride that Ursa feels self-conscious.

Siv raises an eyebrow at it when she comes to dress Ursa: she is as strict a Lutheran as they come, and wears only brown, and a square of starched white on her greying hair. She sniffs as she puts away the pale pink cotton Ursa was to wear, and crosses to the heavy armoire they used to share with Mother.

It is cherrywood, stripped from a ship come from New England, varnished with a dark brown that drags the colour out of it: much as Siv's clothes do her. But at its hinges and the battered carved nubs of its feet, the wood is deepest, softest red.

Siv draws out Mother's favourite gown: yellow and gathered at the sleeves. "Your father wants you in this," she says, reluctant. "You're to meet a gentleman."

"A gentleman!" Agnete is propped on her pillows and clasps her hands. "And in Mother's gown, Ursa. I'm so jealous I could spit."

"Neither jealousy nor spitting are virtues, Agnete."

"What gentleman, Siv?" says Ursa.

"I don't know that. Only that he's a good Christian. Your father saw fit to tell me that. He's no Papist."

Agnete rolls her eyes as Siv turns to unhook the buttons from their loops of silk. "Did you find out anything important, Siv?"

"I can't think of much more important than that."

"Oh, but is he tall, or rich, or have a beard?"

Siv purses her lips. "This will be a little small, but I have no time to adjust it." She motions for Ursa to crouch, and hauls the dress over her head.

Ursa waits in the rustling gloom of its skirts while Siv's hand searches, and makes no move to help. She breathes deeply, hoping for the lilac scent of Mother to come to her in the dark. But it smells only of dust.

•

The drawing-room door is open when she is summoned, the firelight glowing across the hallway carpet. They heard him arrive, rushed to the window to spy a wide-brimmed black hat standing beneath the windowsill, removed just in time for the door to be opened and the head disappear into shadows. Agnete squeezes Ursa's hands.

"Remember everything."

The banister is very smooth, and throws up the scent of beeswax Siv has not buffed off fully. She hopes they will not have to touch. Of course they will not. But all the same she imagines him reaching for her hand and sliding right off, greasy with wax. He has no face and she realizes he soon will. And a body, a voice, and a smell.

It is her first time meeting a suitor, and she wishes Father had come to tell her something of him, or how he met him, or even if he is someone she knows. Herr Kasperson perhaps, Father's clerk, with his rosy cheeks and shy smile. He is twenty-five, only five years older than Ursa. She thinks she could like a man like him, though he has a strange habit of rubbing his lip with his thumb, which makes him look shifty. She could ask him to stop that if they were married. He seems the sort of man who would listen.

The patched step creaks. She looks up to where their bedroom door stands ajar, imagines Agnete listening for her, holding her breath. Ursa lit as many candles as she could before she came down, but still Agnete had been swallowed by shadow. It has been a long winter, stretching out over spring and freezing the windows closed. But then, this house is always dark at its edges, even in summer, even with all the drapes thrown back and the light so bright it makes Ursa sneeze. She may never spend another season in this house. Would she miss it, or only the people inside?

She turns from the staircase and rolls her shoulders back. Walking feels strange in her narrow silk slippers, with the weight of Mother's dress slipping close to her shoulders.

Deep voices flicker with the firelight. It isn't Herr Kasperson's voice that answers Father's, or anyone's voice she knows. It isn't, she notes as she readies herself to enter, even Norwegian. *English*, she thinks, dredges it up from the small, painful place where she keeps all her memories of her mother. Her mother couldn't read or write but, being the daughter of a merchant, she learnt English well enough and brought Ursa and Agnete up with it too. They used to speak it around the dinner table, practising their accents until they were smooth and only slightly inflected. Ursa clucks her tongue, once, twice, and steps across the threshold.

He is as tall as Father, and broader than any man she knows. He bows as Father places a firm hand at her back and sweeps her forward into the room, so even as she sits she has not seen his face.

The men have been sitting beside one another in the crimson-flocked chairs with the carved arms, and she is left to settle opposite them on the armless chair, careful to keep her back straight, hands folded in her lap.

"Ursula. After the saint, I presume." His accent means she has to listen carefully to understand each word, though he doesn't speak fast. If anything, he speaks too slowly, and it distorts the words. He is turned in his chair, sideways towards the fire and her father. His voice sinks and burrs. She feels a blush rising at her throat.

Father jerks his head. She is meant to answer, then, though his tone gave no hint of a question.

"Yes, sir. And the stars."

"Stars?"

Father coughs awkwardly. "Ursula, this is Herr Cornet."

"Commissioner Cornet," corrects the man. "Absalom."

It takes a moment to comprehend this must be his given name, because he says it like a hallelujah or an *Amen*. She looks up more boldly.

He is tall, dark-eyed. She can't place him in age: not so young as Herr Kasperson, not nearly so old as Father. He is handsome, in his way. His austere, well-cut clothing can't hide how he carries a little weight around his middle, though not so much as she. Ursa watches his profile, the workmanlike heft of his jaw and brow made fine by his straight nose, his dark, slightly curling hair.

"Commissioner Cornet has come from Scotland," says Father. "He is to take up a prestigious post in Vardøhus."

"Sent for by John Cunningham himself, who is upon the orders of your King," says Cornet pridefully. She has not heard of John Cunningham, or of Vardøhus. "And I'm in need of a wife."

It is a moment before she realizes this is the marriage proposal.

"The wife of a commissioner," says Father gladly. "Ursula?" She can hear the question in his voice, knows she should look up and smile, reassure him that she is glad too. She searches herself, regards her lap. Her knuckles are white. "We will arrange it at once."

They talk back and forth, Father asking about the commission, Cornet enquiring whether it is true there are no trees so far north. Their passage will be on one of Father's ships, and Ursa listens to the rising rush in her ears. Siv laced her in to the joins, and she can't inhale fully. She thinks of Agnete, her wet breath. North. Ursa never guessed marriage would take her so far. She imagines ice, and darkness. Finally Father seems to remember her there, dismisses her. She stands so quickly her head spins, and trips from the room.

The wife of a commissioner. She knows she couldn't wish for better, but still her skin crawls with nerves. Since Mother's death, Father has made bad decision after bad decision: she sees it in the dismissal of all clerks except Herr Kasperson, the letting-go of all servants but Siv, the visits from the doctors reduced from weekly to monthly. She can read it in the drawing room shuttered up for all but the best visitors and Christmas, in the settling droop of Father's shoulders and the beer on his breath. This is a good marriage, will bring a little coin with it perhaps.

She passes the rack and leans towards Cornet's coat. It smells of wet leaves and her fingers twitch towards the pockets, but she can't bring herself to touch it.

Ursa makes for the stairs, taking them too fast and too loudly. Agnete looks startled as Ursa closes their door, starts immediately to grapple with the buttons.

"What's the matter? Was he ugly?"

The dress has to come off. She can't breathe in it. She is growing bigger inside it, or it is shrinking, and her head is gripped by the hairstyle and she has to be loose of all of it: her sister's careful braid, her dead mother's dress. How has he come here? How has he found her, in this quiet house on an unquiet street in Bergen?

"Can you help me?"

She sits beside Agnete on the bed, and her sister struggles to a sitting position, fumbles with the fastenings, but it is too tight about the waist. "We need Siv."

Ursa feels sick at the way it presses her. She goes to the

window, watching for him to leave. Her heart is loud as a clock.

"Ursa? What happened?"

The door opens, and her betrothed steps into the street, doesn't call for a carriage. She watches his black-hatted head fade in amongst all the other black-hatted heads.

"Ursa?"

Absalom Cornet. It sounds less like a prayer, and more like a knell.

EIGHT

Ursa expects to wake feeling different, but there is nothing to mark the next day as special. Siv rouses them early as usual, throwing back their curtains, though since they were swapped for cheaper cotton the light leaks right through. Ursa can remember the fine blue velvet ones she grew up with, hiding in their long folds while Mother sat at her dresser, brushing out the thick blonde hair that both daughters inherited. But they had to be sold five years ago, along with that dresser and the silver-backed combs, when Father made another poor investment. This room that was once her mother's dressing room is now their bedroom, the top floor shuttered up.

"It makes no sense with Agnete as she is," Father told her when Ursa complained about moving from her large room. "All those stairs. And it is too costly to run the fires, keep all that furniture in those empty rooms. I'm selling much of it, though we may yet rent it out."

Ursa is glad the lodger is yet to materialize. She doesn't want a stranger sleeping in their house. And now, she won't have to worry about it ever again, for soon she will be sleeping beside a stranger in her own house. When she thinks of this, her hands shake. She hopes Absalom Cornet won't remain unfamiliar for long.

Siv sets a breakfast tray before Agnete. It's the same silver one she served the tea on yesterday and Ursa smiles at her, noticing the effort. Agnete has had another bad night, and the sheets are twisted about her legs. Ursa smooths them and helps her sister into a sitting position as Siv clears her spit bowl, brow creased with concern.

"Another dose of the vapours after breakfast, I think."

"No, please, Siv," says Agnete. Her voice is thick, her chest wheezes. "I am fine, really."

"Her nose is still sore from last time," says Ursa. "Can we not leave it today?"

"We have orders from the doctor," says Siv. "You know it helps."

"It hurts," says Agnete when Siv has gone to fetch the vapour bowl. She touches the tender red place beneath her nose where the skin is cracked and irritated.

"I know," says Ursa, smoothing back her sister's hair. Despite her bath, it is already rank with sweat. "We can cover your nose with one of Mother's silk kerchiefs."

"The blue one?"

Ursa stands at once and goes to their mother's armoire. On the shelf above the rail there is a wooden box of kerchiefs and other effects that survived Father's purge, and she takes Agnete's favourite from it. She pins back her sister's hair as Agnete presses it to her face, running it through her fingers.

"Eat, Agnete."

"We should be speaking English," says Agnete. "To help you practise."

"He is Scottish."

"But he speaks English, still?"

"Yes."

"Well then."

"Well then," says Ursa, in English. "Eat, Agnete."

Agnete nibbles at the knekkebrød. "It's so dry."

"There is no blessing so complete as bread," says Ursa, mock sternly, imitating their housekeeper's intonation. But it is increasingly hard to keep Agnete happy, with all her pleasures slowly being strictured. The doctors stopped her eating anything wet about a month ago, and she is still adjusting to it. Ursa suspects they are making up much of Agnete's treatment as they go along. She doesn't think her sister's poor lungs are caused by too much stew.

Siv brings back a cloth and a large bowl of steaming water, and the small bottle brought by the doctor. She starts to unstopper its lid but Ursa holds out her hand for it. "I can manage, thank you, Siv."

Siv eyes her. "Seven drops, the doctor said. Seven drops or else there's no point."

"I know."

The housekeeper puts the bottle into her outstretched palm, presses a brisk kiss to Agnete's forehead, and leaves the room.

"You won't do seven, will you? One is fine," says Agnete, peering anxiously at her. Ursa shakes four drops of oil into the bowl, swirls it so the yellowness spreads about on the water. The smell hits her nostrils and makes her eyes sting. She sets the bowl on the table beside Agnete, helps her sit up so she can lean over the steam, kerchief clutched tight to her nose.

She places one hand at her sister's forehead to support her, and brings the cloth over her head to trap the vapours.

"Breathe deep."

She places her palm on Agnete's back, hearing as much as feeling her slow, painful inhale, the wet rush of her exhale. She counts aloud to one hundred breaths, and Agnete emerges red-faced from the steam, eyes streaming, the kerchief damp. She coughs, spits into the clean bowl Siv brought on her breakfast tray.

"How does it feel?" asks Agnete, as Ursa covers the bowl, and sets it aside.

"I was about to ask you."

"It stings and it's horrible and I wish the doctors would listen when I tell them so. Now you."

"How does what feel?"

Agnete rolls her watering eyes. "Being engaged to be married."

Despite her complaints, Ursa can hear that Agnete's breathing is easier. "Much the same. Would you like to go downstairs today?"

"No. Tell me, what he is like?"

"I do not know much of him yet," says Ursa. "Only what I told you yesterday."

"Tell me again?"

•

She has told her meagre story three times before the day is done. Father doesn't call on them that day, nor the next, and Siv tells them he is out to decide details at Absalom's place of residence, leaving Ursa to withstand Agnete's disappointment at the lack of courtship.

"Why does he not write?"

"It is only two days since we met."

"Still."

"What use would a letter be? I cannot read."

"A song then. Something."

Ursa shrugs.

"Perhaps it doesn't matter," says Agnete. "Perhaps it is enough that he saw your face and wished to marry you."

Ursa supposes there is a romance to that. For someone not even to know you, and yet to love you.

"Do you think Father wrote to Mother?"

"She couldn't read, either." Agnete's face falls, and Ursa takes pity on her. "Maybe. You should ask him."

She knows Agnete won't. She won't, either. Father crumples whenever Mother is mentioned, even after all these years. Lately Ursa has caught him looking at her with an awful sadness in his eyes—she knows she is looking more like her mother with each passing year. Perhaps that is why he stays so much away from her these days, though he used to speak to her on all manner of things. They were once so close, and now, his silence is catching.

Ursa wonders how different this moment would be if Mother had not died bringing their brother into the world. If both of them had lived, and there were a boy running about the house. If Father had not lost all his money, and all three of the siblings were hiding in the velvet curtains, watching their mother brush her hair until it crackled. But Agnete would still be ill, and she would still be marrying a stranger, going with him to a place she has never heard of.

Agnete reaches out suddenly for her.

"You will miss me?"

Ursa wants to tell her yes. She wants to tell her sister she is as air to her, that she couldn't have a better friend in the world. But she only takes Agnete's thin face in her palms and hopes she knows what it means.

•

The night before the wedding, they lift Agnete down the stairs in her chair to dine with them for the first time in months. It is an inelegant task, and all of them are sweating by the time Agnete is ensconced closest to the fire, wrapped in shawls. Siv watches her, poised, as though she may keel over like an upturned boat at any moment.

But Agnete sits straight, and barely coughs, and Father pours Ursa a small glass of akevitt. It tastes bitter as medicine, but she swallows it down, the burn turning to a gentle warmth in her belly.

Emboldened by the akevitt and Agnete's presence, Ursa asks Father how it came to be that Absalom Cornet arrived at their door, and Agnete stops chewing to listen. Ursa knows her sister has imagined all sorts of fanciful things.

"I met him at the harbour," says Father, not looking at Ursa. "He approached me, admired my cross."

Its chain glints from his waistcoat pocket. Ursa knows he often takes it out and keeps it held in his hand without even thinking about it: piousness as a tic.

"He told me of his posting to Vardø, his calling from God to serve there."

"I thought the Lensmann had called him?" says Ursa, and winks at Agnete. But Father does not catch the tone, pours another akevitt.

"The Lensmann is beneath the King, and the King beneath God."

"Your husband must be verily crushed," says Agnete, winking back. Ursa clasps her sister's hand beneath the table. It is so soft she wants to bring it to her cheek, to kiss it and not let go.

"He was in need of a ship, and a bride—"

"In that order?" whispers Ursa, and Agnete snorts so suddenly she begins to cough again. Siv rushes forwards with her spit bowl, and Ursa tightens her grip on her hand until the worst is past. Father drains his akevitt, speaks more to himself than to his daughters.

"I gave him a good price for his passage."

And for me, Ursa thinks.

Agnete must be carried up, and Ursa insists upon doing it, tucking up her skirts so she will not trip on the stairs. Her sister is hot and too light, like a newborn pup. Agnete wraps her thin arms around Ursa's neck.

"Not very romantic, is it?" she murmurs, her chest rattling.

"It'll do," says Ursa. Agnete wrinkles her nose in disappointment.

For once, Agnete sleeps, but the akevitt fizzes through Ursa's body, leaves her legs restless. She stands to pace their room, presses her forehead against the cool glass of their window. She can see as far as the harbour, the ships like toys on the horizon. There are always men there, always busy and moving. *The world goes on*, she thinks, and beneath the weight in the pit of her stomach that is half Siv's cooking, half dread, she is glad she will soon be part of it.

•

Leaving their house in the morning is like walking through a dreamscape: everything familiar and made completely strange by the fact that she will not see it again, not for a long while. *Ever?* She banishes the thought. She is the daughter of a ship-owner: of course she will come back.

Father stops her in the hallway with a rare clasp of her hand.

"Your mother," he begins, and she hears the catch in his throat.

She thinks he will not say more, is hopeful of it because her eyes are swollen enough by her tears with Agnete, despite Siv's cold compresses. But instead he draws her into the dimness of his study, lights a lamp and pushes the door to.

"You must have this."

It is a small glass bottle, the one that always stood on

Mother's dresser before it was sold. Ursa takes and unstoppers it, presses the smell of stale lilacs into her wrists.

"Thank you, Father."

She hopes it will make it easier for him, now there is one fewer to clothe and feed. Perhaps he can employ someone to help with Agnete. For although there has been no time to announce it in the society pages of the paper, and though her dowry comprises mostly of their passage to the North, some fragrance and her dead mother's dress, it is a good marriage. Her husband is a commissioner with a letter from a Lensmann in his pocket.

Father kisses her on the forehead. His hand trembles and he smells of old beer: yeast and sharpness. Later, her husband kisses her on exactly the same spot to seal the marriage, and he smells of nothing at all. Clean as snow.

NINE

It is still early when Cornet holds the door of the tavern he has booked a bed in open for her, and goes to the bar while Ursa retires to their room.

She prepares as best she can, presses the lilac water to her wrists, and at the place where her pulse moves the thin skin beneath her earlobe. She imagines that he will kiss her there, and it makes her hands quake. The linen of her nightdress scratches at her shoulders and breasts. It has a high neck and doesn't seem to be designed to lie down in, but as it is Siv's wedding gift, perhaps that is the idea after all.

Siv starched it herself, and Ursa knows that was a luxury of time she did not have. Ursa smelt the boiling bran, saw Siv soaking it the three days between betrothal and wedding. The nightdress still smells of sour water, though Siv had worked it across the slickstone to take out the worst of it; it still crunched the first time Ursa laced the ribbons at the front.

Agnete gave her the blue silk kerchief, her favourite of Mother's. It clinked when Ursa took it. Inside were five skilling, Agnete's share of what they were given following the sale of Mother's things.

"I cannot take this."

"You must not go so far without the means to come back."

"I can ask Absalom for the money."

"You should have your own," Agnete said, though she had no idea of the cost of such a voyage, any more than Ursa did. "Just in case."

Ursula's eyes are small and mean in the dark, greasy window: her lip trembles like a sulking child's. She draws the thin curtains.

Her husband, for all his pride in his title, is obviously not the lavish sort. Their lodging is within smelling distance of the trade port, with its perpetual reek of tobacco and decay. It seeps in through the rotten frame of the window on the bleak chill and she presses her wrist to her nose.

The lilac brings back easier days, before Mother died, when the house was lit like a Christmas tree throughout the cold winters and long, luminous summers, and all of them dressed and fed by four servants and a cook. Mother and Father had dinner parties with other merchants and their sparkling wives, and Ursa would be permitted to sit up with them in the drawing room before they descended into the dark glitter and chatter of the dining room.

She never had much thought for her wedding breakfast, but supposed it would be something like one of those parties. She'd certainly imagined guests beyond Siv, Father, and Agnete made breathless by the cold air. Though she had no friends to speak of, Father having withdrawn them so much from society, still she'd imagined women like Mother used to dine with, their long bare throats backed by bright collars, golden hair twisted about their heads. Men in fine suits with ruffs jutting at their necks like well-wattled birds, bearing gifts of sugared plums and silk. Pomade and lavender in the air, a table laid with roasted goose and creamed spinach, a whole salmon poached with lemon and chives, carrots heaped with butter. Candles burnishing the scene golden and precious.

Not the back room of Gelfstadt Tavern, convenient to the kirke and the harbour, a bottle of brandy between the men, Father misty-eyed and remembering. He looked old in the glow from the draughty fire that kept spluttering soot and chill wind through its fireguard. The candles were stubs melted together from many ends: yellow and gutting.

When the time for goodbyes came, Cornet turned his back as though her tears were something indecent. Agnete stood without aid, to show she could, leant only a little on her on the walk to the carriage. Father had drunk too much and they had already said their goodbyes in his study. There was nothing Ursa could say to Agnete but they clung to each other until Siv pushed them gently apart.

"Take care, Mistress Cornet."

And then they were away.

She imagines her husband downstairs, the band she placed onto the base of his finger clinking against his glass, perhaps toasting her. And because they will use his customs for naming, she is Mistress Absalom Cornet. Herself, lost inside his name.

She hopes to please him, and knows some of this begins tonight, in this square room with its overlarge bed, here in this tavern on the Bergen docks, their ship to Finnmark waiting outside on water so chill she hears men at the hull breaking ice from it. An accusatory Siv told Ursa a little of what to do, cheeks flushing—*nightdress, bed, don't watch him for it is too wanton, prayers when it is done.*

She removes the chamber pot from sight, slides the warming pan from one side of the bed to the other. There are pale stains on the mattress, and the straw has broken through in places. She can't face the greying pillow and so wraps her old night-dress about it.

She lies ever so carefully, makes sure her hair is about her shoulders the way Agnete told her makes it look like she lies in a field of shining yellow wheat. Lamplight comes irregularly from the dock, and through the wooden walls she hears coarse voices speaking English and Norwegian and French and other languages she can't recognize.

Beneath it all sits a creaking sound, like their stair at home, or Father's knees when he sits. For a long while she can't place it, and wonders if it is inside her own mind. But then she realizes: it is the ice, relocking about the ships.

Soon she will be on that sea, and moving further and further from Agnete and Father and Siv, from their house on Konge Street, and from Bergen with its broad, clean roads and busy port. Leaving the finest city of the world, and all she has ever known, for what? She has no picture of Vardø, the place she is to live. No idea of the house they will share, the people she will meet.

The creaking grows until it is all she can hear. She presses her lilac-scented wrist to her face, and sucks in air like water.

•

The rasp of a door and gutter of a candle wake her, and she rolls over, reaches for Agnete. Her nightdress is creased beneath her cheek, hands frozen on the sheet. And in the small circle of the candlelight, Absalom—her *husband*—is undressing, the dark nap of his head bowed as he sways and struggles with his belt.

She doesn't stir. She barely breathes. In her sleep she has ruined her careful arrangement of hair: it is about her neck like a noose. Her nightgown has rucked up to her waist but she dares not move to pull it down.

Absalom Cornet has removed his trousers, and now that her eyes have adjusted she can see his underthings have come off as well. He is even paler beneath his clothes, like a sea creature winkled from its shell. She closes her eyes as he comes towards the bed, and the straw wheezes staleness as the weight of his body falls upon it.

A rush of cold air sweeps beneath the blankets as he moves under them, and she feels her cheeks flush when she realizes what he must be able to see: her underthings, childish with their ribbons drawn through. The room is filled with a sharp smell of alcohol and smoke. She had not taken him for a drinker. Her heartbeat is painful in her ears.

Nothing happens for a long while, and she wonders if he is asleep. She opens an eyelid and sees his eyes are still wide and staring at the ceiling. He is taking deep breaths, his hand clutching at the blanket, white-knuckled, and it comes to her that he is nervous. That is why he has drunk so much and come so late. She is likely his first. She is readying herself to reach out to him, to tell him she is shy of it too, when he turns his head and looks at her.

She knows the set of his eyes, has seen it in the men who arrived at the dinner parties steady and clear-eyed, but left staggering. Something sharp enters his gaze as he props himself sideways. She remembers Siv's instruction not to look him in the eye, and with an urgency that is almost painful her hands contract about her nightdress, pulling it down.

He rolls himself suddenly on top of her; so clumsy and heavy her breasts are crushed. The possibility of breath narrows to such a point that it is only when she feels the hardness of him already on her thigh that she thinks to take one, a gasp that heightens to a cry. He is fumbling with the ribbons, then lower, at the seams. He pulls: it gives. He moves along her, and her body doesn't give so easily.

Another cry comes, a sound she has never heard herself make before. It frightens her more even than he does. He has cut her, she thinks wildly, he has stabbed her. There is a centre to her she never knew existed: a bright, throbbing place so sore she could sob.

His face is in the pillow, and he is breathing bitter breath against her ear and hair. His arms are braced either side of her shoulders, and his chest knocks against hers with an awful force. She drags her awareness away from the hot point of hurt as he burrows further into her, sending it to the ache of her legs, caught and cramping beneath his. When she tries to move them he raises himself slightly and lays one arm flat across her collarbones, and she knows he means for her to lie still.

The bed makes a wild squeaking sound, like an animal in a trap, and finally tears come hot from the humiliation of it, the tearing of it. His whole body bucks. A moan hits her ear.

The coming-out is nearly as painful as the going-in.

He stands unsteadily and pisses in the bedpan: she can hear he misses. There is something warm between her legs: blood and something else that doesn't belong to her.

When he has dragged on his nightshirt, blown out the candle and slumped into bed with no part of them touching, she rolls the other way and brings her legs up to her belly, trying to soothe the stinging.

She couldn't have guessed at it: this hollow knowledge that wives must carry with them, that their husbands tear themselves a place in their bodies. Is this really how babies are got? She bites on her hand to keep from crying. How is she to tell Agnete of any of this—how is she to warn her that even with a man appointed commissioner, with a beard that smells of clean snow and who prays hard as a minister, there can be no safety? Beside her, with the first light of morning coming through the thin curtains, Absalom Cornet opens his mouth wide, and begins to snore.

TEN

There is a hierarchy to a ship stricter than in the finest house. It is close to covenant, and Ursa decides, for all her limited knowledge of the world, that there must be no country run harder or neater than a ship.

In place of beasts are the monkeys, the boys of twelve or thirteen who climb the rigging and swab the decks: even the ship's cat is treated better. They accept beatings and yellings dumbly as horses, are as pitiable. Then there are the sailors, older, rougher. They are skilled and coarse, going about their tasks with a rhythm inscrutable to Ursa's eye. The captain, it seems, is higher than a king, though lower than God. The sea is that to them, giving grace or committing violence, always spoken of in hushed, reverent tones. Ursa isn't sure where her husband and she fit—she supposes they do not.

Why any man would choose a life at sea is beyond her. From the moment she steps aboard the *Petrsbolli*, she wishes to turn around and step straight back off it. Everything, from its dark wood to its slimed guard rail, seems glowering and forbidding.

It is a rudimentary ship, even to her untrained eye. It isn't that Father has not made an effort: there are clean linen sheets on the bunk, made double size for their marriage bed, and he has sent a tiny clothes chest of cherrywood, same as Mother's armoire, fitted with a brass lock for which she has the only key. In it she keeps Mother's lilac water and blue kerchief, Agnete's money. But these fine details make the whole thing worse. It is dark, the floor is slippery with unknowable grease, and it is tiny—her husband could brush the walls with his outstretched fingers, and when they lie down his feet will dangle over the end of the bunk.

This, she knows, is the best they could do. They can't afford passage on a better ship. She wonders if Absalom regrets her father's offer. It isn't even a merchant ship made for fine goods: their cargo is local wood, milled in the forests of Christiania and brought by fjord to be taken north, where there are no trees. This thought is as strange to her as the sea: all about Bergen is forest.

Not for the first time, she is glad she was not Father's son, and had no need to be trained in the shipping business. The ground never steady beneath your feet, so that at one moment you may be taking tea below decks with your husband and the captain in his cabin and, despite the swaying of the minute horn lantern and the cups braced by small lips to keep them from sliding about the table, almost imagining yourself in some sort of decent society, and at the next the whole world is tipped sideways.

And then there is the sound. Not only from the sea, which her night in Gelfstadt Tavern gave some notion of, but from other people. The sound of so many men: their heavy tread on the boards above and below; men's laughter, always too loud and too long; the grunt of men's effort as they haul ropes or clean decks or move cargo. The cargo must be turned and checked for rot every other day, the ship's cat loosed to flush out rats.

This isn't a ship made, nor fit, for passengers. Their cabin has been nooked out of the men's sleeping room, marked off by thin walls of cheap wood that sway and strain in the joins. They share a doorway, left to the cabin, right to the large space of the men's room. She waits to rise until most of them are up at work, but on a ship no one sleeps all at once so she still catches glimpses of hammocks strung like great cocoons fore-and-aft, two or three sleeping as close as bats clustered in the dark. But worst are the noises of night-times, the snoring and other bodily effects, occasionally sounds that make her cheeks burn and her body tense.

The men, for all their coarseness, still call her "Mistress Cornet" when they pass each other below decks, but in bed she knows her true place. At first she thinks she must be doing something wrong. Though her husband gives her time to take off her underthings after that first night together, and though she learns to keep her legs open so as not to feel so trapped, and pins her hair back so it doesn't catch beneath his hands, there is always pain. There isn't always blood after, but there is a constant soreness.

Every morning, every night, and after each meal, he drops to his knees and prays so fervently she doubts she could pull him from it were there fire licking his soles. He prays with a care and focus he does not show her, his lips working, his forehead pressed against his clasped hands. Inwardly she rails against Agnete's beloved stories, at Mother's tender glances at Father, at the bawdy laughter of the kitchen maids back when they had them, when the delivery boy came calling.

Did they all know what love was, and lie?

•

To survive, she is cultivating distance. Even before Agnete was born, Ursa craved company, always shadowed Father and played in the same room as Mother, always talked too much though she knew it risked being banished to the playroom with its dolls and blocks. Now, she is making a silence of herself.

She barely speaks, barely opens her mouth wide enough to eat the small squares of tough meat and wrinkled carrots, the mush of oats or fish, made edible with fresh herbs that quickly wither and turn brown. She is working on turning invisible, sits very still at the formal meal, which they take daily with the captain, her mouth a dark line like a closed hinge. Even when she joins Absalom on the floor to pray, the wood hard beneath her knees, she is sure not to raise her voice above a whisper on the *Amen*.

Sometimes Captain Leifsson and Absalom have whole conversations without so much as gesturing at her. The captain's English is heavily accented, and Ursa must listen as carefully as she does to Absalom. Her husband is often boastful of his appointment as commissioner: she learns a little more of him this way. How, at thirty-four, he is the youngest commissioner Lensmann Cunningham has selected, that he comes from the same area of Scotland, though is lower-born. That his name has been mentioned to the King himself.

"And why is he bringing you?" asks Captain Leifsson. "It is a long way from Scotland."

"We are to root the Church more fully into the land there," says Absalom, with the same passion with which he prays. "And destroy its enemies."

"I am sure you will not find many of those," says Captain Leifsson, sipping from his cup. Ursa can see a small smile at the corners of his lips. "There is barely anyone there."

She keeps all this information held hard in her mind. She wants to take as much from her husband as she can, without having to give too much of herself in return—she feels the scales must eventually tip in her favour, that soon she will have some power in their relations. That he desires her is obvious, but tenderness seems distant as their destination. Perhaps by the time they reach the edge of the world, they might draw closer together, but then again, she is not sure, any more, that this is what she wants.

What she wishes for, prays for, is some sort of control. She finds it only alone, in the cabin that has been her world at sea so far. Her husband goes elsewhere in the days. He is exactly as his profile suggested to her in Father's sitting room. Brutishness made palatable by touches of fineness and manners.

Their journey is punctuated by stops along the coast. They are to be at sea over a month—"Perhaps two," shrugs Captain Leifsson, unconcerned as Ursa feels herself blanche—though the journey would be far quicker aboard a ship that did not have business at seemingly every port. Ursa supposes Father must exploit any opportunity for trade.

Each day, though she spends them mainly alone, she dresses carefully as Siv taught her, hooking the buttons with a claw designed for this purpose. Siv must have one, to dress herself— or does her dress do up at the front? Ursa wrinkles her nose, tries to remember. She wants no detail of home to slip away. The monotony is broken by occasional nausea, which she eases by lying back with one foot placed on the floor.

It is ten days since they left Bergen, and she is arranged just so when there is a knock at the thin door. Captain Leifsson stands crouched beneath the low beam, smiling.

"We are about to enter Christiansfjord, Mistress Cornet, to begin our approach to Trøndheim. It is fair weather, and the cliffs standing clear. Perhaps you should like to come and see?"

He has a voice like a minister, or a judge. A voice that makes a suggestion into an order, impossible to disobey. He is a head shorter than her husband, and with a thinner beard, blond where Absalom is dark. He is kinder-eyed, too. She wishes Absalom would look like that at her, wonders if this is her lot now, judging all men against the length and breadth of her husband.

He waits while she slides on her cloak and follows behind him. The passageway is busy as ever, men coming running along the length and pausing to allow them past, before disappearing into the shadows again.

"I hope you are finding the journey comfortable?" says Captain Leifsson.

"Most comfortable, thank you, captain. I hope we are not too much of an imposition."

"It is your father's charter." She notices he doesn't say that it is Father's ship. "It is good," he continues, perhaps to soften his sentence, "to have reason to light the lamps in my cabin, and I know the cook enjoys the challenge of creating such culinary delights as are appropriate for a lady from Bergen." He turns briefly back to her, a twitch of a smile in his beard. "And besides, I have not gone so far as Vardø since my whaling days. Here we are. Might you wish to ascend first?"

The ladder is steep, barely slanted. She would like to go ahead, to have someone behind in case she loses her grip, but her dress means it would be improper. She gestures for him to go. The rungs are slick and chill, seeping instantly through her gloves and thin soles. Could Father not have sent her with boots?

Captain Leifsson waits at the top and helps her up, taking her weight where she stumbles slightly on the iced-over top step. Though his touch is gentle it feels bruising even through clothes: she can't suffer a man to touch her, however well meant. He leads her to the raised back of the ship.

The day is impossibly bright: the sort of crystalline clarity that comes when winter still sits in the air. They have already entered at the narrow mouth of the fjord, and the cliffs rise sheerly either side, a clean hundred feet, the black rock raked with lines of lighter grey. The sea is green and glitters with chips of ice, and as soon as the wind bites at her face and brings up its blood, chilling her lungs, she feels better than she has since she left home.

"They are magnificent, are they not?"

"They are," she breathes, and is embarrassed by the keenness in her voice. "Though you must have seen mightier, captain?"

"I take each sight for itself alone, Mistress Cornet. Come."

He offers her his arm. She looks about for her husband, but can't sight him. The deck is full of men, leaning out each side of the ship, calling back in a chain of voices to the second mate, Hinsson, who stands steering at the whipstaff towards the rear. The sail stands over them, snapping in the wind like a canvas cloud: monkeys scurry up and down the rigging, and stronger sailors sit astride the beams, adjusting the vents of the canvas to control their speed.

It feels good to be amongst such action. Ursa takes the captain's arm out of necessity more than anything, and they begin to walk. Her legs are stiff and soft all at once, begrudging and grateful of her weight.

"You should come up here more often," he suggests. "It would be perfectly appropriate for you to walk the stern, even alone. No one would trouble you."

"I'll think on it," says Ursa. It sounds harsher than she meant, and she adds a hurried, "Thank you, captain."

"Have you been a-sea before, Mistress Cornet?"

"Never."

"I am amazed," he says. "Your father was so often at sea. To travel seemed his great passion. I would have guessed at him sharing it with his kin, girls or no."

"Father has not sailed for years," she says, surprised. "He gave it up when I was born, and once my mother..." She hesitates. The clean air brings confidences up easily, and with the wind snatching her words from her as soon as they are out she doesn't feel as though she need conceal it. "Mother grew frail, he did not wish to leave her."

"Ah, yes. I heard Merida had passed. I started to write, many times, but..." He gestures about him, and she thinks she understands what he is trying to say. A ship feels a different place entirely. "Six years?"

"Nine. Forgive me, I did not know you were so well acquainted with my parents."

He stops. "Do you not recognize me, Ursula?"

Her name, unshrouded by her husband's for the first time in ten days, is a shock. But she finds nothing familiar in his face. She shakes her head.

"I am sorry, captain. Should I?"

"I dined at your house on several occasions, when Merida was still living. You were often at play about us, getting beneath our feet. I sometimes passed you food beneath the table, like a dog..." He stops again and turns to her, eyes wide. "I did not mean offence, only you were a mischievous child." But she is smiling at his alarm, gives his arm the lightest of squeezes.

"I take no offence, captain."

"You are up, wife." Absalom Cornet is before them, sudden as a squall, leaning on the guard rail, with his face to them. How decent he looks. But something in her throbs with panic. She gives no sign of it, but the corner of her eye starts to flutter in time with her heart.

"The captain willed it, husband. He wished to show me Christiansfjord."

Absalom eyes the cliffs as though they just occurred to him to be worth looking at. "Named for your King, I suppose."

"There is some debate over that." Captain Leifsson's voice is firm but light.

"That they are named for him?"

"That he is our King. Some still rebuke the treaty."

"It is law," says her husband without humour to match that in the captain's voice. "There is surely nothing to rebuke?"

"Of course." The captain gives a neat bow. She realizes she is clinging to him and eases her grip. A muscle is working in Absalom's jaw. "We are walking the deck, if you would care to join us."

Absalom gives a tight shake of his head and turns back to his staring. She notes that his hands are clasped on the rail and wonders if he has been praying.

Silence falls between them. Their exchange with her husband has reminded her to feel afraid. The back of her neck creeps as she catches the smell of ice on the air: of clean nothing. The knot that had eased in her belly is done up tight again and squeezing, even as they walk away from Absalom. The fjord slides a mighty shadow over them, and in its jagged cool she tries to relax.

"You do not remember, then?" Captain Leifsson's voice is soft, as though he recognizes her panic.

Those dinner parties were over with by the time she was eleven. Even without the fug of distance, the faces of adults were all the same, all glamour and whiskers and age. She never watched them with any specificity, only revelled in her access to this world of laughter and smoke. She barely remembers hiding beneath the table. It must have only been on one or two occasions, when Father was too involved in conversation to notice, Mother turning a blind eye.

"I am sorry."

"No need, no need." But she is sure she has disappointed him somehow. Wanting to pull him from it, she casts about for another question.

"Have you been to Vardøhus before, captain?"

He gives a tight nod.

"Is it a castle as everybody says?"

"Of a sort. It is certainly a sizeable structure to have been built so far from anything."

Her dismay must show clearly for he pushes on. "But I have heard it is to become grander beneath Lensmann Køning. He has the King's ear, and I hear he has great plans for Finnmark. What has your husband told you of it?"

"Very little."

"Your father, perhaps? I know he ran whaling boats at Spitsbergen. Did he go east to Vardø?"

She bites the tender inside of her cheek. "Not that he spoke to me of, captain."

They are approaching the whipstaff, where Second Mate Hinsson lifts a meaty hand in greeting. Before him, one of the monkeys, a thin boy of about Agnete's age, is sorting frayed ends of rigging.

"Would you tell me of Finnmark?"

"I only know it from the sea."

"I know of it not at all. I have not been north of Bergen a day in my life."

They have reached the stern, where St. Peter for whom the ship is named is carved in miniature with brute efficiency and attached to the rearmost mast. Piles of rope are stored in tight whorls big as barrels. The captain lets go of her arm and leans against one, looking back over the stern. Behind, the boat is throwing out long draglines of froth. The captain withdraws a stained pipe from his jacket.

"Do you mind?"

She shakes her head no. He brings out a small pouch of tobacco and tamps it down, strikes his lighting flint, shields it from the wind. The sudden flare of the tobacco catching makes her realize it is growing dark again, the bluish light fading to a darker spread of deep blue. Soon the first stars will be out. She has not seen them in days.

He takes a long drag, exhales white smoke. "What do you wish to know?"

Ursa considers. "What's the furthest you've been?"

"From where?"

Ursa flushes. "From Bergen." She had forgot it was not the centre of the world for everyone.

"Spitsbergen, as I said."

"Is that very far?"

He chuckles, a throaty sound made mellower by his mouthful of smoke. "The furthest most go north."

"And Vardø is not so far as that."

"No, not so far."

That comforts her, a little. "What is there?"

"Whales. Ice. Some Sámi cross the ice in winter to summer there, return when the sea refreezes."

"Sámi? You mean the Lapps?"

"No, I mean Sámi," Captain Leifsson replies, firmly.

"You've met them?" The thin skin at the edges of her eyes stings.

"Some of them."

"What are they like? Are they fearfully wild?"

"No more than the next man." Something between them shifts. He seems annoyed with her, and Ursa grapples for something to say to pull herself back into his confidence.

"Is there anything beyond Spitsbergen?"

He sniffs, rubs at his nose. The moment of uneasiness passes. His pipe has already gone out and he empties out the burnt endings, refills. For an instant she wonders what it would be like to be married to a man such as this, who speaks to her so easily and takes her arm so gently. He strikes the flint, and the tobacco flares in the dark hollow of his palms.

"Educated types say there is a black rock there. A mountain, high as the sky, made out of magnetic rock, and that is why our compass needles drag north. Some think the sea pulls towards it the nearer you get, too. That if you cross the gulf, you will be carried along on its current, all the way to the black rock."

"And you'll be dashed upon it?"

"Sucked down." He takes a long draw. "They think the sea stops before it, drops like a waterfall, right through to the bottom of the earth. But I do not believe it," he says, straightening and rolling back his shoulders. "The Sámi do not speak of it, and they go further than any Norseman has."

"What do you think is there?"

"Perhaps there is a black rock. It makes sense that the compasses point that way for a reason. But I do not believe the sea turns river and drops away. I believe it flows all the way around." The bowl smoulders redly. "And that is quite terrifying enough."

He tamps out the pipe, pulls another pouch from another pocket, loosens the drawstring, and holds it towards her. "Aniseed?"

"What is it?"

"A herbal seed, from Asia. It's sweet." Ursa holds out her palm and he tips a small greenish seed onto it. When she bites into it, it's bitter and she grimaces. Captain Leifsson laughs.

"You are meant to suck upon it. See?"

He places one in his mouth. His cheeks hollow in. Ursa turns away to spit the seed into her palm, throws it over the back of the ship. The captain gives her another, and she sucks, very aware of his eyes upon her mouth.

"Wife." The word is curt, a summons. "Captain, we should ready ourselves to dine." Her husband stands with his hand outstretched. "Come."

She had not been conscious of how close she and the captain had been standing. She steps away.

"Thank you for the company, captain."

"A pleasure, Mistress Cornet."

When Absalom takes her hand, his grip is too firm. As soon as they are out of hearing distance, he bends his head towards her.

"Do not speak Norwegian with him in my presence. A man should understand what his wife is saying." He drops her hand. She follows him at as much of a distance as she dares, and they ready themselves in silence for dinner.

His mood seems to pass quickly, and he calls her beautiful when they are both changed, her hair freshly combed and pinned. He places his hand at the small of her back when they go to the captain's cabin, sits close to her at the table.

"I have been thinking, captain. I should like to make further efforts to learn Norwegian. I hear you butcher my language enough. It is only fair I have a turn at yours."

"Certainly," says Captain Leifsson jovially. "I'll speak with Dr. Rivkin, he has some experience teaching, I believe."

Ursa feels a noose slip about her neck. Soon she will have nowhere to hide, not even her mother tongue. She excuses herself early, leaves them talking in the lamplight. She feels, once again, quite alone.

ELEVEN

They arrive at Trøndheim in the dark. Her husband still hasn't come to bed from the captain's cabin, and despite herself she wishes that he, someone, were there beside her as she listens to the boisterous noise of the port.

She tries to sleep, but before the light arrives she gives up. The men's room is empty, the sacks of the hammocks hanging loose in the scant light. The lanterns aren't lit in the passageway, but the captain had taken her along a straight route to the ladder. The terror of the dark almost sends her back, but she can hear Agnete's voice in her head, urging her on.

Feeling along the rough wooden walls, she begins to make her way to what should be the hatch to get above deck. The sounds guide her and soon she is at the ladder. The trapdoor is closed and she is in near blackness, but starts the climb anyway. About halfway up there is a sudden light, and a crash rings down as the hatch is opened.

A bare foot slaps on the top rung.

"Wait," she calls out. "I'm coming up."

A thin face looks down, and she sees it is the boy she noticed yesterday sorting rope ends.

"Sorry, Fru!" He hurriedly vacates the top of the ladder, and when she reaches it his hand extends and, thanking heaven for her gloves, she takes it.

"Thank you." She smooths her skirts. "Have you seen my husband? Commissioner Cornet?"

"He's gone ashore, Fru Cornet."

"Mistress Cornet," she corrects, and looks about her. Trøndheim is ablaze with lamps and a winch is being rolled to them on the low stone harbour, the ship ready for unloading. The harbour curves fully about them. From here, it looks similar to Bergen, and she is heartened. "Is Captain Leifsson about?"

The boy shakes his head. "No, mistress. Ashore."

"Do you know where?" She had imagined one of them would be here.

"No."

"Then I shall go ashore also. Would you find someone to escort me?"

He gives a short nod and darts off. The sky is lightening, and she can see that the houses lining the harbour are as brightly painted as in Bergen.

The boy is back. "Second Mate Hinsson says I am to assist you, mistress."

"Is there no one else?"

"No one else to be spared." He has a slight lisp, and she wonders if he is in fact younger than Agnete, still losing milk teeth.

"Do you know Trøndheim?"

"No, Mistress Cornet."

"Well," she says, resisting the urge to throw up her hands. "Shall we?"

He leads the way along the narrow gangplank, darting ahead with his bare feet. She should have at least asked him to put on shoes—the ground must be freezing.

She scrambles after him, the ship made unsteady by the unloading. The men crossing the gangplank stop to allow her across, but as soon as she steps onto the damp wood, a slam of wind pushes her sideways. She grips the rope so tight her palms ache, and regains her balance, but the pins are pulled from her hair, sending it in a whipping sheet across her face.

Teeth chattering, she edges her way forwards until she reaches the harbour edge. The ground is so still it makes her stumble, and for the second time that morning a small, dirty hand steadies her. "Careful, mistress."

"Are you all right?" A man stands a respectful distance off, hand half out as if he is about to offer to help.

"Quite all right." She manages a weak smile. "Is there anywhere we may have something to eat?"

He points to a narrow wooden structure painted an uneven yellow. A murky sign depicting a bell sways slightly in the wind. She nods her thanks and, trailing the boy behind, takes several uncertain steps to its front door. The open sewer before it is frozen and she averts her eyes as she crosses the plank and pushes her way into the inn.

It is near full though the hour is early, but the boy finds them a small table in a corner furthest from the fire. There are some finely dressed women dotted throughout the crowd, accompanied by their husbands, and she knows it is irregular for her to be there without Absalom. But she is frayed from her sleepless night, and sends the boy to the bar with a skilling of Agnete's gift to buy light beer and a plate of whatever they have.

He returns with her change and some raspeball, which are hot and surprisingly good, filled with highly salted meat, the potato well cooked and warming. He hovers uncertainly as she begins to eat, and she has to pull him bodily onto the stool beside her and place a dumpling in his grimy hand before he will eat anything. She smiles at the boy and he looks so surprised she wonders what her face has been doing before now. In an effort to reassure him she asks his name, and he tells her it is Casper.

"How did you come to work aboard the ship?"

He shrugs, looking at the raspeball, and she pushes the plate towards him. Silence is fine with her.

As they leave, one of the sailors opens the door with a mock bow and though she doesn't dignify it with an acknowledgement she leaves with a smile on her face.

"The way they were staring," she says to Casper, "you'd think they'd never seen a lady before."

"There were ladies in there," says Casper. "But they were not the same sort."

"Same sort?"

"The sort such as what you are, mistress."

She recalls their rouged cheeks, the bright colours of their dresses. Finally understanding, she flushes and wonders if the sailors took her for a whore, too, and whether those women at least receive something for their shame.

They make their way through the slowly waking town. The streets are narrow and the houses seem to lean in either side, as if conspiring. It isn't so fine as Bergen, of course, despite it being their capital.

They find a market in a large trading square, and Ursa buys boots and a vizard, and though he protests, a pair of gloves for Casper.

"I saw you sorting those odds of rope. These will keep your fingers nimble."

She tries to offer him boots too, but he refuses to try any on, which the cobbler seems glad of. "It is better to be barefoot, mistress, while I'm still growing. I'll be out of them in a month. That's what Second Mate Hinsson says."

When they return to the ship her husband is waiting at the top of the gangplank. He clips Casper lightly about the head and the boy disappears into the bustle of the ship, which has been emptied of much of its wood and sits higher in the water. Absalom glowers at her packages.

"It is the first day we have had a kirke at our disposal. The very kirke where your Kings are crowned, I believe. And you take the chance to purchase *things*." He jerks his head at her full arms. "Where did you get the means for those?"

"My sister gave me a little coin."

"A husband should know of his wife's money," he says, turning his dark eyes on her. "Your father should have told you that." He holds out his hand and after a moment's pause she reaches out to take it, but he flinches away. "The money, wife."

Later, when he is snoring beside her, she will dig her finger-nails into the soft place beneath her ear, and curse herself for handing it over. Because though the lie would have come easy—"I am sorry, husband, I have spent it"—she doesn't speak it. Something in him compels her, even as it repels. She reaches into her belt and passes over Agnete's coins.

He turns and leads her down the ladder, to their corridor. She wonders if, as he has been at kirke and so it is a sort of Sabbath, he will not lie with her that night. But he does, and it is as if he is trying to bed down something into her, plant her penance deep.

•

Ursa often wonders what she would say to Agnete, were she here. She doesn't have the words for the confusion of it: the way her body has become something unhomed, how she has already learnt the way to wield silence like a weapon.

She withdraws again from Captain Leifsson, though he has

been nothing but kind, even giving her a pouch of aniseed. She can trust nobody with her thoughts: fearful and limited though they are. Inside her, they are safe, a locked box stronger than her father's cherrywood gift. She needs them, every word, to herself.

But she does have somewhere, at last, to go. The day after they leave Trøndheim, she clothes herself as warmly as she can. She slips an aniseed onto her tongue, pulls on her boots and, tucking her vizard under one arm, opens the cabin door.

The trapdoor is closed, so she knocks until it is lifted, and doesn't take the hand that offers to help. She looks for Casper but he isn't above decks, or at least she can't discern him from the other monkeys scrambling in blankets up the rigging, unfurling the *Petrsbolli*'s sails to take them north.

Moving along the ship without Captain Leifsson's arm to steady her is disconcerting, but she doesn't trip as she had on the gangplank. She returns to the rear of the ship, just behind the mast where St. Peter holds out his placating hand. Reaching the thick coil of rope twisted into a seat of sorts, and checking no one is nearby or watching, she heaves herself up.

She rests her feet primly on another coil of rope, and sits bundled in her coat and with her vizard over her face, the hard bite of her teeth against its holding bead comforting as a sweet. Through its narrow eye slits, everything feels more manageable. She wonders if this is how a horse feels, blinkered from the sights either side, only able to look ahead. She can see Second Mate Hinsson at the whipstaff, but he pays her no mind. As they move further north, she turns her thoughts before them, to the edge of the world.

TWELVE

Baby Erik is approaching his eleventh month when Pastor Kurtsson receives a second letter from the Lensmann, telling them the commissioner has started his journey from Scotland, and they are to make the second boathouse ready. It is to be converted into a home for the commissioner.

Pastor Kurtsson, to everyone's surprise, seeks out Kirsten at Wednesday meet, and asks her to help.

"He tells me I am a calming presence," says Kirsten to Maren and Mamma as they leave Fru Olufsdatter's. "I wonder what has possessed him?"

"He likely wants allies before this commissioner arrives," says Maren.

"Toril will not be pleased," says Kirsten, smiling.

"Toril cannot ready a house. Our minister neither," says Maren. "You can, Kirsten. Toril knows her beloved Pastor Kurtsson has not offered the same steadiness as you."

Kirsten shrugs off the compliment. "He is sending men from Kiberg to help, but the commissioner is fetching a wife from Bergen, so she will be in need of some comforts. There is a limited purse, and Lensmann Køning has sent wood. I am to slaughter enough meat to last them the summer, and I thought you could stitch the pelts into something?"

Maren looks up at her, surprised.

"Toril is the best one for such a task," says Mamma.

"Perhaps," says Kirsten. "But Toril is like to weave bitterness into it along with pretty patterns, and I would rather give the coin to you."

It is decided then, that Maren will fetch the hides the following week, and the meat is to be salted and smoked in the shed Dag built.

"Very well," says Kirsten. "Between us, we'll make that boathouse fit for a commissioner."

It is a kick to hear it, though of course the boathouse was never Maren's. It was a kindness that Dag's mother even allowed them to lay their dead there. Maren has no claim to it, and yet she still takes routes past it wherever she can, touches the carved runes of the door frame, and Herr Bjørn's carvings beneath. She still walks its circumference in the blue nights when she can't sleep because Erik is crying, or Mamma is crying, or Diinna's silence is too accusing. Now it is truly lost to her.

"What about fishing?" asks Maren.

Something troubled crosses Kirsten's weathered face. "No more of that, I think. Not while things settle."

Maren nods, suppressing a sigh of disappointment. "I'll come for the furs next week."

Kirsten waves them farewell, turns for home.

"We have forgotten our place in the world," remarks Mamma as they walk the other way. "That Kirsten Sørensdatter ought to be careful. She thinks herself our Lensmann, I can see that arrogance in her."

"She has been, of sorts," says Maren, as they pass the second boat shed. "Kirsten kept us alive. She is a better Lensmann than the one soon to sit at Vardøhus."

"Lensmann of what? A place of women. We are no better than a pack of cards to that man. He has allowed us to build ourselves higher than we thought we could, and he may choose to knock it all down."

It is the most Mamma has spoken in weeks. Her grief seems unending, and at times Maren wants to shake her, just to shock her from her weeping. During the long winter nights now thankfully past, when Mamma had latched onto her side like a babe with its mother, Maren longed to dash her mother's hands from her, to sling her from the bed. The frustration is edged with hurt, she knows: hurt that Mamma seems not to acknowledge that Maren has lost just as much, and a near-husband besides, and with that a home of her own.

Maren is grateful that her mother has found her voice again, but she thinks her worry misplaced. Their seagoing will not be found out, and if it is no one can begrudge them trying to feed themselves. The commissioner's anticipated arrival marks a change: an investment of sorts being made in the village. They are not forgotten after all; whether for good or ill they will soon see.

Diinna is outside the house, running a slickstone over the boards of the steps. Maren can hear baby Erik wailing from within, and feels a sharp stab of alarm.

"He's crying," says Mamma, rushing forward.

"He had a splinter," says Diinna. "I removed it."

"But he's still hurting," says Mamma. "You should calm him."

"I am smoothing the steps, so it will not happen again." Diinna doesn't look up, even once. She is bent close over the slickstone, intent on her work.

Mamma mutters something Maren can't catch and treads deliberately over Diinna, foot very close to her hand. There is a tension between them as balanced as an oar in its thole:

they are close to losing balance. It is left to Maren to act as bridge between them, and she is close to abandoning her patience with them both.

She feels worse for baby Erik, who does not seem to soothe any of the unspoken hurt. Where Toril walks about with her bundled child on her hip easy as a basket made for her, on Diinna's narrow body Erik looks like a burden, or a growth. Diinna doesn't call him Erik, which Mamma insisted on, but Eret, which is the Sámi way of saying it.

There is something unnatural in how she is with him. Maren thinks Diinna watches him with her hooded eyes as a wolf watches another wolf: he is kin, but she is wary. It is as if he takes something from her she doesn't want to give, from her breast, from her arms, with his hands tugging at her hair. She never shouts at him, but watches. There's no cruelty there, but there is also little warmth, other than in the quiet times at night, when through the wall Maren can hear Diinna singing to him, always the same song.

"What is that lullaby?" Maren asked once.

"His *joik*." Diinna narrowed her eyes. "It is not a lullaby. It's his song, the one I made for him."

"Do you have one, too?"

"We all do."

"Do I?"

"No." She offers nothing further, and Maren must soothe herself, make tender excuses in her head: *I am not Sámi, that's all*. But Diinna's constant refusal of their familial connection wounds her: Maren thought their bond stronger, able to survive without her brother. She was wrong about so many things that she feels she must each day assess her life anew. Sometimes, Diinna straps her son onto her back in a reindeer-pelt sling and walks—Maren watches her take the road to the headland, or sometimes even a boat to the low mountain, and she comes

101

back smelling of heather and clean, cold air of the kind you get only there.

Maren loves the boy with a fierceness approaching violence, though she worries there is something truly the matter with him, that they harmed him in his coming. He doesn't smile, or wail, or throw things in anger or frustration. When Diinna leaves him with Mamma and Maren, he mostly sits in the soft corner of the house Mamma made out of blankets and hides, and watches mutely.

Erik would have loved his son. Maren sometimes lets the full pain of what could have been come to her, when she watches the baby blow bubbles of spit from between his pink lips, or raise his small arms to her to be held.

"Was it a bad splinter?" she asks Diinna, watching her work at the step. Erik has already stopped crying: was obviously calling for attention rather than out of pain.

Diinna shakes her head. "A scratch."

"We have been at Fru Olufsdatter's," says Maren.

"I know. It is Wednesday."

"Kirsten says there is to be a commissioner, come to live in Vardø. The Lensmann soon to be in Vardøhus has sent for him."

Diinna continues to work the stone: the noise is loud in her silence. The step sags beneath the force.

"He is to live in the second boathouse. He has a new wife."

Finally Diinna sits back. She is squatting, long skirts making it just about decent, but still Maren wishes she wouldn't do things that give Magda and Toril reason to whisper about her. Diinna replies with the frankness she has had since childhood.

"Your and Dag's house?"

Maren feels a warm tingle of gratitude, thinking Diinna understands, perhaps, how hard it is. Diinna nods back, briskly, and rises to her feet.

"Makes sense. It is a good space. It will be a good home."

Diinna's hair is loose and falling across her face. She bends to give the step a last swipe and Maren can only gape after her as she takes up the slickstone and turns to move inside. She doesn't follow Mamma, but enters her own door, leaving Mamma to deal with the baby.

Maren doesn't want to go in at all. She had thought, for a moment, that Diinna would ask her how she feels. That perhaps they would talk as they had when she and Erik were first married—like sisters.

She stands on the polished stair a long while and lets the hurt stab at her chest. She doesn't go in until she is numb with it and the cold, and can feel nothing at all.

•

As promised, Maren goes to Mads Petersson's farm eight days later. She still thinks of it this way, though it is nearly a year and a half since Kirsten moved in. She knows it is time to fetch the skins because the night before the wind was coming in hard from the east, and Maren heard the sharp panic of the reindeer as Kirsten picked which were for the slaughter. Maren hummed tunelessly to drown it out but Diinna went outside with Erik and stood on the step while the cries dropped like stones against the windows.

Maren takes the fastest route, through the centre of the town. The warmer weather has brought the women outside, and they sit about on stools, draped in shawls, stopping their chatter when she passes. Toril sniffs as she goes by, pointedly stabs her needle into the pillowcase she is darning. So the news that Kirsten came to Maren about the skins has reached her. Maren takes delight in smiling broadly at the woman.

The Petersson farm is hunched at the opposite end of the village to Maren's house, its boundary sprawling across a mix of sown fields and scrubland to the sea. Maren spots the rein-deer grazing the slope before she sees the house, their white and grey pelts showing more clearly now the ground is turning green, and heather is beginning to arrive. Their smell comes too, musty and full, following the same passages of wind the cries of their slain companions had the night before.

The house is set apart from the village, its front door and windows turned to the sea. Maren doesn't know how Kirsten stands it: when she moves to knock on the door, her back is directly turned to Hornøya with its hundreds of shrieking birds and its stac. Mads Petersson likely had the best view of all of them of the whale.

When Kirsten answers, she is flushed and smelling of blood. Crescent moons of crimson sit beneath her fingernails as she gestures Maren inside.

"Nearly done. I've slaughtered six, so there are enough for the bed and the floor."

The room is bright and cluttered, almost as large as the second boathouse. There is game hanging from the ceiling: rabbits stripped of fur and pale as naked babies. A side door is open, and beyond it Maren can see the herd moving across the field, and in the near-distance the purple and yellow mess of the skinned reindeer waiting to be hung. Maren remembers the foxes on the headland, but can see no sign of dolls like Fru Olufsdatter has.

What she does see is Kirsten, in trousers. She stops just inside the door, staring down at them.

"What?" Kirsten looks down at herself. "Oh, come now, Maren. You're not going to faint, are you?"

"Of course not," says Maren. She has seen Sámi women in trousers, after all. Diinna wore them all her childhood. But there is something about Kirsten, standing as she is with her legs wide apart like a man, which unnerves her.

"They're Petersson's," says Kirsten, pulling Maren in so she can close the door. "I don't think he'd mind."

"You should be careful, Kirsten," says Maren. "What if it had not been me at the door? What if it had been Toril, or Pastor Kurtsson?"

"They most certainly would have fainted," says Kirsten breezily. "It's no matter, Maren. Do you want beer? I have cheese, too. Made this past month."

Maren nods to both, and carries her meal out to watch Kirsten finish flensing the skins. Fat is still looped in yellowish strings against the smooth underside of the hide, and Kirsten scrapes a seal knife across it.

"No time for tanning." Kirsten is not even looking at her work. She is looking out towards the sea, her profile strong and hawk-like. She is Mamma's age, but her skin has the weathered aspect of a man's. It makes her look older and timeless, all at once. This farm life seems to suit her, and when Maren tastes the beer it's good: free of the bitter aftertaste Pappa's brews always had.

Maren knows from gossip that Kirsten has lost four children, delivering them herself before they were formed properly. But Maren can't imagine her a mother anyway. She isn't exactly a friend, either: Maren feels for her as she once felt for their previous minister, Pastor Gursson, who went down in the boat with her father and brother. He had the same calm energy, the same solid centring to him. He had sharp blue eyes like Kirsten too, that Maren couldn't look long into without blushing. If Kirsten were a man Maren thinks she would be more than an unofficial leader of their village, rather a minister or a man of the law, perhaps even a commissioner.

"I've had more from Pastor Kurtsson," says Kirsten. Maren raises her eyebrows. "I know. He held me back, after kirke. Toril hovered like a hawk. I think you were right, about him wanting allies. I think he anticipates some sort of tussle with this commissioner."

"Will you back him?"

Kirsten snorts. "I'll back myself. And you. But I've a sense the commissioner will be a hardier man than Kurtsson. He is a Scotsman, like Lensmann Køning. And his wife is a ship-owner's daughter from Bergen."

Maren's eyebrows work their way higher, and Kirsten laughs, a throaty sound, mimicking Maren's expression as she strips another length of fat from the fur with a ripping sound. "I know. Shipowners' daughters aren't common in Finnmark, are they? They tend to stop at Tromsø, or Alta at the very least."

"I wonder what the Lensmann promised to warrant a lady to leave her city life."

"Perhaps her husband is very handsome." Kirsten eyes her slyly, and Maren sees her chin is speckled with blood. "Do you think it a shame, that he is bringing a wife?"

Maren frowns. "How so?"

"Perhaps he would have picked one here."

Maren feels a blush creep to her cheeks, brushes at them as though she could wipe it off easy as blood. "I doubt I'd get far even if he had."

"Dag Bjørnsson liked you well enough," says Kirsten, and her voice is gentler.

"Yes." Maren swallows. "I suppose most men would prefer a city lady."

"You're a good woman, Maren. Good enough for anyone."

Maren can't meet her eye, feels her blush deepen. "Is he a sailor, like the Lensmann?"

"A godly man."

"A minister?" Maren sucks in her cheeks. "No wonder Pastor Kurtsson is worried."

Kirsten stabs the blade into the ground at her feet, and dips her hands into a bucket of water beside her, already rusty with blood. "He is not of the cloth but he does God's work."

"A pious man who can marry? Toril will be pleased. The wife should watch herself."

Kirsten snorts, and stands to stretch, reaching towards the sky. "They arrive within the week. The Lensmann, though, he's already being felt in Varanger and Alta. In Kirkenes too. There have been arrests."

"Arrests?"

"Witchcraft," says Kirsten. Her voice is grim. "Sámi."

Maren's heart thumps as she thinks of Diinna. "What for?"

"Wind-weaving, drums."

Maren swallows. "Wind-weaving is for sailors."

"And drums?" Kirsten collects the pelts, heaping them so the fur is touching fur, and skin touching skin. "Don't worry. I'll keep a weather eye out."

"Toril has a loose tongue," says Maren. "Perhaps I should ask her—"

"Ask nothing of her," says Kirsten, holding out the pelts. "There's no reasoning with such a woman. It will pass. The Lensmann only wants to flaunt his power. But we would all do well to mind ourselves."

"It is you who must learn to mind herself most of all," says Maren, glancing down at Kirsten's trousers.

Kirsten doesn't reply, and Maren reaches out to take the pelts. Instead, her fingers wipe the smear of blood from Kirsten's chin. The action surprises them both equally, and Maren can't meet her friend's eye as Kirsten hands her the pelts. They are heavy and smell strongly of raw meat and the sweet air of approaching summer.

"Shame there's no time for tanning." Something drips and lands at her feet. "Scraping's the best I can do."

"That is good enough." Kirsten leads her around the side of the house. The sea glimmers about the stacked rocks. Maren wants to ask if it scares her, if the whale comes to her at night. But looking at Kirsten, hands in her trouser pockets, she thinks Kirsten sleeps soundly as baby Erik.

"You should get out of sight," she says, and Kirsten laughs, tucks a wind-caught lock of Maren's hair behind her ear.

"And you should not worry so much."

Maren can feel Kirsten's eyes upon her as she walks home, laden by the skins. Bright spots of red sprinkle the ground, and trace her path like stepping stones.

THIRTEEN

Now that Ursa has her place above decks, she is better able to bear what happens below. She never before would have guessed she was someone happiest outdoors: felt sure she was bred for parlours. But though the ship's stern is just a larger cage than her cabin, the air it moves through is free and clear, and it is easy to imagine any number of things being possible.

The sun starts to stick better to the heights of the sky, and on the skin about her eyes uncovered by the vizard, she sometimes feels its warmth, like Agnete's laboured breath at night. She wonders if Absalom can taste the sea salt on her skin, if he notices the ring of reddened flesh about her wrists where her coat and gloves do not quite meet.

The *Petrsbolli* stays close to the shore, keeping it within sight on the clear days. At the horizon, the smooth plains about Trøndheim give way to a snarl of mountains, rising sheer as waves at the sea's edge. When they slip into the orbit of the Arctic Circle there is little change in the view. Trees crouch at the throats of the fjords, still thick enough for Ursa to make shapes and troll faces in them; snow settles the crowns of the mountains. She watches islands slide by, defiant juts of land.

As they make their turn east, she sees her first iceberg, a

massive siding of white so bright it is blue and green, big as their house in Bergen, moving impenetrable as rock through the water. Captain Leifsson orders the ship in a wide circle about it and tells her that what is beneath the water is the most dangerous. She imagines it stalking her all the way to Vardø.

After stops at several minor ports, they reach Tromsø. She doesn't go ashore, but watches from her place on deck as they approach the port in a bluster of wind and sea spray. The town stands small on a rocky island that seems to slam against the water as much as the waves slam it, grey upon grey. They stay long enough for her husband to pray in the crouched kirke, and for fresh supplies to be brought aboard for their final push to Vardø.

At the last moment she sees Casper crossing the gangplank before it is drawn up. He stands a little hunched, clutching a bundle and still shoeless. Ursa removes her vizard, leans across the side of the ship and calls out to him, but he has already turned and gone. She feels something close to panic, a hot shard in her ribs. She approaches the second mate, pokes him in the shoulder like a hoyden.

"Herr Hinsson, Casper is left behind."

The second mate turns and looks at her blankly. "Mistress Cornet?"

"Casper. The boy, the boy who was always sorting ropes."

"Sorry, Mistress Cornet, I'm not sure which boy you mean."

She points at his usual place. "There, he'd sit there."

"We let the boys come and go according to where there is work for them. After this we are on to Spitsbergen and some aren't made for whaling grounds."

"I did not know this was a whaling vessel."

He shifts his feet. "We do whatever is profitable. Bergen is flooded with cod, and your father wants something more in demand."

There is something in his tone she doesn't like, but leaves it unremarked. "He did not want to go whaling?"

"Or he was unsuited. Not strong or some such." He looks back at the deck, and she realizes the crew are poised, ready for him to take his place at the whipstaff.

"But I did not..." She lets the sentence slide back down her throat. Second Mate Hinsson is unlikely to care. She isn't certain why she does, so much. But the sight of Casper's bewildered face, his bare grubby feet cringing against the harbour—he looked so insubstantial. And now the second mate turns away from her, their conversation finished, and she glances back to the port. It is as though the boy was never there at all.

She is sorrier than she can explain that he didn't say good-bye, though they had not talked since their day in Trøndheim. She had thought, with a comforting vagueness, that he might stay in Vardø and be a sort of houseboy, and was going to ask Absalom or at least try to make him suggest the idea. It was a thought left unfinished.

They are drawing away from the harbour now. She can feel the ship swaying, the men back at their practised posts, heads already turning to sea. Soon they will be at Vardø, and it will be she who is left behind.

•

A few days before they are due into the harbour at Vardø, Ursa feels an ache in her stomach.

It spreads along her back and into her head, pushing its blunt fingers into her temples and down the backs of her thighs. A griping sensation grips her body, and sweat comes cool across her top lip, beneath her arms. She looks about for the captain, wishes Casper were still aboard. She thinks of calling out to Second Mate Hinsson, but something within her stays her voice: a dark, animal sense, that tells her not to share that she is hurt.

She lowers herself from the ropes, and a spasm crosses her back, so sudden she bites her lip. Is she poisoned? She straightens, breath coming fast through her mouth, just catching it when the pain builds suddenly again, and crashes against her lower body like a white-hot wave.

This time she knows better than to move before it recedes. As soon as she can, she begins a slow edge along the deck. The bead of her vizard is clenched between her teeth and so no one sees that she is sweating, that her eyes are smarting, filling with tears.

The ladder down might as well be a mountain. She counts beneath her breath from ten to one and again and again until she feels floorboards beneath her, closes her eyes and stumbles along the passage, focusing on controlling the pain when it comes, breathing through it.

It is less of a confusion now: she can trace its origin; map its sear across her body. It's a little like her monthly pains, but tenfold. Beginning at the space her husband has made inside her, it sends shockwaves rippling first down her legs and lower back, and eventually up to her head. It feels as though her insides are trying to come out, and she wonders if her husband has torn something vital, or even if the ship's cook's culinary experiments have killed her at last.

She fumbles the lock of their cabin, fingers slick with sweat and numb with cold, bolts shut the door and crawls to the chamber pot. It has not been emptied that day, and a yellow pool lies at its base. The pain fades and ripples, like water settling.

Finally she blinks and is clear-eyed again. She is crunched between the bed and the wall, knees imprinted against the wood frame, spine flush against the thin divide. She wonders if she made any noise: she can't remember. Her skirts drop about the chamber pot, and she doesn't look as she wipes herself carefully.

She throws the rag over the chamber pot and it drops a little, soaks red. She holds her breath and lifts it, looks. Beneath the rag is a soft blot. She saw enough of her mother's difficulties to know what it is.

She should cover it over again, unbolt the door. The cabin will be near empty: she could go to the porthole and empty the pot through it. The contents would barely mark the water with their entrance.

But she can't carry it, can't touch even the pot, which she places in the dark corner of the room, beside her chest, then lies down on the bunk fully clothed, sleep coming choppy as waves.

·

When she wakes she can hear snoring through the thin wall, and her husband is already sleeping beside her. She sits up with panic, and, careful not to wake him, moves to the chest. The chamber pot is empty. Her heart races painfully. Absalom must have removed it, and let her sleep on.

A rawness opens over her breastbone, and she presses her hand to it. She slides back into bed, lets herself move a little nearer to his slumbering warmth. He rolls over and slides his arm beneath her, gathering her in close as a stowed sail.

ARRIVAL

FOURTEEN

They arrive just ahead of the rain. Mamma fetches Maren out to watch, and together with baby Erik and Diinna they go closer to the harbour edge, standing beside Magda's house to see the ship approaching. Behind it a great bank of cloud is building, already swallowing the horizon with grey slathers of sleet.

Magda's son stamps his small feet and claps his hands and cries, "It's giving to them whalers, it's giving to them good!" without thinking about the fact that it will be giving to them just as well within the hour.

"They'll never get in," says Mamma, and it's true that even at this distance the ship is incongruously large, the neck of the harbour shrinking smaller as it nears.

Maren makes no effort to answer, only watches the huge sweep of cloud. The last time they had all stood watching the sea like this it had folded itself entire over forty men. She clenches her teeth.

The wind picks up, and the ship drops anchor outside the narrow mouth of the harbour. Pastor Kurtsson strides out from the kirke, a dark cap clutched to his head. He looks like a doll, like one of Fru Olufsdatter's poppets, and Maren imagines the wind filling his clothes and flying him into the sea. He has moved into the weather too early, and now stands awkwardly at the harbour side. There is no movement from the ship for a long while. Mamma begins to tremble.

"You should go inside," says Maren, but doesn't move to usher her home.

It is shameful, but she can hardly bear to touch her mother now. There is something indecent about how obviously she wears her grief, and Maren is worried that whenever they touch it will leach into her skin. She wants to be away from the house, or wants it to herself. If it weren't for baby Erik she might have already done just that, and gone to lodge with Kirsten. It has been a low taunt to see the second boathouse made fine enough for the living of a commissioner and his wife.

At last, there is movement on the deck. Maren can see dark figures against the grey sky and then, incongruous as the sun in winter, a burst of bright yellow appears from somewhere below deck. It isn't a colour Maren has seen before, and she keeps her eyes upon it, almost hungry.

Five of the figures, including the one in yellow, are lowered slowly in a rowing boat. There is a spray of white against the sea as the boat is dropped onto the waves. The yellow figure makes a jerking movement, as though about to fall.

"Nearly," says Diinna. Erik is dozing over her shoulder, and she has one hand on his back, patting irregularly.

At the harbour side, Pastor Kurtsson is stamping his feet and blowing on his hands. He is always telling them how God's love is the only warmth needed to weather the cold, and it gives Maren a little twist of satisfaction to see him shivering. Kirsten joins him on the dock, and hands him a coat. Maren can see the reluctance in his stance as he takes it and puts it on.

In the boat, two have taken up oars and are rowing towards

shore. The yellow figure sits in the stern, wind blowing their hair about their face, and now the boat is closer it is obviously the new wife from Bergen. Her outfit is an absurdity, especially in bad-tempered weather.

Beside her, steadying her, must be her husband: their commissioner. He is stocky and upright, turned slightly towards her. Between the oarsmen sits another man, his broad back to land. As the boat draws alongside the dock and Pastor Kurtsson raises a hand in greeting, he turns but doesn't return the gesture.

The oars go up like flagpoles, and it is Kirsten who catches the rope and knots it about the mooring.

Mamma sucks in her cheeks. "She should be careful."

For once, Maren agrees. They all know things must change now, even Kirsten, with a direct eye from Vardøhus amongst them. The usual hierarchies must be observed; the ones usual to the world rather than to Vardø. A lift of panic quickens Maren's heart as she thinks Kirsten may offer her hand to help the passengers ashore, but Kirsten steps back and allows Pastor Kurtsson forward, grown large inside his borrowed coat.

The broad-backed man steps heavily from the boat, leaving it rocking in his wake. The woman clutches at its wooden sides. Maren is too far away to make out his face clearly, but his features are even, lower half obscured by a black beard. The woman's companion steps nimbly from the boat and shakes Pastor Kurtsson's hand before turning to help her. She shakes her head, says something.

"She wants to go already," says Diinna drily. "It's a long way back to Bergen."

Pastor Kurtsson beckons Kirsten forwards and she bends her head down to listen, then looks up suddenly towards the houses. Her eyes find Maren's and though Toril is closer, she starts to walk towards them.

"What did you do?" says Mamma, but Maren takes two steps towards Kirsten.

"Coat," Kirsten says, voice thrown by the wind. It makes no sense for Maren to go, their home being furthest from the harbour, but Kirsten is looking directly at her, so Maren pushes her way through the gathered women and runs to their house, the wind at her back. She takes up her winter coat from its hook, lined with the fur of rabbits snared on the mainland, brings it out, slamming the door behind her. She runs against the wind and skids back into place, making Mamma jolt.

Kirsten stands a little way off, Mamma eyeing her with open dislike. Maren folds the coat over her arm and steps clear of the women, narrow skirts whipping about her ankles.

"What is it?" she asks when she reaches Kirsten, who turns and starts again to the harbour.

"The wife is worried her skirts will fly up." There is a smile in her voice. "And I can't say I blame her."

The woman in the boat looks abruptly towards them, and though there is no way that she could have, Maren feels that she heard them. Maren sees a plump face, with large, light brown eyes and very blonde hair that is whipped to froth about her face. She looks at once insubstantial, as though she might fade at the edges and become sea spray, and overly large, garish in her yellow dress.

"A coat, Fru Cornet," says Pastor Kurtsson, pulling it from Maren's grip and offering it spread across both arms. "Not so fine as you are used to—"

"But it's clean enough," says Kirsten, and Maren's cheeks burn as the broad-backed man turns his gaze on them. He is forbidding up close, as dark as the woman is pale, holding space easily, the same way Kirsten does. She feels herself shrink a little, rounding her shoulders against his scrutiny.

"My wife," he says, in heavily accented Norwegian, "isn't used to the cold. And shall be addressed as Mistress Cornet."

This is her husband? Why did he not sit beside her, offer his hand to help her? The woman's lips are trembling, and part slightly as though to say something to her husband, but she instead looks past Pastor Kurtsson, straight to Maren.

"Thank you." Her voice is steady and there is a sudden set to the soft line of her jaw, a muscle working in her cheek.

She reaches out for the coat, and the man Maren took for her husband, but whom she now sees is old enough to be her father, motions Kirsten and Maren forward. "Here, please."

They stand before the rocking boat, and the man gestures at the oarsmen, who obey so immediately Maren realizes he must be high in their chain of command. The captain, perhaps. They look down, shoulders still heaving from the effort of the row. They will be against the wind on their return.

"Give her the coat," says the captain to the minister, and Maren takes the coat back from the frame of Pastor Kurtsson's arms. There are two pink blooms high in the woman's cheeks as she takes the captain's arm to steady herself in the rocking boat, and, keeping her other hand tightly clasped about her bunched skirts, stands quickly. Kirsten moves to block the woman from view as her skirts swirl about her in the wind. Her grip is white on the man's arm, and the set of her lips pressed thin.

She is embarrassed, and Maren is embarrassed for her. She has never seen so much cloth, has a job scooping the woman's shaking frame into her coat's sleeves, stiff with their fur lining.

The woman is shorter but plumper than Maren, and the coat sits rigid about her, arms held at an angle and straining across the back. In that moment, though her body is a woman's, the dress cut to emphasize her shape, the dazed look in her pale eyes makes her look like a girl. But once Maren has helped her with the buttons, the dress is kept down about her knees, and she can at last step from the boat.

"Thank you," she says again, her hot breath hitting Maren's cheek. There is something sweet on it, so unexpected it makes Maren's mouth tingle.

Maren nods, keeping her own lips firmly shut about her teeth. Even aboard a ship this woman has kept herself better than any of the Vardø women, and it is Maren's time to blush at how she must look. Only a moment ago she had felt sorry for this woman, and now she feels a sorry sight herself in her shabby skirts and Pappa's coat, made no more fragrant by months of her seagoing.

The woman's husband has watched the whole scene dispassionately. When his wife is at last steady on the dock, he turns to Pastor Kurtsson. His eyes don't fall on him though: they search the houses clustered about the harbour.

"You the minister?" Maren isn't entirely convinced that his curtness is only due to a lack of confidence in their language.

"Yes, I am, Commissioner Cornet. Welcome to our—"

"Thank you, captain, for our safe passage."

He offers his hand to the shorter man, who still has the wife attached to his arm.

"Not at all, Mr. Cornet. It has been my pleasure."

He nods briefly and turns again to the minister. "That the kirke?"

"It is. Allow me—"

But the man doesn't let him finish before he turns sharply on his boot and makes for the kirke, long dark coat flapping behind him like a flock of crows. Pastor Kurtsson dithers a moment, and Maren could swear he actually dances from one foot to another, like a child. Though he isn't theirs, not really, she again feels that stab of embarrassment for him.

"You can go ahead," says Kirsten to the minister. "We will take Mistress Cornet to her home."

Pastor Kurtsson straightens, trying to regain some control over the situation. "Yes. I will show the commissioner the kirke, and you can oversee the luggage."

He follows the commissioner without, Maren suspects, fully appreciating what he has just said. Kirsten gives a slight shake of her head and looks to the captain.

"Is that everything, captain?"

The bow of the boat is laden with three cases, a smaller package, and a neat reddish-wooden chest. It is finely carved, and has a brass lock. When the oarsmen begin to unload, the woman flutters about it, one hand clasped at the coat, eyes trained on the chest, brow furrowed.

The captain himself lifts the chest with care, and the men carry the three cases between them. Kirsten takes up the small package, leaving Maren uncertain whether to follow. No one gives her a sign, and she repeats Pastor Kurtsson's dither a moment too long. The five of them vanish between Toril and Magda's houses, the women and their children turning to watch, the snatch and flutter of the woman's yellow skirts disappearing out of sight as they turn towards the second boathouse.

The commissioner's wife doesn't look back, and Maren isn't sure why she wants her to. She feels a detached sort of panic, and hopes Kirsten will be kind.

She leaves the dock, feet crunching over the cold-hardened ground. Mamma has gone, but Diinna still stands behind Magda's house, with Erik slumped over her shoulder, her hand tapping its senseless rhythm into his back. They walk home together, and Diinna doesn't speak until they reach their house.

"This will bring nothing good," she says, gaze fixed over Maren's head, in the direction of the boat straining against its

123

moorings in the harbour. She tilts her head, as though listening, then turns and vanishes around the side of the house. Maren hears the slam of her door as she goes into her and Erik's room.

A moment after, the clouds that had followed the ship open above her head, and rain begins to fall.

FIFTEEN

Though Maren has the excuse to visit the boathouse, the reindeer hides being stitched and ready by the door, she instead spends the three days until Sabbath pacing their house like a tethered beast. The rain is fierce, churning the softening ground to mud, and she doesn't want her first visit there to be as a bedraggled mess.

Everything is made blurred and grey by the weather, and the commissioner's wife has set an uneasiness rocking inside her, though she can't name why. She feels she must know her. The yellow dress ghosts through Maren's daydreams: she has become obsessed with recalling it. How soft and giving the woven fabric was against her wrist as she pulled tight the coat, how bright it was, how much was gathered into its loose pleats, enough to wrap three people. The woman's sweet breath, her fingernails pale and delicate.

Maren's own clothes are stiff and itchy about her, the reek of herself so apparent she wonders how anyone can stand to be near her. She washes in the grey water from chores, tries to work her hair into a neater tie. The place where the needle pierced her hand the night of the storm has faded completely, but she worries at the thin webbing between forefinger and thumb until it is raw again, skin shrinking over her hands. Her fingernails are brittle and greyish, her mouth furred though she brushes with a birch twig until her gums sing and she spits the copper of blood into the mud. She wonders if she will ever be clean, has ever been. She takes to cleaning baby Erik more often too, but even his breath is foul with Diinna's milk, his hands mucky with crawling. Perhaps they are born to it.

The rainclouds affect an odd light on their house; the glow of snow gone and inside drab and dark. Maren used to welcome this restless time, the whole village stretching out from winter and everything being readied beneath the never-set sun before they begin their slow dance back together, cold forcing them once more into each other's pockets. Now, it is a reminder of how different their lives have become, and how, with the arrival of the commissioner, they are set to change again. *Just as we've found our feet*, Maren thinks.

When Pappa and Erik lived, they would take the boat for days at a time, and Maren and Mamma would strip the house of all its furs and cloth, beat them out and scatter fresh rushes on the floor. Last summer it had been Maren who had gone to sea, and the house had stayed closed and cloistered, furs collecting dust until Maren grew certain she inhaled lungfuls of herself. Soon there will be excursions across the sea to the low mountain, and the traders will come from Kiberg and Varanger. But the rain has trapped her, and though Mamma is gladdened by how it will ready the soil, encourage moss and lichen, Maren is bored. She unpicks the hem of the reindeer pelts, stitches them back together with more careful hands, burns the last of the dried heather and places the hides over the smoke to try to get the musk out.

•

Sabbath dawns dry, and almost painfully bright. Maren goes ahead of Mamma, passing close by the second boathouse, slowing slightly to try and divine if the commissioner and his wife are inside. The house is still, the flat sunlight hitting the high windows and making them inscrutable. She picks up her pace against the mud.

A group of women are already clustered about the door of the kirke: Maren can see that at their centre is Kirsten, standing a head taller than the rest. They are gossiping, she can tell, because as she draws nearer the women turn to check who is approaching before leaning back towards each other. It isn't a warm day, and they have to shuffle about lest the mud suck at their feet, but none of them want to miss the arrival of Commissioner Cornet and his wife.

"And what did you make of her?" says Toril the moment Maren arrives at the group. "What did she say to you?"

"Only 'thank you,'" says Maren. "Not enough for me to know the make of her." She looks to Kirsten. "What happened after you took them to the house?"

Kirsten shrugs. "I stayed long enough to show the stores and light the fire. She didn't say a word. The captain was nice enough."

"And her husband?"

"Not back from the kirke before I left."

"Pastor Kurtsson says he prayed for hours before he visited Vardøhus," says Toril, sickly with admiration. "He will be a goodly thing for us."

Maren feels pity for his wife, left alone in her new house while her husband prayed.

"Did you take the hides?" says Kirsten. Maren shakes her head. "I told her to expect you."

Maren grips at the sore skin between her forefinger and thumb, is about to say something about the rain or the mud or the re-hemming, but is saved from it by the sudden hush falling as a broad figure comes striding into sight, trailing a shorter one wrapped in Maren's coat, flicks of dark blue kicking about her ankles.

The women draw apart from each other: Maren drops her head without quite knowing why. The commissioner's muddy boots move in and out of her sight, the slippered feet of his wife a few paces behind.

Maren looks up in time to see a pale halo of hair disappear into the candlelit dark of the kirke. She seems so small against the bulk of her husband, and Maren imagines her walking into the belly of a whale. Kirsten follows in after, the women peeling off in a mute stream.

Maren waits another few minutes for Mamma to arrive. She comes huffing, hair unbrushed.

"Have I missed them?"

"Everyone is inside already. Is Diinna not coming?"

"She says she doesn't feel well." Mamma's disapproval drips.

Pastor Kurtsson has abandoned his place by the door, is bending to speak to the commissioner, who sits in the front pew. Maren manoeuvres Mamma until they are sitting across and behind, so she can keep them both in sight. The pews around the new arrivals are crowded, though usually they spread out. The candles splutter as Toril performs her usual duty of shutting the door, and Pastor Kurtsson takes his place at the pulpit.

Maren barely hears the sermon. Her eyes are trained on the commissioner and his wife. All about her, heads are similarly turned, and when they pray Maren wonders if the other women are also trying to pick out the thread of the wife's voice in the knot of theirs.

Absolute quiet comes when they have said the final *Amen*. Maren's eyes are fixed on the back of the commissioner's head, which remains bowed for a full minute past the prayer.

"Surely he will say something?" Mamma's voice is quiet as the spit of the candle.

Pastor Kurtsson has vacated the pulpit, stands uncertainly before the commissioner. His wife stares straight ahead. Her collar is high about her pale neck, the roundness of her cheek made copper in the candlelight. The sort of skin that will change to suit whatever light hits it. Maren looks down again at her chapped hands, raw and ruddy, Mamma's just as coarse beside her.

At last, the commissioner straightens his neck, stands. The kirke is so quiet she hears the movement of cloth against cloth, the swallow of his throat before he turns to them to speak. His feet plant in a wide stance, hands clasped behind his back, and she wonders if he was a sailor or a soldier. Again Maren feels that strange pull of energy from him she had felt in the harbour, something coiled and magnetic, almost dangerous in the size and heft of him.

He wears a suit of black cloth, not so fine as his wife's clothing but well fitted: though it is sombre he wears it like an aristocrat. He has trimmed back his beard, revealing even, heavily bowed lips and a strong jaw.

Maren supposes he is handsome, but there is something wild there too. Something kept back that when left unchecked could turn his face cruel. Mamma draws closer to her and Maren doesn't slide away.

"I have only a little Norwegian. Pastor Kurtsson will translate as necessary. My name is Absalom Cornet, and I am from the northern isles of Orkney, Scotland. This—" he draws out a letter from his pocket, creased with rereading—"is my commission from Lensmann Cunningham, stating that I have been appointed Commissioner over Vardø, and so you all."

He changes to English. She knows only brief words of it, what she has picked up from rare whalers blown off course from the main trading routes, or those who settle in the larger towns nearby.

She listens carefully, picking up unconnected words like driftwood on the current of his voice. Pastor Kurtsson is stumbling in his translation, and Maren suspects his English isn't as good as he led the commissioner to believe. His brow is furrowed with concentration, giving no particular emphasis to the words so it is left to them to decide what is most important.

He tells them it is his duty to be the eyes and ears of not only the Lensmann John Cunningham, which Maren realizes must be Hans Køning's English name, but also those of God.

"Does this mean the Lensmann will not come at all?" whispers Maren to Kirsten, but Kirsten ignores her, eyes narrowed at the commissioner. He tells them a little of his life before, in Orkney and then Caithness, places Maren has never heard of, and of his involvement with the trial of a woman. He says that it is this that brought him to Finnmark, to Vardø. He says that he knows they lost many men to a storm; there is a ripple around the room, a collective reel at the mention of their men in this stranger's mouth. He says that he will make a register of all their names, a census, for the Lensmann so he knows how many and who they are.

"This should have been done before," translates Pastor Kurtsson duly, without noticing the barb in it.

The commissioner asks his wife to stand and she does, turning her moonish face to the congregation and dipping a curtsey that makes Mamma snort. He introduces her as Mistress Cornet and Maren whispers it under her breath, wonders what her given name is.

The woman's gaze barely lifts. The skin beneath her chin creases when she nods her acknowledgement, her pale hands stark against her dress. Her hair is neatly pinned though slightly lopsided, and Maren guesses she is used to using a looking glass, if she is used to arranging her own hair at all. She wills the woman to look up, to see her and know her as the one who placed the coat about her shoulders, but Mistress Cornet sits as soon as her husband motions her to do so, several moments before Pastor Kurtsson's translation catches up.

"Think of me as a Lensmann of sorts, a judge. You can trust me as you do your minister. Too long you have been left here without guidance. I am here to offer it, and I must ask you be vigilant."

Commissioner Cornet returns to his clumsy Norwegian.

"I will take the names, now. And any questions and issues that have arisen—I hope to be a mediator."

In many ways what he describes should be the duty of a minister. Perhaps Lensmann Køning realizes he sent a weak man, and is now trying to remedy it by sending a strong one. Hands have been raised, and the commissioner gestures to the back of the kirke. Toril's voice comes loud behind them.

"What of those who do not come to kirke? Should we give you their names?"

His face is so still Maren wonders if he has not understood. Pastor Kurtsson obviously assumes the same and moves to speak in his ear, but Commissioner Cornet turns to fix him with such a stare that the minister draws back.

"There are those who do not come to kirke?"

Maren notices a patch of damp plaster beside the cross, dark on the wall.

"Not many," says Pastor Kurtsson. "Lapps, some old—"

"There will be no more of that," he says, looking to the back, to Toril. "Give me their names."

SIXTEEN

Ursa's husband is furious. Their house is stale with it, a thick fug of tension that roils from him like a storm cloud. The news that he has heathens among his people is only the latest of it—it began the day they arrived, and he was turned away from Vardøhus.

They had dropped anchor and Ursa had been almost afraid to look to land. The fortress was built of grey stone, visible from the sea, as high-walled and forbidding as a prison, which Captain Leifsson told them it oftentimes served as. Further along the coast were nooked a collection of houses at irregular intervals. Without trees the land seemed flat and featureless as a blank page.

As they had rowed ashore in that terrible wind, Ursa had wanted to cry. Captain Leifsson was sitting beside her and she trained her eyes on his knees as the wind slapped their cheeks.

Absalom was coiled as a spring, though lately he had been almost kind, albeit not in ways that others would notice. He had started calling her Ursula instead of "wife," asking how she was feeling in Norwegian, small gestures at effort, perhaps even affection. Since the night she was unwell he hadn't touched her, and as they approached Vardø, he requested that she change into her yellow dress, placed his hand beside hers on the guard rail and moved it so close she could feel the dark heat and bristles of his hands through her thin gloves.

The women who helped her at the dock were snow-burnt and smelly. The larger woman, who introduced herself as Kirsten, had been brash and brusque. The other, similar in age to Ursa, bundled her into a reeking coat. This young woman looked haunted, her grey-blue eyes the same shade as the sea, her cheeks hollowed. But Ursa had come to feel grateful for the loan of the coat when they were shown to their house.

House. Now, the word burns in Ursa's stomach as she watches her husband pace the short length of the room where they must sleep, eat and otherwise exist—she isn't sure a life spent here is worthy of the label of living. She had thought their circumstances in Bergen were grave since Mother's death, with only one servant and rooms kept closed, but this is another thing entirely.

It has only four high, small windows that she can barely see through. The bed is large and takes up a full side of the room—above it are beams and long loops of rope from which hang rough curtains to portion it from view. The fire takes up another side, two pans and a large pot arranged on the drift-wood shelf. There are no rugs on the floor, only unnailed boards suspended over dirt. The ground beneath sends up a fierce cold though Kirsten, who showed Captain Leifsson and Ursa to the house, said that they have arrived into summer.

There is a second door at the back corner of the room. When Kirsten opened it, Ursa could have been sick. Great headless carcasses hang there, split from neck to belly and restitched.

"Enough there to last to winter," Kirsten had said, before setting a light to the heaped moss in the grate. Captain Leifsson set Ursa's chest down in one corner. He couldn't meet Ursa's eye.

"Mistress Cornet, it has been a pleasure."

He gave her a formal little bow and she wanted to throw her arms about him, cling to him. He held out a black pouch and she loosened its string tie.

"More aniseed," he said. "I know you like it."

She didn't trust herself to speak, even without Absalom there, and gave him a nod of thanks. She wondered briefly if he would tell her to come with him, if he could take her back to Bergen. But he walked out with Kirsten, leaving her to this room with its small windows through which she watched his retreating back. He didn't turn. Within the hour the ship weighed anchor and was gone into the rain-smothered horizon. She sat heavily on the hard bench beside the table, folded her hands in her lap, and waited for Absalom to come.

Without a sunset Ursa feels untethered. She cannot think how long she sat there that first day before Absalom arrived to find her still on the bench, the room barely warmed by the low glow given out by a nearly spent fire. He didn't scold her, only heaped it again and said, "Are you hungry?"

She shuddered no, thinking of the slaughtered beasts next door. He nodded tautly, looked about the room. "Not like you're used to." There was something close to an apology in his voice.

She was fearful he would be angry at her disappointment, but instead he sat across from her at the broad table, and took out a letter.

"I had thought myself made," he said, and not entirely to himself. She waited. "I went to Vardøhus. The Lensmann isn't yet at seat there. There was hardly anyone there at all. I spoke with an old man serving as a guard. They do not know if he will even come, may keep his base elsewhere." His fist clenched upon the table. "He mentioned none of this in his letters."

Absalom looked up so suddenly Ursa flinched, but his face

was closed off and sorrowful, and she could almost bring herself to reach across the table to him.

"I grew up in a house like this," he said. "On an island not much bigger than Vardø. I got out as soon as I could, went to the city. There I made something of myself." His fist hits the table. "But here I am back again."

Ursa didn't know where the words came from, but she said, "You may make something more, here."

Absalom's expression changed, as if a light were lit beneath his skin. He looked at her, seeming to see her for the first time. And then he stretched his long arm across the table, and took her hand.

They sat together, rain falling heavy on the roof. It must have been past midnight when he called her to bed, though the grey light outside was of a perpetual dusk. He was gentler than ever before, but still she couldn't ignore the rigid frame of the bed beneath her, the rain coming hard against the walls, and so sent her mind far away.

SEVENTEEN

Absalom leaves the house twice a day in the three days until Sabbath, for hours at a stretch. Each time he comes back sopping.

"No one there," he says. "Not at kirke, not in Vardøhus." Ursa knows he wants comfort, but it is something she can't give him. The look on his face when she had soothed him on their first night had made her afraid: he is hungry for her approval and she has no idea why. She wants to go back to being invisible.

She senses his mood deepen, but when the rain clears on Sabbath it feels like a sign that all may yet come good. She puts on her darkest dress, and follows her husband into the mud.

As they walk, he tells her their nearest neighbour is Fru Olufsdatter, a woman who, like so many of them, lost her husband and son in the storm. Her house is easily the finest: a two-storey stabbur with thick turf overlaying silvery birch. Carved wooden pillars fence the porch, and through its light-framed windows Ursa sees colour: yellow and red adorning the walls. She wonders whether she can ask Absalom if they might decorate their house. She doesn't think she can stand another moment of its bareness. Otherwise the houses are square, windowless, and single-floored, none so large as theirs.

The kirke is of a good size, standing high as their house in Bergen and in a style more ornate than the new Lutheran churches in her city. It looks older too, all dark wood angling at the sky like an ancient ship brought to settle on land. A dozen women wait outside, and from the way they fall silent and spin away from each other on their approach, Ursa can tell she and her husband are the subject of their talk.

She shrinks inside the borrowed coat, feels all their eyes scratching over her. Kirsten is there, and so is the young woman who helped her with the coat. Ursa wonders about smiling at them, thinks better of it. She feels ridiculous in her mud-clad slippers, should have worn her boots from Tromsø. She hardens the set of her shoulders as they walk past, and then wishes she had smiled. She will need friends here, or she really will go mad.

They are greeted by the obsequious minister, who seats them in the front pew. There are lighter patches on the walls behind the wooden cross, as though something else had hung there, and a massive dark stain beside it that Ursa sees all sorts of patterns in. All through the service she feels a sort of warmth upon her, a scrutiny that has an almost physical weight.

Her husband's eyes are fixed upon the minister with an intensity he usually reserves for the middle distance. His hand is motionless on his knee: he barely seems to breathe.

She tries to look more alert when he rises to address the congregation. Pastor Kurtsson's translation is rudimentary, and the dissonance between them grates on Ursa's nerves so that she nearly misses her cue to stand and show herself to the people of Vardø. Their collective gaze falls against her like stones. She should straighten her back, meet their eyes. She dips a little, out of politeness, hears a faint snort from the back of the kirke. Before Ursa takes her seat again she looks briefly: the thin woman who gave her the coat sits beside an older, thinner version of herself, their twin sets of blue-grey eyes on her. Was it her who laughed? Ursa feels a betrayal though she owes her nothing. Heat rushes into her cheeks and the back of her neck as she waits for her husband to finish.

It takes a full hour to collect all the names for the census, though they are so few. Some women are keen on speaking with him: he turns his steady gaze on each of them, even lets loose an easy flash of teeth. He trimmed his beard ready for the service, and is wearing the suit he wore to meet and marry her. The ship's diet has shrunk his middle, the morning's prayer given him a softness about his brutish jaw which fades and re-hardens only when there is mention of those absent from kirke, candlelight finding red-gold darts in his beard.

Briefly Ursa can see him how she thinks they must. A town of women, with only a weak-chinned minister and two old men amongst the congregation, the others boys: a man like him is welcome here. And as she trails him back to their house, she knows that she isn't. They watch her go like an unkindness of ravens: as soon as the kirke is out of sight she hears them cawing.

In the stark daylight he looks older, the furrows in his forehead deepen. "Six not come," he says. "How has the pastor allowed it?"

Ursa's lips twitch: she still doesn't know if his questions are for her. She assumes this one wasn't, for he doesn't break his stride. He knows the route already from his twice-daily prayers and pilgrimages to the fortress, past three blocky houses close together, between two larger ones, boundaries marked with rocks.

Ursa tries to learn it, commit it to memory. The village has the curious sense of being crammed together and spread widely out: it bunches and then releases, land standing uneasy between buildings of wood and stone, turf and mud. Absalom has told her next to nothing of the town, only that it was the worst hit by the storm, and that it is a place of women now. She had imagined sisterhood, but is now uncertain if there is anything for her here at all. A single tern wheels ahead, climbing into the sky.

Outside their house he stops so suddenly that she must swerve, catches her hip against his.

"Husband?"

His eyes are narrowed. "There. See?"

Ursa does, but isn't sure what she is seeing. Over the lintel, roughly carved into the wood, are a scramble of shapes. A circle, with lines waving from it. A sun? And beside it a fish, as basic as a child's. They are in turn obscured by more carvings. At first she thinks someone has tried to erase them, but the crossings-out are too regular, deliberate.

"Runes," breathes Absalom, and there is something in his voice so foreign she doesn't at once recognize it for what it is. His hands clasp his jacket convulsively. Her own fear rises to meet his.

"Husband?"

"They are runes," he says, and his voice is shaking. He turns and scans the houses about them. Ursa watches as he strides to the nearest and knocks on the door. No one answers: they are probably still gossiping at the kirke. He comes back.

"It is as the Lensmann said. Worse, perhaps." His gaze has taken on a feverish edge. The mud has started to swallow Ursa's slippers but she doesn't want to go inside.

There is a squelch of footsteps behind and two figures approach, one supporting the other. Ursa sees it is the young woman whose coat she wears, and the older woman who shares her thin cheekbones and eyes: her mother.

"You," says Absalom. The women's heads were down, and now they jerk to a stop.

"That," he says, and his fear has resolved into something Ursa understands better: anger. "Why are they there?" He points at the marks over the door. "Runes, yes?"

The young woman follows his finger. She nods.

"Who put them there?"

"Diinna," says the mother. Ursa looks to the young woman.

"You are Diinna?" says Ursa, and the young woman shakes her head, doesn't meet Ursa's eye.

"This is my daughter, Maren," says the mother. "I am Freja, and my son's widow Diinna made those marks." It is not lost on Ursa that she introduces her daughter-in-law so, at such a distance. "We gave our names and hers to you just now."

"Was this Diinna not at the church?" says her husband. "Why?"

"She is sick," says the daughter, Maren. "She has a small boy— she must get better for him." Freja looks at her sharply.

"Why are they there?" His finger jabs at the air, his voice disgusted.

"This was the resting place for my father and brother," says Maren. "For her husband." She looks from Ursa's face and back to Absalom, sees they do not understand. "After the storm, this is where we brought them."

Dead, realizes Ursa, and something inside her twists. Drowned people have lain in their house, on that floor. She thinks of the hanging carcasses in the store, and bile stings her throat. *For God's sake, do not be sick.*

"Why were we not told?"

"It was a resting place, only." Maren must scent danger, because her whole stance changes. She makes her slight frame smaller, rounding her shoulders. "Commissioner, we mean no offence. This was once a boathouse, the only place in the village we thought large enough to befit you."

It is artfully done, thinks Ursa. Absalom's stance softens in the face of the woman's obeisance, and she wishes she could bring herself to be like that for him. She feels always either too bold, or too meek.

"We should have been informed." He turns and looks up at the carved figures. "These aren't Christian symbols."

"Diinna is Sámi," says Freja. Maren's jaw clenches, bone pressing white against her pale skin, and Ursa knows she would not have wished this to be revealed.

"A Lapp?" He shakes his head suddenly, a bull throwing off a fly. "They had Lapp rites?"

"No," says Maren, earning another pointed glance from her mother. "They only watched the bodies. They did no harm."

"Anything that isn't the dominion of the Lord is harmful, however it comes. They used no drum?"

"No."

He narrows his eyes at her. "I'll be telling the Lensmann of this."

He goes inside. Maren's blue-grey eyes have a bright intensity to them, a skein of panic. Ursa fights an urge to reach out to her.

"Ursula!" Absalom's shout breaks their stillness. She thinks to say goodbye but the two women have vanished around the side of the house.

The mud has taken in her slippers, and she imagines sinking down to her knees, her waist and her throat, until she is stuck into the belly of the earth, lying there cool and smothered and safe.

"Wife?" Absalom is in the doorway, the fire coaxed to bright flickers behind him and throwing his broad shape into shadow. In his hand he holds a flat instrument, a chisel of some sort, and beneath his other arm is the bench from their table. "Make dinner."

She looks at him dumbly, and down at her stuck feet. He sighs and places the bench and chisel down, puts his hands beneath her armpits and heaves her free, depositing her in the doorway. Her head spins: how often had she and Agnete imagined a man lifting them into the doorway of the home they share? How different it is, how foolish she feels. Her slippers are ruined, and he closes the door on her.

She makes her dazed way to the cold store. They are almost out of fish and bread, what had been left for them by the women. Soon she will have to make dough. Siv let her household teachings lapse since Agnete's maid was dismissed and Ursa took over her care. She knows how to heat mint oil in water and rest Agnete's head in her hand so she can breathe over it, but can't brew light beer. She can lift and wash Agnete's sore leg, but can't keep a house.

And even if she could remember how to make bread, Absalom will not be happy with only that. Surely he will not expect her to butcher the meat in the store? Her body shakes and she turns her back to its door. She had expected a maid at least. Her father must have too, or else he wouldn't have sent her so ill-equipped for her duties. She hacks at the hard loaf, but her fingers are chilled.

She wishes she could write, and could send a letter to Father. She would tell him Vardø is not fine at all, but an island full of bereaved, watchful women, some of whom are not church-going. That it is cold though it is summer, and the sun doesn't set. That they do not have a house fit for a commissioner, or in fact anything that he would recognize as a house, but a room with runes carved over its door, because it used to hold the dead.

She presses a cold hand to her mouth, breathes the cupped air in and out to warm it. What could he do? She can't leave her husband: the disgrace would follow her like a mangy dog to Bergen. She could not marry again, would be a spinster, a burden. Agnete is unlikely to find a husband of any sort, and Ursa sends up a small prayer of thanks for that.

Scraping sounds filter through from outside as Absalom takes a chisel to the runes. It sets her teeth on edge: her vision flickers. She holds the knife more tightly, until the faintness passes. When Absalom comes inside, the table is laid with its mismatch of crockery. They eat the last of the bread.

•

Each day he strides out to pray, and to learn Norwegian with Pastor Kurtsson, and to stand at Vardøhus's gates for news. Ursa knows he is waiting for a letter from the Lensmann, for an invitation. She wills it to come too, and not only to lighten his stormy mood. She needs to be out of the house, to eat something that isn't tørrfisk, the dried cod that fills their store. Something fresh: a carrot, a herb. She dreams of fruit, of sweetness. She rations each piece of aniseed, places it inside her cheek until it is soft and barely crunches between her teeth. She dreams of a meal shared with anyone but her husband.

But when he leaves to visit, or to check on the unarrived Lensmann, there is worse. Then, she is alone. Even his company is better than her own.

EIGHTEEN

The commissioner and his wife have been here a week, but the stitched pelts are still folded ready by the door of Maren's house. Their exchange with Commissioner Cornet made her uneasy, though Maren knows it could have been worse: she might have been too slow to stop Mamma mentioning the drum.

When she chided her at home, her mother had closed up like a shell, and Maren grew less sure her loose talk of Diinna was in error. She will have to watch them, the women she calls her family—they have grown apart so starkly it feels dangerous. Almost as dangerous as the commissioner's face when the Sámi rites were mentioned.

She knows, of course, that such things are looked down on. Pastor Kurtsson had frowned at the silver-birch shrouds, but he had allowed it. Commissioner Cornet seems not to understand that things work differently here. This was Sámi land, though they would not call it that. Sailors still sometimes call on Sámi for good wind, for good fortune, and Toril, despite all her protests, went to Diinna when she needed help bearing a child. But the commissioner's disgust has sharpened her to things she had not noticed before: how the Sámi who used to set up their laavus on the headland in summer have not come in years, how Diinna is the last Sámi left living in Vardø.

When she tells Diinna of the exchange, she only shrugs as Erik grabs at her thick braid, chewing the end between sore gums.

"I am used to such ignorance," Diinna says, eyes fixed on Mamma's back.

Maren feels alone in her disquiet, as if she is the only one seeing a storm approach.

It isn't until her mother grows tired of tripping on the skins and snaps that she will take them herself, that Maren finally scoops them up and makes for the second boathouse.

The day is crisp and she is comfortable in her woollen dress. The mud has hardened into its churned ridges, digging into her soles. Toril is beating a blanket on her front step and the women studiously ignore each other, Toril sending a cloud of foul-tasting dust into Maren's mouth. She slaps the worst of it from the reindeer skins.

The second boathouse is closed up and quiet, but smoke is rising from the stack and the place where the runes had been is painted in fresh, gleaming white. She isn't sure where they got the paint from: no one apart from Dag's mother insists on a job that only creates more work rather than lessening it. She listens a moment before she knocks, but can hear nothing.

A minute later, the commissioner's wife, Ursula, opens the door, her hair loose about her round face.

"Good morning, Mistress Cornet."

"Maren, yes?"

Her name in the woman's mouth sends a tingling across her breastbone. She nods. "Maren Magnusdatter."

"My husband is not here. He's at the kirke with Pastor Kurtsson." She doesn't meet Maren's eye. Her eyelashes are so blonde they are almost white against her cheek. She is

wearing the dark blue dress she wore at kirke, and there is
mud still about its hem. Maren wonders why she has not yet
washed it.

"I brought these." She holds up the skins. The woman recoils
a little. "The Lensmann ordered them from Kirsten for your
arrival. They're for the floor."

"Oh."

"I stitched them."

"Thank you," says Ursula, but she doesn't reach out for
them. She is eyeing them as though they still have living flesh
inside them, are something to be wary of.

"I can lay them if you like?"

She opens the door wider to allow Maren inside, and her
face is so grateful it makes Maren wince.

The men from Kiberg have made a good job of it. There
is a broad bed across one side of the room, with a curtain for
privacy. There is a solid table and, under it, a bench and an
array of pots and pans hung across the mantel that look
untouched. Beside the grate where Dag used to kiss her is a
wooden shelf set into the wall for the washbowl. A stack of
plates sits beside it. The door to the store where he first took
her hand has a cobweb growing across it. She digs her fingernails into her palm. Though it looks well, there is something
decidedly unhomely about it. Aside from the crucifix over the
fire, there is no ornament. The fire has been fed poorly and
is smoking, giving meagre light and heat.

She can feel the cold of the floor leaching through her boots.
No wonder Ursula is shivering, though she tries not to show
it. A rough woollen blanket is thrown over the back of one
of the chairs and she wonders if Ursula had been wearing it
when she knocked, had taken it off for appearances' sake.
When Maren looks about her she sees that the washbowl is
full of grey water. More cobwebs lurk in the corners of the

room, above the bed, and the rushes beneath her feet are muddy and wilted.

The house smells of closed-up must, but there is no trace lingering of the rot that Maren smelt the last time she stood in this room. Of course there wouldn't be, it is eighteen months since her father and brother lay there—her eyes flick to the spot before the fireplace and it seems to her the ground is darker there. Ursula follows her gaze.

"Is that where?"

Maren nods before she can think better of it, and Ursula sways. She is paler than before, Maren thinks, and shadows are pressed beneath her eyes, though her cheeks are still plump. "Are you all right?"

"I'm sorry," says Ursula. She places her hand upon her stomach. "We were not informed. It is something of a shock to know there were dead kept here."

"There's nothing bad in it," says Maren. "The dead are often rested inside in winter. Usually we would have kept them at home but..." But there were two of them. They would have taken up the whole room. "This was a boat shed, once. We did not know it was to be your home." She wouldn't have allowed cobwebs to settle across the doorways and ceilings. There would be woven curtains at the windows, the pots hung over the fire and full of reindeer stew.

She needs to be out of this house.

"Where do you want these?"

Ursula looks about her, as though she has misplaced something. "I..." She gestures to the floor before the fire.

"There are two. Perhaps," says Maren, "one there, and one before the bed? It is not nice to place your feet straight from the warmth of bed onto the cold floor."

Ursula flushes as she nods, and Maren wonders if she is shy of her mention of the bed. Perhaps in Bergen they are more private about such things: she knows that Dag's father insisted on two levels to his own house, so their bedrooms could be separate as in their house in Tromsø.

Maren takes up one patchwork of skins and lays it before the fire. It is fine fur, and she has worked the white breast of each animal into the corners so it looks almost like a design. She smooths it, looks to Ursula for approval; but the woman's eyes are far away, and she is still holding herself about her waist.

The second stitched pelt she lays beside the bed. It is made, but the blankets are rumpled. Before she stands, her back to the room, Maren places her hand over the place: it is still warm.

Ursula is raking the fire, poking through the smoking ash. It is perhaps not her place, but Maren can't watch without commenting.

"You need fresh." She gestures at the store door. "There'll be plenty in there, Kirsten saw to that."

"Yes, I..." Ursula stands: her eyelids flutter. Maren hurries forward and hooks her hand beneath her elbow, feeling the gentle give of her arm. Ursula places her own hand on Maren's shoulder to steady herself, and Maren is taken back to their first encounter on the dock, the woman's hand soft and cold upon her.

"Are you all right?"

Ursula's eyes are closed. Her lids are palest pink, like the insides of seashells, or a newborn's fingernails. Her breath is coming a little too fast and uneven: there is still that sweetness upon it, and it sets Maren's teeth on edge.

"Yes. I'm sorry." She takes her own weight, and Maren lets go of her elbow, places her hand at her back. "I am a little faint."

"Would you like some water? Some bread?" Maren manoeuvres her gently to the nearest chair, places the blanket about her shoulders. She turns before Ursula answers, is already at the pitcher—it is empty.

"You're out of water."

"Bread too." Ursula's voice is flat and quiet. "I don't know how."

"How?" Maren looks closer at the washing bowl: the water has a skim across it. The house isn't simply poorly kept—it is squalid.

"How to—" Ursula breaks off with a sharp inhale of breath.

The tingling point in Maren's chest squeezes as she takes up the pitcher. "I can fetch water. You stay there."

"I'm sorry, I should—"

Maren hears a rustle of skirts. Ursula has braced herself on the table. The soft skin at her wrist is creased, her face crumpled. Maren looks away again, addresses her feet. "You should sit. Rest. I'll not be long."

The chair creaks and Maren goes out into the bright day, relieved to be outside the house, and urgent to be back. She takes a deep breath of fresh air and hurries home. Toril has gone inside and the rug she had looped over her gate to air has fallen onto the ground: Maren stomps over it.

Mamma, who is watching Erik play beside the fire, looks up sharply when Maren returns. "You were gone a while."

"I went in to lay them."

"She's too fine to lay her own rug? How is the house?"

"She's not well. She's feeling faint." Maren crosses to their drinking bucket, fills the pitcher. "The house is..."

She doesn't know how to speak it, the sadness she felt, coming from Ursula and the dusty floor and the warm bed, the whole place seeming more abandoned than it ever had when she and Dag were there, or even when Diinna and Varr watched over their men. Erik grips at her skirt as she passes him to take a loaf of black bread from the basket.

"What's that for?"

"They have no bread."

Mamma snorts. "The commissioner, out of bread? His fat wife likely ate it all." She narrows her eyes, the hollows of her cheeks showing. "We don't have it to give."

"We have enough for the week," says Maren, wrapping the bread in cloth and placing it over the mouth of the jug. "They will give us the loaf in return, when it's made."

"Lazy dritt," says Mamma, so viciously Maren stares at her. "What else does she have to do all day? Not like her husband, out all hours visiting."

"He visits?"

"Toril and Magda said he prayed with them. And I imagine he has his eye on Diinna too." Mamma licks at the corner of her mouth, the skin there dry and weeping. "He'll maybe come soon."

"Maybe." Maren disguises a shudder as she drapes her shawl over her shoulders. "I won't be long."

She gives Toril's house a wide berth. She wonders if he is in there now, praying with the family instead of keeping his wife company. She walks across the fallen blanket again, grinding in her heel.

The door to the boathouse is ajar, and the crisp chill is seeping inside, making the struggling fire stutter. Ursula is sitting where Maren left her, knuckles white and clasped about the blanket. Maren swallows down her impatience—why could she not have closed the door?

"Here," she says, putting the pitcher down heavily on the table. Ursula starts as Maren closes the door. "Water, and bread. Where are the knives?"

"There."

Maren sweeps the stale crumbs from the chopping board. The knife is dull and she can see no sign of the sharpening stone. She saws two pieces roughly from the loaf, brings them on the cleanest plate she can find and sets them down along with a horn cup that has a stain about the rim.

She is wondering whether she will need to place the woman's hand upon the food, perhaps even feed her, when Ursula blinks and looks up at her for the first time, her hand taking Maren's.

"Thank you," she says. "I'm sorry, I—" She breaks off, swallows. "What must you think of me."

"Not for me to think anything of you," says Maren, feeling her cheeks redden. Ursula's hand is warm from the blanket, and so soft she can't find a bone in it. Maren feels her own all angles, hard and dry and cold as the dirt outside. She pulls from the grasp. "It's no trouble."

"I can pay you." Ursula makes to rise. "My husband...I can ask him..."

"All I ask is for a loaf in return."

"Yes, of course. Please, join me."

Maren could laugh at that, being invited to share in her own bread and water, but instead she sits in the chair beside Ursula, takes a slice.

She watches how small Ursula's bites are, dainty as a bird's. Her teeth are very white, her lips pinker now she is warming beneath the blanket.

Maren hesitates as Ursula takes another bite of bread, a sip of water. "If you don't mind me asking, Mistress Cornet."

"Ursula, please. Or Ursa."

"Ursa?"

"You can call me Ursula if you'd prefer, of course. But those I'm close with call me Ursa, and now we have broken bread together..." She smiles weakly and Maren smiles back, her face feeling tight.

"Ursa." She tries it. "If you don't mind me speaking plainly. There's plenty of flour, and Kirsten left five carcasses in the store." Ursa stiffens. Maren hurries on. "I only wondered if everything was well."

Ursa chews a long while, until the bread must be mush in her mouth. Her swallow is loud in the silence. She meets Maren's gaze again. Her eyes are very light brown, almost gold. "You must think me very foolish—"

"Not at all—"

"But I cannot make bread."

Maren's lips form a silent *Oh* as Ursa speaks on. "I cannot butcher meat, have never seen a dead animal whole, cannot bring myself to even enter that room. I can barely keep the fire going, and my husband must start it when it dies. I cannot keep a house." She gives a wild little laugh, and Maren's pulse quickens. "I am not much of a wife."

"I am sure that isn't—well, that is not so..." Maren wants to reassure her, but how? Butchering she can understand, perhaps: her mother was squeamish about such things, and leaves even the fish to Maren mostly. But bread, a broom? They aren't such hard things to know.

"It is bad," Ursa interrupts, and her face flickers with anger that Maren knows is for herself. "But I do not know what to do about it." She reaches out again for Maren's hand, clasps it in her own. "I need help, that much is evident, I'm sure. And we have some coin. I wonder if you...might you help me?"

"Help you?"

"Teach me. You would not be a maid so much as a friend, a teacher. Unless it is a silly idea. You can tell me."

Maren wonders if she should feel offended. It sounds exactly like being a maid. "I am not the best housekeeper myself."

"The standard is not so high." Ursa gives another weak smile. Maren looks about her, at the dying fire, the windows grimy with smoke, the cobwebs. "Of course, if you do not want to, it is all right. I do not even know if Absalom..."

She trails off, her face sombre again, loosening her grip on Maren's hand. Maren tightens hers in response.

"Yes," she says. The word is out before she can really think about it.

"You are certain?" Ursa smiles. "Thank you. I'll speak with my husband."

Maren rises suddenly. "I'll tell my mother."

"Yes."

"See you on the Sabbath. You can tell me what the commissioner says."

"I will." Ursa follows her to the door. Her brown eyes are bright with relief. There is a crumb caught on her lower lip, and Maren must clutch her skirts to keep from brushing it off.

"Thank you, Maren."

The door closes, and Maren feels it is she who is plunged into an airless room.

NINETEEN

"I know we aren't so fine as her from Bergen but we are no servants." Mamma is pacing the small floor of their house, licking at the cracked edge of her mouth, glaring at Maren. "Whatever possessed you to say yes to that fat dritt?"

But Maren can't explain it. She knows they have enough trouble with baby Erik and Diinna to keep them busy, enough work to do in the remaining month of the midnight sun to ensure they survive the winter. There are crops to be planted, last year's harvested. They will have to go to Kiberg for fish, sell furs to trade, make trips to the low mountain for fresh heather and moss for the roof where last winter ice found its way in and swelled, letting in damp when it melted.

This means Diinna will have to pick up the slack Maren creates, as will Mamma. And Mamma is getting older, getting frailer, and inside her is growing an anger towards Diinna that frightens Maren when she sees it, even more than her mother frightens her now.

As Mamma tells her over and over how foolish she is, that she supposes there is no way out of it without offending Mistress Cornet and so the commissioner, Maren can't disagree. She can't explain what happened, why she felt she had no choice in the matter. The only thing she could offer—though she will not offer it—was that when Ursa loosened her hand, she felt as though something important was slipping away from her and that she must grab it. She had to say yes. She had no choice.

Though something is decided, she is unsure how the arrangement will work. It feels strange to take money, but Mamma will not accept her helping for nothing. She doesn't know how to broach the subject, or whether she should go unbidden to the house. It is only another day till the Sabbath— she supposes she will hear more then.

She tries to go about her tasks with her usual care and attention, but the thought of being out of the house has sent something singing through her blood, something restless and hot and almost painful. Though she isn't to go to the sea to fish as they had before the commissioner arrived, it is still a change of scenery, and a place where she had kissed her betrothed and watched over her brother and father. In another version of her life, the boathouse is hers, and now she has a chance to claim a small ownership to it.

And Ursa—she too sets something moving through Maren's body. It feels almost like the ache when she watches Erik sleep, but it is ridiculous to harbour such tenderness towards a grown woman, even one seemingly clueless as a child. Maren is startled by her. What kind of life must she have had in Bergen, to arrive so unprepared? Though it is as unthinkable as Mamma says, Maren feels no scorn, only a crushing pity.

The day that passes between the making of their agreement and their meeting in kirke is filled with thoughts of Ursa alone in her large house, sitting still as stone by the table beneath the blanket, or lying in bed once her husband has left. Maren imagines her bare toes falling on the pelt she stitched, the gentle attention of her eyes as she slices the bread Maren brought her. The birdlike close of her lips about it.

•

Though Maren is in a hurry to get there, she still knocks at Diinna's door and urges her to come to kirke on the Sabbath.

"He doesn't approve," says Maren, "of people not attending."

"What do I care for his approval?"

Maren can't make her dull-eyed sister-in-law understand, that he isn't like the minister, how this man's favour has a heft to it, that to fall out of it would have an even greater weight.

She hasn't told Diinna what Mamma said to him about the runes and the rites, though she supposes she may have over-heard them discussing it, through the wall. But Diinna gives no sign that she has heard, gives no sign of caring what anyone says, even Maren. The dislike between her and Mamma pulses, is growing teeth. Maren reaches out for her hand. It is sticky with something.

"Please, Diinna. You should come. He may have more ques-tions for the census."

She shrugs. "He knows where I am." Her dark eyes slide to the wall. Perhaps she did hear after all, knows Toril gave her name and that Mamma confirmed she lived here.

"At least let us bring Erik," says Maren, impatient to get away.

Diinna holds him out, a wordless *Take him*. So Maren takes the boy, places him gently on the floor. He sits heavily, like a child much younger than his near fourteen months. *He should be walking more, and babbling*, Maren thinks, *or at least trying to*. His small face regards hers seriously. He has Diinna's eyes, his father's narrow face and lips. The lower one trembles, but he doesn't cry.

"Hello, Erik. You're coming to kirke with me. Would you like that?" His gaze moves to her face, then slides away.

Diinna shuts the door and Maren hoists Erik back to her

hip, carries him to their house, kisses him upon the forehead. The smell of clean cotton is long gone: he smells of wet wool, and his hair is greasier than it should be. She calls for Mamma to hurry up, and bring a blanket for Erik. He has been handed to her in a shift. Mamma comes out grumbling.

"She should take her own child to kirke. And what's she thinking of, sending him out in so little?" She doesn't bother to keep her voice down. "The Devil's in that woman."

"Hush, Mamma," snaps Maren, glancing around. "Don't say such things."

Mamma tuts as she wraps Erik in the blanket, swaddling him like a newborn. He struggles briefly to free his arms as Mamma takes him. She babies him, and Diinna treats him as though she can't wait for him to be grown up and out of the house.

What will become of him? Erik's child, who is as serious as his namesake. She and her brother lived lives apart from a young age, Maren inside the house, Erik learning the land and, later, the sea. They played at the headland sometimes, in those rare, in-between years when they were old enough to be un-supervised and young enough to be more use out of the way than trusted with housework. Whole worlds sprang up from Vardø's flat ground—troll lands and faerie kingdoms.

In company outside of her own, he was quiet and she always talked for her little brother. Now she remembers it, Erik did not speak until late, two or three. But that was because Maren did it for him. Who will speak for his son? As an adult, Erik was a man of few words. Even Diinna, always bright and laughing in those days, could not make him speak beyond what was necessary. And now his wife is silent as he was, and sullen besides.

•

The novelty of the commissioner and his wife has not worn off enough for the women to go straight inside. They are ranged about the door of the kirke again, Kirsten a head taller than everyone else. Pastor Kurtsson is there too. As Maren draws closer, she can see there is a faint break between the groups—most have set themselves close to the minister, but a handful, mostly the seagoers, are speaking with Kirsten.

Mamma makes for the minister's group, Maren moves towards the other. She hears the women make half-hearted coos over Erik, though he is too large for them, and she knows most do not like Diinna any more than Mamma seems to.

"No Diinna?" says Kirsten, watching Mamma's back. Maren shakes her head. "You should have made her come."

"I can't make her. I tried."

"You should have tried harder," says Kirsten. "Edne managed to bring her father though he is nearly blind. The census..." She lowers her voice. "It would be good to have her say her own name. Especially with the killings at Alta and Kirkenes."

"Killings now?" Maren feels a chill steal across her neck.

"Three Sámi, all weather-weavers."

"But Diinna doesn't—"

"It doesn't matter much what Diinna does, only what she is. This Lensmann, he is determined to put a stop to the old ways."

"He is not even at Vardøhus."

"Nor at Alta," says Kirsten. "But he has his commissioners, and Cornet should see Diinna in kirke."

Maren understands. To not come to kirke is one danger; to be Sámi and not come is another. "I've no time to fetch her now."

"Perhaps he won't notice," says Kirsten, but Maren knows as well as she that he is the sort who notices. It is why, when she sees him striding towards the kirke, Ursa in a lighter blue dress behind him, she shrinks herself small as she can.

"Good morning," he says. The women chorus back like girls. Kirsten grimaces.

"Good morning," says a quieter voice, a voice Maren feels is just for her. Ursa has stopped beside her and Kirsten, is smiling nervously. Her hair is neater than last Sabbath's Day— she must be getting used to the lack of a mirror.

"Good morning," says Kirsten.

"I was hoping we could begin our arrangement tomorrow?" says Ursa.

"Of course."

Ursa smiles more broadly, showing even teeth. "I have not forgotten the loan of your coat. Perhaps I could buy more skins from you, Fru Sørensdatter?"

"Certainly," says Kirsten. "I can bring them tomorrow, if that is agreeable."

"Most agreeable. And maybe Maren could give you a list of what more we need—I understand you have a good store of grains and the like. You sound most enterprising."

"Thank you very much, Mistress Cornet."

"Ursula, please."

Maren becomes aware of others watching them, Toril's attention torn between the commissioner and their conversation with his wife.

"Until tomorrow," says Ursa, following her husband inside the dark mouth of the kirke.

"You have an arrangement?" says Kirsten, the curiosity apparent in her voice.

"She needs help with the house," says Maren. There is a spiralling in her stomach. It feels like a strange sort of triumph. "I offered." Kirsten's eyebrows are raised. "She's paying. Good coin. Bergen coin."

Kirsten nods slowly. "Get that list to me after kirke. And Maren?" She looks intently at her, her eyes direct as her words. "Be careful." She squeezes Maren's upper arm, and goes inside before Maren can ask of what.

TWENTY

Absalom leaves early the next day for Alta, before Ursa can ask him for his approval of her plan to bring Maren into their home. He has a new tactic, he tells her.

"I am done with waiting at the fortress gates day after day. Until the Lensmann arrives in Vardøhus, I will make myself useful. There has been some action at Alta that I am keen to gain the measure of."

Ursa guesses he is also resolved to meet the other commissioners to get some idea of their relationship with Lensmann Cunningham. She knows it enrages him that others may be in communication with the Lensmann while he is left in Vardø, and Ursa hopes their situation is common among the commissioners, prays he will not return with even more anger in his heart.

He tells her he must take a small rowing boat a few hours up the coast to Hamningberg, manned by a fisherman from there, where a larger whaling ship will carry him on to Alta, which lies two days to the west. They must have passed the town on the way from Bergen, but Ursa doesn't remember stopping there.

The journey and visit will keep him away at least a week,

and she feels the same mix of relief and anxiety she felt the night he didn't come to her on the ship. The house is already becoming familiar, seeing as she doesn't leave it all day, but at night, even with him snoring beside her, she thinks of the bodies in the store, the runes painted over the door, and the space before the fire beneath Maren's hide covering, where drowned men lay.

Though she has not told him of Maren, he was impressed by the coverings and so agreed when she asked for some money for additional pelts and supplies promised to her by Kirsten, and guessed at a little extra so she could pay Maren. She can't think he would have denied her: the embarrassment of their home was suddenly apparent after Maren's visit. It had been all right when she had been left to sit in the creeping squalor alone. But when Maren had come, holding the skins that now adorn the floor, she had noticed the disarray for the first time.

She had done her best in the small time between Absalom's departure and Maren's arrival, sweeping with the bristle broom and sending plumes of dirt and dust into the air. She had fetched water from the well, and tried to scour the mud from her blue dress with a brush and board. She imagined Agnete's raised eyebrow, and most of all Siv's thin, tired face, her hands blistered and cracked, her nails kept so short the sisters would laugh about them being mannish.

Ursa's face flushes with the memory, the casual cruelty and complete stupidity of it. Her arms ache from the minutes over the scrubbing board, and she feels her hands greasy with tallow soap, stained with ash. She should ask Absalom to write to Siv, so Ursa can thank her for keeping them clean and fed and, in her own stern fashion, loved. Ursa longs to feel this way again, and for the bathtub before the crackling fire, the warmth that easily reached her bones. The press of her sister's bony spine against her back as they sat facing away from each other in the tub, the buzz of Agnete's laboured breath like bees cupped against her ribs—

Maren is on her doorstep before Ursa has washed the tears from her face. In her hands is a bundle of cloth, and she sets it on the floor beside the table with great effort, bending carefully. Ursa offers her tea.

"With what?" says Maren, looking at the meagre shelves.

"My husband brought bilberry leaves from Bergen. I'm sure he can spare us some."

Maren nods, and moves to the fireplace.

"Let me," says Ursa. "I know how to make tea."

It is the simplest of tasks, but she has not been watched doing it before, and she can feel Maren's eyes upon her just as she had in kirke. It makes her stand a little straighter, take the cups from their shelf with greater care, flourish a little with the leaves as she drops them to boil. She enjoys the woman's attention upon her: it doesn't feel like malice, as though she is watching for her to make a mistake, but rather more like care, the way Siv would supervise Ursa with her needlework.

Maren takes the cup between cold fingers—Ursa notices the nail beds are raw pink and stretched as though freshly scrubbed. The pads that brush against her own hands are rough as her husband's. She feels shy of her own palms, soft and unskilled as a baby's, hides them in the folds of her skirts. They must be of similar age, but they are made so differently. Ursa feels too big in Maren's presence, cumbersome and absurd in her petticoats. Maren's eyes are large and softly coloured, but her gaze is sharp and clever.

The last time they had been together in the house like this, Maren had taken charge immediately, and Ursa waits for her to do the same again now. But Maren seems uncertain of herself, her eyes lowered to the steam of her cup. It sets off uneasiness in Ursa, a discomfort. She becomes aware of her breath, too loud in the quiet, tries to breathe more shallowly, which makes her chest tighten.

They sit wordlessly together at the table, and Ursa realizes that though she is vague on the perimeters of their relationship—Maren isn't a servant, like Siv, and so she isn't this woman's mistress—she must be the one to speak, to begin.

"Thank you again for coming."

Maren's eyes are still fixed on her cup.

"I am glad your mother could spare you. With luck I will be quick to learn and she can have you back. Summers must be busy here, being so short."

Maren is bent so low over the steam of her cup, perhaps warming her nose, that Ursa can see the small hairs pulling at the back of her neck where her bun is tight, the collar of her dress creased and worn, the nubs of her spine beneath. The bundle sits at her feet, lumpen.

"What have you brought?"

Maren bends, brings it up to her knees, the cloth and her arms straining, the hollows about the base of her throat deepening. Ursa reaches out to help, catching her hands beneath it to help raise it to the table.

"Why, it's heavy as a rock," says Ursa, standing now beside her chair, and Maren's narrow fingers work at the knot, tightened by the strain put upon it. Her ragged nail catches and she sucks in a breath. "Shall I cut it?" She fetches a knife, but at last Maren is roused to speech.

"No, if you'll please, Mistress Cornet." There is an urgency beneath the formality, and both surprise Ursa. Maren's cheeks are red, and she moves so the bundle on the table is hidden behind her, as though protecting a small child from Ursa's blade. "It's my mother's."

Now it is Ursa's turn to flush, and she takes her time

returning the knife to its place. It isn't Maren who put the distance back between them at all, but her, treating the cloth like something that could be easily got, easily disposed of, easily replaced. *That is your old life*, she tells herself.

By the time she turns round again the cloth has been carefully eased out from under its cargo, and folded neatly beside. Ursa had not been wrong in her first estimation: beside a smooth column of stone that she recognizes as a rolling pin, sits a rock, grey and shaped like a mound with a flattish top, about the size of her mother's belly when she was pregnant with the brother that wasn't to live.

"Is it a slickstone?" she asks, and Maren snorts, an abrupt sound, bringing her hand up to her mouth.

"I am sorry, it's only..." Another snort escapes her, followed by a thin peal of laughter. She looks immediately contrite, which makes Ursa laugh, too. "I am sorry, I am sorry."

"Do not be sorry," says Ursa, feeling the distance closing between them again. "Only, please, explain to me what this is. And perhaps," she smiles, "why it is not a slickstone?"

"A slickstone is for smoothing, or for starching. It fits like a hand in a hand, just so—" Maren holds out her palm, and in a gesture that is more reaction than intent, Ursa reaches her hand out too, and places it atop Maren's palm. She barely feels the cool dryness of it, the rough callouses, before Maren jerks away, clutching it to her as though burnt.

"I—"

The door is knocked upon: three sharp raps displaying a confidence that sets Ursa in mind of her husband. Her chest thrums, but Maren recognizes the sound.

"Kirsten Sørensdatter," she says.

She knocks like a man, thinks Ursa, as she opens the door. Kirsten stands there, her arms piled with bundles, a covered bucket hooked over her elbow, and two skins tied like a cape about her neck. She doesn't wait for an invitation to enter, only strides inside and drops the whole lot upon the table.

"Good morning, Ursula, Maren." She stands smiling at them both, as though aware she has walked in at a strange moment and understands it better than Ursa herself. Ursa is again prompted to draw a line between Kirsten and her husband: she is so certain of herself, so solid in the middle of the room that Ursa fancies she can feel the air pushing itself backwards to make more space for her. And though Maren's exclamation comes immediately, it still takes Ursa another moment to register that the woman is wearing trousers.

"Kirsten, are you mad? I told you this must stop."

Maren is standing before her friend, and though Ursa can't see her face from her place beside the open door, she can hear the fear upon it.

Kirsten looks down at herself. "What would be madness is slaughtering in skirts."

Ursa notices the dark stains over her thighs, speckling the bottoms of the trousers, which are a little short, the waistband tied with rope. She checks outside the door: there is no one looking from the neighbouring windows, no one on their steps. She closes it and moves back to the table quietly. Maren is mouthing wordlessly, standing very close to Kirsten, as though to shield her from Ursa's view. There is something between them, she thinks, a deeper friendship than two who gossip outside kirke once a week.

"No one was looking," Ursa says, hoping to break the thread between them.

"Still, someone will have seen." Maren clutches her hands together as though in prayer. "Someone always does. What if word gets back to Pastor Kurtsson, or to Commissioner—"

She gasps and wheels about to Ursa, who recoils. Maren's energy feels dangerous and desperate, like a fox in a trap.

"Mistress Cornet, Ursa, you will not..." She gathers herself. "Please, would you please not..." She turns back to Kirsten. "You have come to the commissioner's house, Kirsten. The commissioner's house, in trousers!"

"They are my finest trousers," says Kirsten, her voice mock-affronted.

"And yet you slaughter in them?" says Ursa, playing along. Maren's face is still wretched, and Ursa tries to soothe her. "I will not tell my husband, Maren. Fru Sørensdatter, you have my word. Or should it be Herr Sørensdatter?"

Maren doesn't laugh, but Kirsten lets out a boom and doffs an imaginary cap. "Milady."

"Do you not see how dangerous this is?" Maren twists her hands into her skirts. "It was one thing in your own house—"

"What is dangerous is your glower. If the wind blows the other way you shall be stuck like that, and even the trolls will run away."

"Trolls are for children," says Maren. "This is serious."

"And yet you leave crumbs out every midwinter."

"We do not follow such customs." Maren's voice has a note of hysteria, and Ursa finally realizes that she is again the cause of Maren's distress. It is her husband Maren fears, his displeasure at the runes and, no doubt, at trolls. Ursa despises him at that moment: how she wishes these women knew that she is as scared as them. This time she comes close to Maren and places a hand upon her shoulder.

"Please, Maren, you do not have to worry. I will not tell my husband of any of this. He is in Alta this week, and no doubt Pastor Kurtsson is taking full advantage of his absence to rest from his Norwegian lessons. And besides—" she gives her a hesitant smile—"I, too, leave food out for the trolls in midwinter. In fact, my sister and I would insist on whole herring, prepared with a potato, and a sweet cake."

"I should like to be a troll in Bergen, to eat so fine as that," says Kirsten, and though Ursa decides to take it in good humour she hears the barb in it, chides herself again for her display of extravagance.

Maren searches her face and, at last, seems to take her at her word. She nods carefully, her pointed chin uncreasing. "Thank you."

"All the same, Kirsten," says Ursa, determined to take charge, to show confidence so Maren can take assurance from her. "You had better borrow something to return home in." She lifts the lid of her cherrywood chest, draws out her grey wool skirt. "This is a little long anyway." She holds it out to Kirsten, and for the first time sees uncertainty cross her broad face.

"I can't wear that," she says. "It is too dear."

"Nonsense," says Ursa. "I insist."

"I will muddy it with my boots."

"I am learning how to take mud out of cloth. It is no trouble."

Kirsten takes it with reluctance, and removes her boots before stepping into it. It comes up a little short, but the trouserlegs come up shorter.

"All this worry over some trousers," says Kirsten, relacing her shoes. "I am like to cause as much of a fuss in so fine a skirt as this. Best be careful, Mistress Cornet, or you'll have the kirke-women at the door, begging alms of lace." She straightens. "I brought everything you asked for." This to Maren. "Flour and such. And even found some fennel seeds among Mads's things. I have no use for them."

Ursa fetches what she owes Kirsten for the supplies, and the woman places the coins into her trouser pocket beneath the skirt. "Thank you. I hope your lesson goes well, though why you have picked such a teacher I will never guess." She smiles warmly at Maren, whose face still holds the last vestiges of worry. "I will see you on Wednesday."

TWENTY-ONE

Maren could weep. Damn Kirsten, with her arrogance and her stupidity and her need to be seen. She doesn't believe for a moment her attire was only for the slaughter. It was as much for show. She wanted the measure of the commissioner's wife and now she has it. Maren hopes she is ashamed.

The door closes heavily, and Maren jumps.

"Please," says Ursa. "You must not worry."

Maren tries to smooth her face, which aches with the effort of it. She isn't used to being noticed in this way. But Ursa is looking at her as though she could see straight through her skin to her thudding heart. Maren brings her arms across her chest, holds herself.

"I am not worried." She clears her throat, gives herself a sharp pinch beneath her shoulder blade, and then moves back to the table where the rock sits. "Will you help me move this to the fire?"

"We are to burn it?"

"Rocks do not burn," says Maren carefully, checking Ursa's face for jest, and finding it. She smiles back. "It is a baking stone." She unties the nearest bundle, checks inside and brings out a closely woven packet of something. She opens it carefully, rubs it between her fingers, feeling for the grain. "It is good Kirsten brought fennel, all she has given is potato flour." She dusts off her hands. "We are going to make flatbrød."

Ursa nods. "I think I have had that, at Christmas time with herring and onions."

Maren winces. Flatbrød is what they eat more than anything, and certainly never with onions. She hopes Ursa likes it—there will not be fresh bread waiting in her pantry often.

She doesn't elaborate, doesn't tell Ursa that the reason she has chosen this for their first meeting is because even a child could make it, as it is near impossible to burn or make bitter. She has been making it with Mamma for as long as she can remember, since before her brother was taken by Pappa to hunt or to fish. They spend a whole day on it every few months, Mamma rolling and Maren baking.

"This kind of stone, it holds warmth very well. We use it for our beds, on very cold nights."

She used to go with Mamma, sometimes even Pappa, to the low mountain looking for these rocks. Firestone, Pappa called it, because it was warm from even a touch of sun. She strokes her hand across it. This was their second baking stone, more recently fetched, ten years ago perhaps. The one left at their house is better, scooped like a bowl from years of use. She thought to make this one a gift for Ursa, is shy to propose it. Mamma is unlikely to notice it gone. She notices nothing much at all any more, as though a film has grown across her eyes and thickens every month.

"Like a bedpan?"

Maren doesn't know, nods anyway. "It keeps the heat even, keeps the air out of the dough. The bread will keep for months, years."

They heave it up between them, Ursa exclaiming at Maren's ability to carry it alone to the house, and settle it atop the grate. "It will take a while to heat, but we can begin anyway."

She lays out what Kirsten has brought: there is plenty of flour, a bucket of kjernemelk with a thin skin on top that makes Maren's mouth water just to look at it. Kirsten, Maren realizes as she unpacks smaller packets of seeds and even a small hard crystal of salt, is even more comfortably off than Maren guessed.

She fetches Ursa's pestle and mortar, made of cool grey stone, and sets Ursa to grinding the fennel seeds while she begins measuring and sifting the flour. The seeds will be too overpowering whole, will throw the balance of the bread out and make the places where there is none taste lacking. That is how she feels, standing beside Ursa: chalky and thin as plain flatbrød.

Ursa scatters the ground fennel into the mix and Maren must start to sift all over again: Ursa has not put great effort into it and the seeds aren't of the fine powder she would have preferred. But the woman is looking anxiously into her face and so Maren nods and says thank you. When the flour mix is a little less gritty, she has a small mound of fennel husks beside her on the table. Ursa reaches to sweep them away and Maren puts her own hand out. She is prepared, this time, for the contact, doesn't feel the surge that came a little like panic when Ursa had placed her hand in her palm.

"Keep them. We can use it all."

Ursa does something very strange. She covers her face, makes a sound of irritation, much like a chided child.

"I am sorry," she says. "I feel so foolish. You must think me awful, to be so wasteful."

"I think no such thing," says Maren. "I only think you lived differently in Bergen. I hope you will come to like your life here." She feels heat flush her neck. "Not that I think you are struggling."

Ursa lets out a hollow little laugh, a wretched sound that pulls at Maren. "Oh, but I am."

It is a moment of confidence that fills Maren with tenderness. "All will be well, Ursa."

Ursa looks at her with such simple gratitude that Maren blushes. "You are so kind. I am so glad of you."

She reaches out to Maren, and though Maren doesn't hold people easily—the last time was perhaps with Diinna when she lay collapsed on their floor as Mamma held the newly born Erik—something compels Maren to let her.

There is no reluctance or self-consciousness in the way Ursa folds into her arms, fitting beneath her chin, her hair smelling of sleep and perfumed water. Ursa mentioned a sister, and has perhaps missed holding her, for she clings to Maren with an unsettling need.

For her part, Maren grows bolder, and tightens her grip about Ursa, feeling the softness of her shape beneath her fine dress, the gentle swell of her shoulder blades, like low waves across her back. She doesn't want to breathe, to create the space between them for her chest to grow into. But then Ursa is loosening her grip and pulling away.

"Thank you," says Ursa, and turns back to the fennel husks. She seems soothed by the embrace where Maren has been disquieted. "Should I grind them finer?"

There is a double pulse in Maren's body. She motions yes and begins adding the kjernemelk, skimming the butter from the top to reach the liquid below. The action requires focus, and calms her. She wraps the butter in the clean cloth Kirsten has given for this purpose, and the creamy smell coats her nostrils. They went without butter last year, and she has missed the richness of it, the salt dried from a pailful of sea and churned until it is golden and smooth and perfect.

When she has added enough buttermilk she mixes it in

carefully, tilting the bowl so Ursa can see as she stirs it about until the mixture is firm and consistent, sitting mounded like a small mimic of the baking stone heating in the fire.

She scatters flour over the tabletop and Ursa passes her the heavy rolling pin. It is made from a different rock than the baking stone, cooler, to keep the dough from sticking. She portions palmfuls of dough, sets one before Ursa.

"You want it thin as a biscuit."

Ursa nods, but the moment she starts rolling Maren knows she has not made biscuits before. The shape that forms is nothing like a circle. But when she looks to Maren for approval, a flour stain on her forehead near her hairline, Maren smiles encouragingly, watches as she carries it carefully to the baking stone and drops it on top. It is off-centre, one side edging over towards the licking flames, and Maren already knows it will burn there and cook unevenly elsewhere.

"How long?" Ursa is staring at the baking stone.

"We wait until all the water is gone, until it is crisp and good for cracking. Will you watch it?"

With Ursa given her task, Maren takes up the rolling pin. It holds none of the warmth from Ursa's hands. She rolls out the remaining dough into neat discs. She isn't so skilled as Mamma, but they are even and speckled like the rare eggs they find tucked in the gaps between rocks in the cliff below their house. They have not checked since the storm. Perhaps she should suggest it to Mamma—after well over a year undisturbed the birds will likely have forgotten the danger of people.

After a few tries of Ursa rescuing the flatbrød too early or too late, she learns the point at which she must clamp the breads between the tongs and rest them to cool. They find an easy rhythm between them, do not speak except through glances and nods, and when the dough is rolled and stacked, Maren takes up the pot without asking and begins to brew some more tea. The fireplace is double width, as Dag intended, and so they can stand shoulder to shoulder before it. By the time the tea is brewed the first breads are dry and cool.

Ursa prods them. "They are good?"

"One way to discover it."

They sit together at the floury table. Ursa takes her own attempt and cracks it, sending crumbs and flakes of seeds scattering into her lap. She brushes them carelessly to the floor as she chews.

"They get better the longer you leave them," says Maren.

"They are good already." Ursa's smile is broad and Maren returns it gladly. "There is no blessing so complete as bread."

"What?"

"Something Siv used to say."

"She is your sister?"

"Servant." Ursa seems to catch herself. "But also my friend. Agnete is my sister." She blinks, her pale lashes brushing her cheek. "She's ill."

"I'm sorry."

"She was near drowned when she was first born. The doctors say it's because she came in my mother's bath, and there's still water on her lungs. I used to care for her."

Maren can't think what to say. She takes some more flatbrød, catching the crumbs neatly in her palm and placing them atop the flour.

"They did not think she would see her first birthday, but she's thirteen years old now. She will be grown when next we meet."

The silence widens. Ursa doesn't finish her piece, only passes it between her fingers, hand to hand. In her face is pain so apparent it feels indecent to witness.

"My brother was younger, too," Maren says finally. "By a year. But still he was married before me."

"At least I have beaten Agnete there." Slowly, Ursa meets her eye. "You must miss him."

To that there is nothing Maren can say. She feels a dark draw of energy from the spot before the fire, where Erik lay in his greenish skin and seemed to shrink before her eyes. She couldn't bring herself to touch him in the weeks he'd lain there, had not thrown herself over him and keened as Mamma had. Though the Kirke talked of souls, Varr and Diinna of spirits, from the moment she saw him dead she had felt there was nothing left of him in this world, or any other. There was only a body, empty as the shapes in the store. Erik was not this shrunken form, was not caught like a bird fluttering at the windows, was not in the sea or the whale or the sky. He was gone, and Maren could find no comfort for it.

"I'm sorry," says Ursa. "I have spoken out of turn. Agnete and I, we did not converse much with others beyond Father and Siv."

"We don't speak much at all in our house," says Maren, briskly. "We should store these. You have bread barrels?"

"Not that I have noticed. Though perhaps..."

Ursa looks towards the store. The cobwebs have gone, but Maren suspects they have been cleaned away rather than broken by entry.

"I'll fetch them," says Maren, rising to her feet, but Ursa stands with her.

"Let me." There is that determined set to her chin that Maren noticed when she stepped from the boat in her yellow dress. "I can do it."

She crosses the room, places her hand upon the latch. Maren watches the small lift of her shoulders as she takes a breath and opens the door, leaving floury smudges on the frame. The store has a small, narrow slit of a window set into the far wall, and the light filters through the hanging shapes of the carcasses to illuminate the wispy hairs that spring up about Ursa's ears, escaping her neat knot.

She hesitates a moment before moving further into the store, and out of Maren's sight. She sees the sway of the slaughtered reindeer, their bodies dark red and sinewy. They will be gamey now, rich and salty. She should offer to teach her how to butcher, but perhaps that is too much too soon. There's a scraping sound and Ursa comes back out, rolling a barrel before her, flinching as the swing of a carcass brings it brushing against her. She pulls the door closed behind her, lips a thin line, and rolls the barrel to the table, righting it and resting her palms on it.

They wrap the flatbrød and stack them inside the bread barrels. When it is done, they wipe down the table, sweep the floor. Maren washes the cups in the grey water of the bowl, her hands wrinkling as she rubs a fingertip across the lip of Ursa's cup.

They edge the stone out of the fire using the pokers. "Leave it until tomorrow," says Maren. "It will be cool by then."

"Shall I bring it to you?"

"You can keep it. And the roller. We have another."

Ursa reaches out with her easy familiarity, and takes her hand. "Thank you."

"I don't have to go just yet," says Maren, though it isn't true. She had promised Mamma she would be home for their own baking. But returning to their small house, full of silence and sadness so thick it reeks, feels an impossibility just now, in this warm room, with Ursa's soft hand in hers. "We could make a start on those hides."

"How thoughtless of me," says Ursa. "You must be missing your coat."

"Yes." It is an easy lie; she has her father's at home. "It would be good to have it back."

"But won't your mother be needing you? I could do without the coat. I have nowhere to go but kirke. Besides, it is a few days till Sabbath and warmer all the time."

Maren feels her chance slipping. "I wouldn't want to leave you without it. It will not take long for me to teach you. Though of course it would be quicker with two. We could have it made before turn of day."

Why does she not just say she wishes to stay? This isn't how they speak here, if they speak at all, this to-and-fro like currents whirled away and together again by a quick wind.

"It is no trouble for me if you stay. In fact I would prefer it, with Absalom gone to Alta." Her eyes shine as she turns them upon Maren. "We could sit beside the fire together, talk a little as we sew. If you would like it. You don't have to..."

Again Maren feels that reach from inside her, a third, ghostly arm stretching out to seize hold of Ursa, as though she were drowning and found a raft among wreckage.

"Yes," she manages. "Yes, I can stay."

TWENTY-TWO

They spread the hides out upon the floor, and Maren fetches a knife to score them at the right points. She must reach about Ursa with string to measure her, and even this makes her flush. She slices the hides into various shapes, and as Ursa watches her, Maren can feel she wants to say something.

"Is the Wednesday meet a regular occurrence?"

Maren stops slicing, rests on her heels.

"The Wednesday meet Kirsten spoke of," says Ursa. Maren can barely recall any of Kirsten's visit. It feels a great distance away. "Is it just the two of you?"

"No. Many of us meet, in Fru Olufsdatter's house."

"She is our neighbour, yes? I perhaps could come. I should like to meet some people outside of kirke."

Maren flinches.

"I won't mention any of this to them if you do not wish it. I could pretend not to know you at all."

Maren knows she says it in jest, but still she is too slow to hide the hurt in her face. "You may do as you like."

Ursa rises and goes to her cherrywood chest.

"Aniseed?" Ursa tips two smallish seeds onto her palm, holds it out to her. "You place them on your tongue. They taste

178

strange, but good." She takes one and puts it in her mouth, sticks her tongue out to show it. "If you do not like it," says Ursa, covering her mouth, words slightly stilted by the aniseed, "you can leave it."

Maren takes it from Ursa's hand, closes her lips around it.

"It is good, yes?"

"I have never tasted anything like it. From Bergen?"

"Asia. Captain Leifsson, who ran the ship that brought me. He gave me some."

They set to work again, Maren bringing the sleeve pieces together to the table for them to stitch, one each. She makes holes with a pointed bore, shows Ursa the cross-stitch she must use to make them strong.

"I hope you do not mind me asking about the Wednesday meet," says Ursa. "I should understand if I were not welcome. It is only that I have so enjoyed this day together, and I should like to meet some others, if they are all as kind as you."

How can Maren explain the knot in her chest at the thought of Ursa becoming friends with others? It is childish to feel jealousy over such a new friendship. And there is the complication of having the commissioner's wife in such an informal atmosphere. She trusts that Ursa will not tell anyone about Kirsten's trousers, but what else will she hear?

"I understand I am a stranger here," prompts Ursa, "but I should dearly like not to be."

"Come, of course."

"Will you fetch me? I should not like to arrive unannounced the first time."

Maren can do nothing but nod.

"Good," smiles Ursa. "It's settled." She turns her attention back to her work. "Now, where have I gone wrong here?"

The answer is immediately, and Maren helps Ursa unpick her work, shows her more slowly so she can follow along. The fire burns down twice before they are done. The world is still and grey at the small windows, the night so quiet it is as if everything living is holding its breath.

Ursa's thumb is reddened and bleeding from pushing the needle through the coarse hide without a thimble. Maren will bring her a piece of leather next time, she thinks.

"You should try it on." She holds the coat out for her, and Ursa slides it over her arms.

"How do I look?" Ursa asks, spinning. "Like a Vardø woman?"

She looks nothing like them, any of them. Maren's chest aches and she dips her head to mask her confusion, begins to ravel the remaining gut thread.

Ursa takes the coat off, hangs it from the hook beside the door, takes the one beside it and holds it out to Maren.

"Thank you for the loan of it." She crosses again to the chest. This time there are two seeds in her palm, and coins.

"Here."

The coins sit in Maren's hand, cold and glinting. "This is too much."

"Not with the stone and the rolling pin and so forth," says Ursa. She closes Maren's fingers about them. "We have done far more than I ever thought to achieve. Why, I am nearly a housekeeper already."

"And the aniseed—"

"One for now, one for later. Until Wednesday?"

Maren wants Ursa to stay her yet again, to barricade the way, to keep her at least until the day returns. But she only opens the door, and lets her disappear into the misty, sunlit night.

Her time with Ursa makes her feel noticed in a way she has not since Dag came to her trembling, and asked to marry her. Even her friendship with Kirsten, though dear, is built on different terms.

The money is more than she has ever seen before, their village running more on trade than coin. It jangles in her skirts like a taunt. It makes their time together nothing more than a service, she nothing more to Ursa than Kirsten is. Still, she knows it is too much, will pay many times over for their usual orders from the traders from Varanger when they come in midsummer. And besides, Mamma will not allow her to return empty-handed, would forbid her from going back.

Would Maren listen? She doubts her mother's disapproval could keep her from that house, from Ursa. She is the first friend Maren has made in years, and untouched by the hardnesses of a lifetime in Vardø. Even before the storm, none of them were so soft as her.

When home is in sight, light leaking from its windows and making it seem a ship poised on a fogged sea, she takes three of the smaller, heavier coins from her pocket, and moves them to the other, stifling them with a scrap of cloth. She doesn't know what they are worth, can't make sense of their surfaces, but something in their heft and colour makes her sure they are the most valuable.

These she will keep for herself, for some purpose as yet unclear to her. Perhaps she will go to Trøndheim and buy woven cloth, make herself a dress in the style of Ursa's dark blue one, with a collar that scoops daringly close to her shoulders, and has a trim of lace about the cuffs. She wouldn't fill it so pleasingly, but it would be good to have something new, something that isn't frayed about its edges and seams. She squeezes the coins until they grow warm at her touch, looks up to the sky. The sun is low and diffuse, its light shifting always to the corners of her sight. Perhaps she could even build a house of her own some day.

Her mother is awake and standing before the fire, the baking stone crouched in the flames like a toad, a stack of flatbrød beside her, more dough on the table. She doesn't look around as Maren closes the door. The room is close about her after a day at the commissioner's house, and though it is well swept, there is a smell that she has never noticed before: smoke and unwashed hair. She clears her throat, tastes aniseed.

"Mamma?"

Her mother reaches with her hands to the baked bread, taps it, and flips it out onto her palms. It is steaming but she takes her time carrying it to the rack, lowers it gentle as a prayer. *There is no blessing so complete as bread*, thinks Maren, as her mother takes up another circle of dough, lays it atop the stone.

"I'm sorry I'm late," says Maren, taking off her coat. She is caught suddenly about the chest, remembering Ursa. How she had made the new coat look like something rare and lovely, the way a bird wears its feathers.

She doesn't know that Maren stitched two small runes into her sleeve, the ones Diinna once taught her meant protection from harm, and care. It pleases her to think of it now, like messages scrawled in invisible ink, worn against Ursa's pale wrist, the smooth passages of her veins green as meltwater.

Mamma still doesn't speak, but there is a tense set to her shoulders, inched up towards her ears, and when Maren moves to the fire there is a grim twitch in Mamma's jaw as she flips the bread. Her hands are so used to the motion she doesn't look down but straight ahead, the heat bringing sweat beading about her face. Her skin glows with it, the constant scab at the edge of her mouth flaking. She looks like a stranger.

"Mamma?"

Maren holds out the coins, and at last Mamma looks at her, then at her hand. Wordlessly she nods towards the pot where they keep their meagre purse, the string of beads that came from Diinna's father on her marriage to Erik, and the grey pearl their father found in the mouth of a shell that she thought to give Dag as a marriage gift. Maren adds her coins, and comes to hand Mamma the next flatbrød.

They work shoulder to shoulder, and the silence is both harder and easier than it was with Ursa. They have done this together so many times, they are like parts of the same body.

"What is she like?" says Mamma, eventually.

Maren thinks of Ursa's soft hands, her smooth cheek, the crease of her chin when she thinks or is embarrassed. She thinks of the aniseed on her breath, how she shares it now, like a secret. "She is not as you would expect."

Mamma snorts her disbelief.

"You will know her soon enough," says Maren, passing the last of the uncooked breads as Mamma moves another to the rack. "She is coming to the Wednesday meet."

The mention of it brings the same confusion she'd felt when Ursa had raised it. Their friendship is still new and unformed, not yet hardened into something solid enough for her to feel confident in it. What if Ursa finally realizes that she has chosen someone wholly middling to assist her, when she could easily have her pick of teachers? Toril is the most skilled at needlework, Gerda the fastest at churning, Kirsten the best at butchering. Her mother is better at cooking, baking—Maren doesn't even have as good a temperament as most.

"Is she now?" Mamma's eyebrow rises. "That will be interesting. What will your Kirsten have to say on that?"

"Why would she have anything to say?"

"She likes to be the centre of it all, doesn't she? With the commissioner's wife there, she will not be able to take charge so easily."

"She will not mind. She is the one who mentioned it in front of her."

"We will see," says Mamma. She begins to stack the breads into their barrels, and Maren moves to help. Through the thin wall, Erik is at last quieted, and Maren hears a low song coming, Diinna speaking in her language. Erik's *joik*.

They go to bed just as the morning slips its noise beneath the door, and Maren must wait until Mamma is asleep before she takes the remaining coins and aniseed from her pocket and places them in the rip in her pillow. She shifts the aniseed so it will sit small and hard against her cheek, and she fancies she can smell it through the greying cloth. She should make the most of one of the long summer days, row to the low mountain. She has not replaced the heather since the storm, and it is as crisp as burnt bread. Perhaps now that Ursa has her coat, she will want to come with her.

Diinna's singing still comes through the wall. Erik must be waking, and Maren places her palm against it, letting her eyelids close against the brightening day. She sinks, and the whale that came for her father and brother surfaces, calling her to the sea.

TWENTY-THREE

Mamma works Maren hard in the day before the Wednesday meet. She is sent to Toril's to fetch mended winter vests, and the woman is stiffer with her than ever. Toril was always a difficult woman to like, cool even to those she had known all her life, but since the storm she has taken to wearing her faith like armour, wielding her piousness like a blade. Maren counts five crucifixes on the shelf over the fireplace, ranged like newly forged weapons. More line the walls, delicate fashionings of woven sea grass and twine.

"That for Commissioner Cornet?" Maren nods at them.

"For God. He comes most days," says Toril.

"God?"

"The commissioner." Maren sucks her cheeks to keep from laughing at Toril's furious face. "Though not today. Today he is in—"

"Alta."

Toril's knuckles turn white on the vests in her arms. "He told you?"

"You aren't the only one who knows things, Toril," says Maren, irresistibly reminded of how Kirsten took the wind from Toril's sails with her information about the Lensmann.

She holds out her hands for the pile of restitched cloth, but the woman doesn't pass it to her.

"He has not visited you."

Maren shrugs.

"I know he has not. He would never, not with that Lapp and her bastard under the roof."

Anger comes quick and hot to Maren's chest. "Erik is no bastard. They were married, you yourself danced at their wedding feast."

"I did not dance," says Toril. "I would not dance at such a devilish union."

Maren's palm itches. She longs to slap Toril across the face, to tear at her hair. But she only snatches the vests from her. "You had best mind your tongue, Toril Knudsdatter."

Toril loses her balance and stumbles, her shoulder catching at the shelf beside her and sending several of her crucifixes to the floor. Maren turns and leaves her scrabbling about on the ground for them, heart thumping.

Vardø is busy in a way it only is in summertime, women sitting outside their houses with butter churns, scaling fish brought from Kiberg. The smells, the low talk, familiar as it is, can't soothe her. She goes straight to Diinna's door, knocks with her elbow.

Diinna takes her time answering. She is sallow-skinned, mouth a tight line, her hair loose and lank. Maren is minded of her expression the day Kirsten dug her from the snow that first winter. Behind her, the room is dark and airless, and smells of sour milk. Maren can see the small figure of Erik still tucked into the blankets, the slow rise-fall of his breath just visible.

Diinna reaches wordlessly for her vests, but Maren shakes her head, gestures for her to come outside. The door closes softly behind them, though Maren wishes she could tell her to leave it open, to let some fresh air into the room where her son sleeps.

"I have just come from Toril's house."

"So I can see." Moved fully into the daylight, Diinna looks more wretched than ever. Her eyes are pouchy and deadened, and if Maren didn't know that there was no way for her to have gotten hold of any, she would have thought her drunk on spirits.

"She has been speaking of you. Speaking unkindly."

"What does it matter?"

"She said you and Erik were not married, not truly."

Pain crosses Diinna's face. She puts an end of her hair into her mouth, sucks upon it. "She was there, she saw us marry."

"She called it——" Maren lowers her voice so Mamma will not hear——"a devilish union."

Diinna shrugs. "She has always been like that. Even when we were children. She threw a hot potful of water at me once." Her hand goes to her shoulder where the scar tissue sits like lace across her shoulder, and Maren remembers at last that it was indeed Toril who inflicted it. "Why are you coming to me with old tales?"

"But this is no idle chatter," says Maren. "She has the ear of the commissioner now. He sits with her most days to pray."

Diinna snorts. "Is that what they are doing all hours?"

Maren lets the vests drop to the ground, takes her by the shoulders. Her bones come hard beneath her fingers. "Diinna, please. Come to kirke on the Sabbath. He should see your face, see you there."

Diinna shrugs her off. "I send Erik, for you and for your mother. That should be enough."

"It is not for me." Maren wants to shake her. "It is for you, and if not for you, for Erik. It is in the commissioner's census that you do not go to kirke."

"Census?"

"In his book. It is written, and once written, things aren't easily forgotten. And you are..."

"A Lapp?" Diinna's eyes are narrowed.

"I would never use that word. But I told you what Kirsten said of the Sámi men put to death in Alta, and another in Kirkenes."

"They were wind-weavers only." Diinna's carefully smooth face creases in sadness for a moment. "Innocents."

"That is exactly why you must be careful." Maren grits her teeth. "And at his first meet," she continues, remembering suddenly, "Commissioner Cornet spoke of his involvement in the trial of a woman. It may not be all he is here for, but it is some of it. You must come to kirke."

"Seems to me the best idea would be to stay far from his sight."

"But he knows of you. Toril spoke your name in the kirke, and it sounds as if she speaks it still to him."

"I should have put a hole in her tongue when I threatened it," says Diinna. "It would do us all good."

Maren had forgotten that warning made in those terrible, early days after the storm, and it sends a fresh broil of nausea through her.

"You should not say such things."

"Why, do you think me a witch, too?" Diinna's gaze is unblinking.

Maren digs her nails into her palms, desperation verging on annoyance. "You will not come?"

Diinna looks into the middle distance.

"It would be good if you would come more often to see the others at least," she says. "You used to like some of us."

You used to love me, she thinks, collecting up the vests. Diinna doesn't move to help. She still has a slick snake of hair trailing from her lips, and the sound of her sucking it fills Maren's own mouth with bitterness.

"Perhaps come on Wednesday? You used to come. Toril doesn't attend, nor most of the kirke folk."

"Your mamma does, though. And I thought you were all kirke folk now." Diinna's voice is dry.

"You know I am not one of them," says Maren, straightening and holding out the vests. "Kirsten and Edne and many of us, we aren't like them."

"Yes," says Diinna, taking the soft garments. "But I am not one of you, either."

Inside, Erik begins to moan.

"You'll come to the meet?" says Maren, desperate as Diinna opens the door and turns to close it behind her. She gets no answer.

She paces back and forth before her door. She feels it, a trap being set about them, has felt it since Toril gave Diinna's name in kirke. The news from Alta makes it worse. That the sailors have been going to the Sámi for weather charms since they settled here held no currency in the court. Kirsten said they were sent to their deaths within a day.

She knows it is against Diinna's beliefs, against the Sámi ways, to go to kirke but she cannot help that it matters less what they believe now than what they pretend to believe. She sometimes wonders if she is pretending a little, too. The eye of God feels turned from her, has done since the storm, and since the commissioner's arrival she fears Cornet far more than any God.

Inside, Mamma is wrapping salted fish in clean cloths. They are spread across the table, a dissemblance in various shades of white, blanched by salt. The bones sit in a wispy pile, ready to be sorted into those that can be used as needles or combs, and those that will be boiled for soup.

"What was that about?"

Maren places the vests on the shelf, comes to join Mamma at the table. "Diinna will not come to kirke."

"Nothing new there." Mamma turns a sharp eye upon her. "Why did you try?" Maren takes up a fish and some tweezers. She doesn't want to go over it again.

"Ah. Toril?" Maren nods, and Mamma sucks her teeth. "I told Erik when he married her there would be talk. And now he is not here to protect her from it."

And you do nothing to help her, thinks Maren, pulling bones from a butterflied cod. "I invited her to the Wednesday meet."

Mamma's eyebrows raise. "Her, and the commissioner's wife? You think that a wise combination?"

"Urs—Mistress Cornet is not like the commissioner. It will be fine."

"We will see." There is something glinting close to excitement in Mamma's voice, and not for the first time Maren considers that her mother's dislike for Diinna has grown more akin to hatred. Whereas before Mamma worried about Diinna disappearing to the low mountain, now Maren suspects Mamma would prefer it, so long as Erik was left here.

"Besides—" Mamma's tongue flicks at the corner of her mouth—"whatever will come, you can be sure Diinna brings it upon herself."

TWENTY-FOUR

Though Ursa had been worried about sleeping alone, her body is so unused to any sort of exertion that it drags her down into a deep sleep as soon as she closes the door on Maren. She wakes in confusion early the next day, her head throbbing, in her swept and tidy house, the new coat hung like a presence behind the door.

She wonders about putting it on, going for a walk perhaps, maybe to find Maren. While it would have been unthinkable for her to go out unaccompanied in Bergen, in this place of women it seems to hold no cause for gossip. But she doesn't know the way to anywhere but the kirke, and she has no desire to go there.

From Wednesday, she tells herself, she will know more people, and perhaps can go visiting. With her coat and boots, she feels steadier. She makes herself tea, eats a square of flatbrød spread with some of the butter Maren skimmed from the kjernemelk. Even a day with Maren has given her fresh eyes, and where before she saw no work to be done now she knows she must replenish the fuel for the fire, and perhaps use some of the leftover flour to make small fresh loaves that she and Absalom can eat together upon his return.

It comes far sooner than she's prepared for. On Wednesday morning, she is up early and dressed, boiling water for tea, when the door opens roughly behind her. She turns, thinking it might be Maren, come early to collect her for the meet, but the doorway is filled by Absalom Cornet, taking off his black hat.

"Husband." She catches her smile before it drops. "Back so soon?"

"The wind was against us, so I took measure of the situation in Alta from Hamningberg." After all that, he had only reached the next village up the coast.

Ursa studies his face, but there is no sign of temper. He is looking her up and down. "Have you been to the kirke, wife?"

"Forgive me, no, husband. I only wanted to look present-able."

His thick eyebrows rise. "For whom?"

"Later I am to meet with some of the other women."

She had feared his reaction, but he nods. "That is good. Did Toril Knudsdatter come to invite you?"

"No, husband."

"Sigfrid? They spoke of doing so."

She shakes her head. "I do not know these women."

"They help at the kirke, and I have been overseeing their spiritual teaching with Pastor Kurtsson."

Ursa pours the boiled water, sending the leaves spinning.

He frowns as she passes him a cup of fresh-brewed tea. "Who, then?"

"Our neighbour, Fru Olufsdatter." She doesn't want to give Maren's name, and certainly not Kirsten's.

"I see." He takes a sip.

"How was Hamningberg?" Now that he has not raised an objection outright to her attending the meet, she wants to move him from the subject.

"Fine, fine. The commissioner from Kiberg was also stuck there. Larsen. He's a good enough man, though a little full of bluster. Had all the news sent from Commissioner Moe in Alta. The trial was a clear-cut one."

"You were to attend a trial? What for?"

"It was already over—I only wished to take measure of the situation. Though they have two more Lapps in their gaol, so I intend to return when the wind blows more favourably."

"What did the Lapps do?"

"It is not so much what they do as what they are born to. Sorcerers."

"They are witches?" Ursa's arms come across herself.

"Often as not," says Absalom. He is flattered by her interest, she can tell.

"How is it proven?"

"There are tests." He leans forwards, and though there is an undeniable frisson of excitement in his voice, there is fear there, too. "Our King James in Scotland has written a book on how to spot and test a witch, but the Lapps are easy enough to catch. They have drums of stretched skin, and they beat them to summon demons." He crosses himself, and Ursa feels a chill slide beneath her skin.

"Demons? They can do that?"

"Surely as a minister can call on God," says Absalom gravely. "Old times, before King Christian ordered it, they were not even bound by law to destroy such instruments. Moe's letter says they have one they seized—they dare not burn it in case it releases something."

Ursa shivers. "You truly think it possible?"

"I have seen such things are possible." Absalom's voice is a whisper. He is remembering something that makes him afraid, and it unsettles her. "In Scotland, we had a great many trials. I did not need to make such a journey to see another, but I thought I could learn something from Commissioner Moe's ways of operating. I certainly can have no knowledge from Larsen." He leans back in his chair. "He had not even thought to conduct a census before I suggested it."

"He has seen the Lensmann?"

"He has, in Alta." Absalom's face closes back to its usual inscrutability. "A lot of the other commissioners, they are old friends, old seagoers."

"Then it is a great honour, is it not, husband?" He looks up at her. "That you have been brought all the way from Scotland, on your reputation alone."

His shoulders straighten a little, and he looks at her with the ghost of a smile at the corners of his lips. "That it is, Ursula."

He drains the cup, stands with a renewed vigour.

"I am to kirke. I hope your meet is pleasant—but, wife?" She looks into his face. "Keep your ears open. If you hear anything of use..." He trails into silence, and then he is gone again, closing the door behind him.

Ursa can breathe again. She did well with him there, showing an interest in Alta and the trial, though it turned her stomach. Devilry felt a more distant thing in Bergen, but here? Perhaps such things are possible. She cleans his cup immediately, and makes another pot of tea. She doesn't want to drink from the same dregs.

•

When Maren arrives just past high sun, she is trailing two others. Ursa recognizes Maren's mother, and makes a neat curtsey that the woman doesn't return. Instead she looks past Ursa, into the house, and there is such hostility in her gaze that Ursa doesn't invite them in, only slips on her coat and closes the latch.

All three have bundles strapped to their fronts, and Ursa recognizes the cloth she thought to cut, bound to Maren's mother. She hopes Maren did not tell her of her ignorance. The sky behind them is grey and blue, like a day-old bruise, their misshapen figures pegged out against it.

"This is Diinna," says Maren, strain apparent on her face.

The other woman meets Ursa's eyes steadily. She is carrying a bundle big as her torso, and has a broad face and high cheekbones. Ursa has not seen her in kirke, realizes this must be the Sámi woman who Maren tried to protect from her husband's questions. The one who drew the runes over the door.

Though she is thin as Maren and her mother, she suits it better, carries herself with more ease. Her hair looks stringy and long unwashed, matted into knots at its ends. She jigs the bundle on her front, and it is another moment before Ursa realizes it is a young child, but not so young as it should be carried like a baby.

"This is Erik," says Maren. "My brother's son."

"And mine," says Diinna, the edge of a challenge on her tongue. There is something disconcerting about the three of them, and Ursa walks beside Maren the short distance to her neighbour's house.

The door is ajar and chatter comes from within, along with the now familiar smells of fresh bread. There is no time for Ursa to gather herself before Maren pushes the door fully open, and plunges into the yellow room.

There are benches set along the sides, women ranged on them in clumps, chattering with needlework on their laps. There is a shelf set into the wall with what looks like an assortment of pale stones upon it. The table is pushed before the fireplace, and laden with bread and fish, and jugs of water and light beer. She wonders then if she should have brought something, whether she should fetch the small loaves she made yesterday.

At first the talk goes on, but heads turn as Ursa enters, faces she knows from kirke but for which she has no names. Finally there is silence apart from the children playing on the floor at their feet. It feels like the first time in kirke, and Ursa shrinks, studies her skirts.

It is Kirsten who breaks the quiet. "Did I not tell you she'd come?" she says to a mousy-haired woman beside the fire. "I'll bet you're glad of your good platters now."

The woman rises to her feet, crosses to Ursa, hand out in a gesture of welcome. Fru Olufsdatter, the owner of the house. "I am very glad you have come, Mistress Cornet."

"Ursula, please. Your home is lovely."

"My husband's father built it," she says. She moves to her right slightly, and Ursa wonders if she is trying to obscure the shelf beside the fire. At Ursa's side, Maren shifts from one foot to another, but the woman's focus is fixed on her, almost reverent. "Thank you for coming."

"It is Maren who invited me," says Ursa, still keen to prove the validity of her presence. The woman studiously ignores Maren, and Ursa realizes that something is between them, some distance.

"I am glad," she repeats, motions towards the table. "Would you care for something to eat, to drink?"

"I am a little thirsty," says Ursa, and the woman bends to the table to pour from one of the jugs. She takes the opportunity to look more closely at the shelf—the objects aren't all stones; she can see two figures carved roughly from bone placed in the centre.

Fru Olufsdatter straightens and brings her a cup. It isn't water or tea, which is all she has drunk for weeks since the akevitt on the ship, but some sort of clouded liquid. Ursa sniffs at it, not wishing to be rude.

"It's sorrel water," Maren tells her. "It's a little sharp, but I think you'll like it."

With Maren so close, Ursa can smell aniseed on her breath. It comforts her and she takes a sip, tries not to wrinkle her nose. It is very bitter, but with an ending of sweetness, like the cooking apples Siv buys for Christmas time. Agnete loved them before her doctors imposed her diet of dry food, used to chomp through them like a horse, pulling her lips from her teeth. Ursa's insides clench with missing.

Fru Olufsdatter peers at her anxiously, and so she smiles and nods for more, though it will take some getting used to. Room is made for them on a bench to the right of the fire, and though there is space enough for Diinna's slight form, she stays standing beside the door even once she has deposited Erik with the other children. Her presence has as much effect on the others as Ursa's. Though Ursa feels badly for Diinna she is glad that the attention on her is closer to wariness than open dislike.

The chatter starts up again, but it is quieter, each speaking to her neighbour and not across the room as before. She looks at Diinna from over her cup. Herr Kasperson, her father's clerk, had spent some time in Spitsbergen as a bookkeeper at a whaling station. He told them Lapps were short and wild-looking, with teeth tiny and needle sharp, that they dressed in knotted wolf tails about their necks, and pointed hats on their heads. But there is not much to mark Diinna out as different, beyond her darker skin, higher cheekbones, and the other women's attitude to her. Ursa thinks of the trial in Alta, wonders if Diinna knows about it.

Erik too sits a little apart from the other children, legs straight out in front of him. He is more markedly distinct: there is something slack about his jaw, a looseness. Ursa wonders if there is something wrong with him. Agnete, too, had been a slow child. But despite her illness, her mind had grown sharp. Perhaps it is the same with Erik.

Maren takes out a large piece of cloth from her bundle, unwraps a fine needle and piece of thread. Kirsten has a pair of boots—large as a man's—on a low stool before her, and is cutting pieces of fur to line them. Ursa realizes she should have brought something to do, too.

"Would you like some help?" she asks Maren, who looks at her, surprised. Ursa supposes she is remembering her handiwork at the sleeves. But she must also recognize Ursa's need for something to focus upon, and passes her a smaller piece of cloth, a pillowcase perhaps, and a thicker needle that will not so easily sink into her fingers.

She is well aware of eyes upon her as she threads the needle, finds the worn patch and takes up a fresh piece of cloth to cover it. But just as she is about to make the first stitch the door is opened again.

A pinch-faced woman comes in with two children, another woman following behind accompanied by a young girl with matching blue eyes and thin lips. This silence is more abrupt than the one that greeted Ursa's arrival. Kirsten moves aside the stool with the boots, stands with her arms folded.

"What are you doing here?"

"Last I checked this was not your house to ask such a question, Kirsten Sørensdatter." The woman is carrying two baskets, and she lifts back the cloth atop one, holds it out to Fru Olufsdatter. "I do not come empty-handed."

Fru Olufsdatter doesn't take it. She looks caught by some invisible current, pale and suddenly afraid. Her eyes flick to the spot on the shelf beside the fire, where the small bone figures and stones are arranged. The woman purses her lips, and places the basket on the table. Ursa notices she wears a cross about her neck, realizes she is one of the kirke-women her husband keeps council with.

"Sigfrid and I only came to keep company. And to speak with Mistress Cornet."

It is a few heartbeats before Ursa realizes that she is Mistress Cornet. The name still doesn't feel as though it belongs to her: it is a thing apart, like the needle in her hand, and as sharp.

"Me?"

"What are you wanting with her, Toril?"

Maren has stiffened beside her, and out of the corner of her eye Ursa can see open dislike on her face.

"That is no matter to you," says Toril.

Ursa touches her leg against Maren's to stay her. "How may I help you, Fru...?"

"Knudsdatter." Toril frowns. "I thought your husband mentioned me."

"And me," says Sigfrid. "He wished us to come and keep company with you."

"She has company enough," says Kirsten, gesturing around. The other women are looking shiftily about themselves, and Ursa isn't sure whose disapproval they are shrinking from, Kirsten's or Toril's. There is obviously some struggle for power between them, though they seem very unmatched to her. She would wish to stand beside Kirsten any day.

"He hopes for a better sort of companion for his wife," says Toril, and Ursa's cheeks flush with Absalom's interference. She should not have spoken of her plans with him. Toril stands before Ursa, and eventually Maren's mother moves along the already cramped bench. Toril sets her other basket down on the floor and slides in beside her.

Fru Olufsdatter still looks imperilled. She has again positioned herself before her shelf, and Ursa notices her move a jug to cover the bone figures.

Sigfrid too finds a spot on the bench, knocking over Toril's basket, sending scraps of lace and spooled thread tumbling.

"I'm sorry," says Sigfrid, crouching to right it. There is much tutting from Toril as some of the women rise to help gather everything together. Ursa notices Kirsten doesn't, nor Maren, and so she stays in her place.

Diinna retrieves a needlecase, holds it out to Toril. Toril looks at her sharply, and makes no move to take it. "Do you threaten me?"

"Threaten?" Diinna snorts and drops the case into the basket.

"I've not forgotten how you thought to thread a needle through my tongue," spits Toril, and the room ripples with muttering.

"Toril," says Kirsten, warning sharp in her voice. "She was only helping."

"I need no help from the likes of her," says Toril. Maren is tense beside Ursa. Diinna looks as though she may say something, but she only sucks her teeth, and scoops up Erik. She leaves the house without a gesture of goodbye, letting the door bang behind her. Maren starts, looks as though she may go after her, and Ursa is certain it's only her presence that makes her stay.

Toril meanwhile makes no attempt to start a conversation with Ursa. She just sits, a little too close, and brings out some cloth to darn. It is immediately apparent that she is very skilled at it, her narrow fingers working deftly and closing the tears at the edges, frilling it with a stitch she has not seen before.

"So, Ursula." Kirsten's voice is like a bell, ringing into the hushed room and bringing it to silence. "What has Maren taught you so far? I can see you have a fine coat from the hides I brought."

Beside her Maren shrinks a little. Perhaps it is as Ursa feared, that she is embarrassed by their arrangement. But it is too late now.

"She is a fine teacher. I have enough flatbrød for a decade, I feel, and the coat will serve me well."

"A coat," says Toril. "You?"

She speaks past Ursa, who wishes she were thin as Maren and could press flat to the wall. Maren doesn't answer, keeps her eyes fixed to her work, but Ursa sees the slight shake of her fingers.

"Yes," she says. "Maren helped me make something warm. I did not bring anything suitable from Bergen."

"Mistress Cornet, I would be happy to help you with any clothes-making. It is something of a speciality of mine. It is well known throughout the village."

No one speaks in her favour, though Sigfrid nods like a lackey.

"I am happy enough with what I have, thank you, Fru Knudsdatter."

"Toril, please." She moves, if it is possible, even closer, her knee angled towards Ursa's thigh. "Your husband thought it would be pleasant for us to meet together regularly. He thought you would need some more educated conversation, being from Bergen. My own mother was from Tromsø—"

"Fru Olufsdatter is from Tromsø," interrupts Kirsten. "If Mistress Cornet wants educated conversation she should not come to you, Toril. Unless she wants her Bible learnt by heart."

"You say that as though it is a bad thing, Kirsten Sørens-datter," says Toril, snappishly. "You forget who our commissioner is. As much a man of God as Pastor Kurtsson. He wishes his wife to have better companionship than this and, most like, a better coat than Maren Magnusdatter can manage."

Ursa thinks she should speak in Maren's defence but her voice feels as caught as her skirts beneath Toril's thigh. The woman seems to gather herself, her voice turning sickening sweet again. "Perhaps you would like some company in the days. I know he is often at kirke or on important business in the district—"

"I have company, thank you, Fru Knudsdatter."

She feels Toril's gaze pierce through her and into Maren, who has still not spoken a word in her own defence.

"Very well," says Toril, and there is a break in her voice.

"Is that it now, Toril?" says Kirsten. "Can we all be free of your kind company?"

Toril throws her needlework into her basket, then pauses, running her fingers over the scraps.

"Who took my lace?" She scans the room.

"Lace?" Kirsten sounds bored.

"Was it you?" Toril squares up to Kirsten, the mismatch in their heights like a child to their parent. "I had lacework in here."

"What use have I for lace?"

Ursa holds her breath, but Toril seems to think it not worth the fight. "Elsebe, Nils, we are going."

She stands suddenly and gathers up her children, who follow her mute and neat as her stitches. She turns in the doorway, Sigfrid hastening to pack her things and usher her daughter out.

"Don't think I have not seen what sits aside your fire, Fru Olufsdatter, and who fled your house when we arrived. The time for such things is past. Commissioner Cornet has not the patience for it. There are men burnt at Alta—"

"My husband," says Ursa, temper flaring, "doesn't mind how people keep their houses."

The room seems to hold its breath. Ursa is aware of absolute silence as Toril turns her imperious face upon her. She is minded of Siv when she is back from kirke and the prayers still sit fresh in her: unbowed, strengthened by them.

"As you say, Mistress Cornet. I will tell him you have chosen your company."

"I can tell him myself." Ursa's heart is thumping. Burnings? Absalom had neglected to tell her this detail.

Toril stands aside to let her children out before her, speaks again to Fru Olufsdatter. "You would do well to use my gift for you." She jerks her head at the table. "I'll have the basket back. God bless you."

TWENTY-FIVE

Once the door has slammed shut behind Sigfrid and her daughter, Maren feels she can breathe again. Kirsten slaps her hands together and lets out a hoot.

"Mistress Cornet, you have a heat to you that I confess I hadn't foreseen."

"I only spoke my mind," says Ursa steadily, though her body trembles. Maren wants to take her in her arms and rock her like a child. "It is no business of hers how I choose to spend my time."

"The poppets," says Fru Olufsdatter. Her voice reminds Maren of a worn-out rag, her face as grey. "I had forgot them, Mistress Cornet. They aren't—I had them given me after my boy and husband died. Many of us had them…"

She looks about for support: heads bow to their work.

"They do not mean a thing. I should throw them in the fire." But she doesn't move, only looks at Ursa with desperate eyes.

"I do not mind what you choose to keep in your house, any more than I would wish you to tell me how to attire my own."

"Sounds as if that is what Maren has been up to," says Edne. Maren casts her a sharp glance.

"I am only helping a little."

"Who was that woman?" says Ursa, and Maren is pleased to hear dislike clear in her voice.

"She helps Pastor Kurtsson at kirke," says Kirsten. "And seems to me she is now your husband's anointed emissary."

No one else would have dared such a remark, but Kirsten is rewarded with a sudden peal of laughter from Ursa that sends an echoing ripple around the benches, and a jab of envy through Maren.

"Do not worry on your poppets, Fru Olufsdatter," says Kirsten. "Ursula doesn't mind them, and she knows her husband's thoughts better than Toril Knudsdatter."

Ursa doesn't laugh this time. A crease appears between her eyes.

"What gifts has she given you?" asks Edne.

Fru Olufsdatter doesn't move to look in the basket, so Kirsten bends over it, snorts and brings out a cross of cloth and twine, like those Maren had caused Toril to knock from her shelf. "There must be near two dozen in here. Enough for all of us."

She throws one to Maren, who catches it without thinking. She places it into her bundle, wanting to drop it as quickly as possible. It feels a threat, rather than a gift.

Their meets usually go on until evening, but Maren has no stomach for food or conversation. It is a relief when, after a period of uneasy silence, Ursa begins to shift uncomfortably, leans in to her, says, "Shall we go?"

Mamma is talking to Edne and so they go together, rising to another silence, and leaving in an outbreak of whispers. Fru Olufsdatter sits crumpled in her place, watches Ursa leave like a thing hunted.

As they reach Ursa's door she hesitates, her jaw tense. Maren listens, hears a low rumble that must be the commissioner, and a woman's voice answering. Maren recognizes its syrupy undercurrent: Toril, speaking to authority. Ursa begins to back away, but her foot creaks upon the step and the voices stall. Heavy tread on the floorboards, and then Commissioner Cornet is at the door, brows pulled down over his eyes.

"Wife," he says, ignoring Maren completely. "Inside."

Ursa's face pales, but she straightens her shoulders, turns to thank Maren before stepping through the doorway. Maren can't see past his bulk, but Toril's greeting to Ursa reaches her clearly. The commissioner slams the door on Maren, and for a moment she waits. But what will she do? She will not push open the door, nor listen at the latch. Over the door the runes are not fully smoothed out. Their shadow is still visible, showing beneath the whitewash like scars.

She could go back to the meet, but the poison Toril had spread about the room remained. Mamma never used to like Toril, but recently Maren thinks that has changed. She noticed the look of satisfaction on Mamma's face as Toril delivered her speeches, and at Diinna's departure. Toril was always against the Sámis visiting the village, and Kirsten was always headstrong. But the women and their divides have strengthened, are growing swallowingly large, deep and dangerous as a pit.

Even Kirsten is irritating her with her brashness. Maren is still not over her appearance at Ursa's house in trousers—at least Toril had no mention of that, and so must not have seen it. She wouldn't have missed the opportunity to spread such a piece of gossip.

Maren barely notices her feet carrying her home. She is pushed far inside her body, hearing only the jumble of her thoughts tangling like a fishing net. Diinna's departure was delayed just long enough for her to give Maren a look of such venom that if Maren believed some of the kirke-women's stories of the Sámis, she would have thought herself cursed. Diinna can't think that Maren knew Toril would come?

She speaks this through Diinna's closed door, though she will not answer. There is no noise from Erik either. Diinna's silence is a wall that grows into a wave, pushing Maren from her door and onwards, out past Baar Ragnvalsson's house, the roof rotted and collapsed in, the stones scattered about as though thrown by a troll. It was a fine house, once, but when he started spending summers with the Sámi on the low mountain it became less a place where he lived, and more a place where he existed. She would see him outside in his embroidered tunic and hat, sitting in even the coldest weather, with his head tipped to the side, eyes closed, as though listening for something.

The memory hits her like a blow, and she presses her fist to her heart. She never mourned for him, though his body lay beside Erik and Pappa's all those months. She can't even recall his injuries, if he had any. Perhaps that is better. She says a small prayer to the wind, which has begun to gust full behind her, like an insistent hand at her back, throwing her skirts before her. Her hair is across her face so she must focus on her feet and can't see the tumble of Herr Ragnvalsson's house any more, or his remembered form outside it.

She walks past the boundary wall and on to the green, boggy land beyond. How quickly what little grasp they have on the land vanishes, as though beyond the boundary there were never people there at all and she has wandered full into the land of trolls. As children, she and Erik used to go hunting for them, under pretence of foraging for the sweet clover that sometimes grows here, and that their mother would boil until the leaves softened and leaked milky liquid, good for settling stomachs sore through hunger. They would comb through the moss and short grasses, searching for marks and stone circles, for small doors set into hillocks and rocks. They'd speak half-sentences, telling each other that they'd trodden on a knoll and were cursed to death, losing each other in the mists that sometimes stumbled over the headland from the sea.

She remembers finding herself suddenly alone in one once, all about her an endless grey, chill soaking through to her bones. She should have stayed still, crouched to keep warm, but she carried on walking until she thought she had crossed over. The terror of it had struck her dumb, and when the mist lifted, sudden as a skein of birds taking flight, she found herself a mere step from a drop of sixty feet, the sea churning white at the base of the rocks. Erik came running over the spongy ground calling for her: he had done as she should have, stayed still and waited. His cheeks were snot-streaked and blotchy with tears and she had shoved him and called him a coward, though he wore her face, had her frighted heart beating in his narrow chest. It was one of many small unkindnesses she wishes she could take back, thoughtless moments or worse, instances engineered to hurt.

Her feet have brought her here, to that spot. Now the sky is clear and crisp, the light that bluish grey that means they will find frost on the inside of their doors though winter is months away. She goes as close to the edge as she dares. Sometimes, in that terrible year when the pain was so immediate it was like living with a knife through her chest, she came here and stood with her toes so far over that one good gust of wind could cause her to fall. It would be quick enough, faster than a blade or some nightshade steeped like tea and drunk. This place is out of sight of the village, and the current that keeps the channel clear of ice would drag a body clear into open sea. It was something remarked upon by them all, that it was lucky the storm had not occurred this side of Vardø, or they never would have had their men brought back.

When she stood there it was both challenge and offering. She was waiting, like Baar Ragnvalsson, to be given permission to go home and continue living, though she often wondered if she wanted that at all. Since the storm, there has felt so little to exist for. But something has changed that; she feels it now, certain as seasons. Someone has changed that.

There are small yellow flowers growing on wiry stalks at her feet. She uproots one for her father, one for Erik, and a third. This one she cups close to her lips, as she lets the wind carry the others before her, over the edge.

•

The whole week Maren fears a knock at her door, telling her she isn't needed, that Toril has managed to take her place in the commissioner's household. She must bear this alongside increased hostility between her mother and Diinna, who on Friday have a disagreement over Erik's lack of movement, which grows to a fight of such ferocity that Maren scoops up Erik and walks him ten times around Herr Ragnvalsson's house before they are done.

But the knock doesn't come, and at Sabbath, though Ursa is locked tight to her husband's side, and though she is greeted by name by Toril and Sigfrid, it is Maren whose face she seeks out, Maren who she makes for after the sermon while her husband is engaged in conversation with some of the women.

"You will come tomorrow?"

Maren can barely speak.

"He is usually away by mid-morning." Ursa brushes her fingers against Maren's, a gesture meant as comfort. There is a circle of bruises on her wrist, and when she notices Maren looking she snatches her hand away. She pulls down her sleeve and is beside her husband again so fast Maren feels she may have imagined it.

The next day she arrives at Ursa's door with her frame

loom tucked beneath her arm, feels her body unknot as she steps inside and it is just her and Ursa. They spend the day weaving cloth for curtains, slow and full of mistakes and easy silences, easier touches that make Maren feel loose and formless as Ursa's weave.

"What did Toril want?" she says. Ursa is frowning at the loom as though it has betrayed her, her tongue a pink blot between her lips.

"She lost some lace at the Wednesday meet. She said she wanted to borrow some of the lace Kirsten gave me, but I think she thought Kirsten had stolen it."

Maren sets down her shuttle. "Did she say so in front of Absalom?"

Ursa nods, focusing on the loom. "Don't worry, I set her right. I am sorry that Absalom was rude to you."

"I did not mind." She had expected no less. "Did she tell him of the poppets?"

"Perhaps," says Ursa. "He was certainly displeased to hear of Diinna's attendance. I told him the meets are nothing, that they are harmless." She puts the loom onto the table with a sigh, at her trouble with it or Toril's interference Maren does not know. "And that Toril should not be taken from her study with him, and her Christian duties are much fulfilled by her work for the others. That it wouldn't be fair to have her all to myself. You, on the other hand," she says, with a sly smile, "are completely dispensable. Cheap, too. And perhaps we can save your soul from living with a Lapp."

The word is ugly in Ursa's mouth, but the rest of what she says so pleasing that Maren doesn't speak against it.

"Moreover, he agreed that you must come twice a week from now. The more you are out of that house and influence the better, don't you agree?"

Maren's face aches from smiling, the dry skin of her lips

stretching, but as Ursa reaches for her loom, she again sees the bruises, dark as dirt about her wrist.

"What happened?"

Ursa looks down at her wrist as though it does not belong to her. "Nothing." Maren stares at her. "Absalom, sometimes he does not know his own strength."

"It was not because of Toril, because of me?"

"No," says Ursa, cheeks flushing. "It was not done in anger."

"He should not touch you like that," says Maren, understanding. Her rage is quick and frightening, hot as a brand inside her.

"Isn't it a wife's duty to be touched by her husband?"

Maren's cheeks redden at her frankness. "I would not know of it."

"You were never married, before the storm?"

Maren doesn't want to call Dag to her, not now. She shakes her head. "No."

•

From that day on she is at Ursa's house Monday and Thursday, watching for more bruises, finding none. She wonders about the pale expanse of Ursa's body, if she is marked in places Maren can't see.

Wednesdays Ursa comes to the meets, her presence quickly losing intrigue. Maren notices the poppets and runestones are gone from Fru Olufsdatter's shelf, one of Toril's crosses planted in their place, but the benches are less full. Toril and Sigfrid do not return, Edne no longer comes, and after a couple more weeks, nor does Maren's mother.

"Toril is having a meet at her house," says Mamma. "The commissioner will be there, to lead us in prayer. You should come, Maren. No doubt his wife will."

But Maren knows Ursa will not, and so goes with her to

Dag's mother's house, where Kirsten holds court and makes ever-cruder jokes about the kirke-women, and Maren tries not to imagine what is said of them in return. Ursa seems unfussed by the rift, perhaps doesn't notice it, or maybe feels herself above it all. She doesn't speak against Toril except to Maren, and she suspects that she alone is the recipient of Ursa's true thoughts.

Twice a week is too much for a household of one room and a family of two. Maren herself generates as much mess as she helps sort out. They get their work done slowly, Ursa more and more capable so that she is like not to need Maren there at all, but there is no suggestion of her stopping coming. They butcher two of the reindeer, make stews with cloud-berries that Ursa leaves too long on the fire so they must spend hours scouring the pots with sand. Maren teaches her to bank the fire so in the mornings she can break the crust and it will be fierce enough for boiling water almost straight away.

Beyond the faded bruises, Absalom's presence is merely an impression upon the house: she doesn't see him but at kirke. Ursa speaks a little of him, tells her of his growing frustration at the lack of communication from Vardøhus, and Maren doesn't ask more because she doesn't want to hear it. She changes the sheets and helps with the washing, knows Ursa's bloods come monthly upon her, allows herself to hope that they do not lie together much at all, though there is only one bed and no chair suitable for a man to sleep.

When they are alone she can imagine that it isn't the commissioner and his wife who live there, nor even another version of life in which she and Dag made their home here, but rather she and Ursa. And though she knows it is a wrong thought, a dangerous thought, she allows herself to slip into this dream more and more as their weeks together stretch to a month, and they begin to span their time into the late, light evenings when Absalom is away travelling to Alta or elsewhere. Maren does not care where he is, only longs for him never to return.

In these times they walk through the village together, when most are inside or sleeping, the distance between them stinging like a hook in Maren's side. They speak of their childhoods. Ursa tells her that once their family was rich and now they are not, and when she mentions Agnete, Maren can feel the sorrow coming from her like cold. Maren tells Ursa about troll-hunting with Erik, and it makes Ursa laugh.

She takes Ursa to the headland, watches how the colour of the thin skin at her throat changes in the endless low light, how the wind throws her dress more tightly against her body, as it did the day they met and Maren thought her as much a fool as Mamma still does.

Ursa is telling her about the black rock at the end of the world, that pulls currents towards it.

"Captain Leifsson, the captain of the *Petrsbolli*—you know, the ship we came in—he thinks there are no waterfalls, perhaps no rock at all." She turns to Maren and her eyes shine. "But I think there is. I should like to see that rock, some day."

Maren wants to reach out to Ursa and hold her, but not in the easy way they embrace now when she arrives or leaves. She wants to press her whole form against her, like Dag in the boat shed.

Sometimes this thought comes to her at night, and she feels a low throb in her belly, and must keep her hand from moving to herself. Even with her mother snoring beside her, it isn't easy, and her dreams are full of slick mouths that moan her name, sometimes in Dag's voice, more often in Ursa's, her face smooth against her, her almost-boneless hands supple against the blunt thinness of Maren's ribs.

She thinks she keeps it well from the world, speaking as

little as she can to Mamma or Ursa, and even less to Diinna, who would see something on her face or in her voice, she is sure of it.

Most of all she guards it from Ursa, knowing the absurdity of what she feels. But she doesn't pray for it to pass, doesn't pray at all but for Erik and Pappa in kirke. The secret doesn't gnaw at her. Rather she feels strengthened by it, forged into something glittering and rare. She doesn't tell herself she loves Ursa, but knows it is something closer to love than she has ever known. With it inside her, she feels bold as Kirsten in trousers, and though she relishes the feeling, she knows it is just as reckless, as dangerous.

TWENTY-SIX

The letter from the Lensmann comes almost four months to the day after their arrival in Vardø. Ursa's time is pegged out by her days with Maren, and the others which she must survive without her. Maren is now where she flies to in her head, when her husband moves upon her. Walking with Maren, into the wind on the headland, the ground so uncertain beneath her she never fails to stumble and reach for her friend, gasping with laughter, Maren's strong hands holding her steady as his grip leaves more bruises on her wrists.

The nights they lie together he doesn't have the same anger in him, though it is still nothing pleasurable. He doesn't even make much sound, and she wonders if it has become a duty for him, whether it would be best for them both if she were to bear a child, and then maybe they could be done with it.

She tries to imagine her life with a baby in it, but that again is another country, much how she felt about Vardø before they arrived. She supposes she would adapt as she has to this place, and with Maren to help her in this as well perhaps it wouldn't be so difficult, but the thought of her soft belly hardening and filling makes her queasy to the point of dizziness.

As for the coming of it, the little she knows of that was

learnt from Mother's birthing of her many dead siblings, and
Agnete. Even a living baby brings so much blood. She wonders
sometimes to speak with Maren about it. Her reaction to the
bruises had made her think not, though she doesn't think Maren
would be prudish. She would have some knowledge, what with
Diinna and Erik, but there is always something more important
to speak of, or a silence to be had, so comfortable Ursa feels
she could stretch out in it for ever.

Maren has never spoken of a betrothed, or a want for one.
Spinsters were a rarity in Bergen, but then, so were widows
before middle age. Men, sailors mostly, come to Vardø's
harbour to sell fish, to shelter their boats in squalls, to trade
for furs and needlework. But they stay at the boundary, not
even leaving their boats sometimes, and Kirsten strides down
to meet them. Ursa thinks there must be some talk of this
island, with all its drowned men, that keeps the living ones
from it.

Absalom is like to hear of such talk. He travels successfully
to Alta, and on his return sometimes speaks of more trials,
more Sámi arrested, and now Ursa knows that this means
burnings she doesn't ask for details. She could almost forget
there is a world outside Vardø, especially on days when the
sea sends a mist creeping over everything, and she and Maren
must knot arms and stay close, walking slow along the headland. It is a strange landscape even on a clear day. No forests,
no shrub above hip height, and even in the time of the midnight
sun it was cold enough for her to need her coat most nights.

Now the weather is turning properly, and winter will arrive
soon. Ursa has no guess at its brutality, though as the days
shorten, the cold digs so sharply into her joints they seem to
creak. In Bergen they would close off half the house, heat the
remaining rooms to such a peak she and Agnete would have
worn nothing but their shifts had Siv allowed it. Here she will

wear her coat all the time, even in bed with her husband, the reindeer hides pulled over their bodies.

She receives no word from her father or sister. She supposes she could send some pressed heather from the headland, or some of her poor weaving, ask Absalom to write her a note, but she does not. Now they are at a distance of months she almost wishes she could forget their faces, the way her sister's rattling body felt curled at her side, knees digging fit to bruise, how their bed was clean every night, and at dinner there was cheese and meat that she didn't have to cut from carcasses herself. She misses her life in Bergen as impossibly as the landscape misses trees.

Absalom writes many letters, to the other commissioners and the Lensmann, she assumes, but receives few, and so when he strides into their house waving a square of paper, an invitation is the furthest of her guesses.

"Lensmann Cunningham has arrived!" His face is slick, his eyes radiating triumph. "He is at Vardøhus, and we are invited to the fortress, to dine."

They will be there a night at least, Absalom tells her, will be expected to stay though it is a mere mile away. Ursa has no overnight bag, only her chest and her large case, and so gives her fine dress, petticoat and underthings to Absalom to pack in his case. It makes her queasy to think of their garments pressed together. She escapes the house when he goes to kirke to tell Pastor Kurtsson the news, and hurries to Maren's home.

Maren looks harried when she opens the door, but her expression softens when she sees who has knocked. "Thank goodness. I was about to wring my mother's neck. Walk?"

Ursa wishes she could say yes, but she shakes her head. "I only came to tell you, we are invited to the Lensmann's. To stay the night."

Maren raises her eyebrows. "In the fortress? But it is so close."

"I know," says Ursa, "but Absalom is greatly excited."

Something crosses Maren's face, a shadow, as it always does when Ursa mentions Absalom.

"All right," she says. "Will you send word when you return?"

Ursa nods. "I will, of course."

Maren glances back at her house, and Ursa clasps her hand the better to impress upon her what she says next. "You should go for a walk, though. It would do you the power of good." She raises her eyebrows at the raised voices issuing from inside. "Better than being held for murder."

A brief smile flickers on Maren's cheeks. Her sea-tinted eyes are inscrutable. "Be well," she says.

"Be well."

•

The next morning, Absalom has her up early and in her boots to walk, but they are only steps from their house when there is a noise Ursa has not heard since Bergen: the clack of horse-shoes, the rattle of a carriage. Absalom is gleeful as it draws up.

"We are made now, Ursula."

She changes back into her slippers before they step out to the carriage. The horses look half starved and sway in their harnesses: they must have been brought by sea on one of the ships passing by, and it has not suited them. But the carriage is made of light wood and covered over so it is better than a cart. All about them, their neighbours are coming out to watch as Absalom helps her inside. She leans forward to look out, to try to sight Maren. She would like her to see, so they can laugh about the absurdity later, their mile-long carriage ride. But Maren is not there. She instead sees Toril standing mean-eyed, and Fru Olufsdatter already shrinking back inside her fine house.

The fortress is visible as soon as they are out of the village proper, a bank of earth and tufty green shielding grey stone walls, the whole thing rising from an otherwise flat and featureless plate of land. It is entirely underwhelming, though she knows from Captain Leifsson this place was the subject of a brief struggle between Novgorod and Norway–Denmark, this land fought over, and that is why the Lensmann was installed.

"Were it not for the fishing and whaling, I doubt they would have bothered," he'd said. "But whoever runs Vardøhus controls passage through the Barents Sea, and come summer there'll be thousands of skilling made." It doesn't look like a rich place to Ursa, but the Lensmann is only just arrived.

The ride is over as soon as it is begun. The Lensmann isn't there to greet them, and though her husband doesn't say anything, she feels the cold throb of his disappointment fall over her like a rain cloud. The bank, she notices, is raised by grey stones of the same kind as the walls. Maren has never brought her here on their walks, and Ursa realizes that she has held a horror of it since sighting it from the ship. She shudders as they pass through a slice in the fortification, manned by two guards. She has seen more men in the past few minutes than she has for months. They are led across an empty moat on a road of flagstones, slick though it has not rained the past two days. Ursa must take Absalom's arm to keep from slipping.

At the base of the wall, a door sits mounted on metal hinges. A barred grate is set into it and they are eyed before it is opened. Once they are across the threshold, the door bangs heavily shut behind, and Ursa jumps.

"Feels like a prison," she says.

"It is," replies Absalom.

It isn't the castle she had imagined. Inside are several build-ings, arranged along the edges of the wall. Absalom points out one, speaks to their guide to confirm. "That is the gaol, yes?"

The guard gives a brief nod. "The witches' hole."

"Any witches?"

Ursa's attention piques as she regards the structure. She has never seen a prison before. It is long and narrow. Bars line small, high windows.

The guard gives a slower nod, shifting his shoulders. He answers in the rough English many sailors learn. "Two. Sorcerers. Lapps from Varanger."

"May I see?" Absalom's voice has something tight in it. An excitement.

The guard indicates the largest of the buildings. "Lensmann Køning wishes to meet you, and then it will be time to dine. The Lensmann likes things run to time." The man's stance sharpens. "He was a captain of our fleet. Ran the pirates out of Spitsbergen."

"We have corresponded," says Absalom, defensive. "I know."

The guard gives a deferential nod, and Ursa is reminded of Maren, making herself small in her husband's presence.

Turning their backs to the gaol, they cross the slippery flagstones to the main house. It stands taller than the other buildings, built in a style unfamiliar to her, broad at its front with the door set in the centre, made of stone like the wall, but with wooden touches about the windows and even carved gables beneath the roof. The guard doesn't knock, but opens the door and leads them into a wide corridor. It doesn't look as though it has only recently been inhabited. There is a woven rug beneath Ursa's feet, its pattern a garish pink and yellow, its softness disarming.

The guard takes them left, into a room where a fire is

crackling and china cups have been set out on a low dark-wood table. There is smoke-stained wallcloth, and the windows have heavy curtains and sashes of red that clash with the rug. There is even a vase on the table beside the teapot, with five lilacs standing from it.

"Please, wait here." The guard closes the door softly behind him. The settle is upholstered in the same colours as the rug, but its pattern is faded and threadbare, stuffing frothing from the arms as she arranges herself upon it. It is hard beneath her, like a church pew.

She looks closer at the lilacs: they are paper. She can see now that the vase has no water, and that dust has settled in the petals' creases. But still, it cheers her to see them, and the gesture at homeliness.

Absalom doesn't sit, nor move to pour tea. Ursa watches, throat dry and tongue thick from sea salt in her mouth, as her husband paces the broad width of the room, his long black coat setting the fire to quiver every time he passes.

He is nervous, she thinks, and wonders whether to say something to calm him before realizing it is exactly this power she lacks. Her mother could settle Father with a touch of her fingertip to his wrist, with a soft exhale of breath. He'd bend towards her like a reed bowed by the wind, the lines of his face loosening. Absalom notices her staring at him. He frowns and turns his face away.

The door opens and she rises hurriedly, but it is only the guard.

"Apologies, Commissioner Cornet. The Lensmann has urgent business and will be delayed. Perhaps——" he notices the untouched tea——"you would like some biscuits while you wait?"

"No," says Absalom, a muscle in his cheek working beneath his trimmed beard.

"Mistress Cornet?" The guard turns his gaze on her.

Ursa's mouth floods with want, for butter and sugar and perhaps some currants—

"No, we are fine." Her husband casts her a stern look. The door closes.

Ursa wonders if they will ever have an easy silence, akin to those she shares with Maren. Absalom sits and pours her a cup of light brown tea that smells of damp wood and something medicinal. She drinks it in small sips—it is already cold, but it is something to do—while he fixes the door with such an intense stare she wonders if he is trying to summon the Lensmann. She thinks of the witches in the gaol, the...what had the guard said? Sorcerers. Absalom shifts in his chair, takes a swig of tea, grimaces, sets it down.

"Do you like that stuff?"

He says it in Norwegian, and his accent is improving. His address is always a shock to her body, a cause for her heart to race and her palms to sweat. She sets down the cup so it will not rattle against the saucer. *Calm*, she tells herself.

"It is all right."

"Why do you do that?" He is leaning back in his chair, looking directly at her. She wills his attention to return to the door. "If you do not like something, you should leave it."

There is disapproval in his voice. She can't be right, can't please him. She takes the cup back up, finishes it. "I like it now."

He crosses his arms, goes back to eyeing the door. They are left perhaps another half an hour—there is no clock in the room—and this time when the door opens it isn't the guard but a woman trailing a serving boy.

"Commissioner Cornet, I am Christin Cunningham." She inclines her head as they both stand. "You must excuse my husband. Some trouble with tax, I suspect. It usually is." Her voice has only the touch of an accent to it, Danish, Ursa thinks, like her father's once-associate Herr Brekla. Her eyes are large and framed by thick, straight lashes. She flicks them towards Ursa.

"You must be his lovely wife fetched from Bergen." She holds out both her hands and Ursa takes them, feeling embarrassed and buoyed by her familiarity. "Forgive me, I do not know your name."

"Ursula, Fru Cunningham. Ursula Cornet."

"A beauty," smiles Christin. She has a motherly warmth to her, Ursa decides, though she can't be much more than thirty. She is wearing a white cap of the sort Siv wears, but it is trimmed with white lace and stylishly starched, pushed back off her forehead so the neat parting of her dark hair is revealed.

"You have done well, commissioner." She turns to the boy. "Oluf will take you to John's study. And we—" she tucks Ursa's hand beneath her arm—"we can go to the kitchen. It is cosier there."

She guides them back to the corridor, and the serving boy takes Absalom ahead and to the right, while the Ursa and Christin go down a small set of stairs into a squarish space only slightly smaller than the drawing room. Two women look up from peeling carrots. A large stew is bubbling over the fire, and everything smells rich and nourishing.

Christin switches to Norwegian, and her accent is more pronounced. Ursa is relieved not to have to attempt her clumsy Danish, learnt from brief exchanges with her father's clerk.

"It is very good to have you here. Many of the other commissioners are churchmen and not much interested in wives, or else they are old or live far away."

Christin leads her to a couch beside the fire, and one of the women stops peeling to bring them more tea and—Ursa's stomach clenches—round, dark biscuits, which she sets on a low table before them.

"I hope you do not mind this," says Christin, pulling off her cap. Her hair is drawn into a neat coil. "I much prefer it to upstairs. We sent ahead to have it redecorated a little but it still feels drear, don't you think?"

Ursa catches herself. "It's very fine, Fru Cunningham."

Christin waves her hand in a parody of graciousness. "Christin, please." She takes up the plate of biscuits, holds them out. "Pepperkaker? More suitable for Christmas time I know, but it's still cold enough to be Christmas here, don't you think? They are my favourite, and John gets a good supply of ginger from his connections in Bergen—" something twists in Ursa's chest at mention of her city—"though we are running a little short. Did you bring spices with you from home? No? Pity." She takes a biscuit as well, eyes it critically. "They are a little burnt. Fanne, you must take more care."

But Ursa can smell the ginger, is so grateful for its sweetness she doesn't mind the bitter foretaste.

"Now, you must tell me all about yourself, and your husband too. Handsome man, as these Scots often seem to be, if a little..." She wrinkles her nose, lets out a little, high laugh that sets Ursa's teeth on edge. "And you are so lovely. Wherever did he find you?"

"Bergen."

"Yes, Bergen I know, but where? How?"

Ursa recounts their meeting.

"Did he tell you what it was like here?"

She shakes her head. "He knew little of it himself, I think."

Christin sighs, a theatrical sound such as Agnete might make while throwing herself back, hand to forehead.

"I did warn John, I told him to tell everyone. But he's a seaman, he's used to it. You've heard about Spitsbergen? Not that it will make a difference if you have or not—he'll tell you all about it himself at dinner."

Her dark eyes glitter, but there is no malice there. It is

strange to have found a woman like this in such an austere place. She is fey and sharp all at once. She is just the sort of person who would have attended their dinner parties in Bergen, been friends with Mother.

"He's the King's favourite, if you can believe it. And this is where the King's favourites end up—can you imagine where the enemies go."

Ursa notices the servants eyeing each other, and suspects they do not approve of their mistress.

"How long have you been here?" she asks, feeling a little bolder in this room of women, with the taste of sugar still on her tongue. "We did not see you arrive."

"We came in at night, two weeks ago," says Christin. "You are surprised?"

Ursa hopes her husband does not know it was so long between their arrival and his invitation. "Only that the house seems so settled."

"Castle," says Christin, a little too sharply. "That's what the King called it. Vardøhus Festning." Her eyes go a little far away. She is not quite right, thinks Ursa. Her brightness is too keen, a little slanting and strange. "We were wed in Copenhagen. A captain! I'd thought…"

Ursa knows, because she had also thought. She has a compulsion to reach out to Christin with both hands, as Christin had to her in the drawing room. Male voices fill the corridor upstairs, and Christin seems to snap from herself. "Dinner soon, yes?" She stands and smooths her dark skirts. "I must ask John something."

They go up into the corridor and see the front door close. Absalom is there with another man, perhaps ten years his elder, with a weather-beaten, bearded face like Captain Leifsson's, which broadens into a smile.

"You must be Ursula." His Norwegian is flawless. Absalom

isn't looking at the women, but at him, with rapt attention. Ursa guesses he does not know of the delay in the Lensmann's contacting him. "It is very good to meet you." Cunningham switches to English. "Tell me, can you sing?"

"Sing?"

Absalom gives a simpering laugh. It is so unlike him it causes her to stare, but his eyes are fixed on the Lensmann, who claps him on the back, chuckling.

"Never mind, never mind. You must be ready for dinner. I like to dine at seven o'clock sharp, just like we did on the *Katten*. My second ship, you know. The one I took to Spitsbergen. Good to keep a routine, yes? Fanne will show you to your room."

A stone-faced Fanne leads them upstairs. Their room is above the drawing room at the front of the house, and just as faded and fine, though it smells unpleasant, of closed, forgotten cellars and something else more insistent, greasy and cloying, like fat left to congeal at the base of a pot.

It feels half a world away from their home just a mile down the road, though. There is even a tarnished mirror on the dresser. It has been a long time since Ursa has seen her face but in dark windows, and she notes how it has lost some of its plumpness, how the weeks on the ship's deck and days walking with Maren have given her cheeks and nose a smattering of freckles that Siv would have called common. There is a different set to her face too—a worry line has come in between her eyes and she smooths it with her forefinger but the wrinkle stays there, faint as a whisper.

Ursa's dress has been placed on a chair to air, and the overnight bag is empty and sits atop the chest of drawers. Their things have been folded into the drawers and it discomforts Ursa to think of someone touching them, seeing the stains she has not managed to soak away. She used to be so at ease with their bevy of servants, found it a nuisance when they were left only with Siv, but now she is unsure about it again. Someone seeing your soiled clothes, your mucky belongings, the mess of your house and body.

Absalom is happy, perhaps even a little drunk. He sits upon the end of the bed and holds two pieces of paper in his hands, tied with green ribbon and sealing wax.

"Was your meet with the Lensmann good, husband?"

"He has shown me my purpose, wife. He is a greater man than I had hoped for."

"I am pleased for you."

Then Absalom does something that astonishes her. He stands, takes her chin in his hand, and presses his lips to hers, softly, chastely. "God did this, Ursula. I am assured of that now."

She waits until he has turned his back to wipe her hand across her mouth. Still she can feel the tickle of his beard upon her, the gentle press of his thumb under her lip.

It was so tender she wants to weep.

TWENTY-SEVEN

There is a screen in the corner of the bedroom, painted with black birds and slicked in a thick layer of varnish, and Ursa takes her dress behind it when Absalom begins to unbutton his shirt. The mirror and light of the room have made her more conscious of her appearance than she has felt in months, and she can see her shape dimly in the varnish. Though Absalom is nearby, she takes off her underthings and stands regarding the round edges of herself, her nipples like dark holes at the centres of her breasts, the pale fuzz between her legs, the curve of her belly only slightly diminished by her changed life.

It's like seeing a ghost, and she changes quickly, comes out to stand before the mirror again, tries to slick and twist her hair the same way Christin had. The pins bite at her head.

They go down, and find Christin emerging from the kitchen, wearing a deep yellow dress, the velvet so fine it shines nearly golden in the lamplight. She nods approvingly at Ursa's hair, pats her own to show she has noticed.

"Excuse the smell," she says as she leads them towards the drawing room. "My husband accepted tax from the Ruskis in whales. Blubber, oil." She grimaces. "It does reek."

So that is the smoky, greasy smell, so hard to ignore. The

burnt gingerbread roils in Ursa's stomach. They have tallow burners in Bergen, the smell disguised with clove.

"A wise trade," says Lensmann Cunningham, emerging from what Ursa presumes is his study. He is wearing a small ruff over his black tunic: it is a little tight and she watches as his Adam's apple squeezes up before disappearing back down. "Prices are rising weekly now the channels are closed."

"You closed them," says his wife.

"Exactly." He pulls the door to, gestures for them to follow him. "Here we are."

The dining room is wood-panelled, so fresh Ursa can still smell the forest on it, with a table built large enough for thrice their number. Candlesticks line it, and Ursa is grateful to note there are no blubber lamps here, only the candles with their soft light. She feels their glow settle over her like a lick of kindness, smoothing her dry hands, casting her husband in gentleness. There are two rows of cutlery, and polished china plates, a square loaf of black bread on the table with a knife lying beside it.

They sit with the Lensmann at the head of the table, his back to a large window. The curtains have not been drawn, and the darkness seeps into the room, edging at the candlelight. The women sit together, facing Absalom.

Fanne enters with a tray of small glasses half filled with clear liquid, etched about their rims. It is sharp, herbal-smelling. She leaves the bottle on the table beside the Lensmann, an elegant, long-necked thing of blue glass.

"Akevitt," says Lensmann Cunningham. "Normally an after-dinner sup, I know, but it's a habit I got into aboard the *Katten*. A glass before food wakes the tongue. *Skol!*"

He raises his glass, drains it in one. Absalom does the same and begins to cough. Lensmann Cunningham slaps him between the shoulders as Ursa looks to Christin for guidance, but her glass is empty, too. Ursa sips at the akevitt, winces. It burns down.

Beside Absalom there are two seats empty. "We are to have company?" he says, and Ursa wonders if Lensmann Cunningham can hear his disappointment too.

"Commissioner Moe from Alta," says the Lensmann, taking up the knife and beginning to slice the bread. "I believe you have met? And Herr Abhorsen, a wealthy trader up from Bergen." He nods at Ursa. "I thought it would be nice for you to hear the gossip."

Ursa nods back politely. She never heard gossip when she lived there and was old enough to care. She and Agnete speculated, but their father couldn't employ a chaperone after Mother died, and so they were mostly left inside with their imaginations and chatter.

"But they must be delayed coming from Alta. We can begin without them." He pours more akevitt, this time filling only his and Absalom's glasses.

"Tell me, Ursula," says Christin, resting her hand lightly upon Ursa's. "What of your family? What does your father do?"

"He's a shipowner, wood mostly. From Christiania."

"Oak, then?" interrupts Cunningham. "*Katten* was a pine ship. Lighter, faster."

Christin speaks as though her husband has not. "Have you brothers, sisters?"

A bitter taste fills Ursa's mouth, and she takes another sip of akevitt to wash it away, welcoming the burning channel it carves down her throat, the heat it brings to her stomach. "A sister." There is a silence, so she heaves up her name too. "Agnete."

"She is crippled," says Absalom. Ursa flinches. "Something wrong with her leg, her lungs."

"She is well in her mind," says Ursa. "She is thirteen, nearly fourteen."

"So much younger," muses Christin. Fanne enters with a plate of something silvery and gelatinous and sets it at the centre of the table, leaning across between Cunningham and Absalom. The Lensmann's eyes follow her out of the room. "Why did your mother wait so long?"

Ursa checks her husband's face. But he is looking off over her shoulder, his attention sleeping until it is called to wake by his master.

"She had several losses, I know."

"Any boys?" Cunningham asks, reaching forward to spear a chunk of silver herring from the plate before them.

"I do not know," says Ursa. It is strange to be discussing her mother's failed birthings at dinner with near-strangers, but she doesn't feel she can refuse the information.

"What does she think of you living up here?" He is now mashing the fish flat on a slice of bread with the back of his fork. It pulps and glints. Ursa feels nauseous.

"She's dead," interjects Absalom, but it isn't done to save her, only to get a foot in the conversation.

"I am sorry," says Christin, moving her hand from Ursa's and taking up the plate. "Herring?"

Ursa takes some, the jelly sliding through the tines of her fork and soaking the rye bread. They chew and Fanne brings a small platter of sliced onions.

"These are to come out with the fish next time," says Christin. Fanne bobs, brings around a flagon of honey-coloured liquid and pours each of them a large glass though the akevitt is still on the table, Absalom's second glass full and untouched.

"Your husband has told me some of his suspicions of Vardø," says Cunningham. The contents of his mouth churn in the candlelight. "What is your opinion?"

"My opinion?" repeats Ursa.

"Of the women." He swallows; his Adam's apple wrestles its way past his ruff again. "Women often see things we miss, don't they, sweetling?"

"And things you hope we would miss," says Christin, voice arch as Fanne leaves the room again, the Lensmann's eyes trailing her.

"They seem..." Ursa searches for the right word.

"Do not worry about tact, Mistress Cornet. I have encountered enough of these Finnmark women to know they are a hard sort, and those from Vardø have a special reputation even here. After the storm—you'll have told her all about that, I'm sure." This he addresses to Absalom. But her husband has told her nothing. What she has heard she gleaned from Captain Leifsson, or else from Maren's mention of her father and brother.

"It killed a handful in Kiberg, made widows. They remarried. It struck worst here. But the women of Vardø..." He chews, shakes his head. "About six months after the storm, I received a letter from their minister. Pastor Kurtsson—what do you think of him?"

Absalom shrugs his broad shoulders. "He is a good-hearted man, but not a strong one."

Cunningham nods until the movement takes on its own momentum, tears another piece of bread. "He sent me word the women were planning to fish for themselves. Can you imagine?"

"I can, actually," says Christin. "Women are different here. They till the land, tend the livestock."

"Peasants do that all over," says Cunningham. "But none go to sea."

The runnels of their exchange sound smooth, as though they have gone over this ground many times.

"What else were they to do?" says Christin. "Starve?"

"I provided for them."

"How?"

"I sent money to Kiberg for them to send fish and grain."

"You were not here," says Christin. "How can you be sure it reached them?"

"I did not need to be here to do my duty." Cunningham's voice rises. "They would not defy my authority. A woman has no place on a boat. And besides—" he takes another bite of bread, eyes Ursa—"that storm was no ordinary one."

Her heart pounds in her chest, and in the corner of her vision she sees Absalom lean forward, elbows on the table.

"You are certain of it?" he asks, his breathing a little ragged.

Cunningham does not look away from Ursa when he answers. "Quite certain. I have been a-sea more often than on land for most of my life. I know what the weather can do, and what it cannot. Forty men, dead in a moment?" He shakes his head in disbelief. "And after what your husband told me of the runes..." He crosses himself, his hand clutching bread. Absalom follows suit, and finally Cunningham turns his attention back to her husband. Ursa can breathe again. "You can surely see why I posted you here? We have some handle on it in Alta, in Kirkenes, but here..."

Ursa waits, but the end of the sentence doesn't come. The door opens and Fanne enters. She is carrying a broad polished tray with five bowls of the stew they had smelt in the kitchen earlier. "Commissioner Moe is here, Lensmann. He's just washing for dinner."

She sets them down, and one at the place beside Absalom. They wait, the smell of the stew making Ursa's stomach murmur inside her dress, until Commissioner Moe arrives.

"I beg your pardon, Lensmann Køning," he says in Norwegian. "The crossing was rough as anything. Waited for it to calm and it only got worse. Daniel begged off the journey and has gone to Hamningberg. You know these Bergen folk." He winks at Absalom, who looks back blankly. He has whiskers like her father's, and their disarray attests to the rough crossing. Ursa places him about the Lensmann's age, and he is her height.

"It is good to see you again, Commissioner Cornet," he says, changing to English as he bows to Absalom, who nods shallowly back. "And this must be your charming wife."

Ursa can't imagine he got that description from Absalom. "Commissioner."

"Moe, please. Now then—" he slaps his hands together— "what are we having?"

TWENTY-EIGHT

The three men speak so loud and continuously, over and around each other, it is like listening to ten. Christin barely touches her food, takes the occasional sip of mead, and watches them, eventually leaning in to Ursa and saying, "He doesn't speak Norwegian?"

"He has a little. He is working on it with the minister."

"Could you not help him?"

"I am not sure he would like that."

Christin nods, and Ursa knows she understands her meaning. "Tell me then, truthfully. How is it in the village? My husband has told me enough to ensure I am unlikely to visit."

"It isn't so bad."

"You aren't afraid?"

"Of what?"

"Cornet wrote to us of the runes, of the poppets. Well, he wrote to my husband, but John reads me many letters. He loves an audience."

Ursa takes another mouthful of ptarmigan. "I am not afraid. Do you not feel afraid, with the gaol so near?"

"Ah, yes." The woman sips her mead, but her voice remains

dry as ever. Perhaps this is the key to surviving here—emptying your glass. "The Lapps. My husband has a particular fascination with them."

"My life's work," booms the Lensmann. Ursa jumps—she had not been aware they were being listened to. "The reason I am here. My predecessor but one was not so lucky."

"Kofoed?" says Moe. "Knew him as a boy. Nasty business."

"What happened?" says Ursa.

"Lapps got him," says the Lensmann darkly. "Cursed him. They say he shrivelled like an uprooted plant. Overnight."

Commissioner Moe makes the gesture of the cross over himself. "Watched the burning of Olson myself. He was the ringleader. When they lit him the smoke burnt black as hellfire."

Ursa puts her fork down but the others carry on chewing, eyes intent on Commissioner Moe.

"Were there other signs, before Kofoed?" asks Absalom.

"Oh, yes," says Moe darkly. "Livestock deaths, put down to wolves until Olson confessed. Girls pregnant without husbands. And those who watched him burn, we were all of us sick for days after. It felt as though I had blots upon my lungs."

There is a heavy silence. Ursa feels sick, the akevitt turning her stomach. She drinks more.

"You have two sorcerers now," says Absalom to Cunningham. "What are they imprisoned for?"

"Wind-weaving," says Cunningham, and Ursa can't stop the small laugh that escapes her lips. The others look at her with implacable faces. She can't tell them she had been thinking of her weave, large enough for fingers to move through, how Maren had waggled them at her and said they won't be setting any ships to sail with them.

"I am sorry," she says. "I have never heard of such a thing before today."

"It is nothing to be laughed at," says Lensmann Cunningham,

and Ursa feels like a child chastised. "Weather has always been their weapon of choice. You should know it, living in Vardø."

"Perhaps it is only that we do not have witches in Bergen."

"That may be so," says Cunningham seriously, his eyes unfocused, his grip on the arm of his chair unnaturally tight. "Though there was a witch's hill near Bergen, was there not, Moe?"

"There is. Lyderhorn, I believe."

"I read of it," nods Absalom. "Mons Storebarn and Mons Anderson met there, plotted against the Kirke."

"Said he was good, didn't I, Moe! We know our stuff, we Scotsmen." He reaches across to clink glasses with Absalom. "But still, they usually lurk at the edges of the world. That's what I told you, isn't it, Absalom?" Cunningham is leaning forward in his chair. "In our letters. The candle's light is weakest in the corners. We are here to shine the light more fully, to seek out darkness and burn it up. Swallow it with the fire of God's love."

His eyes are shining. Though he speaks to Absalom, his gaze is fixed upon her. He looks possessed, and Ursa has a sudden terror he will throw himself across the table at her, grip her about the throat and squeeze and squeeze. But he only slumps back in his chair, motions for his wife to pour another glass.

None of the others seem to notice they are caught in this room with a bear.

"That is why the King placed me here, over one of your own." He nods at Moe. "In Scotland we are gaining ground, but of course that is without the complication of Lapps to contend with. I knew we had to meet sooner rather than later, especially after your last correspondence, Absalom. The news of the Lapp, the poppets."

Ursa's skin crawls. She had hoped Christin's reference to

the poppets earlier had been conjecture, but Toril has talked, as Maren feared. And the Lapp—she must tell her Diinna has been mentioned.

"Until now our concern has been with the Lapp sorcerers, the men—they call themselves noaidi, you know the sort. Shamans, like Olson, the two in the gaol. But the women have become trouble too, and not only the Lapps. Your husband—" his eyes are again upon her and she hears her heart loud in her ears—"is a man of particular talents, as you no doubt know." He raises his eyebrows at her blank face. "Surely you know that is why he was sent for? One of the very finest, even amongst us Scotsmen."

"I am sorry," she says, looking to Christin for support, but she is looking at the middle distance, her lips slightly parted.

Cunningham turns to her husband with a theatrical look of alarm that makes Commissioner Moe guffaw, the sounds choked by his mouthful of bread. "Absalom, do not tell me your wife doesn't know of your achievements?"

Absalom shrugs modestly, and Ursa could hit him. "I have not spoken of it."

"Well, then, I must speak of it. Tell me, Ursula, have you heard of a woman named Elspeth Reoch?"

"Forgive me, I have not."

"Forgive me, for I am about to tell you." His voice is full of relish, and Ursa determines to meet his eyes, to not look afraid. "She was but twelve years old, was she not, Absalom, when she made promises with the Devil? Twelve years old when she washed her eyes in his tears to make herself see what it is ungodly to see. She compacted with him. You know what compacted means, Mistress Cornet? What a woman must do to gain such powers of witchcraft?"

"I am sure she can guess at it," interrupts Christin. "Do not be so vulgar, John."

"But it is vulgar." Cunningham slaps the flat of his hand upon the table. "It is depraved, disgusting. She bore him a child, did she not, Absalom?"

"Two," says Absalom gravely. "Though her secret was not found out until the trial. She claimed to have lost her voice, lived as a mute for years after her pact. Her brother tried to beat the voice from her—he was a godly man, brought her to Coltart's attention."

"Coltart," spits Cunningham, dislike apparent in his voice. "A fraud if ever there was one. It was you who was the power behind his conviction, and do not deny it. Modesty is a fair trait in most cases, but this is not one of them."

"How did you make her speak?" says Moe.

"Ducking. Irons."

"You bound her?"

"Branded her. With crosses at her throat and arms." Absalom is not looking at Ursa. She hopes it is because he is ashamed, but she hears none of that in his voice.

"Go on."

"She cried out in a demonic language, and then sang like the Devil's bird she is." Ursa's dress feels very tight as she watches him enjoy the Lensmann's attention. "Confessed the whole tale, to seduction of four men and to theft, to a half-dozen meets with the Devil."

"But what marked this so apart was her execution—a masterful stroke," says Cunningham.

"You did not burn her?" asks Moe, as though enquiring as to the weather that day.

"We did," says Absalom.

"They did," echoes Cunningham. "But first, to make right her crime of deceit in her claim of muteness, they strangled her. Did you not, Absalom?"

"Yes." Now he looks at Ursa quickly, as though he wishes

239

she were not here, and she realizes they have not yet heard the worst of it. She presses her palms very hard against the table, bracing herself.

"Go on," smiles Cunningham. "Tell them how."

"With a rope, sir," says Absalom, and finally she hears the looked-for shame in his voice.

"And your involvement?"

Absalom's voice is barely audible. "Had hold of one end of the rope myself, Lensmann."

"See," says Cunningham, leaning forward to slap Absalom on the shoulder. "A man of quality. Not many men could mete out their punishment themselves. I'll bet it was not Coltart who had hold of the other end of that rope."

"It was not, Lensmann." He does not look at Ursa again, and she is glad. She could not hide what she is feeling at that moment, not for all the world.

"That was when I knew I must have you here," continues Cunningham. "In the heat of it. Anyone can set a fire—it makes killing no harder than boiling a cup for tea."

"The kettles shriek louder," says Moe.

"Please," says Christin.

"Sorry, sweetling," says Cunningham, a smirk at his bearded mouth. "Moe, you must not forget our company."

Ursa can't speak. She hates him, she knows now. Hates all of them. She knew of the trial from Absalom's mention of it in the first kirke meeting, but had not guessed that the woman had been put to death, that her husband with his own hands murdered her. *Branded. Strangled. Burnt.* The words repeat like a child's rhyme. She shudders, and it doesn't escape Fru Cunningham's notice.

"It is brute to hear such details, but you must feel no pity for a witch, Ursula," says Christin, sympathetically. "It is through the soft places that they take hold, through the hurt heart, the tender mind. Even in Tromsø, in Bergen, we women must be taught this."

"And you need fear them less than most," says Cunningham. "With such a man for your husband."

Ursa watches Absalom across the table. She had not guessed at the pride he takes in the telling of this story. She can feel his pleasure in the admiration from the others coming off him, tangible as the smell of drink off Lensmann Cunningham.

Talk turns to the fishing channels, to the whaling at Spitsbergen and, finally, endlessly it seems to Ursa, to Lensmann Cunningham's time on the *Katten*. The dinner closes with a rømmegrøt of such proportions the candlesticks must be moved further apart so the great dish of cream can be placed between them.

Ursa takes enough to seem polite, but the cream feels wrong in her mouth, too rich after months of ship and then Vardø food. All this time she had been craving tastes like she used to have at home, cream and cinnamon and sugar, but it slides down thickly, sits heavy and malign in her stomach.

She notices that Absalom barely touches it either. His hands, large as hams, are resting on the table, the small hairs at his knuckles catching the candlelight like cobwebs. She feels tightness in her throat.

Commissioner Moe excuses himself soon after, red about the nose, citing his long journey. "I am invigorated," he says, grasping Absalom's hand. "Let us get to work."

Christin has grown very quiet beside Ursa, and she suspects it is the effect of the same drink that makes the Lensmann so expansive. Ursa too has drunk more than was perhaps polite. Her mouth feels tingling and raw with the liquor. As the plates are cleared and Absalom and Lensmann Cunningham rise to retire to the Lensmann's study, she brushes her fingers across her lips. They feel very soft, and not her own.

"Ursula?"

Christin is standing behind her pushed-in chair, watching her. "I hope you do not mind?"

"Mind?"

"I am quite tired. Would you like me to see you to your room?"

"Oh..." Ursa hurries to stand, her skirts catching beneath the chair legs as she moves it backwards, Lensmann Cunningham moving too slowly to help. "Thank you. Thank you for the dinner. It was very fine."

"We found Fanne in Alta," says Lensmann Cunningham. He is standing a little close to her, and she can smell sourness and cream on his breath. "She is a good cook."

"I wouldn't go so far," says Christin crisply. "But I am glad you enjoyed it."

"Do you have help?" asks Cunningham, squinting at Absalom. "Any Vardø women know how to keep a home?"

There is a leer in his voice that makes Ursa's skin crawl.

"My wife has some aid," Absalom answers. "Though not of my choosing. She is kin with a Lapp."

"They are not kin," says Ursa, fear making her bold. "They are not blood. She comes to kirke, husband. She is a good woman."

Absalom looks as though he will say more but Cunningham waves his hand diffidently.

"It is best to leave such matters to the women," he says. "You have enough to worry yourself about, especially with our conversations to act upon."

"Shall we?" Christin is all but tapping her foot. She is obviously anxious to be abed, and Ursa doesn't mind. She longs for the oblivion of sleep, for it to be morning and to return to their house, to Maren. In her blurred mind she tells herself that there are things she must warn her of, like the mention of Diinna and the poppets. She digs her fingernails into her wrist, to make herself remember.

They go out into the corridor and say their goodnights to the men, who are already back into conversation, breaking off only briefly, Lensmann Cunningham to bump his mouth against his wife's high cheekbone, Absalom to give her another disconcertingly soft brush of lips, this time against her cheek.

"You must be proud, to be wed to a man such as that," says Christin as she leads her up the stairs. Ursa wants to laugh, to ask which part she should be proud of—his slavish attention to the Lensmann, his intimate part in a woman's death, or his satisfaction in it?

"Your husband really had no say in the appointment of your servant?" Christin continues.

"She is not so much a servant, more a companion."

"It is best to keep such people apart from yourself. And from your husband," says Christin as they reach Ursa's bedroom door. Christin opens it, stands aside. As Ursa moves to walk past her Christin brings her hand up, brushes Ursa's neck where her knot has slipped its pins. The spot feels tender. "Though you are so lovely, I am sure you do not need to worry."

Ursa feels a blush rise up her constricted throat. "Worry?"

"Drink, cards." She blinks slowly at Ursa. "Serving girls. Even great men have weaknesses. And it is we who must bear them."

Ursa suddenly wants to confide in her, of her life with Absalom, all its small terrors and confusions, but Christin has already dropped her hand and is moving off to the other end of the corridor. She is not unsteady, only too careful.

"Goodnight, Ursula. I will put you in my prayers."

Ursa closes the door. Light is coming around the edges of the drawn curtains, and the bedspread has been folded back, the linen smooth beneath. Can it be true, that Fanne and the Lensmann lie together? Perhaps in this bed, when there are no visitors.

She lets her hair down, collecting the pins in her hand as she crosses to the window, hooks aside one heavy drape with a finger. The other buildings in the complex are still lit, with the exception of the gaol. She listens: is that the sound of men moaning, or only the wind, the sea? The dark windows seem to stare back, and she lets the curtain drop, hurries to complete her ablutions, anxious to be asleep when Absalom comes to bed.

Before she slips between the clean sheets, she kneels beside the bed, the way she and Agnete used to, says a prayer for the sad-eyed Christin, for Maren out in the dark somewhere, and for herself. And though it may be an unnameable blasphemy, for Elspeth Reoch, who died at Absalom's hand. Witch or no, she wouldn't wish it on anyone.

TWENTY-NINE

Ursa thought the worst of the evening was behind her, but she doesn't manage to sleep before Absalom comes to bed. The noises of the house are too strange, the sea much closer and the sound of it against the shore unsettling. She thinks she hears his hand on the door many times before he actually pushes it open.

"You awake, Ursula?"

There is no point pretending. She pushes herself up, pulling the sheets to her chin. He removes his boots, goes to the chair by the fire. He has a small glass in his hand, more folded paper in the other.

"I hope you enjoyed your dinner?"

"It was very rich, I have become unused to it."

He sets his glass down on the fireplace, ducks his head so she can see his face only in profile as he gazes at the flames. When he speaks, it is into the flames too, and she doesn't catch his words.

"Sorry?" she says.

He speaks a little louder. "I had not meant you to find out like that."

She thought she would feel afraid upon his return, but now

she is full of the same righteous anger she felt in the dining room. It makes her bold.

"That you murdered a woman?"

The silence stretches, yawns like a pit. Ursa can hear her heart louder than the sea in her ears. She wishes she were wearing more than her cotton nightdress.

Finally, slowly, he straightens, turns back towards her, the flames glowing about his legs. His lips are pressed together thinly, and when she drags her gaze to his eyes, she sees they are glassy, a little unfocused. Is he drunk as the Lensmann?

"Murdered a woman?" he repeats, unable to make sense of the words. "No. No—" he shakes his head as though dislodging a fly—"I tried a witch, wife. She was sentenced to death by the court of my country. She was guilty, in the eyes of the law, and of God. 'Thou shalt not suffer a witch to live.' God commands it."

"But you, husband. You had to be the one to kill her?"

He looks pained as he lifts his small glass from the fireplace, and, still clutching the papers, sits heavily in the chair beside the fire. "It was a grave matter. I took no joy in it, though she deserved to die, and I prayed for it after. God forgave me. I am not an arrogant man, Ursula." She stops herself from snorting. "But I am proud of my service to God. I hope for my wife to be so, too."

She knows the wisest thing is to say she is proud, as Christin thinks she should be. It would dispel the tension between them, and perhaps he is drunk enough that he would not remember the detail of their conversation in the morning. But she says nothing, only watches him.

He tilts his head against the hard back of the chair, so she can see only a little of his eyes, which seem almost black. "I do like that you are from fine stock, Ursula. I could hardly believe my luck when your father told me of you. A shipowner's daughter." He sucks in his breath. "You are better than I could have hoped for."

She wishes he would stop speaking, stop looking at her. "You are a commissioner. You could have chosen finer." She wishes he had. In that moment, though it would mean she would never have met Maren, she longs to be back at home with Agnete, tucked up in their shared bed, unwed and unaware of Absalom Cornet.

"I did not start so high," says Absalom. "Not like the Lensmann, lifted already at birth. I was the son of a sheep farmer, did you know that?"

"I did not. You have never told me." *Careful*, she tells herself. *Not so sharp.*

"You have never asked." He pauses, as though waiting for her to do so now, but she doesn't trust herself to speak.

He takes a swallow from his glass. "I was born on a tiny spit of an island. Only a bit larger than this, as I once said. Nothing but sheep. It stank. And then they built a kirk on the next island over, and that was clean and smelt of candles. It was the finest place I'd ever known." His eyes close, as if he is picturing it. "The minister there, he could see something special in me. It was he who recommended me to Coltart, when the witch was caught."

Bile rises in her throat.

"Isn't that a miraculous thing? The son of a sheep farmer, become a witch-hunter, and then a commissioner?" His dark eyes gleam at her.

"It is, husband."

He shifts in his chair. "Why do you not call me Absalom?"

"I will if you prefer it, Absalom." She can feel a great sort of danger approaching, is searching for how to avoid it.

"Do you know what my name means?"

She shakes her head.

"Father of peace."

Ursa almost laughs, catches herself in time.

"That is all I want. To rid the world of witches, so we can all live in God's peace. And if the only way to it is through war, so be it."

He closes his eyes again, and does not say anything for a long time. She thinks he is asleep, and the knot in her stomach loosens slightly. But a moment later he speaks. "I was destined for this, Ursula. The Lensmann has great faith in me. He sees me as special, just as the minister in Orkney did."

He stands, so suddenly Ursa can't stop herself from jumping. He drains and sets down the glass, comes to the bed and sits beside her. His breath is hot on her cheek. "Do you think me special, Ursula?"

She turns to face him. Her hands tremble on the sheet. "Yes, Absalom."

He closes one of his hands over hers. It is warm and strong and dry. He holds up the folded pieces of paper. "The Lensmann gave me these. They have been arriving the past two months at Vardøhus. Letters, from Bergen."

Her heart leaps. "From my father?" She wants to reach for them, but her hands are held steady by his. He nods, drops them on the bedspread.

"They are opened," she says, recognizing her father's writing, but nothing of what he says.

"A husband should know what his wife's affairs are."

"They are my letters," Ursa says, trying to stay calm.

"Can you read them?" His tone tells her he knows she can't.

"Can you read Norwegian?" she snaps, the words out too fast to catch them. His hand is upon her shoulder and squeezing before she can pull away.

"Careful, wife. They are in English."

"I did not mean—of course my father knows you would

have to read them to me." The pressure on her shoulder is painful. "But could you not have waited until we were together?"

"It was my duty to read them. What if there had been bad news I had to prepare you for?"

Ursa's heart thumps. The fine dinner churns in her belly. "There is bad news?"

He says nothing, only lightens his grip on her shoulder.

"Please." She feels as though she is about to cry. "Absalom, is it Agnete?"

He reaches for the letters again, plucks them from her hands. He sorts through them, and she grows certain he is searching for the one that brings news of her sister. Of her death.

The tears are already spilling down her face when he shakes his head slowly.

"Nothing like that. All is as it was." He rifles through the sheaf. "Your sister has a new doctor. They have bought a new rug for her room. Small, petty things like that. They want to know of your life here."

She wipes her tears away, trembling. "Can you read them to me?"

"It is late."

"Just one, then. The latest one." Ursa feels desperate as a starving animal. "Please, husband—Absalom," she corrects, "please would you read one to me?"

He looks at her a long moment, then reaches out and touches the last of her tears. He rubs it between his fingers, considering, then takes up one of the letters. She wants to weep again, with relief, but controls herself.

"This was sent on the twenty-third of May."

"But that is months ago," says Ursa before she can catch herself.

"We are months away. Letters are slow to arrive." He is placid at her interruption, but she reminds herself to not speak further. "It says, 'Dearest Ursa'—" he pauses. "Is this what they call you?"

She nods.

"It is inelegant. 'Dearest Ursa, you are not long gone but already we feel your absence sharply. The days are a little drabber, the house a little less full of light.'"

Ursa closes her eyes, tries to imagine her father's voice.

"'Though it is a comfort to know you have taken your brightness north. I think they may need it even more than we. Agnete is no worse. Siv is thinking of employing a kitchen girl, so she may be more of a maid to her. Though Agnete insists that no one can rival you for a nurse. She wishes you to know that she loves you, though she is missing the blue kerchief, and would rather like it back.'"

Ursa smiles as Absalom stifles a yawn.

"It goes on so."

"Please, a little more." She places her hand on his, hating herself for needing him so. "Please, Absalom."

He fixes her then with a more focused look, and she recognizes his desire, rubs her thumb slow across his. He resumes, and she removes her hand as fast as she dares.

"'I hope Captain Leifsson cared for you well. He will be returning to Finnmark in early next year, and we will send gifts. Do let us know if there is anything particular you require. Should Absalom's business bring him south, be sure to accompany him. Ursa, it is only now that I realize how much I relied upon you. You can be sure that I am loving Agnete for us both, and am resolved to be the father she needs in the absence of her much-loved sister.'"

Ursa can't stop the tears this time. The words are so lovely she knows Absalom has not made them up: her father really has written just what her husband has read out. She feels nauseous with relief.

"Told you, nothing much to report." Absalom throws the letter to the bed, reaches for her. But she is too slow to act: she flinches, still raw from her father's words, the obvious love and care in them. His gaze sharpens further, and he gathers up the letters. They scrunch between his fingers.

"Careful," she pleads, but in one fluid movement, he stands, crosses the room. She knows his mind in an instant, rises from the bed, runs to stop him—but it is too late. He throws the letters into the fire.

She presses her hand to the sore throb beneath her breast as he turns to her. He takes her head between his hands, so large they encase her cheeks, and raises it so her neck is bent, arching up to him. She imagines him squeezing, her skull caving, but then he brings his mouth down on hers and kisses her, so softly it makes her skin crawl.

"I will write to them for you," he says, breath hot against her cheek as he brings his lips again to her. She can feel his hardness pressing against her belly, and knows there is a silent condition to his offer.

Behind him, the letters from her father shrivel into ash, and are carried up like smoke signals to the night.

HUNT

THIRTY

Though Ursa is only gone Wednesday and Thursday, it is twice what Maren had prepared for, and she feels each moment keenly as a blade. The meet is full of speculation on their Lensmann, on the gossip Ursa will come back with, and at every mention of her, Maren's nape tingles.

She doesn't know how she existed before her, now that mere days feel interminable. She matches Mamma for skittishness, Diinna for irritation, Erik for silence. She goes about her tasks with a caught anger that makes her fast, escapes to the headland, the only place she can see over the walls of the fortress, and watches the lights from the windows. She can see the whole of Vardø spread out in its gentle roll of valley, the two halves of the island matching each other almost exactly, like a book opened. Both nights she paces the cliff edge until the grass is flattened and churned.

She hears they are back on Friday morning, when Kirsten comes with salt and blood for blodplättar, and a message from Ursa. Mamma will not speak with Kirsten, barely speaks to Maren any more.

"Be sure she tells you all," says Kirsten from the threshold. "I am interested to have a measure of our Lensmann."

"If you came to Toril's meets," says Mamma to Maren, pummelling the butter churn though Maren can hear the thud that means it has been overworked, "you would have heard all already. Commissioner Cornet speaks often of the Lensmann's work, his plans for us all."

"I am interested in Ursula's measure of him, though," says Kirsten. "I will see you Sabbath Day, Maren."

"What plans?" says Maren when she has closed the door and set the pail of blood upon the table, though she doesn't much care to hear. The sound of the over-churned butter clagging in the milk is pounding in her head and it is all she can do to keep from knocking the paddle from Mamma's hand.

"Good things. Godly things." Her eyes flick to the place where her cloth cross from Toril is hung from a nick in the wadding of the wall. She had left one outside Diinna's door too, and Maren had found it unravelled and left in a pail of water two days later. Diinna must have been using it as a washcloth.

When did Diinna's dislike of Mamma grow to be such a monster? she wonders. Not that Maren's dislike is much less. She tries to quiet it, but sees only the vile cracking beside her mother's mouth where she constantly licks, the narrow hard face too like her own, the sweat coming heavy through her work dress. Is this the woman who used to soothe her pains, who laughed and span her when she came home with news of her proposal from Dag, who made her brother and delivered his son with gentle hands, that now sit crabbed about the paddle? Even her breath scratches at Maren's ear, loud with effort.

Maren doesn't ask anything further, but begins on the blodplättar, her stinging heart soothed a little by the knowledge that Ursa has been returned to her, is nearby at this very moment. When she has mixed the flour fully with the blood, she goes out with a rope to the cliff and ties it about the post Erik knocked into the ground for this purpose five years before.

She lets a basket down, and her eyes linger a moment too long on the rocks below. The whale has come to her less and less, but now she sees it sprawled on the toothed jags, its sides heaving. The smell of salt and rot comes into her nostrils, and she wipes it away, blinks until the vision is gone.

She bends and ties another rope over this one, tugging the knot to make it strong. The other end she knots about her waist, tucks her skirts up into the rope and takes the easy route down to the nearest guillemot nest, her mind too full to attempt the trickier path. The birds lift, shrieking, and her head rings with their cries. She works methodically, taking five eggs from three nests, extending mercy to the smallest ones, the ones with fine freckles or that are pale as cream. Below it is low tide, and she remembers pulling Toril's son from the waves, his body slack and moving about on its bones.

She climbs up quickly, brings up the basket, and goes back to the house. She cracks the eggs one after another into the blood and flour, the shells breaking easily and speckling the mixture so she must scoop with her fingernails, draglines of blood drying quickly beneath them.

They have a blodplättar between them for lunch, the house filling with the smell of iron and salt. Her mother is mercifully silent as they eat: Maren knows she will be thinking of Erik, how these were his favourite. When Maren wraps one, still steaming, in a piece of cloth to take to Diinna on her way to the headland, Mamma doesn't raise an objection.

•

"Thought I could smell blodplättar," says Diinna. She is sitting on her step, Erik playing in the earth below. She takes the cloth carefully. "Saw you going to the cliff. Did you check the knots?" She unwraps it, breathes it in.

"No need to thank me," says Maren, her annoyance a bubble bursting. She turns to go, but Diinna reaches out with her strong hand, grasps her softly about the wrist.

"Thank you, Maren." It is a shock sudden as a slap to see Diinna's dark eyes shining. "If you need me to help you next time, ask. I am a better climber."

Maren nods, swallows. She rubs the top of Diinna's hand. "I will."

As she steps from the shadow of their house, she hears Diinna coo softly to her son.

"Come, *ráhkis*. Come and taste. Your father loved these."

As Maren walks she thinks only of Ursa: whether she will be at their agreed meeting-place, what she will do if she isn't. The alternate pleasure and panic have her almost breathless, so when she sights Ursa's figure in a light grey dress at the headland her head spins and she must slow her tread to keep from stumbling.

For a thin moment the double trick of the low sun off the sea is dazzling, and she thinks perhaps it isn't her at all. The face is mask-like at this distance, the pale blonde hair whipped to frenzy about the head, the dark eyes two holes set deep and swallowing beneath knitted brows. But in another moment Ursa is smiling, herself again, and raising one hand to wave, the other at her swirling skirts, and it is all Maren can do to keep from running to her and sweeping her up in her arms.

She stops short of embracing her, for though Ursa's mouth is wide her eyes are strained, hollows like bruises beneath them. Maren resists the urge to reach up, place her thumbs at them to soothe them.

"Kirsten found you then? I thought it best not to come directly, but did not wish to wait till evening."

"You are unwell?"

"It is so obvious?" says Ursa. "I kept to bed all day yesterday. It is why we were another day delayed. I hope you did not wait for long."

Maren says nothing of the night before, her anxious pacing of the cliff. The ground at their feet is scuffed and worn by her tread, and she shifts to cover the worst of it.

"What ails you?"

"A poor stomach, only. You have given me a peasant's appetite." She smiles more weakly. "The cooking at Vardøhus did for me. And, perhaps, the drink."

Maren imagines her made slack-limbed by it, like Pappa at midwinter.

"You are shocked?" says Ursa. "You would have drunk in such company."

"Your visit was not good?"

"My husband would say it was. The Lensmann is a great admirer of his deeds."

"That is good for you. It means you are like to stay?"

Ursa looks at her, forehead creased.

"The Lensmann was a beast. All of them were, even his wife." She takes in a sharp breath, holds her hand to her side. Maren moves closer.

"Perhaps we should go somewhere to sit? You are very pale."

"My husband is at home. He is writing, some edict or another. We will hear all at kirke. But I wanted to tell you— Diinna is mentioned."

"Mentioned?"

"My husband told the Lensmann of the runes, and he was not greatly pleased. The poppets too. I have a thought to tell Fru Olufsdatter, but I wanted to tell you about Diinna first."

"You think it a bad thing?" says Maren, though she knows

it is. She is trying to grasp the edges of the situation, feel out what sort of trouble Ursa's confidence holds.

"My husband will not tell me more, but there was talk of witchcraft. There were two men in the gaol. Lapp men."

"It is not witchcraft, what Diinna does. The runes were only what prayers are to us."

"You should learn a better argument," says Ursa. "It wouldn't please him to hear you say such a thing. I have certainly spoken well of her to my husband, but the Lensmann has his mind and I discovered he has some past in dealings with witches."

"Diinna is no witch," snaps Maren, her panic making her voice harsher than she meant it to be.

Ursa's voice is deliberately calm. "Perhaps she should come to kirke?"

"I will have no luck with that." Maren's throat feels tight. "Especially after Toril turned up at the Wednesday meet. She doesn't trust my opinion on such things."

All her joy at seeing Ursa again has been snatched to pieces by this news, and she begins to pace a small path before her, a route in miniature of what she trod waiting for Ursa.

"Perhaps I could speak with her?" Ursa's hand rests upon her forearm, stilling her. "I really think it important."

Maren can't imagine it having more of an effect, but her touch sets more nerves jangling. "What else did they say of her?"

"Nothing. But the talk... it was none of it good." Ursa brings her hands up suddenly to her face, speaks in a strangled voice. "Forgive me. I did not know the man I married. If I had, I would have warned you, wouldn't have brought you close to me, to us."

Maren holds herself. "I was mentioned?"

"Goodness, no," says Ursa. "I would never have let your name be spoken in such a way. I wouldn't have allowed it."

She takes both Maren's hands in her own, holds them tightly. "You are very dear to me, you know that, do you not? I could never let harm come to you."

This is the time, thinks Maren with Ursa's fierce, lovely face before her, their gazes locked, that she should kiss her. The thought is terrifying: but Maren is certain that if she were a man, she would close the distance and press her mouth to Ursa's, stop up her words with kisses. But she only nods. "I do."

"Shall we go then?" Ursa says, the moment broken. "To speak with Diinna?"

"It will not do any good," says Maren. She doesn't want their time together to be over so soon, to go back to the village and to other people. But she allows Ursa to lead her back anyway, her head dipped against the wind so the creamy nape of her neck shows.

"What more of Vardøhus, of the wife?" Ursa asks.

"Nothing. It is a drear place however mightily built. And she..." She hesitates, reaching for the right word in a way that makes Maren think she has not thought long on her after. It makes her very glad. "Is lonely there, I think. I did not care for her."

It was not a danger she had considered, that Ursa might like Fru Cunningham enough to take her into her confidence. Maren feels a swooping sort of relief, as though a pit has been narrowly avoided.

"Are runes really only like prayers?" Ursa asks. "Aren't they meant to call things, summon things? They spoke of wind-weaving."

"Diinna doesn't do that. The runes were harmless." To guide Maren's brother and father's soul to safety. She had believed it, because in those months she was grasping for something, anything, to order the chaos that the storm set amongst them. From Varr's drum to the runes, she had found comfort in it.

Though she could swear against it in a court if she must, it would be a lie.

Does Commissioner Cornet also know of the runestones left on the headland, of the skinned foxes and the talk of five-finned whales? With Toril close in his ear, she can't doubt it. None of that was Diinna, Maren is almost certain, but blame could easily be laid at her door. It can be claimed as simple superstition, of course, but now she sees it was ignorantly done, just as the fishing had been. And Commissioner Cornet's arrival, though it has brought Ursa to her, has pulled back that protective veil in a way that Pastor Kurtsson's presence never did.

Diinna is still on her step, Erik on her lap. His head is drawn into her chest, and Maren realizes suddenly that Erik's mouth is around his mother's nipple. Ursa comes to a sudden halt, her purpose fading as a blush reddens her cheek.

Diinna looks up at them both, and Maren, suddenly, sees her as a stranger would, as Ursa must. Her legs apart the better to bear the weight of her too-grown son, her heavy breast slipped between the folds of her jerkin. Veins stand out, rivers against the thin skin. Her hair is greased and flat to her head, her eyes dark with challenge. With Erik clasped to her, she looks like some sort of deity, powerful and strange. Maren can't stop her eyes going to her breast. She turns away, her mouth dry.

"We should not be here."

"She should not be doing such a thing outside," says Ursa, voice faint. "What if Absalom were to see?"

Maren looks about them. They are shielded from all houses but the ruin of Baar Ragnvalsson's, the wheeling birds their only witnesses.

Diinna has moved Erik from her breast and set him on his feet. She rebuttons her jerkin. She doesn't look even a little ashamed.

"I had thought you would be away for longer," she says as Erik reaches up to her front. She pushes his hands away, stands. "You are usually a long time at the headland."

There is a sharpness to her voice that makes Maren uneasy. "Mistress Cornet wished to speak with you," says Maren. She feels furious, and isn't sure why. "You have a perfectly good door—why do you not use it?"

"What is it you wish to say?" Diinna turns her heavy-lidded eyes upon Ursa. "Mistress Cornet?"

Ursa gets straight to it. "I have just come from Vardøhus. My husband was invited to dine with Lensmann Cunningham. There was talk of you, at dinner."

Diinna does not expect this, Maren can tell, though she hides her surprise well. There is only a slight movement at her jaw and Ursa, missing it, tries harder to impress upon her the situation.

"There were two Lapps in the gaol there." Her jaw tightens further. "They were wind-weavers."

"I do not do that," says Diinna.

"But the runes were mentioned, Diinna," says Maren. "The poppets too."

"Fru Olufsdatter made those herself," she says. "I only told her which herbs to burn for remembrance."

"And she is like to be in trouble too," says Maren. "But it is you we must concern ourselves with."

"You need not concern yourself with me at all. The time for that is long past."

"It is Ursa who wanted to tell you," says Maren, turning away so Diinna doesn't see the hurt in her face. "She thinks it important."

"You should come to kirke," says Ursa. "I do not think the situation beyond remedy."

"You don't?" says Diinna, disbelief in her voice, and Ursa

shifts, uncomfortable beneath her gaze. "With two Lapps, as you say, in the gaol, no doubt waiting to burn?"

Maren waits for Ursa to refute it, feels a mounting pressure in her throat when she doesn't.

"I do not believe my husband to be above mercy." There is nothing convincing in Ursa's voice.

"I have heard what happens when my people throw themselves upon the mercy of men like your husband, Mistress Cornet." She bends and picks up Erik, holds him at her hip. "I wouldn't be so certain."

Diinna strides across her threshold and closes the door. Maren hesitates a few moments before she follows her. She doesn't knock but pushes full inside, catching Erik on the leg with the door so he lets out a soft wail. Maren shuts Ursa out, and turns to the room. It has been years since she has been in here, perhaps even since it was newly built and Diinna and Erik just married, and she filled the room with small white and yellow flowers, helped bring them their gifts of skrei and strung them from the rafters like miniature sails.

There are no flowers here now. What had felt cramped for a newly married couple feels somehow tinier with a mother and her son. The fire is banked and a thick blanket is hung at the window, so the whole room is in shadow and Diinna blinks at her through the gloom like some nocturnal bird. Erik goes to a corner that is scattered with small cloth shapes, some sticks, like a nest. It smells of off milk, and blodplättar, seeping in from their house. Her brother's boots are beside the fire, in echo of where Pappa's are next door. One is unlaced, its tongue gaping, the inside dark as a mouth.

Maren had come to accuse Diinna of rudeness, to tell her she spoke falsely when she said she was no longer Maren's concern, but in this room that feels impossible. They have failed her, failed Erik, failed Erik's memory.

"Diinna..."

Then she sees a knotted figure over the fire, wrapped in Toril's missing lace. The sight makes Maren stumble. There is a silver needle, stuck into its side.

"What is that?"

Diinna follows her gaze, then takes up the poppet. "Nothing. A doll for Erik."

"That is Toril's lace."

Diinna pulls the needle from it, unwraps the scrap of lace. "You want to give it back to her?"

Maren shakes her head, and Diinna drops it onto the fire. Maren makes a convulsive movement, as if to rescue the fabric, but it has caught, is already twisting and curling up.

She looks about the room, spies runestones beside the bed, a handful of rabbit spine bones next to the empty boots. The hairs on her arms lift.

"Diinna, what is all this?"

"All what?" Diinna lays the poppet at the centre of a large square of cloth spread flat on the bed. On top of this she puts a fox-tail scarf, thick mittens, her knife, a tunic.

"What are you doing?"

"You must not tell anyone," she says, not stopping. "Not even her."

"You can't go." Maren feels a flutter of panic. "Diinna, you are no witch."

But there is uncertainty in her voice, and Diinna looks up at her sharply. "You don't sound so sure."

Maren's hands tremble, and she realizes she is a little afraid. "The poppet—"

"A doll," says Diinna. "For Erik. I took the lace out of spite, and to make the fabric less coarse."

Maren's eyes trail to the bones, the runestones, and Diinna lets out a sad, low laugh. "I remember once when runes gave you comfort, when sailors came to my father to cast bones and tell them of their time left to come. They are a language, Maren. Just because you do not speak it doesn't make it devilry."

Maren nods, ashamed. She wants to apologize, but knows it will sound weak. Instead she repeats herself. "You're no witch."

"It doesn't matter what I am, only what they believe I am."

"Ursa thinks it will be all right, thinks he will—"

"What does she know of any of it?" Diinna's voice frays. "What do you know? I have stayed for you, so Erik may know his family. But it is not safe here."

"You aren't taking him?"

"He is my son," she says. "You can't think me able to leave him behind."

"How will he survive, on the low mountain?"

"We will have to go further than that," says Diinna. "But wherever we land he will survive better than he has here." She looks about the squalid room. "This is no place for a child. He needs air, he needs trees, he needs people who will not look at him as though he is something broken, or half made." She shoots a poisonous look at the wall through which Maren can hear her mother still at work with the butter churn. "I should have taken him when his father died."

Maren catches Diinna's hand, tries to delay her. "Please, stay."

"It isn't safe."

"I can keep you safe."

She shakes her head, brings her hand up to Maren's cheek. "We are nothing to them. We are as men to the sea, caught on their currents." She rests her forehead against Maren's. Her skin is dry as sand.

"You could come too," she says. Maren jerks away. "Varr summers beyond the low mountain, in the forests south. They will not follow there, and if they do, we know how to hide if we must."

"I can't leave Mamma." She can't leave Ursa. "And there is no danger for me here."

Diinna looks as though she wants to say more, but she only knots the first bundle, takes another blanket from a shelf, and spreads it out to start another.

There is so much Maren wants to say, manages only, "When will you go?"

"Tonight. I will take Baar's boat—"

"It's a ruin," says Maren. "Take Kirsten's. I know she will not mind."

Diinna nods. "She can say I stole it. I'll leave it safe on the shore."

Maren scoops up Erik, holds him to her, breathes in his milky smell. "I have something for you. Some coins—"

"Keep them," says Diinna. "I'll have no use for them in the forests."

"What if you are caught—"

"Tell no one," says Diinna. She comes before her again, wraps her arms around them both, and Maren clenches her jaw so hard she hears something pop.

"Be careful," whispers Diinna, her breath tickling her ear. "Even of her."

She draws back, places her thumb on Maren's forehead. "Should you need to find me."

Maren clenches her eyes shut, remembering Diinna pressing the same thread to her brother's forehead before he left that Christmas Eve. "Diinna…" Maren catches her hand before she draws it away. "Will you sing it to me? His *joik*?"

She is sure Diinna will deny her, but instead she brings her mouth close to Maren's ear and sings. The tune is lilting and soft, and Maren recognizes some of it from through the wall, but it is altogether stranger and more beautiful against her cheek. When it ends it feels as though something has been snatched from her. Erik is calm and smiling after the song, and Maren presses a last kiss to his cool cheek, breathes him in, before passing him back to his mother.

She tumbles from the house bewildered, a sob caught in her throat. Ursa's hair is bright after the gloom.

"Will she come to kirke?"

"She will," says Maren, because it is easier, and Ursa's face lightens at the lie.

●

That night, Maren hears no sound though she sleeps in her old bed, presses her ear to the wall. She thinks Diinna must have changed her mind, goes at first light to her door.

It is unlatched and opens at her touch. There is nothing within but Erik's boots, empty beside the dead fire. Maren goes to the neat bed. She wants to throw the curtains wide, to let air and light touch the places so long held in dark. But she doesn't.

She only closes the door behind her, sits heavily on the bed. This is where her brother lay, where her nephew was got. She spreads wide her palms, presses them to the frame, trying to call something of them to her. Maren feels suddenly alone, as she had in the mist when she lost Erik on the headland. But this time, the mist will not lift. There is no one coming for her. Not her sweet, quiet brother with his heavy brows and slow laugh. Not Pappa, not even Mamma.

Her cry catches, sharp as a hook. She touches her fingers to the spot Diinna placed a thread to reel them together again, and something in her knows that just as it did for her brother, the cord has already been broken.

THIRTY-ONE

Absalom spends the following day at home, sitting at the table. Ursa is unused to his company, can't settle to any one task. Their trip to Vardøhus had been illuminating and horrifying in equal measure, and now she feels she can never come close to liking, let alone loving, him.

He is absolutely focused, the two letters the Lensmann has given him lying with their seals broken before him, while he brings out the census he made in kirke the first day and runs his fingers down what she knows to be the lines of names, then writes on a third piece of parchment in small, cramped writing.

"What are you working at, Absalom?"

"A list."

He is excited: she can feel it sloughing off him, just as it had in the Lensmann's dining room, and it makes her afraid. She wishes she could escape to Maren, but doesn't want to draw his attention to their closeness, not with Diinna in her perilous state. She feels as though they are all of them balanced upon a precipice, and her husband is chipping at the stone beneath their feet.

"A list?"

"For the Lensmann. You will see."

That night he wants her fully naked despite the sucking cold of the dark room, and when he moves into her, he places his hands beneath her shoulder blades, moves his thumb up and down their length. It feels to her as though he is fingering a wound, making her skin raw. She thinks he is trying to be gentle, but she can't make herself open enough for him, and he must push in a way that makes her lock up further.

When he is finished, he watches as she pulls the nightdress back over herself. He doesn't roll over to sleep, but takes her hand and looks up to the ceiling. She lets it settle in his vast grasp, turns her head away, feeling his stickiness coming from between her legs.

"Will you have a child soon?" His breath is still heavy. "The ship. The chamber pot. That was one lost, was it not? Are you like your mother?"

"I hope not, husband," says Ursa.

"I hope not, Ursula," he repeats. "I shall want sons, five sons. I had four brothers that lived. We were all of us the terror of our town. It was a good way to grow."

"We couldn't keep five boys here," she says, faintly.

"That will soon be sorted."

She doesn't like the way he says it, as though he has a secret.

"Have there been more?" he asks.

"More?"

"Losses."

Her cheeks grow warm. She doesn't want to speak of such things, not with him. "No."

"I hope you are praying for our sons."

"Yes," she says, though she knows she will not pray for five. She wouldn't mind one, hopes he will be no terror. If she were to bear Absalom a child, she would wish for a daughter, with Agnete's smile and nothing of him. Though the world is not tender for girls, she would want someone to understand her the way Agnete did, to love her as she loved Mother.

"Pray with me now." He rolls onto his side so they are facing each other, catches her hands in his and closes his eyes, mouthing silently. She studies the brute force of his face, made restful in prayer, repeats his *Amen*. He smiles at her. "We will have a legacy fit to match my work here. I will write that letter for you soon," he says. "Is there anything you would like me to say especially?"

"I will leave it to you."

"Good," he says, plants a final kiss on her forehead.

They drop hands, roll to their sides of the bed, and she presses her hand to her lower belly, willing his seed out of her.

•

Ursa wakes to an empty house, a dirty cup on the table, shudders when she thinks of him watching her as she slept.

She climbs from the bed and pours water still hot from the fire into her washbowl, scrubs at herself with a rag, reaching up inside until she is as sure as she can be that she is free of him. She begins to dress, fast in the cold room, thinking to walk to Maren's, to check that Diinna has taken her words to heart, but there is a cry from outside, sounding very close by, which spurs her into action.

The cry comes again, and outside it is louder but she is less certain of its source. Someone comes running past her—Ursa can't remember her name: Edne, Ebbe?—holding her skirts clear of her legs. She is running towards Maren's house, and for a terrible moment Ursa begins to follow her. But a loud sob, imploring, comes from behind.

Fru Olufsdatter's door is wide open on its hinges and slapping at the wall. From this angle Ursa can see nothing within, but as she watches, a man she doesn't recognize, slight and tall, comes to the doorway and closes it. A semicircle of women stand about outside. She is too far off to note their expressions, but several have their hands at their mouths.

She sees other faces at other thresholds, other shapes moving between houses like animals between trees towards the sound. She wants to go back inside, makes for the door. Fear grips her at the backs of the knees, loosens her legs, and for a moment she must cling on to the latch.

The women's attention breaks from the house as she approaches. Several scatter, faces downturned, but Toril walks towards her, grips her upper arms painfully, delight plain on her thin face.

"He has acted, at last! Mistress Cornet, it is a blessed day indeed."

Ursa shrugs her off. "Acted? What is happening?"

"Surely he told you?" The woman doesn't even bother to hide her smile. "Mistress Cornet, he is in there now, with Fru Olufsdatter. He is arresting her."

Her heartbeat becomes painful. "Arresting her? What is her crime?"

"We do not know exactly," Sigfrid says, coming to stand beside Toril. She is paler, less triumphant, but her voice is breathless with exhilaration. "But no doubt her crimes are numerous. Their workings are apparent once you spot them."

Toril squeezes Sigfrid's shoulder. "We will be safer now, my friend."

Ursa looks to the other women. She knows none of them well—one, Gerda, comes to Wednesday meets but doesn't speak much. The others must be the kirke-women, as Kirsten named them.

The door is thrown open, and Fru Olufsdatter comes out, bound at her wrists with the thin stranger beside her, a stripe of blood upon her white apron though she looks unhurt. Absalom walks close behind, his sheaf of papers tucked to his chest. His face is grave, mouth twitching with excitement. He spots Ursa—she sees his sharp intake of breath—but doesn't speak to her, only brushes past.

"Husband," she says. "Absalom. Where are you taking her?"

"To Vardøhus." He speaks not only to her but lets the words ring out. "To the witches' hole."

"She is no witch," says Ursa, desperate, remembering the squalid building where the Lapps were kept. "I have been often to her house, prayed there often—"

"I knew her for it," says Toril, a sheen on her upper lip. She is rank with agitation; Ursa can smell it in her sweat. "Witchcraft. Her fine house—how would she keep it so well alone, other than with help from familiars? And the poppets—"

"And the marks upon my arm," says Sigfrid. "Twelve small black holes, like a beast's bite marks."

Ursa blinks at her. She sounds mad. But Absalom nods gravely at them, places a hand upon each of them as though in benediction.

"You will be called for testimony," he says. He follows as Fru Olufsdatter is pulled away. She is weeping, bound hands scrabbling at her face. Ursa can't bring herself to go to her. Instead she rounds on Toril and Sigfrid.

"What are these marks? Show me."

"It isn't decent," says the woman, flushing.

"God damns a liar, Fru Jonsdatter."

"She is no liar," says Toril.

"Was it you who told my husband of the poppets? They were gestures of remembrance, nothing more."

"They were poppets," says Toril. "We all saw them for what they were." The other women nod. "She got them from that Lapp. She is next, no doubt."

Ursa runs, skirts pulled over her knees. Maren's door is open too and for a terrible moment she thinks she is too late, her husband's men already inside, but as she calls for her Maren emerges, Edne's frightened face pale within. Beside her sits Maren's mother. The relief stabs at her side like a stitch and she grasps at her ribs.

"She told you?"

"Yes."

"You must warn Diinna. I thought she had time to make amends, I thought—"

"She's gone." Maren says this low, so only Ursa can hear.

"Gone?"

Maren holds her finger to her lips. "In the night. They will not catch her now."

Ursa sways, her breath still difficult, and Maren steadies her with a hand beneath her elbow. Her words and touch are so welcome Ursa wants to catch up her hand and kiss it.

"Come inside."

Despite their months of friendship, Ursa has never entered Maren's house. It is laid out similarly to theirs—a single room with the fire at one end, a bed at the other, and a narrower bed snug in a corner—but it is barely a quarter of the size. With the four of them inside there is hardly space to crowd around the table as they sit, knees knocking together.

"What happened?" says Maren's mother. "We can get no sense from Edne beyond that your husband is coming."

"They have arrested Fru Olufsdatter," says Ursa, the words feeling unreal in her mouth. "For witchcraft."

Maren's mother inhales, her breath a hiss through gapped teeth. "Does Toril know of this?"

"It was Toril who accused her."

The woman's tongue darts out the side of her mouth, licks the sore spot. Ursa looks away.

"You knew this was coming," says Maren, her hands clenching compulsively on the tabletop. "Didn't you?"

Her mother's silence is confirmation enough, and Maren flies to her feet, knocking her chair to the floor. Ursa rises too, ready to get between them, but Maren only begins to pace the short length of the room, finger pointed in accusation at her mother. "And you would let them take Diinna too? Leave your grandson without a mother?"

"Better no mother at all than a witch."

The knock comes into Maren's stunned silence, and Ursa is the only one who moves when it comes again, harder this time. Absalom is there, his eyebrows rising.

"You are here, wife?" He strides inside. The remaining air is squeezed from the room. "Where is the Lapp?"

"Next door," says Maren's mother, standing slowly. "I will show you, commissioner. My grandson may be upset. I will keep him safely."

Edne follows them out, scurries back to the other houses. Maren is frozen by the door, and Ursa can hear her husband's heavy tread, his heavier knock, and the lifting of the latch.

There is a moment's silence, and then a wail, high and anguished from Maren's mother, words fading in and out of understanding.

Absalom's tread comes faster this time and he is back in the room, face furious. "Where is she? Where has she gone?"

"She is gone?" says Maren faintly, and if she had not whispered the news to Ursa a few minutes previously, Ursa would have believed her shock. "And Erik? My brother's child, is he there?"

The tears that come to Maren's eyes are as real as any, and Ursa can't stop herself reaching for her across the table. "Absalom, please. This is a terrible shock for them."

He snarls with rage. "She can't be far. We will find her."

He storms from the house, leaving the door wide open, and Ursa can breathe again. Maren's tears do not stop for a long while, and through the wall comes a high keening, like an animal in pain. Maren presses her hands over her ears, jaw clenched.

"Maren," whispers Ursa. "Let's go. Come, let's go."

Maren lets Ursa help her to her feet, and she is barely any weight at all. Though Maren is the taller, she slumps against Ursa, drags her feet as they pass the open door where Maren's mother sits on the floor and weeps.

Ursa considers their options. They could go past the ruined house and into the wild land. But already Ursa can see small shapes upon it, more men dressed in black, looking for Diinna and her son. The sight sends a terror through her, the swarming men dark as insects on a carcass.

Though all she needs is a quiet place, a lonely place, she turns them for home, keeping her head down, Maren's hand shielding her face. As they reach it, there is the sound of raised voices, and they round the house in time to see the same group of women who watched Fru Olufsdatter be led away gasping and parting as the solid, unmistakeable figure of Kirsten shoves another black-clad stranger full to the ground.

"Kirsten!" cries Maren. She straightens, hurries forward. "What are you doing?"

"This dritt thinks he can lay hands on me."

"He is the commissioner's man, the Lensmann's guard!"

"He is not my husband," says Kirsten, looming over the man, who is skidding backwards on his heels. "And should not touch me."

The guard gets to his feet. He is a head shorter than Kirsten, as shrunk by her rage as she is grown by it. But more strangers are coming from the direction of Vardøhus, more men than Ursa has seen since the ship. They must have been sent from elsewhere, Alta or Varanger.

And there, emerging awful as a nightmare from between two houses, her husband, approaching Kirsten with triumph glinting in his eyes. How had she ever thought him handsome? His face is brute and cunning as a wolf's.

He closes the distance, more men at his back. How long has this been planned? she thinks. How long has the noose been closing without her, who was closest to it all, guessing at it?

"A step ahead of me again, wife?" he murmurs as he passes her.

"You are not to resist," says the thrown man, emboldened by Absalom's presence, brushing himself down. "You are accused."

"Who accuses me?"

"I do, Kirsten Sørensdatter," says Toril.

"And I," says Sigfrid.

"And me," says a tight voice behind them. Ursa turns to see Maren's mother, face wild with tears, lift a trembling hand and outstretch her finger. "Witch."

THIRTY-TWO

Maren watches as the word ripples around the assembled women like a current. One by one they raise their fingers, hatred so bald and terrible on their faces it makes Maren's breath catch in her throat. All the kirke-women, Toril and Sigfrid and Lisbet and Magda, and even Edne, who came to warn her of Fru Olufsdatter's arrest, who sat beside her in the boat and rowed until their arms ached and grew strong.

Maren tries to catch her eye, but Edne looks about the group, to Kirsten and to Absalom. His gaze falls upon her in return, and Edne, too, raises her hand, so fast it is as if it has been pulled on a string. Kirsten stands alone in the centre of their arrowing hands, and the fight seems to flood from her sudden as blood.

"Of what am I accused?"

"You will hear your charges in court," says Absalom. "But they are most grave."

Maren can't let her stand alone, starts forward, but Ursa catches her about the wrist, digs her fingernail in. "No, please."

No one else could have stayed her in that moment. But she is helpless at Ursa's touch, undone by the need in her voice.

She watches, betrayal thumping its drum in her chest as Kirsten is bound at the wrists and led in the direction of Vardøhus.

With the focus of their accusation removed, the women drop their hands, blink about them as though emerging from a daze. Edne is breathing hard, places her hands on her knees and retches. Toril rubs her back, satisfied.

"You did well, girl."

Edne pulls away, straightening with the same jerky motion that made her raise her hand. "I am no girl. I am a woman same as you."

Edne looks around, and Maren knows she is looking for her. Their eyes meet, and Maren sees the wretchedness in Edne's face. It sends cold fury thrumming through her, and her hands itch, but she dare not approach with the men still circling the village.

"Come away," says Ursa, perhaps sensing her impulse and pulling softly on her.

Maren follows her to the second boathouse. The door closed, Ursa pulls Maren in to her, tucks her chin over her shoulder, murmurs nothings into her hair.

Both of them are trembling, and Maren lets herself be swept on the tide of Ursa's voice, lifts her hand slowly to Ursa's soft hair, coming loose from its hurried knot, the smooth rope of it like fine cloth between her coarse fingers. She breathes her in, her lips a moment away from Ursa's neck, and as her friend releases her, Maren lets them brush against her, so slight that she could have imagined it.

Ursa gives no sign of noticing as she settles Maren in a chair, begins to brew tea. Her hands shake and clatter the cups. "You must be careful."

"I need to speak with him." Maren voices the thought before it is fully come.

"Who?" says Ursa, and there is a challenge in her voice, as though daring Maren to say.

"Your husband," Maren pushes on, the idea taking hold. "I need to tell him he is wrong."

She rises to her feet and Ursa hurries to her, places her hand on her shoulder to force her back down. Maren lets her. "That would be a mistake."

"This is all a mistake." Maren clenches her fists to stop her fingers shaking. "It's Kirsten, Ursa."

Ursa turns away, back to the hearth. "You must not draw attention to yourself." Her hands are white birds, fluttering about the pot. "A trap is set, and I will not have you be the next to walk into it."

"Then I should not be here," says Maren, "in his house."

Ursa stays her with a look. "You are perhaps safest here, with me."

Maren can barely sit still. Her leg jigs beneath the table. "What will we do for Kirsten?"

"Do you not hear me, Maren? We can do nothing for her but wait."

"With such a chorus against her?" Maren shakes her head. "Someone must speak for her."

"Then it should be me, not you," says Ursa, bringing cups to the table with shaking fingers. In her distress she has not added leaves, sits with hot water steaming before her. "Your position is not good, Maren. Even I can see that. You should leave, perhaps, like Diinna."

Maren looks at her sharply. "Leave?"

"You could go to Bergen, to my household. My father could keep you safe."

The terror of leaving Ursa comes harder than that of the arrests. "How would it look, if I fled? I am guilty of nothing, Ursa."

"No more than Kirsten and Fru Olufsdatter?" she snaps back. "And see where their innocence has got them."

There is sense in what she says, though Maren would wish it different. She would wish it all different.

"They cannot hurt them," says Ursa. "Not for nothing."

"You know they can," says Maren, her anger flaring at Ursa's suggestion of leaving. "You are the one married to a witch-hunter."

Ursa flinches, and Maren wishes she could draw her words back inside her mouth.

"He is as apart from me as Toril or Sigfrid or any of them," says Ursa. "You cannot think I knew."

Maren slumps, ashamed. "Of course I don't. My mother—" she winces at the sharp pain in her chest—"oh, God, my mother."

"She is not herself," says Ursa. "Even I can see that. She is taken in by Toril. Toril is the true evil at the heart of it, alongside my husband. And the Lensmann, who sent him. This was his plan all along, to make witches here in the North. He thinks the whole place corrupted."

"I have been blind," says Maren, sunk deep inside her own thoughts. "I did not guess at their hatred of her."

"Kirsten?"

Maren nods. "Even Edne—"

"Nonsense. You warned Kirsten, but it did no good."

"And Fru Olufsdatter," says Maren. "Why is she accused? She has done nothing to draw attention to herself."

"They said she bit them."

Maren blinks at her, astonished. "*Bit* them? Fru Olufsdatter?"

Ursa gives a shaky laugh, then seems to catch herself. "I am sorry. It's only...it's absurd." Ursa wraps her hands around her cup. "The poppets too, and they mentioned the house, how large and well kept it is."

"Toril always had an envy of it."

"You think envy enough to cause this?"

Maren doesn't want to say it, though she does think it. "She is no witch. Those things they said about her, the bite marks. It is all lies."

"I had thought there was something between you and Fru Olufsdatter?" Ursa is watching her closely.

"Between us?"

"A bad air. A dislike."

"I have never disliked her," says Maren. "She does not like me, that is true."

"Why?"

Maren sighs. "Her son, Dag Bjørnsson. He was my betrothed. She did not think me right for him." She looks to the spot where the bed is now nooked beneath the broad beams, remembers Dag's hands hungry upon her. "Did not want us to have this house."

"This house?" Ursa looks aghast, mouth slack. "You mean, this was to be your home?"

Maren nods.

Ursa covers her face with her hands. "How stupid I have been. To make you work like a servant in the house you would be mistress of."

"I thought," says Maren, "I was here lately as a friend."

"You are." Ursa reaches for her. "The greatest friend I have ever known."

Her touch is warm from the cup, and Maren feels as though she is ice pooling into water. Her whole body loosens, and she wants Ursa to hold her as she had when they first entered the house. But Ursa lets go a moment later, looking down at her cup.

"No leaves," she says, letting out a brief, empty laugh. "Why did you not tell me?"

"I didn't notice," lies Maren. "Besides, I'd rather beer if you have it."

Ursa shakes her head. "Nor akevitt."

Maren rises suddenly, surprising even herself. "Kirsten has some, at her house."

Ursa gapes at her. "You cannot think to go there. Not now."

"Why not?" says Maren, recklessness making her light-headed. "She is not at home, after all."

She lets out a hiccupping laugh, and Ursa stands too, moves quickly around the table and steadies her with a hand on her shoulder. "Maren—"

"Are you coming?" Maren shrugs her off. Her skin prickles. Her need to see Kirsten's house is urgent as thirst.

"Do you not have any at your house?"

"I'm not going back," says Maren, with such vehemence Ursa starts. "Not with that woman there."

Mamma's pointed finger floats before Maren's eyes, and she rubs her hand roughly across her face, to wipe the vision away.

"The men are all over town..." says Ursa.

"So it would be better if I were with the commissioner's wife, surely?"

Maren leaves the second boathouse, not checking to see if Ursa is following. She knows she will. Ursa's footsteps are half a beat behind as Maren strides through the houses. Fru Olufsdatter's door gapes, and Maren can see men moving about inside.

"They are searching," hisses Ursa. "They may well be at Kirsten's too."

Maren knows this is designed to stay her, but she increases her pace, her feet carrying her past Toril's house, which is lit and loud with talk. She wants to push inside and knock a lamp over, spread the embers from the fire beneath their feet, set the whole house aflame. But she hurries on, past the kirke and Sigfrid's house, past the traitor Edne's until she sees the Petersson farm with its reindeer circulating pale as spirits on the fields.

Ursa's breath is coming fast, and Maren can tell she is dropping back, unable to keep up, but she does not stop until she reaches the door set between its two windows, staring blank-faced at the sea. It is still closed up tightly, and Maren peers briefly in. Aside from the loose, foggy light of the burnt-down fire, it is dark and empty.

Ursa catches up, her breathing ragged. "We must not go in. They will be finished with Fru Olufsdatter's home soon enough."

"You do not have to," says Maren, her hand upon the latch.

"What is this about?" Ursa gives a stamp of her foot in frustration. "You can't have me believe you are so desperate for a drink?"

Maren's heart is hammering, and she realizes the walk has wrung out her breath too. The latch is ice beneath her fingers. "I want..." She searches for the words, how to express the want to see Kirsten's home for herself, the thoughts coming clear even as she speaks them into being. "I need to be sure there is nothing here. Nothing for them to find."

Ursa's eyebrows rise. "You think it possible?"

"I know it is impossible that Kirsten is a witch," says Maren. She remembers the runestones in Diinna's room, the casting bones and the needle glinting against Toril's lace. "But they may find things they do not understand, things they can use against her."

"All right," says Ursa, nodding slowly. "We must be quick."

Maren pushes inside. Ursa follows cautiously, as if stepping onto a boat. "What are we looking for?"

Maren breaks the bank of the fire, feeds it another square of peat so it sends up a flare of light and heat. "You will know better than I. Anything that seems out of place to you, that you do not understand."

"Like those?" She points, and Maren follows her finger to two runestones laid beside the bed.

She crosses quickly and scoops them up. There is the mark of safety on one, smooth sea on another, and she knows that together they are a Sámi remedy for bad dreams. She closes her palms over them, wants to weep at the idea of Kirsten alone in this room, caught on the tide of a nightmare. She always seemed so solid, so strong, but she suffered as much loss as any. Did Kirsten see the whale too? Maren wonders.

"Maren?"

Ursa's voice is soft, and Maren turns to see her holding the trousers Kirsten wore to slaughter in. They are stained with rusty splatters, and by the firelight they look ghoulish. She nods. "Take those, too."

"What are we going to do with them?"

Maren eyes the fire. There is not enough fuel to burn the cloth entirely, and whilst it may scorch the stones it would not necessarily obscure the marks fully. She holds out her hand for them. Ursa passes them over. The cloth is soft with wear, and Maren slips the stones into the pockets.

She goes outside, Ursa following, and weights them with more stones from the ground, until the pockets are full. Then she drops them into the sea. They billow for a moment, and then plummet from sight.

"What now?" says Ursa, in a small voice.

Maren rolls her shoulders. They click like the snapping of bones. "Now we can fetch the beer."

•

They pass the group of men on their way back to the second boathouse. Maren keeps her head lifted, wishing the flagon of beer and bottle of clear akevitt in her hands were already inside her, giving her strength. The men's gaze feels physical upon her, and she wonders how she ever tolerated being watched in this way when their village was as full of men as it was of women.

Ursa's presence is protection, and a balm. They walk through the village swiftly. Toril's house is still bright and full of chatter, but Maren doesn't torture herself by looking inside. Fru Olufsdatter's house is quiet, and the door has been left ajar, the fire allowed to go out. Maren shivers.

Ursa stays her a few paces from the second boathouse. "Let me check he is not at home."

She opens the door cautiously, then gestures Maren inside. "He must be at Vardøhus. He is like to be a while if so."

Maren sets the drink down on the table while Ursa coaxes the fire back into full flame, and fetches two cups from the shelf Dag put above the hearth. Maren reaches for the beer, but Ursa points to the akevitt.

"I think it best." A smile tugs at Ursa's mouth. Her lips are very pink, slightly parted so Maren can see the glint of her teeth. Wordlessly, Maren pours a slug of akevitt into each cup. She has had it only once before, at Erik and Diinna's wedding. Maren had not really enjoyed the burning in her throat, the sudden heaviness of her legs and lids, but now she craves it. She knocks it back, and Ursa, after a moment's hesitation, copies her.

Immediately, she bends over, disappearing below the line of the table, and coughs violently. Maren rises, startled, thinking to fetch a bucket, but Ursa flaps her hand above the table, her head emerging a moment later.

"I'm all right," she splutters, rubbing her stomach. Her cheeks are flushed pink as her lips. "That is stronger than I'm used to." She taps the cup twice on the table, a gesture Maren has seen men make. "Another."

Maren laughs, and obeys. Ursa comes to sit beside her as they sip their second cup of akevitt. Maren can already feel the warmth kindling in her limbs. The room feels smaller than usual, and Maren can't stop her gaze drifting to the wall beside the fire, the wall where Dag used to press himself against her. Telling Ursa about him has brought him near again, so she can almost feel his hot breath on her neck.

Ursa is very close beside her, and Maren is not sure if the heat she feels comes from the fire, or her friend's body. She imagines leaning against her, resting her head on Ursa's shoulder. It would not be out of place, not beyond the intimacies they have already shared. But Maren is unsure whether she could rest her head so close to Ursa's, breathe in her sweet smell, feel the brush of Ursa's soft skin against her own dry forehead, and not turn her mouth towards her.

She shakes her head to loosen the thoughts, pinches the skin between thumb and forefinger with her nail. The pain brings her back into her body.

"Perhaps Kirsten will be freed soon," says Ursa into the silence, and Maren watches her profile, silhouetted against the fire. "Especially if they do not find anything at her house."

"Perhaps," says Maren, but she does not really believe it. She doesn't want to think about it, wants this moment to be a respite from the horrors of the day, the horrors yet to come. She takes another sip of akevitt, and Ursa mirrors her.

Their hands rest on the table, the distance between them so small Maren could brush her little finger against Ursa's wrist if she could only bring herself to stretch it fully out. But it is Ursa who closes the gap, taking Maren's hand easily, and squeezing.

"I will speak with Absalom," she says decisively. "We will get Kirsten home."

Guilt floods Maren's cheeks. She should be thinking on Kirsten's fate, on Kirsten's return and how they can help it come about. But Ursa's hand is so smooth, so tight about hers, and the akevitt is a fire in her belly, her head floating upon her shoulders—

Without warning, the door is thrown open. The two men standing there hesitate. Ursa snatches her hand away and Maren's rests alone, beached on the dark wood.

"Sorry, Mistress Cornet. We thought the house empty." He is looking at them both, unsure who to address. "Commissioner Cornet ordered us to begin moving now."

"Moving?" Ursa stands, and they turn their attention to her. Maren scoops up the bottle of akevitt and places it on the floor by her skirts, out of sight.

"Apologies, mistress. Yes. Most he wants kept, but the bed must be burnt."

"Bed..." says Ursa faintly. "What are you talking about?"

"The bed at the witch's," says the other man. "He wants yours brought instead."

"You are moving next door, Ursa," says Maren. She feels sick: her stomach churns about the liquor. "Is she not?"

"Yes, mistress," says the first, clearly unsure of how to address her and of who she is. She thinks he is the man Kirsten sent sprawling to the ground: his breeches are smeared with mud. "To the stabbur. It is only right the commissioner has the finest house."

"So that is it," hisses Maren, and Ursa strides forward to detract from it.

"Might I speak with my husband?"

"He is at Vardøhus, Mistress Cornet." The men are growing bored of explaining themselves, eyes flicking towards the bed, anxious to be on with their duties. "We have our orders."

The bed does not fit easily through the door, and they must take it through the store instead, sending the reindeer carcasses swinging. The cherrywood chest and their cases are also removed. When they are gone for the last time, leaving the door open, Ursa reaches at once for the broom, begins to sweep the mud tracked across the floor from their boots. Maren stands to take it from her, but Ursa resists.

"We are moving into Fru Olufsdatter's house. She will not be back." Her knuckles whiten. She is sweeping the dirt in circles, breaking it apart on the boards and smearing it. "They mean to murder her, like the Sámi men."

Maren can't speak. She is thinking not of Fru Olufsdatter, or even Kirsten. She is imagining Diinna and Erik, already lost to the mountains and beyond. *Stay hidden*, she thinks. *Stay safe.*

"How can I live there, Maren? How can he—" Her breath hitches: she holds herself beneath her ribs, leaning on the broom.

"You must," says Maren simply. "It is as you say—we must be careful now."

Ursa straightens. "I will not spend my days there. We will come here, as before. I cannot live in Fru Olufsdatter's house."

There is grit to her voice that gives Maren hope. "Perhaps," she ventures, "I could live here?"

Ursa blinks at her, dazed. "There is no bed."

"I can't go to my house. I can't sleep near my mother, or in Diinna's room. And then I can be close." The plan is growing roots. "You could tell Absalom you will need me nearby, to help in a larger house."

"It would be a great comfort," says Ursa. She smooths back her hair. "I cannot think he will deny me that."

Even after all this, Maren thinks, Ursa believes herself to have power over him. Witch-hunter or no, Absalom is, after all, still only a man.

THIRTY-THREE

Though there are only two women missing, and four strange men sit at the back of the kirke, at Sabbath service their company feels entirely diminished. Toril and Sigfrid and Edne sit in the front pew alongside the Cornets, and Maren takes a seat apart from her mother. Maren has already moved to the boathouse, and the mere sight of her sets fury coursing through her blood. Mamma keeps trying to catch Maren's eye, and Maren keeps her face turned determinedly away. The absence of Kirsten stings.

Pastor Kurtsson looks a little thinner than usual. Maren wonders what he makes of the arrests. He should be as pleased as the commissioner, but something in his stance is slumped, his face frowning as he preaches righteousness and mercy.

At the end of the sermon the commissioner stands. Always a large presence, he appears gargantuan, and though she tries to summon hatred Maren feels only dread. Pastor Kurtsson keeps to the shadows.

"As you are no doubt aware, Fru Sørensdatter and Fru Olufsdatter stand accused of witchcraft. I will be compiling evidence against them. If you have suffered at their hands, or know of any malignancy relevant to their charges, come directly to my residence."

He bows to the wooden cross and strides down the aisle, the men at the back throwing the doors open for him. Maren shrinks from him as he moves past her. Toril follows close behind with her women, and Maren looks up long enough to glare at her.

"That was not wise," says Ursa under her breath, sliding into the pew beside her.

"Someone should accuse her," says Maren, furious.

"You are best out of it. I will come to you, as soon as I am sure he is comfortable."

She leaves the kirke, and Maren waits until it is empty but for Pastor Kurtsson. He starts a little when he turns from blowing out the candles and sees her still sitting in the pew.

"Maren Magnusdatter." He says her name like it is glass, carefully.

"Pastor Kurtsson."

They watch each other. The man's throat contracts as he swallows. Maren makes her decision and stands, approaching him down the narrow aisle. He stays quite still, and she stops a few paces from him. Maren is not sure how to begin, but it is he who speaks first.

"You have no charges to lay before our commissioner?"

Maren shakes her head. "Have you, minister?"

"No." His pale eyes are weary. There are hollows beneath them.

"You did not tell him of the fishing boats?" Maren can't keep the surprise from her voice.

"There is no sin in feeding yourself," says Pastor Kurtsson. His hands are limp at his sides, his shoulders slumped.

"But you opposed it."

"It was not proper," he agrees. "But I did not think it ungodly."

"Our commissioner might, if he hears it."

"It will not be from me."

"Will he hear anything from you?"

Something pointed enters Pastor Kurtsson's face. "What does that mean?"

Maren swallows. "Will you speak for her? For Kirsten, and Fru Olufsdatter?"

Pastor Kurtsson sighs. "I can speak only the truth, what I know of it before God. I do not see all of it as He does. He is the ultimate judge."

"But you are His servant," says Maren urgently. "You must have some insight, some sway..."

"I know only what He shows me."

"What has He shown you?"

Pastor Kurtsson brings his palms together, clasps his fingers about themselves. "He saw fit to save you from the storm, to guide you through the difficult time afterwards. The mercies He bestowed upon you—I cannot think His eye is turned from you."

Maren wants to push him full in the chest. "You think it mercy, what has happened here?"

"To think otherwise is a sin," says Pastor Kurtsson, moving past her. "I am sorry for your friend. But I cannot judge her innocent. Only God can do that."

But it is a man who took her, thinks Maren. *A woman who accused her*. Though there is no use in saying it aloud. The minister is already out of the kirke door, and she trails after him, before turning to the second boathouse.

There is a line of women snaking from Fru Olufsdatter's house, and Maren shudders each time one steps into the sun-yellow interior, as though they walk across her grave. She knows Kirsten is damned by many mouths, wonders how many others will follow as accusers, how many will be accused.

•

There is a near-month of uncertainty and silence. The winter draws in and locks about them, and Maren keeps mostly to the house, though her legs long for their walk to the headland, her lungs for air.

Now that the boathouse is hers at last, it has lost all its shine. She sleeps on the floor beneath the hide blanket she made, and enjoys the stiffness she wakes with throughout her body, a punishment she feels she must bear. She dreams of the whale and of Kirsten, her proud form bent into the witches' hole, imagines she takes Kirsten's aches into herself and helps her bear them better.

She wonders how Mamma is coping with the change in weather. She has never borne a winter alone, any more than Maren has. Is she, too, haunted by her own breath coming smoky from her lips, the chill seeping mercilessly into her bones? Maren has managed to avoid her entirely, but she is also tormented—what would Pappa think of Maren leaving Mamma to the midday dark?

Maren tells herself Mamma has new friends. Toril's standing in the village is now higher than any except the commissioner, and Mamma sits alongside the kirke-women at Sabbath. She has not come to visit Maren in the second boathouse, has stopped trying to catch her eye. They are becoming strangers, and Maren feels as though all her family are dead, and only Ursa remains.

Two years since the storm, and a new year begins. No more arrests are made, but the men settle in Kirsten's empty house, circle Vardø like bats. She had forgotten what it was like to live among men, their laughs too loud and stares just as disturbing. There are those who visit the stabbur in the day, and Maren watches them watch Ursa as she crosses the short distance between their houses, grinding her teeth at their leers.

Ursa comes as often as she is able. Absalom is keeping her

close, tethered to his side, and Ursa tells Maren she is worried of bringing attention to her by visiting too often. Despite the sapping cloud of threat that hangs over them all, Maren finds she is still lifted by her presence, still sent spiralling by her touch.

She hates herself for it, for the small pleasure she takes from Ursa without her friend realizing, for taking any pleasure in anything at all while Kirsten languishes a mere mile away in the darkness. But she can't help it. Her feelings are as relentless and powerful as the tides. Sometimes, when Ursa and Maren touch hands or catch eyes, she imagines they are matched in Ursa too. That if she were to speak to them, they would be returned. And then what? What could follow?

Maren tries to prove herself indispensable to the commissioner while keeping from his sight, using the second boathouse as a kitchen and sending stews scented with the musty herbs she discovers in jars. One looks a little like dried nightshade, used in small amounts for fevers, and she fantasizes about upending it into his dinner, his face turning puce, his breath stopped and his tongue swelling black in his throat.

It is a daydream she indulges ever more regularly when, on the first day of the year of our Lord 1620, Ursa arrives with news. Maren is sitting at the scrubbed table when Ursa pushes the door open and sits down opposite her, though she can't look Maren in the face. Maren feels a plummeting in her stomach.

"Fru Olufsdatter has confessed," Ursa says. "And is to be sentenced."

"Confessed?" The word is dissonant inside Maren's head. "To what?"

"To witchcraft. To the poppets being tools of her witchcraft." Ursa swallows drily. "I think they used brands. Absalom said it was hard to bring the confession from her without fire."

"And Kirsten?" Maren's chest clenches. "She cannot have..."

Ursa shakes her head, meeting her eye at last. Her gaze is so sad it strikes a tender place inside Maren. "Kirsten would not confess."

"So they will release her?" says Maren, though she knows it is a fool's hope.

Ursa bites her lip.

"Tell me," says Maren.

"I wish it was not so. But she is to be ducked."

"Ducked?" The word sounds comical to her, like a child's game. But Maren knows from Ursa's tone it is no game.

"I did not know the word either. I hoped never to relay it but...you must be prepared." Ursa takes a deep, shaky breath. "They asked her to confess her crimes, and she wouldn't. So they are to test that she is a witch and should be sentenced as one."

A feeling of foreboding crosses Maren's neck, like the bird dark at the window before the storm. "How?"

"They will bind her, and put her in the sea."

"In the sea?" Maren feels her tongue slow in her mouth. "It is freezing. She might drown!"

"It may be better if she does."

Maren gapes at her. "How can you say such a thing?"

"If she floats, they will say she is a witch. They say water is pure and repels the Devil, and so those who float are witches."

Maren wants to be sick. "Who are they? Your husband?"

"He, and the Lensmann. Pastor Kurtsson will be there too, and anyone else who would see it."

The bile stings Maren's throat. "It is to be public?"

Ursa nods. "It must be witnessed."

"Can you not stop it?" Maren knows she sounds hysterical. "Can you do nothing?"

A sob grips Ursa's throat. "What would you have me do? Tell me, and I will do it."

Maren presses her hand hard against the table, to anchor herself. "When is this happening?"

"Next week." Ursa looks at her sharply. "You cannot think to go?"

"I must," says Maren. "She cannot bear it alone."

"Watching will do nothing," says Ursa. "It is better not to see, whatever the outcome."

"How is this godly?" says Maren, eyes stinging with tears. "How can they call their work holy?"

Ursa has no answer, and Maren must leave her alone in the house as she goes outside to heave her guts into the mud until she is hollow, full of nothing but her painfully thudding heart.

THIRTY-FOUR

The day of the ducking, the sky is dark and low. As Maren walks to the harbour, she is aware of the stares, the mutters, feels exposed without Ursa's presence to protect her. A small group are already gathered at the joining of land and sea. Ursa is not among them.

"Absalom says it is not for a woman's eyes," she had said.

"Does he forget it is a woman he means to push into the sea?"

Ursa's brow creased. "Won't you stay with me? There is nothing to be gained."

Though Maren knows it would have been best to remain behind too, she could not. Kirsten can't be alone with a group of kirke-women and men, intent on drowning or damning her. She must bear witness, too.

Seeing her resolve, Ursa had sighed and taken her hand. "Promise me you will do nothing to draw attention to yourself. Stay silent."

Maren heeds her words now, standing a little apart from the others, careful not to catch the commissioner's eye. Mamma is not there, nor Edne, but Sigfrid and Toril are talking with the minister, whose face is pale as milk. All are lit by meagre

297

lamps laid along the harbour, and it is a lamp that signals Kirsten's arrival too. Maren turns to watch it coming from Vardøhus, swaying with the movement of the cart. When it draws close, Maren sees Kirsten for the first time in months. She must bite down hard on her tongue to keep from crying out.

The shape in the back of the cart is slack as a sack. Kirsten is clad only in a cotton dress, skirt dark with stains. Her eyes are shut even as guards and the commissioner haul her to her feet, wrinkling their noses. Maren can smell her friend too, the wind carrying the rust of old blood and piss towards them. Pastor Kurtsson presses a kerchief to his nose. Maren wants to call out to Kirsten, tell her she is there, but her tongue is pressed hard to the roof of her mouth, and she does not think she can stir it into speech.

Another cart follows close behind, a finer carriage, covered over. Maren recognizes it as the one that collected Ursa to take her to Vardøhus last year. The women murmur as a man steps from it, and Maren takes the measure of their Lensmann. He is short and stocky, dressed in a well-cut fur coat. His face is obscured by a beard thick as Commissioner Cornet's, but it is white as lambswool. He strides to the harbour edge, and though Maren feels a building need to flee, she moves closer to hear what he says.

"Will you confess, Fru Sørensdatter, and save us this business?"

Kirsten is trembling so hard the guards are struggling to keep her upright.

"Will you confess," he repeats, "that you are a witch, and did bring down the storm that murdered your husband and many others besides?"

Maren's breath catches in her throat. They cannot think that Kirsten could conjure the weather? She was on the harbour edge same as Maren, same as all of them, screaming as their men were swallowed by the sea. Maren should say so, but her tongue is still latched tight.

Kirsten's hair hangs limp about her face, and Maren wonders if his words can even reach her in her fear.

"Very well," says the Lensmann, and there is a definite note of excitement in his voice. He nods to the guards, and they pull Kirsten's dress roughly over her head. Pastor Kurtsson averts his eyes, and Toril and the kirke-women peer through their fingers, but Maren cannot look away. The wasted mass of Kirsten's body is pitted with scratches, pressed with bruises and burns. Maren wants to wrap her in her coat, and pulls it tighter to herself.

"The rope."

Commissioner Cornet fetches rope from the cart, and ties it about Kirsten's waist. It bites at her white and loosened skin. A lump rises in Maren's throat as she realizes this is to haul Kirsten back out, after.

She looks at the sea. It is slate grey and lifts in gently rolling waves. Ice shimmers in small patches upon the surface. Kirsten will freeze to death, and Maren will watch, and not do a thing to stop it. But her promise to Ursa is not all that stays her: Maren is afraid. Terror has her about the heart, and grips her bodily, sticking her in place.

The rope is tested, yanked twice, swaying Kirsten from side to side. She shakes, her whole body twitching, her face downcast. The commissioner takes hold of the rope, as do two more guards. Pastor Kurtsson steps forward and blesses the water. His words are too quiet for Maren to hear, but his hands are clasped tight as they were when Maren spoke to him in kirke.

He steps away, and, so suddenly that Maren could have blinked and missed it, Kirsten is pitched into the water. The small crowd surges as the commissioner and his fellow rope-holders lean back to gain purchase on the frosted ground. Maren runs, forces her way forward.

Kirsten vanishes beneath the water, which is white and churned by her impact. The cold from the waves slaps Maren's face. She is caught between hoping Kirsten will rise, and praying that she will sink as fast as did the runestones in her trouser pockets. But as Kirsten breaks the surface, her eyes wide and rolling, her breath coming fast and desperate from her chest, a keening sound shrill as the terns overhead, Maren knows she is glad Kirsten still lives, though it damns her.

She is hauled to the harbour, her naked body pale as snow. She is so thin Maren can see every one of her ribs jutting, nosing up through her skin like the tracery of roots through dirt. Maren steps towards her, but a hand, cold as the air, grips her wrist. She sees it is Edne, come after all. Edne's eyes are wide, and she shakes her head, almost imperceptibly.

Maren pulls away, looks back at Kirsten. She is being wrapped in a fur and hauled back to the cart. They do not want her to freeze to death before she stands trial. The exposed skin at her throat and wrists is white as bone.

"A witch, as accused," says the Lensmann, reaching up to clap Commissioner Cornet on the shoulder. The commissioner is panting with the effort of pulling Kirsten up. "A date shall be set."

His words ring in Maren's ears like a beaten drum. It takes three men to lift the sodden figure of her friend back up into the cart, and the other watchers begin to drift away before the horses start up. But Maren comes close to the cart, as close as she dares with the guards watching, and must clasp her hands together to keep from reaching out. The horses are ordered into action, and she watches until the lamp disappears back inside the walls of Vardøhus.

Kirsten never even knew she was there. And what help would it have been? Maren's presence was useless as a shredded sail. She had thought she had seen the worst from this harbour, thought nothing could rival the viciousness of the storm. But now she knows she was foolish to believe that evil existed only out there. It was here, among them, walking on two legs, passing judgement with a human tongue.

Pastor Kurtsson is standing still beside the harbour, clutching his cloak about him. Maren remembers Kirsten striding out to him, placing her coat over his shoulders as they waited for Ursa to arrive. He removes his glove and bends to the water, holds his hand over it. He snatches it back immediately, clamps it inside his coat. As he straightens he seems to sense her watching him, and looks at her. His eyes are shining in the dark, though it may be only from the cold.

He turns his back, and she lets him go without challenge. No matter that Pastor Kurtsson believed their survival after the storm to be a miracle: now Maren thinks that the mercies of God would have been better spent drowning them all.

•

The sentencing is agreed for the approaching spring, two months hence. Ursa tells her this is because men will come from all around, other commissioners travelling to witness the sentencing of a witch. The recent trials have centred around Sámi men, but Kirsten and Fru Olufsdatter are the first Norwegian women accused in living memory, and people are coming from as far as Tromsø, perhaps even Scotland.

Maren knows of no one who has been inside Vardøhus but Ursa, and not even she has seen the courthouse. Absalom, Ursa tells her, has refused to say anything about it, though he has been at work there most days, readying himself for the trial.

"It is almost as though he thinks it a treat," says Ursa, tone bitter with disgust. "As though he wants to keep it a surprise."

"It is his hour," says Maren, kneading black dough with rough punches. "He wishes to please you."

She can recognize this because it is something they share, she and the commissioner. How it would hurt him to know of Ursa's disdain for him, she thinks. How delicious Maren would find it for him to notice.

The night before the sentencing Maren scarcely sleeps. Her mind can't go anywhere but to Kirsten in the hole. Does she even know that the day of her sentencing is upon her? Or have they left her so without news that the days have already lost their shape? Is she still suffering from her time in the sea? Maren imagines the chill, can't summon it. They were taught as children that in winter a leg slipped through the ice meant the end. To be thrown bodily as Kirsten had been, finding the air calling you to life, only to be plunged into death at a man's hand—it is monstrous.

She thinks, too, of Diinna and Erik, prays for them to be safe. She wishes she could hold the boy, breathe him in. Can he speak yet? Will Diinna teach him Maren's name? She is glad he is away from this place. Perhaps he will not remember it at all, will forget her. She has no memories so young. The thought is comforting, and terrible.

Ursa must go ahead with her husband to the trial, and so Maren walks unaccompanied in the crowd that pushes through Vardø's haphazard paths to the fortress. Though she has lived with these women all her life, they seem to wear masks of their own faces, made slick by excitement and fear. And as they break from the houses and the stone walls rise ahead of them, Maren sees more and more men, more strangers, all full of the same chatter. She feels herself separate from it, completely alone.

They funnel inside, kept back from the fine squarish house that must be the Lensmann's by a chain of guards wearing a uniform of deep blue, an emblem stitched onto their chests showing a crest of crowns and lions set about a cross.

"King's men." She hears the mutter go about her. She had never thought much of having a king, felt them here in Vardø to be so far removed from Christiania and Bergen and the other places Ursa speaks of that it is as though their power did not stretch to them, that they were more at the mercy of the sea and wind than King and country. She locks eyes with one of the men and looks quickly away, feeling ignorant as a child.

The courthouse is full already when she reaches it, a mill of people outside churning at the closed door, shouting and barging. Maren stops short of the chaos, cursing her lateness. She should have come last night; she had no sleep as it was. She can't go home to wait for news, and is just looking about for a place to stand when there is a disturbance to her left as two men emerge from a squat, long building, carrying a large bundle.

"Witch!" The shout comes from a cluster of women including Sigfrid and Toril. The bundle lifts its head at the cry, and all of a sudden it is Kirsten, or rather, something like Kirsten. A shadow of her, a mockery. Her friend's face is pale, grime dark against her temples, blonde hair matted to thatch on her head. Maren doubts she has been allowed to wash, shudders as she imagines the salt of the sea still upon her skin after so many weeks.

In another moment they are drawing close, their route taking them past Maren, and as she sees Kirsten's feet go bare and dragging by her she looks up, hopes she has been seen, or not seen, and then she is following in their wake, the crowd pressing all about them, spitting and aiming kicks, those misjudged landing on Maren and the guards holding Kirsten, and always the hiss, the cry, the screech of *Witch! Witch! Witch!* The assembled masses are mostly strangers, shouting at someone they do not know, who never caused them harm. They put Maren in mind of a herd of panicked reindeer.

And then the doors of the courthouse are opening, and Kirsten is inside, and Maren is held back alongside many others, prevented from entering. She finds her breath at last, fills her lungs, cries, "Kirsten!" and she may imagine the lift of the head, the turn of her friend's face as the doors close and Maren is pushed against the wood, lifted from her feet as those behind surge forward. Maren prays aloud that Kirsten heard her, knew her, felt that she sent her all the hope she can summon.

THIRTY-FIVE

Absalom has made Ursa wear her yellow dress, though she protested it was surely not proper for a courthouse.

"I want you in your finest," he says. "The other commissioners will be there."

He is up early and whistling, helping her with her fastenings, her skin crawling at his touch. The dress is tighter than ever at her waist though she has grown used to the hunger pangs that come constantly.

She prays she isn't pregnant: can't remember, in the disaster of the past few months, whether her bloods have come regularly or not. And her terror at the trial, at what she may witness, means her dreams are full of blood and her mother. She doesn't tell even Maren of these, knowing she has her own horrors to deal with. *Branded. Strangled. Burnt.* And these are the hands that touch her, that may have planted a child inside her.

In some ways, Kirsten's suffering has meant a lessening of her own. Absalom has been distracted by preparations, and made merry by them too. His power has made him stronger, and so he has treated her more kindly. He is happy, and wishes her to share in it. She hates herself for it, but she dissembles, tells him she is proud of him, moans into his ear when he lies upon her. She hates him, but she wants to stay in his good graces. She must protect Maren.

She wonders how Maren can stand to be near her, when Ursa herself is so close to Kirsten's tormentor. But Maren seems to cling to Ursa more than ever, and Ursa finds herself clinging back. It dizzies her, how strongly she feels for Maren. She has never loved anyone so dearly but Agnete, and it seems that their kinship is stronger even than sisterhood.

In the carriage on the way to the courthouse, she lets herself be thrown about on the potholes split wide by winter. There are already people crowded at the castle's gates. They raise bleary faces at the carriage's arrival and she sights the kirke-women at the fore, knows that Absalom has been with them often, praying with them in exchange for testimony. The crowd parts as the carriage pulls up, and she shrinks back into the shadows until the door is opened and she must step onto the slippery flagstones, careful to catch no one's eye.

Absalom guides her into the courthouse beneath the crook of her elbow, as though accompanying her to a dance. It is sparse and clean as a kirke, all angled towards the altar of the Lensmann's seat. A small square demarcated by wooden rails is set before it—this, Absalom tells her, is where the accused will stand. There are rows and rows of seats like pews, and a gallery set elevated to the back of the room where usually the women must go, but as there are mostly women, even with the additional visitors to the island, the rules will be bent this once.

She is led to a smaller gallery up and to the side of the dock, so she will see all in profile and be separate from most of the—what are they? An audience? Witnesses?

"Christin will be here shortly," he says. "Perhaps some of the other commissioners' wives." He kisses her chastely on the cheek, and it feels as if she really were in kirke. "I must prepare."

He pauses as though for a response, but what can she say? *Good luck, go well*: these would feel false. She can say nothing that would please him, and so he goes without her blessing.

She doesn't have to wait long for Christin. She is wearing a dress of deep purple that only serves to make Ursa's dress brighter, like contrasting crocuses in a field.

"These seats are so damnably uncomfortable," she says by way of greeting, after they have curtsied to each other and settled back down on the pew. "I should have brought a cushion."

Ursa is saved from making conversation by the arrival of two more women, Fru Mogensdatter and Fru Edisdatter, both older than Christin, who are the wives of Commissioner Danielsson from Kirkenes, and Commissioner Andersson from Kunes. They are introduced but neither seem interested in her. Fru Mogensdatter looks as peaky as Ursa feels, and she wonders briefly if she has found someone as appalled by this as she, but it is only from the travel.

"Why the seat of power must be on an island in the middle of nowhere, I do not know." She shudders. "I cannot imagine how you stand it, Christin."

Christin waves airily. "We were much away before this business, and intend to be after it is concluded. I never step outside Vardøhus unless I can help it. You grow used to it."

Below them, the commissioners are assembling. Absalom stands taller than the rest. He is younger too, and Christin points him out to Fru Mogensdatter and Fru Edisdatter.

"That is Commissioner Cornet, who has brought the trial. He is something of a prodigy. I fancy my husband has found him a successor already." The other women exchange glances, and Ursa wishes she could disappear inside the voluminous skirts of her dress.

From outside, noise builds and at ten of the clock, the doors are thrown open. Instantly women begin to pour in, the few men amongst them led to the front of the room. The crowd fills the remaining seats of the lower pews and upper gallery. They stand pressed against each other, rowdy and hullooing, calling up and down between levels. The men put their heads together and chatter like crows.

There is no sign of Maren anywhere. Perhaps she did not get in, for it sounds as though there are still many outside. Ursa can feel a headache building behind her eyes, a spasming point of pressure that opens and closes in time with her heartbeat. The dress bites into her ribs.

"Are you quite all right?" says Christin, her tone more curious than concerned. Ursa realizes she is breathing raggedly and nods, shifts in her seat.

"It is warm in here."

"Would you like something to drink?" Christin raises her hand to gesture at the guard stationed at the entrance to their gallery but Ursa shakes her head.

"I'm fine."

There is the sound of the doors being opened once more, and the noise from outside rushes in. Ursa thinks she hears the name "Kirsten" shouted, and a moment later two men enter, dragging her with them.

It is worse than Ursa had guessed at. Kirsten is shrunk inside herself, filthy and broken-looking. She looks down at the ground as the hisses start, and so Ursa can't see her face, only her dirty curtain of hair and bound hands, gripping the wooden rail for support. She sways and Ursa can't help but whisper to Christin, "Will they not give her a stool?"

Christin frowns at her, shakes her head.

"Your husband is here," says Fru Edisdatter to Christin, and they lean forward as the Lensmann, dressed in long black robes, strides along the centre of the aisle, trailed by a slight

man with a thick book beneath his arm. The crowd falls silent
as he ascends to his seat, looks about him. He nods to their
gallery and Ursa bites her tongue as Christin gives him a small
wave. He checks that the court clerk is ready, and Ursa fixes
her eyes on Kirsten as Lensmann Cunningham addresses the
court.

"I, Lensmann Cunningham, as appointed by our King
Christian the Fourth as Lensmann over Vardøhus County and
Finnmark, sit in judgement over this court. We are gathered
on the twenty-ninth of March sixteen-twenty, in the presence
of God and the commissioners of Finnmark, to pass sentence
in the case of Fru Kirsten Sørensdatter of Vardø—"

Several people hiss and tut at Kirsten's name, and a ringing
starts in Ursa's ears as Lensmann Cunningham continues.

"—for charges brought against her from a period of near
three years, with particular notice to the twenty-fourth of
December, sixteen-seventeen, and diverse other days and times
as well before and after. These certain detestable acts fall
beneath the King's Decree against witchcraft and sorcery,
enacted in our district on the fifth of January, sixteen-twenty.
Commissioner Cornet arrested Fru Sørensdatter on the eight-
eenth of October of last year.

"She was told she would be spared interrogation if she
confessed at once, but pleaded innocence and was ducked on
the eighth of January of this year. She has since confessed to
several acts of witchcraft. Commissioner Cornet, if you would
please rise and read the confession."

Someone is making low, soft, animal sounds of distress, and
Ursa looks to the other gallery before she realizes it is she
herself. She searches again for Maren, can't find her.

Her husband stands, back straight, and in his clear, low
voice, he reads the charges in his accented Norwegian.

"Fru Kirsten Sørensdatter did confess, on the ninth of

January of this year, her guilt in charges brought against her. She is denounced by Pastor Nils Kurtsson, Toril Knudsdatter, Magda Farrsdatter, Gerda Folnsdatter, Sigfrid Jonsdatter, Edne Gunnsdatter."

He takes a breath, reads more names, intoning that of nearly every woman of Vardø. She hears Maren's mother's name, even Fru Olufsdatter's, and wonders whether her neighbour has saved herself with this denouncement. Finally the names are at an end, and Absalom takes up a new piece of parchment.

"She confesses that Satan did come to her when she was twenty-two and at work tending a calf, and she did ask him who he was and was told he was the Devil. He did offer her his hand to kiss and said upon it that she would be given power over air and the strength of a man if she forswore God and her baptismal pact. And she did take his hand and kissed it and felt very happy after it. She blew breath on the calf and it did die."

The story goes on, a litany of such absurdity that Ursa feels herself almost floating above it. It reads like a list of women's gossip, from arguments over fish-drying racks to saying the Lord's Prayer backwards. But the crowd leans forward as one to the swaying woman in the dock, voices held in check only by the Lensmann's admonishments. On more than one occasion Ursa sees someone reach through the rails and pinch her, but Kirsten barely reacts. It is as if she is asleep, her eyes half closed, mouth slack. What more have they done to her, to reduce her so?

Absalom places the first parchment down, picks up another. "And she confesses that she did, on Christmas Eve sixteen-seventeen, fly to the witches' mountain of Ballvollen and there knot a cloth with five others, and set the storm that drowned forty men, her own husband among them—"

The hissing grows to a sudden cry of rage that echoes about the room, and though the Lensmann shouts for order he must send his guards forward and about the dock to keep Kirsten from being kicked and her hair pulled at. Ursa covers her face with her hands. Christin pats her lap. "Mark her, Ursula. She is smiling."

But Ursa sees only a grimace upon Kirsten's face.

"The names!" someone shouts from the gallery. "Give us their names!"

The Lensmann stands, raises his arms. "I will have the court emptied!"

A begrudging silence falls. Absalom says, "If I may speak on the names, Lensmann." He turns back to the courtroom. "We asked for the names and she says she couldn't see their faces, that they were shrouded in smoke. But we have established Fru Olufsdatter as one, and have her confession, and are working at her on the rest." He looks meaningfully out at the crowd, and Ursa shudders as he raises the parchment again. "And they did raise the storm so they might have property and dominion over their husbands' land."

"And she did steal Mads Petersson's herd which numbered fifty reindeer, and Fru Gunnsdatter was bewitched to row with her and eight others, where they did not lay nets but Fru Sørensdatter called the fish up with her breath. And she did wear trousers and so possessed the strength of a man, and sent terrors to Fru Knudsdatter and did blow upon Fru Jonsdatter and she fell sick with a wasting disease that swelled her belly."

Ursa looks at the kirke-women. Their faces are rapt, as though her husband were a miracle, awful and beautiful.

Absalom rolls the parchment up. "Such are the charges confessed to, amongst other sundry acts as are characteristic of a witch. She lay her mark upon them as an 'X,' and I submit it to the court."

He places it before the Lensmann with a short bow, and goes grandly back to his seat. There is scattered applause amongst the commissioners, which ripples through the room.

"He has done well," says Christin. "You should be proud."

Ursa gives a tight nod as the Lensmann leans forward in his seat, looks directly to the dock.

"Have you anything to say, Fru Sørensdatter?"

Nothing. One of the guards shoves her, the crowd jeers.

"Have you anything to say?"

The guard moves close to her, wrinkling his nose as he listens.

"'Nobody,' she says, Lensmann Cunningham."

"'Nobody'?"

"She says, 'Nobody.'"

"Very well then," says Lensmann Cunningham, sitting back again to address them all. "Fru Sørensdatter, you have been accused of the grievous crime of malevolent witchcraft and sorcery, and upon receipt of your writ confession I am to follow the rule of the King's Decree that, 'If any sorcerer had the sacrifice of God and His holy Word and Christianity, and devoted himself to the Devil, he should be cast down on fire and incineration.'"

"She will burn," says Christin.

The crowd's voice lifts as one, and this time the Lensmann doesn't quiet them, only raises his voice as he sets the date, two days hence. The men take hold of Kirsten, and as they do she at last stirs and lifts her arms.

"May God have mercy upon my soul." As her unbuttoned sleeves fly back, Ursa sees it isn't dirt patterning her arms, but bruises upon bruises, purple and yellow as Christin's and her skirts, petals pressed into her wasted skin.

•

Ursa excuses herself from the Lensmann's lunch though she knows Absalom will be displeased. She claims a headache, but really it is her whole body that hurts. She changes in Fru

Olufsdatter's house, as she can't help but think of it, from her yellow dress into a plainer, looser one, and crosses to the second boathouse. She knocks and, having no answer, lets herself inside Maren's house to wait.

She feels calmer already in that room, amongst Maren's meagre possessions, the noise of the courthouse far away. Now that she no longer lives there it feels more like home than ever. She practises what she will tell Maren, for she is sure she was not inside the courthouse, but when the door opens and Maren enters, the set of her starkly pale face tells her that she already knows what has come to pass.

Ursa reaches out for her, but Maren flinches away.

"Edne told me. They say she caused the storm," Maren says. "And she confessed it."

"She had been beaten, ducked," says Ursa. "She would have confessed to anything."

"Not that," says Maren, her voice flat. "Surely not that. You did not see it, Ursa. So sudden, like a hand scooping up the boats, crushing them." She closes her eyes. "She would not have confessed to that were it false."

Ursa does not correct her, does not tell her of the bruises on Kirsten's arms.

"And it is true what they said of the trousers and the fishing," says Maren. "She alone among us seemed not to grieve."

"You cannot believe her a witch," says Ursa harshly. "You are not so stupid."

"You did not see it," says Maren. "The storm. It was fast as a breath. And we caught fish easy as that."

"You had nets, though?" Maren nods and Ursa snaps her hand to the table. "There, see? They have lied. Edne and Toril, all of them lied. And no one defended her."

"And you think I should have spoken against it?" Maren doesn't shout, but the ice in her voice makes Ursa flinch.

"I did not mean that—"

"You told me not to go to him. You told me not to speak with Cornet, that you would do it, and see what has happened."

"Maren." Ursa has lost her words. She feels winded.

"I would wish to be left alone, if I might, mistress."

"Maren, what are you doing?" Ursa wants to shake her, but can't bring herself to touch her.

"I'll go then," says Maren, moving to stand.

"No," says Ursa. "I'll leave." She pauses at the door. "I will go to watch Kirsten's burning, the day after next." She had decided it as soon as sentence was passed, though no part of her wants to. "It will be hard, but she will need a friend's face. I hope you will come with me, Maren."

Maren sits impassive as stone.

"'Nobody,'" says Ursa, at last understanding. "When they asked her for more names, that is how she answered. She wouldn't take another down with her. She is a good woman, and she loves you."

Maren looks down at her knotted hands.

•

Ursa doesn't go to Fru Olufsdatter's sentencing the next day. She holds her hand to her head and moans softly, so Absalom will insist she rests. He speaks to her more than ever that morning as he dresses. He is happy, and she wishes he were dead. It is a marvel he can't feel the hatred coming from her, like heat as she feels it upon her own skin.

Ursa's anguish keeps her to bed all day, but the exultant, feverish sounds of women returning mid-afternoon tell her that Kirsten will not be sent to the stake alone.

THIRTY-SIX

Absalom leaves early and Ursa refuses the carriage, claims she needs the fresh air after her day in bed. He presses his hand to her forehead, and she knows he will find her warm—the nerves have set her sweating.

"I hope you are not sickening, wife. Or perhaps..." His eyes flick down to her belly. "I have heard a baby can quicken the blood."

She pushes his hand away, but gently, forces herself to smile. "Perhaps, husband."

He kisses her atop the head as he did the day they married. "Captain Leifsson arrived on the *Petrsbolli* yesterday. Perhaps we will be able to send happy news to your father when he leaves."

"Captain Leifsson?" Ursa tries not to let her relief show. "He is here?"

"Staying at Vardøhus. Did I not tell you of it?"

She shakes her head. The last she heard of his possible arrival was in Father's letter that Absalom read to her. Her thoughts of it had gone up in smoke with that and the other letters. "The trials knocked it clean from my mind."

He rubs his beard, blows out air fast through his lips. She

has not seen him nervous before, and it makes her more fearful too. "I should go," he says. "Be sure to stand upwind."

He dons his hat, and strides out.

She dresses in her yellow again. This time she wants to be seen, wants Kirsten to notice her and know she isn't to go to death without a friend.

She walks to the second boathouse and knocks gently. For a long moment there is no answer, but then Maren is stepping from it, her face blotchy. They do not embrace but Maren slips her arm through Ursa's, and they clamp tight together so their hips bump and Ursa's fingers ache from gripping her.

The executions are to take place on the scrubby patch of grass behind Vardøhus, where they will be shielded from the worst of the wind and where the most people can gather. The crowd is already massive, swelled with visitors. News of the details of Kirsten's confession has spread across Kiberg and Kirkenes, who also lost men and boats, though not so many. Their faces are intent upon the brow of the small hill, but they part when they see Ursa in her yellow dress.

A wooden stake, higher than a man, has been erected at the top of the rise, logs and coarse brushes of shrub placed about its base. The sight of it makes Maren falter, and though Ursa feels a twin twinge of hesitation she pulls her onward until they are almost directly before it, right up against the line of guards marking a boundary about twenty paces short. Past this line are Pastor Kurtsson and the commissioners, her husband fore amongst them, speaking with the Lensmann. The *Petrsbolli* bobs in a calm sea beyond, but Ursa can't see Captain Leifsson in the assembled crowd. Absalom notices her, gives her a brief smile.

Ursa feels outside her body, watching from a great height as the noise of the crowd, dissipated by the wind, laps at her ears. Only Maren is real, solid, an anchor against the unreality of the scene.

She considers the stake, hewn from a single trunk, its bark stripped so the pulp stands pale and shining as moonlight. What sort of tree had it been? Was it cut exact for this purpose, brought on her father's ship? Her skin prickles. It must have been sent for months ago. Is that why the *Petrsbolli* came?

She closes her eyes against the horror of the thought, and only opens them when Maren murmurs, "They are coming."

An open cart is pulled the short distance from the castle, Fru Olufsdatter and Kirsten bound back to back. A torch burns in the guard's hand, the spark that will start the pyre. Kirsten is facing their direction and Ursa sees that her hair has been combed and her face washed, and she is wearing—there is a clench in Ursa's chest—Ursa's grey wool skirt. It shows her pale bruised ankles and feet. She wears no shoes.

As they come through the crowd, pails of stinking liquid are hurled at them, and there is spitting and shouting, but the sounds are no longer laced with excitement as they were before the sentencing. It is anger, pure and fierce, that hounds them to the stake. The crowd jostles Ursa and Maren, but they stay locked together as the women pass the line of guards and are removed from the cart.

They are lifted onto the narrow platform. Fru Olufsdatter is limp and must be held in place as the rope is tied about their waists. She hangs almost in half against it, but Kirsten is straight-legged. She looks out to the crowd as more wood and kindling are brought to close the gap left for them to reach the platform. Ursa sees some of her old defiance, and stifles a sob.

Maren's fingers dig into her hand, and she is biting her lip so hard the skin is broken and bleeding. Kirsten sees them, and though they make no gesture at each other, her face loosens a little, and she looks up to the sky.

"It is right we came," whispers Maren, more to herself. "It is right we came."

She keeps up the whisper as the torch is brought from the cart. They aren't asked last words, nor prayed over by Father Kurtsson. The torch doesn't blow out in damnation of the event. It is simply lowered to the base of the stake and Ursa can see the bright snake of it slither through the kindling, gathering at the base of the larger logs, striking up and into a full flame.

It spreads in a circle about the women's feet, as though in a dance, and Kirsten begins to shift and roll her head as the smoke starts to wash up and over them in waves, snatched at by the wind. Ursa can't look away now, and the crowd is almost silent about her. Fru Olufsdatter has not moved from her position slumped over the rope, and even as her hair brushes the flames and begins to catch, she doesn't stir. Ursa prays she is unconscious, perhaps dead already, her lungs thick with smoke.

Kirsten, though, seems to be wakened more and more. Her lips are parted and she may be moaning, her words swallowed up by the wind and the guzzling spit of the fire. Flames are licking the platform, and she lifts one foot, then another.

"Breathe deep!"

The call comes from behind them, a solitary woman's voice that Ursa can't place but that is loud enough for Kirsten to hear. She jerks her head towards the sound, her eyes wide and terrified.

"Breathe deep!" it says again, and this time Ursa follows the thread back into a crowd of kirke-women. It cannot be Sigfrid, who only two days previously sat baying as Kirsten was accused of cursing her? But Ursa sees Sigfrid call again, tears on her cheeks, and Toril cries out too. The phrase is repeated, thrown up about them in a growing chant of many voices. Ursa remembers herself telling Agnete the same thing, leaning over the vapours bowl. But that was to clear her lungs. This is so Kirsten will cloud hers with smoke, choke herself before the flames scorch her to death. Ursa joins in. All of them are shouting it, calling it to her, accusers and friends alike.

They see Kirsten's chest begin to heave, the smoke swirling about her head, tears and sweat pouring down her face. She is speaking words they can't hear and Ursa feels choked, as though her own lungs are filling with hot, acrid smoke, and Maren's nail breaks through her skin as Kirsten gives out a strangled cry and breathes and breathes and breathes.

A smell is coming on the wind now, meat and wood and hair, all of it burning, and at last Kirsten falls forward on her ropes and is still. Birds are swirling the air above the stake and there is a release amongst the crowd, a collective swell forwards. Maren loosens her grip then, and Ursa stumbles without her support, has already lost her in the melee when she turns to follow her. She pushes back against the tide, those further back struggling to see the flame-engulfed stake, until at last she breaks from it and is free, and can just spot Maren's narrow body hurrying away.

THIRTY–SEVEN

No one follows them. Ursa falls further and further behind, her dress slipping beneath her shoes, Maren quick-footed and disappearing into the scattering of Vardø's houses.

Instinct tells Ursa to keep going, past the stabbur, past the second boathouse and the strewn remains of the ruined house, to the headland. Ahead there is the cliff and at its edge is Maren. She is bent double and screaming, neck stringy with veins. As Ursa reaches her she retches, spits up thin whitish liquid that is carried away to the sea below, screams again.

Ursa stands next to her, takes her hand to draw her back a pace. She opens her mouth wide and screams too, their voices seized and spun away by the same wind that fed the flames, that climbed high the smoke, taking Kirsten's last words from them.

At last, Maren stops. She sways on her feet, and Ursa pulls her clear of the cliff edge.

"Come away, Maren."

She allows Ursa to lead her. The village is still empty as a burial yard, and a column of blackish smoke is being swirled about ahead like a flock of storm-thrown birds. Ursa takes her to the second boathouse though it is warmer in the stabbur.

She puts Maren in a chair and breaks the crust of the fire, stokes and feeds it. The heat is harsh on her cold cheek and Ursa shrinks from it. Maren is leaning slightly, barely upright, and so Ursa returns to the stabbur, brings all the blankets she can carry and dumps them on the floor where the bed used to be. From her pocket she takes her last aniseed, holds it out to Maren.

"Come, Maren. Come and lie down."

Maren's teeth chatter. Ursa comes close to her.

"I smell of her," whispers Maren. "She's upon me."

Out of the wind it is true: they both of them are thick with the smell of smoke and its nauseating edge of sweetness. Ursa can smell it on Maren's hair, on her own skin, greasy as oil.

"Stay here then," says Ursa, and Maren snatches at her hand. "Have this." She gives her the aniseed, places it between her lips like a child taking medicine. "I'll not be long."

The washing tub is wooden and heavy, and she leaves long draglines in the gap between their homes. She must do four trips to the well before she has enough water to fill it. Each time she circles back to the second boathouse, Maren has not moved but watches her like something haunted as she sets the pots to boil. Before long the tub is half full of steaming water. In the stabbur she opens her cherrywood chest, removes the lilac water. The bottle is so small and delicate, she worries it will break as she removes the stopper and upends it into the tub.

"Quick then, before it cools." Her voice grates her throat.

Maren crosses her hands at her lap. "I cannot."

"You are not shy of me?" Ursa gives her a gentle smile. "I have a sister."

"I am not your sister," says Maren, sharply.

"I love you as one," says Ursa, coming close to her and settling her palms upon her shoulders. There is something in Maren's face, a deepening pain, and as Ursa rubs her thumbs along her upper arms she flinches.

Ursa sighs. "I can go."

"No," says Maren. "Only maybe look away."

Ursa turns and hears cloth rustling as Maren undresses, her movements quick shadows in her periphery, and then the gentle sound of a body sinking into water.

"All right," says Maren, and Ursa turns. Her body is curved into itself, knees drawn up, and she has loosened her dark hair so it falls to her waist and covers the nubs of her spine.

"Here," says Ursa, passing her the tallow soap, and Maren reaches out to take it. "I can, if you would like."

Maren nods and Ursa moves aside her hair, begins to soap the narrow stretch of her back, up to her nape. Maren lets out a long breath and her head tips forwards, shoulders dropping. Ursa smells aniseed as she works the soap into Maren's hair and rinses with pails of water until the scent of burning is faded to nothing, masked beneath old lilacs.

"Here," she says, standing and holding out the soap. Maren's head is still tipped forwards, her hair in long wet strings clinging to her slender body. Her ribcage presses out, clenches in, and Ursa wants suddenly to rest her palm against it, to feel her breath.

"Maren?"

With infinite slowness, Maren looks up. There is something in her face Ursa hasn't seen before, or perhaps only not noticed. A hunger. Ursa's hand is still outstretched, holding the soap, and Maren uncrosses her arms, reaches as if to take it.

But instead, she takes Ursa's wrist in a gentle hold, so light it is almost not there, brings her lips to it, and kisses it. She looks up at Ursa, who can't move, can barely breathe. Maren shifts in the tub, kneels up.

Her body is like nothing Ursa has ever seen, thin and knotted with muscle at her arms and legs, her hipbones sharp against her skin, the hair between her legs and beneath her armpits dark, her breasts small and shining with water. Ursa feels a stab of something low in her belly. Her breath hitches. The want in Maren's face is so naked Ursa knows she cannot deny her. Is this what Ursa has felt, in these past months as they have grown so close? Ursa has not named it, is not even certain she can, but then Maren takes both Ursa's hands, and kisses each wrist with small, light touches. The soap slides from her grip.

Ursa feels caught, at the wrists and at the legs and chest, as Maren lowers her face again and again, and at last lets it rest in Ursa's palms. The gesture sends a tremor through her whole body. She pulls her hands away, holds them to her. Maren stays kneeling, head bowed, as though in prayer. Her thin shoulders are heaving, and despite her height she looks slight as a child.

"Don't be frightened," she says suddenly, though Ursa thinks it is Maren who looks the more afraid. "I did not mean to frighten you."

Their eyes meet, and Ursa reaches out. She lets her hand rest, not upon Maren's skin, but over it, hovering just at the place where her neck and shoulder meet. She can feel the heat from her. Maren tilts her head and guides Ursa's hand up, to cup her cheek. Ursa moves closer, skirts tightening about her knees. She strokes Maren's face, up and down, and Maren brings her own hand up to Ursa's cheek, to match her movement. Ursa turns her head, and takes Maren's thumb in her mouth.

Maren's whole body shudders in answer, and Ursa feels something white hot pass between them as Maren stands and steps from the bath. She helps Ursa to her feet and moves into the circle of her arms, guiding her until Ursa can feel the hard edge of the table at her back.

Maren lifts Ursa's head so their noses touch. Ursa can smell aniseed from her breath, and tallow and lilac from her skin, and something that is only Maren. Her gasp comes sudden, urgent, and she slips her leg between Maren's, presses her hips forward, skirts rustling. Maren brings her own forwards to meet her.

Ursa plucks at her fastenings and Maren steps back. Ursa feels cold air rush at her body where Maren should be, undoes them with trembling fingers. She barely lets her dress drop before they are pushing their bodies together again, only her thin underthings between them now.

They kiss, and though Maren's lips are rough Ursa feels it is the only good and tender thing that she has known for months. The desire in Maren's touch is enough to bring her own rising to meet it, and Ursa slides her hand down to Maren's lower back, to pull her against her more strongly. Maren trembles and Ursa breaks away, her mouth wide and panting, brings her to the blankets, clumsy in her haste, pulling her atop so their bodies can fit more cleanly together.

Maren slides her hand down past the curve of Ursa's waist, the paleness of her belly, and to the light hair between her legs.

Ursa grows very still, suddenly uncertain. Maren begins to pull her fingers away, but Ursa grasps them and says, "No. Only, slow. Gentle."

She does not send her mind flying away. She is only her body, and Maren's hand upon her, and in her, and she could weep with the kindness of it, the ache of it. She did not know, she thinks: she did not know it could be like this.

THIRTY–EIGHT

By night-time the haze of Ursa's touch has lifted, and the smell of Kirsten is carried all about her on the air, and Maren can't sleep. The windows of the stabbur are lit, and she wonders if Commissioner Cornet is home again, and the thought of him with Ursa makes Maren press the heels of her hands to her eyes until she sees dots of dancing light.

She starts her usual route to the headland. The nights will soon shrink again, and it will turn warmer, and everything that seemed dead will grow, but Kirsten will still be murdered. She keeps her eyes turned hard from the rise where the stake smokes and glows in the darkness.

But Ursa...she can hardly trust it happened. Their lips, finally touching, the moan in Maren's throat returned. Ursa's skin soft as she'd imagined, like the velvety inside of a flower. If not for the throb of want between her legs, Ursa's yellow dress on her floor, she wouldn't believe it.

The villagers are returned and the houses are full of sound. She thinks of Kirsten's home full of guards, and all the reindeer braying in the dark. She had been afraid when she heard her friend's confession, and for a moment wondered at

Kirsten's guilt. That moment of betrayal is a pain she can't yet access, and she feels adrift inside it.

As she passes her mother's house she sees a shape backlit on the porch, the door open.

"Mamma?"

The figure jumps—she had been dozing. Maren moves closer. Her mother is propped against the door frame. The fire is high behind her, and there is an empty bottle of Pappa's akevitt beside her.

"You should not have drunk that. It is years past."

"We were to drink it at your wedding," Mamma says, and her voice is low and thick. She lifts her head to Maren and it is obvious she has been crying.

Maren feels a pointed twist of spite. "You should go to bed, Mamma." She turns to leave her but her mother lets out a wail.

"Maren. Erik is gone."

"Yes, Mamma. And if you had not spoken against Diinna perhaps she wouldn't have had to go."

"No," says her mother. "Erik is dead. And your Pappa. And..." she breaks off, hand rising to her head. "And you will be too."

Maren's breath catches. "You are drunk."

"It is true, my girl." A fresh bout of sobs shakes her. "Your name...it has been mentioned."

Their house is a ship in the pitching night: the floorboards roll beneath Maren's feet. *The whale*, she thinks. *The whale has come.* It is arching its great back beneath their floor, waiting to break through and swallow her down.

"Kirsten?" says Maren, her voice a whisper. "Did Kirsten mention me?"

Mamma shakes her head. "Fru Olufsdatter. Toril says she named you, and Edne. Just before she went to the stake. She says you went with Kirsten to the mountain."

"What mountain?"

"The low mountain. The witches' mountain."

"The low mountain," hisses Maren. "The mountain Erik would fetch heather from, that you and Pappa walked upon. You think it a witches' hill?"

"No. Yes," Mamma's words trip out of her mouth, snot runs from her nose. "Kirsten confessed. Fru Olufsdatter confessed."

"Do you think me a witch, Mamma?" Maren feels oddly calm. "Do you think I drowned Erik, and Pappa, and all those poor men?"

Mamma howls, a sound so raw it tears Maren's own throat. "I do not. We did not know. We did not know, and now see what we have done." Her voice is muffled as she lowers her head to her hands. "The way she burnt, Maren. The way her flesh melted. The smell. Oh, God." She wraps her arms about herself, begins to rock. "Oh, God have mercy on us. We have begun it, and cannot end it."

Maren has heard enough. She breaks into a run, Mamma calling to her. "Maren, my girl, my love. I'm sorry!"

Maren will not wait for them to come for her. She has the money saved from her time working in the second boathouse, can take a boat as Diinna did, find her perhaps in the mountains, or else go to one of the cities she has heard of, where there are so many people you can lose yourself entirely.

But Ursa. How can she leave her, after their time together? She could not ask Ursa to come with her. Maren's breath comes hard through her body, her thoughts chasing her back to the second boathouse, and she hurries inside, closing the door firmly behind.

"Maren," says Ursa's voice.

She is sitting at the table in a thin cotton nightdress, and beside the fire stands Absalom Cornet, Ursa's yellow dress clenched in his fist.

THIRTY-NINE

Maren has walked straight into Absalom's trap, just as Ursa had.

He returned late from Vardøhus smelling of akevitt and meaty smoke, and his hands upon Ursa's skin while the memory of Maren's touch was still bedded into her was too much to bear. She pushed him away and for a moment he watched her in the gloom of their stolen room, so still she hardly dared breathe.

"Why do you not wish to lie with me, Ursula?" She can give him no answer that could keep her safe.

"Do you love me?" He is drunker even than he smells. He sways on his heels.

"Yes."

He kneels, leans forward until he is in her lap. She lifts her hands away from his head, so she does not have to feel his skin on hers. His broad back rises and falls, and she prays for him to sleep and remember nothing of this. But instead he hauls himself upright, smoothing his stinking tunic.

"I have business I must attend to, and upon my return I expect to find you in a better state of mind."

She listens, heart thrumming, as he leaves the house. But his steps do not disappear into the distance. Instead, she hears his heavy tread upon the boards of the boathouse, Maren's house. She runs to the window in time to see him open the door, and vanish inside.

He can't know of them. It is impossible, but still a panic sends her flying from the house in her shift, following after him through the unlatched door. Maren isn't there, but her husband stands by the table, staring at the fire.

"What are you doing, Absalom?"

"What are *you* doing, wife?" He turns, looks her up and down. "You are not decent."

Ursa clutches her hands to herself. "Forgive me, but why are you here? Will you not come back to the house with me?"

"I have business here."

Fear grows hot inside her. "You are drunk."

"I am not so drunk." His voice slurs. "If you had come with me to dine, you would know it."

"I am sorry I did not come. Please, let's go to bed."

She holds out her hands to him, but he does not move.

"I have come to arrest your friend, Ursula. I know you are fond of her, and wished to spare you the embarrassment."

"Maren?" The room spins as though it were she who is full of spirits. "She is accused?"

"By the witch Olufsdatter herself. Her last confession. But tell me, wife. Why is your wedding dress on the floor?"

"I had brought it for Maren to clean," says Ursa. Her hand begins to tremble and she snatches it behind herself. "See, the tub is set ready."

His eyes trail to the tub, still half full of grey water. The smell of lilacs is gone, overwhelmed by the ghastly smoke on his clothes. "Why did you follow me here, wife?"

"Should a wife not follow her husband when he goes at night to another woman's house?"

"Am I to think you jealous of me?" Absalom's teeth glint

in the low firelight. "Because I never have before, and I do not now."

"Can the arrest not wait, husband? Come to bed."

"Sit down, Ursula. I want the truth of this."

"I have told you the truth."

"Sit." He picks up the soiled dress. "Now."

They don't have to wait long, though to Ursa the minutes seem endless. She prays wordlessly that Maren will not return. Her husband watches her, and the door. Maren sweeps inside, and though Ursa tries to warn her, it is too late.

"Hello, Fru Magnusdatter," says Absalom smoothly. "Be seated, please."

Maren doesn't move. "Commissioner Cornet—"

He crosses the room in three long strides and pulls back a chair. Maren's knees seem to give way. Ursa can feel Maren looking at her but she dare not return her gaze. Absalom stares down at Maren, as though she is in a dock. She looks small set against him, a wavering candle against a swallowing dark.

"Why is my wife's dress upon your floor, Fru Magnusdatter?"

"I was cleaning it, commissioner."

"Then why is it upon the floor, and but a little wet?"

"It must have fallen from the chair. I was working upon other laundry."

"Where is the laundry?"

Maren hesitates and suddenly Absalom's wide hands reach down, and are about her throat.

Ursa jumps up, her chair overbalancing and crashing to the floor. "Absalom, no!"

"You have bewitched my wife, have you not?" Spit flies from his mouth, and his eyes glitter wildly. Maren is making small crushed noises, like a dying bird. He lifts her from the chair and drags her away from Ursa. "Tell me!"

"Absalom, she cannot speak!"

Maren's face is turning puce, and her feet are flailing for purchase on the floorboards. Ursa feels as though she moves through mud, slow and useless as she tears at his fingers. Absalom drops Maren roughly to the floor, knocks Ursa with a hard slap to her cheek that sets her head ringing.

"Answer me," he says, finger pointed to Maren's heaving body. "Answer me."

Before Maren can so much as catch her breath Absalom is upon her again. This time he drags her to the tub, and through watering eyes Ursa sees him bend Maren bodily over the water and plunge her in face first. Her legs kick out, and Ursa crawls to them, again tries to break his grip but he is holding grimly, silent now, watching the churning bubbles.

"You will kill her!"

Ursa's mind is full of water. She reaches for her fallen chair, brings it crashing down on his back, but it strikes only a glancing blow before breaking to pieces. Absalom roars and Ursa thinks of going outside and screaming, bringing her neighbours running. But what neighbours are they? None that would take her part over her husband's.

"Please, Absalom," she cries, pulling at his shoulder with all her strength. "You cannot kill her."

He slackens his grip and knocks Ursa back again, sending her head against the shelf beside the fire. Maren comes up, coughing and retching, and Absalom turns to Ursa where she crouches, mind spinning with the impact.

"Ursula," he says, back on his heels, panting. His voice is bewildered. "Are you all right?"

She looks up at him, incredulous, her eyes swimming. He reaches out to her; there is tenderness writ over his face, and confusion. She flinches away, grasps for Maren where she lies bucking on the floor, but Absalom stays her with a practised hand on her wrist, and she is forced to look up at him.

Something calm and black settles on his face, and it is exactly the look that comes over him when he pins Ursa to the bed, pushes his way inside. He grabs Maren by the hair, twisting his fingers until she moans, water mottling her breath.

"Do you confess?" says Absalom. "That you have bewitched my wife, that you brought the storm with Kirsten Sørensdatter?"

"No," gasps Maren. "No."

This time when he dunks her beneath the grey water, Ursa knows all is lost. Her hand reaches for the shelf, closes upon something smooth and cool. She brings it up, arm shaking with the effort, and then lets its weight fall full down upon his head.

The rolling pin smacks at the centre of his skull. It sounds like a bird's egg, cracking, and he lets Maren loose, sways upon his knees. Ursa is dimly aware of Maren scrambling away as she brings it down again and the sound is moister, less crisp, and his black hair is growing wet and he is falling forward into the tub. Ursa brings up the pin again, but Maren grasps at her ankle.

"No."

Absalom's mouth is beneath the waterline, which is reddening with his blood. The back of his head is split and she can see white and pinkness. His left hand is tremoring, fluttering, reaching.

She pulls Maren clear of it, both of them crawling, backing away into the blankets where they lay only hours before, their bodies bare and warm. Ursa's teeth begin to knock together and Maren cradles her though she is the one half drowned, taking her into her thin body and kissing the top of her head.

"Let go, Ursa."

Ursa drops the rolling pin and it thumps and spins away. Ursa can't see Absalom but for his back. It is unmoving.

"Of me, too."

She loosens her grip and Maren crawls forward, moves to the other side of the tub.

"Is he..."

"Yes."

"Oh, God. Oh, God. I did not mean to kill him." It sounds unconvincing even to herself, though she knows she did not, not really. Only meant to stop him. She had to stop him. "What will I do?"

Maren does not answer. She coughs up water, then stands unsteadily, staggers to the table. Ursa clasps her knees. She imagines that any moment Absalom will rear up and seize them. The sound of his skull breaking comes in her ear, again and again, and the wet noise as she struck him a second time, the water on his breath as his head fell forward into the tub. She closes her eyes, hugs her legs to her. Her spine is against the hard side of the wall, and she thinks of Agnete, of their backs pressed together as they sleep.

Maren turns to her. Her face is different somehow, smoothed. Ursa reaches for her and she comes, but there is something stiff in the embrace. Maren draws back quickly. Ursa wipes her face—there is blood on her cheeks and it smears over her hand.

"Do you trust me?" says Maren into the unsteady silence.

Ursa looks up at her, at the hard angles of her face. "Yes."

"Go back to bed."

Ursa draws away.

"Go back to bed," Maren repeats, cupping her face as she had when they kissed.

"What will we do? Can we take the body, hide it beneath the floorboards?"

"No."

"Drop him in the sea, like Kirsten's runestones?"

"What if we are seen? It will not be easily done."

Ursa casts about for another answer, but Maren pushes on.

"And when the commissioner is found missing, there will be questions upon questions."

"Then what?" Ursa's mind is clouded, full of blood and the sound of cracked bone.

Maren's expression is so sad Ursa's own chest aches. "I am going to go away, Ursa."

"Go away?"

"Like Diinna. And they will find his body and think I did it."

"They will kill you."

"I am mentioned."

Ursa feels a bloom of pain in her chest. She had forgotten the reason for her husband's visit to the boathouse. "It's all lies."

"That didn't save Kirsten." Maren's eyes flutter shut. Her eyelids are thin and pink and Ursa wants to press her lips to them. "I can't stay. But you must go now, before anyone sees."

"I will come with you," says Ursa, grasping for her hand.

Maren looks her full in the face. "I do not want you to."

Ursa could swear her heart stops a moment.

"I want you to go to bed, and to report your husband missing in the morning. I want you to say you saw nothing, heard nothing. Even if it takes them days to find him. And then I want you to go back to Bergen, to your father. That ship in the harbour, it is the one that brought you. It can take you back."

Ursa knows the truth of it. When Absalom is discovered, there will be nothing to tie her to Vardø. She will be allowed to go home, and Captain Leifsson will ensure her safety. But something has changed, and she tries to put words to it.

"There is nothing there for me without you."

"There is your sister. Don't you want to see her again?"

Ursa can't answer no. Agnete had been her whole world, but everything is made different since Maren kissed her wrist. Ursa had never dreamt of such a thing until the moment it happened, but now it feels an impossibility that she can live without Maren. It is knowing that all your joy is bound up in another, and to be parted from it would be to live without light for the rest of your days. Ursa closes her eyes against the thought, can feel Maren's sea-grey stare upon her. She meets her gaze, searching for the want that brought them crashing together. "I will come with you."

"It will be easier," says Maren, and now a definite coolness washes into her voice, "if you do not."

Ursa kisses her then, desperately, and Maren doesn't return it.

"Maren, please."

"Go, Ursa. We will lose the night. Burn your nightdress, wash your face."

"I love you," says Ursa, the truth of it sudden as a falling star, bright and painful. "Will you not say it? I love you."

"I cannot say it," says Maren. She stands, hauls Ursa to her feet. Sends her weeping into the night.

FORTY

There is no time for tears. The morning will be upon them soon enough. Maren waits until Ursa is gone and the door of Fru Olufsdatter's house has been closed. It is easier this way.

Maren looks back at the dead commissioner, his head leaking still. The bloodied pin is at her feet and she picks it up, alongside Ursa's yellow dress. She can leave no clues, nothing that makes it simple. When Ursa raised her hand to strike again, Maren had felt it as though it were her own hand flying down, her fingers closing about the smooth column of stone. It seemed as though they acted together, as they had only hours before in bed.

She closes the door on the second boathouse, taking nothing but the dress, the pin, and her money. She turns, not to the harbour, but to her headland. Hers and Ursa's, hers and Erik's. The yellow dress smells of Kirsten and Fru Olufsdatter's pyre, and she breathes it in. The smell, she knows it from before today. From her dreams of the whale, the whale that came to her the night before the storm.

She remembers lying stretched across it as it was taken to pieces. She remembers its blubber burning in lamps before it even stilled. It feels now like a warning. She will not let herself be caught. She had decided this the moment her mother told her she was mentioned. She will not let herself burn, live long enough to smell her own body blazing.

She is alone as she walks the familiar path between the houses. She knows she is rare in not favouring the months of the midnight sun, but she can never be truly settled in that half-light. It reminds her of the lightning, the greenish bodies of drowned men. Here in the total dark, she feels safe.

Her mother's house is dim and still. She prays for her name to be kept out of the mouths of condemned women, prays for them all—Edne, and Gerda, even Toril and Sigfrid. It is too much death. It will end with her. It must.

She keeps her head down as she passes Baar Ragnvalsson's ruined house and boat, not looking ahead, watching for the changing ground, the lifting wind that means she is where the island stops. The sea slaps against the jagged rocks, and she can taste the salt of it, mingling with the aniseed, sloughing the bitterness of the dirty water the commissioner held her in. Here, where the current carries out to the northernmost places, where Ursa told her there is a black rock that sucks all towards it, she prays even for him.

She sets down the pin, and steps into Ursa's yellow dress, the one she first saw her in, first touched her in, first kissed and knew her to be as much hers as Maren was Ursa's. It is large even over her clothed body, and as she'd run her fingers over Ursa's belly, her breasts, she had felt it and known the reason the fastenings were loosed and loosed again. The hardening of the flesh, the making of space. A baby will protect her. It is another reason she couldn't bring her, nor imagine any end but this.

She throws the pin into the sea. She could follow, easy as a step. She would not float, like poor Kirsten. She would sink, just as in her dream, to the bottom. The sharp rocks that snagged their men would pierce her, and then the sea would take her, and if not the rocks, the sea alone, all the way to the end of the world. She always thought that is all there is, all there was for any of them in this place.

But now she remembers past the whale, past the drowning, to the rising at the end of her dream. The air is cool at the back of her throat. The money is heavy in her pocket. She looks ahead, to where the low mountain looms. As she steps forward, her thoughts are of Ursa, how she was the first and only one to ever know her. How that is enough.

HISTORICAL NOTE

On 24 December 1617, just off the coast of the island of Vardø, Norway's north-easternmost point, a storm lifted so suddenly eyewitnesses said it was as if it were conjured. In a matter of minutes, forty men were drowned. In this already remote and underpopulated place, it was a catastrophic event.

This was a time of great change in the country, then Denmark–Norway. King Christian IV, almost halfway through his fifty-nine-year reign, was growing increasingly desperate to make his mark on the world. He had won some indecisive victories at his borders, but his attention was turning towards what was within his rule, rather than without it. A strict Lutheran, he wanted to establish his Church more fully, and finally drive out the Sámi influence in his country's far northern reaches, especially Finnmark, a vast, wild, largely ungoverned area.

This indigenous population, for whom wind-weaving and spirit-talking were commonly used practices, mostly refused to obey his religious reforms, and King Christian brought in a number of increasingly harsh laws that ultimately amounted to state-sanctioned persecution and massacre. He was aiming at a singular, unified society that conformed to his view of the world, as embodied in his Church.

He turned, particularly, to Scotland. King James VI had recently published his treatise on witchcraft, *Daemonologie*, detailing how to "spot, prove, and kill a witch," sparking a wave of witch trials throughout the mainland and islands. Hysteria, together with church attendance, was at an all-time high. King Christian brought in sorcery laws in 1618, closely modelled on King James's.

King Christian also had a close personal friendship with a high-ranking Scotsman, John Cunningham, who had served several years in the Danish navy and driven pirates from Spitsbergen. When the King decided that Finnmark must be brought to heel, it was Captain Cunningham who he installed at Vardøhus.

What followed was a reign of unprecedented length and brutality. Though it was not his only duty, Lensmann Cunningham, or Køning as he came to be known, oversaw no fewer than fifty-two witch trials, leading to the deaths of ninety-one people: fourteen men and seventy-seven women. But Cunningham had gone further than the King had planned: of these, the men were all Sámi, but the women were Norwegian. In a region where there had previously been only a handful of such cases, and only two resulting in executions, it was a stark and telling change.

Their alleged crimes ranged from the mundane—arguments over drying racks, mild blasphemy—to the extreme. The first major trial, in 1621, had amongst its accused eight women charged with bringing about the 1617 storm, which had by then taken on a mythic status even in the minds of those who had not seen it.

The panics follow a similar pattern to those repeated around the world, throughout the seventeenth century and beyond. The trials are memorialized by a Peter Zumthor and Louise Bourgeois installation on the island of Vardø, which was the initial touchpaper for this novel. They are documented by scholars such as Dr. Liv Helene Willumsen, whose kind support, scrupulous research, and books including *Witchcraft Trials in Finnmark and Northern Norway* (2010), have been invaluable in ensuring a historical foundation to what is ultimately a work of fiction, concerned not with the trials themselves, but with the conditions that make such things possible. Even writing at a distance of four hundred years, I found much to recognize. This story is about people, and how they lived; before why and how they died became what defined them.

Kiran Millwood Hargrave

ACKNOWLEDGEMENTS

I am full of gratitude. For my mother, Andrea, to whom this book is dedicated, the best of women. For those myriad women who I depend upon to write, and to survive, and most of all when writing and survival feel like the same thing. For Hellie, my agent, who understands this, and without whom this book would not have been written.

For my father, Martyn, my brother, John, for being nothing like the men in this book. For my grandparents, Yvonne and John, for their vivacity. For my family, especially Debby, Dave, Louis, Rina, Sabine, Janis, and Piers.

For my friends, especially those who read this book and held my hand through its journey: Daisy Johnson, Sarvat Hasin, Lucy Ayrton, Laura Theis, Hannah Bond, Katie Webber, Kevin Tsang, Anna James, Louise O'Neill, Cat Doyle, and Elizabeth MacNeal. For my wider writing community, especially Maz Evans, MG Leonard, Rachel Leyshon, Katherine Rundell, and Barry Cunningham.

For Dr. Liv Helene Willumsen, who I hope will not be too horrified by the liberties I have taken with history in the name of narrative, but who I hope knows my appreciation and admiration.

For Kirby Kim, and the entire team at Janklow & Nesbit, UK and U.S. Every book is a labour of love for you all, and I value that deeply.

For Sophie Jonathan, an editor of rare gifts, and enormous grace. You have taught me so much, and I treasure working with you. To Judy Clain, who has shown this book, and me, such generosity and belief, and Carina Guiterman, for her part in shaping this tale. For my team at Picador and Pan Macmillan, the best possible home: Francesca Main, for looking after me and guiding the book in its final stages, Gillian Fitzgerald-Kelly, Paul Baggaley, Kate Green, Katie Bowden, Christine Jones, Emily Bromfield, Laura Ricchetti, Mary Chamberlain, my amazing cover designer Katie Tooke and Nicholas Blake. For Alex Hoopes, Reagan Arthur, and the glorious team at Little, Brown, Hachette.

For you, the reader, for becoming part of the story. For anyone angry, and hopeful, and trying their best.

For the men and women murdered at Vardø.

For Tom, for saving my life, and for helping me to make something of it.

ABOUT THE AUTHOR

Kiran Millwood Hargrave holds degrees from both Oxford and Cambridge Universities. She's a poet and playwright, as well as an acclaimed children's book author in the UK. Her debut book for children, *The Girl of Ink & Stars* has sold over 100,000 copies in the UK. It won the Waterstones Children's Book Prize 2017, the British Book Awards Children's Book of the Year 2017, and was shortlisted for numerous awards. Her second book, *The Island at the End of Everything*, was shortlisted for the Costa Children's Book of the Year Award and is publishing this month in the US and has three starred reviews in hand. Kiran reviews and contributes to *The Guardian*.